FORGING DESTINY

Chronicles of a Legionary Officer
Book One: **Stiger's Tigers**
Book Two: **The Tiger**
Book Three: **The Tiger's Fate**
Book Four: **The Tiger's Time**
Book Five: **The Tiger's Wrath**
Book Six: **The Tiger's Imperium**
Book Seven: **The Tiger's Fight (Coming 2022)**

Tales of the Seventh
Part One: **Stiger**
Part Two: **Fort Covenant**
Part Three: **A Dark Foretoken**
Part Four: **Thresh (TBA)**

The Karus Saga
Book One: **Lost Legio IX**
Book Two: **Fortress of Radiance**
Book Three: **The First Compact**

Born of Ash:
Book One: **Fallen Empire (Coming 2021)**
Book Two: **Infinity Control (Coming 2021)**
Book Three: **Rising Phoenix (Coming 2021)**

The Way of Legend: With Quincy J. Allen
Book One: **Reclaiming Honor**
Book Two: **Forging Destiny**
Book Three: **Paladin's Light (Coming 2021)**

Nonfiction:
**Every Writer's Dream: The Insider's
Path to an Indie Bestseller**

FORGING DESTINY

The Way of Legend Book 2

BY

MARC ALAN EDELHEIT
AND
QUINCY J. ALLEN

Forging Destiny: Book 2, The Way of the Legend
First Edition

I wish to thank my agent, Andrea Hurst, for her invaluable support and assistance. I would also like to thank my beta readers, who suffered through several early drafts. My betas: Jon Cockes, Nicolas Weiss, Paul Klebaur, James Doak, David Cheever, Bruce Heaven, Erin Penny, April Faas, Rodney Gigone, Tim Adams, Paul Bersoux, Phillip Broom, David Houston, Sheldon Levy, Michael Hetts, Walker Graham, Bill Schnippert, Jan McClintock, Jonathan Parkin, Spencer Morris, Jimmy McAfee, Rusty Juban, Joel M. Rainey, Jeremy Craig, Nathan Halliday, Ed Speight, Joseph Hall, Michael Berry, Tom Trudeau, Sally Tingley-Walker, James H. Bjorum, Franklin Johnson, Marshall Clowers. I would also like to take a moment to thank my loving wife, who sacrificed many an evening and weekend to allow me to work on my writing.

Editing Assistance by Hannah Streetman, Audrey Mackaman, Brandon Purcell
Cover Art by Piero Mng (Gianpiero Mangialardi)
Cover Formatting by Telemachus Press

Agented by Andrea Hurst & Associates, LLC
http://maenovels.com/

MARC'S NOTE:

For clarification purposes, Tovak's tale takes place a handful of years before Karus and the Ninth arrive on Tannis. Both stories also take place on different continents.

Writing with another author is always a unique experience. In my experience, it tends to produce books that have a unique flavor that is distinct from other works. I believe that has only served to enhance Tovak's tale and helps to set it apart from my other work. I know it has also made me a better writer. *Forging Destiny* has been a true labor of love and a joy for both Quincy and myself. I sincerely hope you enjoy this book.

You may wish to sign up to my newsletter to get the latest updates on my writing.

http://maenovels.com/

Reviews keep us motivated and also help to drive sales. I make a point to read each and every one, so please continue to post them.

I hope you enjoy *Forging Destiny* and would like to offer a sincere thank you for your purchase and support.

Best regards,
Marc Alan Edelheit, author and your tour guide to the worlds of Tannis and Istros

DEDICATION

This book is dedicated to each and every fan who ever picked up a copy of one of Marc Edelheit's novels, and specifically those who enjoyed Reclaiming Honor. It is an honor and a privilege to be allowed to play in this particular sandbox.

~ Quincy

A WORD ON THE GREAT MARCH FROM GRIMBOK LOREKEEPER

To all those readers of the common tongue of Tannis who find themselves in possession of *Forging Destiny,* the continuation of the tale of Tovak Stonehammer, know that by this time, his honor had been reclaimed in the eyes of many within the Blood Badgers Warband, but certainly not all. The stigma of Pariah runs deep amongst my people, and for some, the taint of his lineage would remain with him until the end of his days. To his credit, and as was his way, that young, noble Dvergr learned to rise above a lifetime of petty disdain, censure, and abuse. Instead, with every breath he took, he remained steadfast in his service to the Blood Badgers, the Dvergr people, and to the mighty god Thulla, above all.

As in my previous work on Tovak Stonehammer, *Reclaiming Honor,* accommodations were made so that most readers could more deeply fathom the experiences and deeds of young Tovak as my people endeavored to avoid servitude to or extermination by the Horde. I should add that the Great March was only our most recent exodus towards safety, freedom, and, we believed, a new destiny. Just as we had on more than one occasion in the past, we fought against all odds with a stubborn determination which—and

I offer this with a considerable amount of pride—has frustrated our enemies for millennia, and in some cases to the point of literal madness.

You must understand that, long ago, on a distant world, far from but inextricably linked to Tanis, we chose to stand against the oncoming avalanche of the Horde. It nearly destroyed us—all of us. When we were faced with the very real possibility of our complete annihilation, we gathered up what little we had left and moved on. There were those of us, to be sure, who wanted to stand, fight, and die for the sake of Legend, but wisdom prevailed over the desire for honor, and for one reason only. We existed when the Horde was born, and we, as a people, fully intend to exist long after the suns of every world in the heavens have set upon the Horde's utter and—if we have anything to say about it—fiery destruction.

It is often said that history is cyclical, and oft repeats itself. It is because of this one irrefutable truth that, in the time of Tovak, we once again found ourselves retreating in the face of the only implacable enemy we have ever known. The Great March—although I should say *this* Great March, if I am to set it properly within the context of the whole of my people's history—was a thoroughly perilous time for us, not the least of which were the specific events which befell young Tovak on our journey across the Grimbar Plateau and beyond.

It was only known to a select few, but Grata'Dagoth, detailed in ancient prophecy, was always our destination. Though if I am being honest, I must admit that we did not even know how to open its gates were we to find them, but now I get ahead of myself. All we knew at the time was that the mysterious fortress, wherever it lay, might hold within it the salvation of our people. Our pursuit of it was a leap of faith for a people who had lost their own. It was desperation and determination that drove us, to be sure, but in hindsight, I must believe that, although we had turned away from our faith, our faith had not fully turned away from us. For, you see, something stirred within Tovak's breast in those days, and none of us could ever have foreseen where it would lead us all.

So, with only the vaguest notion as to where Grata'Dagoth lay, let alone what might exist beyond, my people steeled themselves for the inevitable trials and tribulations we were certain to encounter as we stubbornly drove towards the hope of a new life. We did so with the Blood Badgers as our vanguard, led by the warchief Karach Skullsplitter, who had and would face a litany of challenges as his warband forged a trail for my people to follow. With one difficult crisis after another, and frequently with Tovak at the center of it all, we also discovered what fearsome odds the universe had set against us. In that realization, we came to understand that if we were to achieve our freedom, it would not be without a terrible and bloody price.

It is, therefore, with humility and respect that I present to you *Forging Destiny*. It is the second volume in the Tale of Tovak, and in it we see the first burning sparks of what lay ahead for both him and our people.

His was the Way of Legend.

Your humble servant,
Grimbok Lorekeeper
Scribe to the Thane Rogar Bladebreaker

TABLE OF CONTENTS

Chapter One 1
Chapter Two 16
Chapter Three 35
Chapter Four 47
Chapter Five 68
Chapter Six 84
Chapter Seven 105
Chapter Eight 116
Chapter Nine 130
Chapter Ten 142
Chapter Eleven 159
Chapter Twelve 178
Chapter Thirteen 196
Chapter Fourteen 212
Chapter Fifteen 227
Chapter Sixteen 249
Chapter Seventeen 269
Chapter Eighteen 284
Chapter Nineteen 304

CHAPTER ONE

"Look, another swarm." Tovak's voice carried over the steady crunch of boots as he pointed towards a cloud of heratta seeming to flow over a ridge to the north.

He let the sight of the swarm push away the feeling of guilt and unhappiness that had filled his heart since the morning's march began, a little over an hour before. The sight of the large insects taking to the air was incredible and the sheer number of them staggering. This was the third such flock they had seen in the last half hour, as the bugs continued their annual migration out into the rich grasslands of the Grimbar Plateau.

Fifth Company, what remained of the Baelix Guard, and a handful of archers were marching along the edge of the vast grasslands that made up the plateau, which was to his immediate left. To his right were the ridges. These led to the valleys and then ultimately to the higher ground of the mountains. Like grand specters of doom, those forbidding mountain peaks rose to near unimaginable heights off in the far distance.

Eyeing the nearest ridges, Tovak felt a sense of unease. After the events of the last few days, he almost dreaded leaving the plateau again, and it was a certainty that they would.

The second of Tannis's suns had only just cleared the horizon. Morning sunlight washed over the marching

1

column of Dvergr, casting long shadows. Although the two suns had begun to warm the land, there seemed no warmth in the hearts of the warriors who marched together in near silence. There were no marching songs or stone flutes playing an inspiring tune to help keep pace. The mood of Tovak's comrades was grim to say the least.

"Bloody heratta," Dagmar grumbled behind Tovak, a little too loud. "I hope they feed on the bones of whatever got Struugar and the Second."

The words sent a pang of worry through Tovak's heart as he glanced back at his squad mate. Dagmar was hobbling along with a noticeable limp, grimacing with each step. The injury seemed to be not as bad as the day before, but Tovak thought it clear the warrior was hurting. Dagmar had refused to be sent back to the warband and had insisted on coming with them.

"Stow that trash," Sergeant Thegdol barked, having obviously overhead the comment. The sergeant marched at the head of the Baelix Guard's column. He turned and glared back over his shoulder at the offender. "First of all, you incredibly dumb durpa, heratta only eat plants," Thegdol growled. "They don't even have teeth for meat and are about the most harmless things in these parts. I thought you might already have figured that one out. All we've been doing these last few weeks has been hunting those very bugs. I swear, Dagmar, there are days I think you must be as stupid as you are ugly."

"Not as ugly as you, Sarge," Dagmar shot back, with a trace of a grin. "Yours is a face only a mother could love."

Dagmar was playing with fire.

"I thought the sarge was your mother," someone from behind called out.

It was the first time in the march Tovak had heard any levity. There were a handful of chuckles that followed, but not many. The grim mood hung heavy over the column.

"One ugly mother, then," Dagmar said. "Tell me you love me, Mother Thegdol. I don't hear it enough."

Though his glare did not soften, Thegdol's beard twitched slightly around the corners of his mouth as he looked back at them.

"Just like any mother and her children, I love all you bastards equally," Thegdol said after a slight hesitation. "I play no favorites, but I do hand out punishment details. And … I feel one coming on." The sergeant paused, his gaze sweeping across the column marching behind him. "Regardless, and because I love you all, I will give it to you plain as its day, boys. Straight and clear, so that even a dumb durpa like Dagmar here can follow." The sergeant's tone softened a hair. "Boys, we have no idea what happened to Captain Struugar and the others. It's as simple as that, and until we do, there will be no speculation in the ranks." The sergeant's tone hardened again. "Is that understood?"

"It's not like they got lost, Sergeant," Dagmar said.

Tovak shook his head. He'd learned that Dagmar often had more brash in him than brains.

"I said stow it"—Thegdol's tone hardened even further, becoming like tempered steel—"or when we get back to the warband, I'll have you shoveling teska shit until those brown locks of yours turn gray."

Thegdol moved to the side of the column and slowed his pace until he was dead center in the middle of the march. He raised his voice so they all could hear.

"The captain is the best company commander in the Blood Badgers. You all know that, and I shouldn't have to say it. Assuming he did run into trouble, I'll bet he's up there right now"—Thegdol jerked a thumb towards the nearest ridge—"waiting for us to come to his aid."

The sergeant turned fierce eyes back on Dagmar and seemed to dare him to say otherwise. This time, Dagmar had enough sense to keep his mouth shut.

"Do you have anything to add?" Thegdol pressed. "Now's your chance."

"No, Sergeant," Dagmar said. "I don't."

"Good," he growled, then raised his voice slightly, addressing the entire section. "Then keep the chatter to a minimum. We're out here to find the captain and Second Section. We're gonna bring them home. Until Karach says otherwise, they are out there somewhere, waiting for us. That we don't have contact with them does not mean they're bloody dead. Understand me?"

"Yes, Sergeant," Tovak and the others replied in unison.

Thegdol raked his gaze across the column. Apparently pleased his message had been received, he gave a sharp nod. With that, the sergeant picked up his pace and resumed his original position at the head of the section's column.

Marching at Tovak's side, Gorabor looked over at him, before leaning nearer and whispering, "It's hard not to think about it. And last night was … I don't know …. I've never felt relieved to be alive, happy that we came out on top, and defeated all at the same time. Gods, it feels good to have survived … but Staggen. I feel so terrible about that … poor bastard. He deserved better than to be bent over an altar and slaughtered like an animal."

Tovak was silent for a long moment as he recalled Staggen's death. It was something he would not soon forget, and he suspected it would be with him to his dying days.

"I know what you mean." Tovak looked over at his friend, even as thoughts carried him to the day before, the rescue of his comrades, the desperate flight from the enemy's camp, the terrible fear, the moment he'd been cornered and known his personal end was at hand. Then, astonishingly, had come deliverance at the hands of the warchief himself and two companies of heavy infantry. It almost seemed like it had not happened, but it had. Tovak had not been dreaming. Just as he'd saved Gorabor and Dagmar, he'd been saved.

After it was all over, Tovak had been complimented for his bravery at rescuing his comrades. It was a new experience for him, being recognized for his worth. He was, after all, a Pariah.

Due to his actions, the warband had won a small victory over the enemy, but in a way, Tovak felt like he had failed. The price had been too high. Not only had the Baelix Guard suffered serious losses in the raid on their camp, but he had intentionally violated orders in going alone to rescue his comrades and best friend, Gorabor.

His gaze tracked to the sergeant's back. It was an unforgivable breach but Tovak had felt driven to make the attempt...compelled even. He had been willing to risk it all to do what was right and it had mostly worked out. Staggen had been the only one he'd been unable to save. That gnawed at him and made him feel like he'd failed. The sergeant had said otherwise.

Thegdol had also given Tovak a stern warning. Should he violate orders a second time, he knew he would not be forgiven. His chance at reclaiming his honor would be done and the warband would cast him out.

"After all that we went through up there"—Gorabor nodded towards the nearest ridges—"do you think they live? Second, that is…. Do you think it's as the sergeant says?"

Tovak glanced in the direction Gorabor had indicated and was silent for a long moment before looking back over at his friend. "For what it's worth, and I can't explain why… I…." Tovak hesitated, then decided to plow ahead. "Something tells me Struugar is alive up there, and we have to get to him… soon. They need our help."

It was more than a gut feeling. It was a *pull* or, more accurately, an almost desperate need to get moving ever since he had risen that morning. Struugar and Second Section were in trouble. Like the elderly could feel a coming rain in their joints, Tovak could feel it in his bones.

He let his eyes run ahead to Fifth Company, who marched to the Baelix Guard's front. Somewhere at the Fifth's head was Karach, the warchief. Tovak thought it incredible that the warchief himself was going after Second.

Tovak glanced back over at Gorabor. "And I feel we're headed in the right direction."

Gorabor gave him a sidelong look, scowling slightly. "You're just saying that because we're moving next to their tracks across the plateau." His friend pointed down at the swath of crushed grass and boot prints, which blazed a trail for the entire column to follow.

"No," Tovak said, more matter-of-factly than he intended. "It's more than that." He tapped his chest. "I feel it."

Gorabor gave a grunt. "I hope you are right."

"How are you holding up?" he asked Gorabor, wanting to change the subject. Both of his friend's eyes were black, his jaw swollen, and his lower lip split and purpled. Thegdol had managed to straighten Gorabor's nose out, but it still looked two sizes too big. The enemy had not been kind to him during his brief stint as a captive.

"Sore, hurting," Gorabor said quickly. "Stiff all over. And my face feels like one big ache. I wasn't about to get sent back with the wounded, though." He patted the hilt of his sword. "I can still fight, and I want to find the captain and Second. Yesterday, you taught me the importance of never leaving comrades behind. It was something I will not soon forget."

Tovak looked away, suddenly uncomfortable.

"By the gods," Gorabor coughed, and as he did, he winced. "By Thulla, I ache all over."

Tovak himself ached from the exertions of the previous day. He had a sudden flash of Staggen and with it came a wash of guilt. Staggen would never feel anything again, not anymore, for dead was dead.

He stole another glance at his friend, whose stare was a long one. There was now a distant look to his gaze. Gorabor had finally seen the horrors the world could offer. It had changed him, much like Tovak's life struggle had changed him. He could see that plainly and felt saddened by it … for Gorabor had lost an innocence that would never be recovered.

Gorabor stretched his neck left and right before moving it from side to side. He winced and let out a long breath. "I hope you're right about the captain and the Second. I really do."

Tovak turned his gaze to the west, where the warband, many miles away, had been encamped. That morning, Karach had ordered the Third Infantry Company to escort the carts, the seriously wounded, and the dead back. They carried with them the maps and documents Tovak had retrieved from the orc encampment. As Thegdol had thought, Karach had been seriously interested in those.

Fifth Company, along with the remains of the Baelix Guard—at least those able to march—and a handful of archers had set out to determine what had happened to Struugar and Second Section. Until Dagmar's comment, nobody had said much of anything, but the worry for the captain was palpable.

What if Tovak was wrong? What if his feeling was nothing more than wishful optimism about the captain and Second Section? With everything he had gained in recent weeks, just the thought of losing Struugar—the very Dvergr who had given him a chance to make something of himself, to stand on his own, after years of being beat down, sometimes literally—was almost more than he could bear. Tovak desperately clung to the hope, propping it up with prayer, that the captain was alive.

"Thulla," Tovak whispered to himself, "grant Your mercy and return to us our captain and comrades. We look to You for our salvation and thank You for Your benevolence and love."

Tovak sucked in a breath of air and slowly let it out. Feeling a little better, he looked at the backs in front of him. He and the twenty-five warriors remaining of the Baelix Guard's First and Third Sections marched in a column of two abreast, just behind Fifth Company's strikers, heavy infantry, and the mainstay of the warband's battle line. Fourth Section, made up of the Baelix Guard's twenty remaining strikers, brought up the column's rear, as did the handful of archers.

Lieutenant Benthok and Corporal Karn had scouted ahead. Tovak wished he had been called to go with them, but he hadn't. In a way, that was not a bad thing. He was tired, more than a little run-down, and despite an hour of marching, still sore and stiff. But like Dagmar with his ankle, Tovak would not have let that stop him. He'd have willingly gone with them, had they asked.

As the suns climbed higher into the sky, the march continued along the edge of the foothills and finally, after what seemed like an eternity to Tovak but had only been a couple of hours, angled up a forested ridge and into a small valley. The column marched through the valley and up along one of the ridges that hemmed it in.

As they moved towards the mountains, the forest grew thicker the farther up they went. Still they continued, climbing steadily higher. The exertion became more difficult, and soon Tovak, like everyone else, was sucking wind and sweating profusely in his armor.

After another two hours, he had tired of marching in the column, a terribly monotonous thing. He craved the freedom scouting brought. Tovak wanted desperately to join Benthok and Karn, desiring to do something—anything—other than follow along in the line of march. Stuck in the column, he felt useless.

As the forest thickened, Tovak and everyone else had to weave their way around trees, step over rocks, or push through undergrowth, some of it prickly. The ground became broken up with rocks, scree, and numerous trees and brush roots that threatened to trip the unwary. Tovak soon lost sight of even the trampled path they had been following, which was the most frustrating thing of all.

He suspected they were now marching directly over the Second's tracks. If true, it meant the company of strikers ahead had obliterated all signs of previous passage. They also kicked up a fair amount of choking dust.

"Column, halt," came a shouted order from ahead.

"Bloody gods," someone behind Tovak breathed, "it's about time."

The column ground to an unsteady stop. Several warriors almost immediately opened and upended their waterskins, drinking deeply. The heat of the day had grown and, though they were under the cover of the trees, was oppressive.

Tovak felt intense frustration at not knowing what was going on. He wanted to rush up to the front of the column and find out, but they'd not been told to fall out. So, he remained where he was.

Tovak turned to Gorabor. "They must have found something."

Dagmar gave a weary shrug. "For all we know, Karach had to take a leak."

Ignoring his squad mate and looking forward, he craned his neck in hopes of seeing what was going on, but all he could see was an impenetrable wall of the strikers' backs to his front.

"Tovak Stonehammer," Thegdol called in a weary voice. The sergeant did not even bother looking back. "You're wanted forward. Get a move on."

Tovak glanced at Gorabor, who merely shrugged as he wiped sweat from his face with a soiled rag.

"You wanted to know what's going on," Gorabor said. "Now is your chance."

"Better you than me," Dagmar said. "If my name had been called, it would have been for a punishment charge."

"It's not too late for that," Thegdol said. "Tovak, stop wasting time and get moving, son."

"Yes, Sergeant," Tovak said. Taking a deep breath, he stepped forward and moved past the sergeant and alongside the column of strikers from Fifth Company. No one paid him any attention as he passed. All of the warriors were equally tired.

Tovak had to negotiate a small stream, which, gurgling happily, ran down the steep slope to his left. When he made it past the heavily armored warriors to the front of the column, he spotted Karach a few yards ahead. The warchief was gazing at Benthok and Karn, who had taken a knee about fifty yards ahead to examine something on the ground with interest. They were so close their heads almost touched.

Benthok looked up and flashed some finger speak at Karach, which Tovak could not catch. The warchief waved a weary hand in reply and gave a nod, then turned and approached Captain Greng.

The captain was standing about ten yards ahead of the column of march and in the shade of a tree. He had been drinking from his waterskin. He offered it to the warchief, who took it and drank a swallow before handing it back. Even though they were under the shade of the trees, both officers radiated a confidence that was as natural as sunlight.

Tovak approached, came to attention, and saluted.

"At ease," Karach ordered, glancing over the column, as if slightly distracted and deep in thought. He turned his gaze to Fifth Company's captain. "Captain Greng, we might be here for a bit. Let us take advantage of the stream. See that waterskins are filled. Put sentries out and have your company and the Baelix fall out for some rest. Might as well get them fed too." He glanced back towards Benthok and Karn. "It's a good time for a break anyway."

"Yes, sir, I agree." The captain pointed towards higher ground. "I'd like to post scouts, several of Thegdol's boys, farther up these hillsides and deeper into the forest, as well as downslope. With all the orc and goblin tracks around, I'd feel more comfortable, sir."

Tovak became alert. He had known the captain was following an enemy raiding party, goblins... not orcs. Had there been orcs with the raiders? He looked down around them and spotted a heavy boot print, mixed amongst dwarven tracks.

"I don't have a problem with that," Karach replied. "Do whatever you think is necessary."

"Yes, sir."

"Lieutenant Belk," Greng called, "on me, if you will."

Karach turned to Tovak as Belk separated himself from the column and started towards them. The warchief's gaze was intense, almost piercing, and Tovak suddenly felt on guard.

"After what you did yesterday," Karach began, "I believe you need rest. I wanted to send you back to the warband. However, Benthok thought you might be useful. And when he talks highly of someone, even if that person is a Pariah, I make sure to listen."

"Yes, sir," Tovak said, not knowing what else to say. He felt honored that Benthok had thought of him.

Belk had joined them. Both he and Greng were watching.

"I expect good things from you, son," Karach said. "Do not let me down."

"I won't, sir," Tovak said, feeling his cheeks flush.

"Well, the lieutenant has asked for you. Might as well join him." The warchief turned away. Tovak had been clearly dismissed.

He gave a stiff salute before starting towards the lieutenant, eager to learn what they had found. It seemed his time of slogging along in the column might be over.

"Tovak," Greng called after him.

"Sir," Tovak said, looking back.

"We're in the field and clearly in hostile territory," Greng said. "You don't salute officers here. That's a good way to see us dead, if there's an enemy about with a bow. One day, I hope to die in bed with my wife, in the wild throws of orgasm. I want to go out with a bang. Understand me on this?"

Karach gave an amused chuckle.

Tovak felt his cheeks burn. He'd been taught such basic protocols back at the Academy and should have known better. "Yes, sir, I do. It won't happen again, sir."

"Right then. We will speak no more on it. Get going." Greng jerked his chin in the direction of the lieutenant.

With that, Tovak moved quickly up to where Benthok knelt, pointing out something on the ground to Karn. They looked up as he approached.

"Reporting as ordered, Lieutenant," Tovak said, remembering this time not to salute.

He briefly met the piercing green eyes of Corporal Karn, who gave him a nod. He had just joined the corporal's squad the day before. Karn's red hair and beard were a stark contrast to the dark blue of his cloak, armor, and helm.

The lieutenant pulled himself to his feet and stepped back a couple paces. Pointing at the ground, he looked at Tovak. "Tell me what you see here."

Tovak didn't hesitate. He moved forward, careful not to tread on the footprints scattered along what was quickly becoming clear was a path through the forest that continued along the ridgeline they had been following.

He examined the ground, his eyes sweeping left to right. He saw prints that had been clearly made by orcs. There were Dvergr boots too, a lot of them, moving in the same direction, down the trail. He judged them to be at most two days old. When he got near the edge of the path, he saw something new. He knelt down, examining the print. It was small, as if a child had made it, although the track was pointed and not rounded. It was also narrow. He found more of the small tracks and some of those had tread over the orc prints too. That told him whatever had made these strange prints had come after both the Dvergr and the orcs had passed through.

Benthok watched him carefully as he scanned the forest around the path. Tovak spotted additional such tracks coming down the hill, with all of them moving in the direction the Dvergr and orcs had gone. It was as if a mass of children had joined up here, before following. He turned around and scanned the other side of the path the orcs and Dvergr had made. Finally, he turned to Benthok.

"Sir," he said, "it's clear that the Second and a large group of orcs went that way." He pointed down the trail. "However, another set of tracks followed after them both. They are smaller, and I believe to be neither orc nor goblin. I've seen a goblin up close, and…well, their feet are webbed. These are not."

"Very good," Benthok said, then looked at Karn. "I told you he could read a trail."

"So he can." Karn blew out a breath. "But we're still gonna have to train some of the Academy out of him, sir. If he is to be useful to us, that is. He bloody saluted Karach out in the field." He looked up at Tovak. "By now, you should know better."

Tovak colored again at that, his cheeks burning. Karn grinned at his discomfort. But then, something occurred to Tovak. He glanced down at the tracks once more before looking at the lieutenant.

"I don't see any goblin tracks," Tovak said. "Some of these orc tracks are older than those made by Second, some newer…. I thought the captain was going after goblins?"

"We thought so too." Karn's grin faded. "He was on to something, that's for sure. We just don't know what, yet."

The lieutenant knelt next to one of the smaller tracks and traced the outline with a finger. Benthok appeared thoughtful as he looked up at Karn.

"Corporal, their presence here means we have a problem, a real problem."

"At least I'm not the one who has to tell Karach the good news," Karn said.

"I could order you to do that," Benthok retorted, "make it happen, if you like,"

"You won't," Karn said. "You like raining on other people's parades too much not to pass this one along personally."

"Sir?" Tovak asked, drawing both of their attention. "Who made those tracks? What are they?"

"Thulla-cursed gnomes made them," Benthok growled, and then he spat on the ground. "The gods must really hate us, for there are a lot of gnome tracks."

"A lot," Karn echoed. He too spat onto the path. "And that's not good."

CHAPTER TWO

"Gnomes?" Tovak looked down at the track again. He glanced back up, not quite believing he had heard correctly. "Gnomes, really? You both are serious?"

Looking grave, Karn gave a slow nod. "I am afraid so."

Tovak slid his gaze along the path ahead of them, studying it yet again. The orc tracks were heavy and somewhat disorganized, as they had worked their way along the path in what appeared to be ones and twos. So too were the Dvergr prints.

He now saw the path with new eyes as his gaze sought out those smaller prints. Amongst his people, gnomes had fearsome reputations as unconventional, bitter, and fearless fighters. He had heard it said the enemy feared them just as much as the warbands. And yet, they were known to work with the Horde.

"It looks like at least two groups of gnomes moved down these hillsides, converging here, before pursuing Second Section farther up the valley." Benthok fixed his gaze upon Tovak. "See that mark on the tree there?"

Tovak turned his gaze to where Benthok pointed. There were two thin lines carved into the trunk of a pine, at about eye level. He'd missed it. The blaze had been made so that it was not obvious to the casual observer, but that was no excuse for not spotting it. In his haste, he had only been

16

studying the ground. That was an unforgivable lapse, one for which he suddenly felt embarrassed.

"You may not have realized it," Benthok said, "but when each section goes out into the field, they leave such markers. When you know what to look for, they are easier to spot."

"That way," Karn added, "if there's trouble, help can find them."

"I see," Tovak said.

"Although Struugar definitely had the numbers to deal with the orcs he was pursuing," the lieutenant continued, "the gnomes are a different matter altogether." He glanced back towards the warchief and seemed to be considering Karach. He stroked his braided beard for several silent moments, then looked at Karn, as if he had made a decision. "I think we need to scout ahead a ways, make sure it's safe and no one's waiting for us down that path."

"Somehow," Karn said, "I knew you were going to suggest that, sir."

"We could have easily been spotted on the way up here," Benthok said. "We need to make sure we're not walking into a trap."

"I agree." Karn gave a nod.

"Good. Time then, I think, to break the good news to Karach. I will be right back." Benthok left them and made his way over to the warchief.

"Lose that pack," Karn said as he began unhooking his own, one clip at a time.

Tovak did as he was told. When he slid it off his back and set it down, he felt light as a feather. As usual, he marveled at the feeling. Karn grunted with amusement as he leaned his own pack against a tree off to the side of the path. He untied his horn bow from the pack, as well as a small bundle of black-fletched arrows. Tovak set his pack next to his corporal's.

"Got your sling?" Karn asked. "And shot?"

"I do." Tovak patted the shot pouch cinched to his belt.

"Good," Karn said, "you might need it."

That was a sobering thought, for he had needed the sling the day before, against the goblins that had been chasing him. Now, he was potentially facing a whole different enemy.

"Are gnomes as bad as they say?" Tovak asked.

"Worse," Karn said unhappily. "The little bastards are nasty business—nasty business. Pray we don't have to fight them. One on one, gnomes usually are not much of a problem. They are easily overcome. However, they are like rats. When you see one, there's always more about."

Looking down at the multitude of tracks around them, Tovak understood, with all the gnome tracks about, Second Section was in a world of trouble.

"What do you know about gnomes?" Karn asked as he pulled his waterskin free and took a deep pull at it. He wiped his lips with the back of his hand and offered the skin to Tovak, who declined the offer by shaking his head.

"Only what I've heard," Tovak said. "I've never seen one myself, and they weren't a topic covered in any real detail at the Academy. Gnomes occasionally work with the Horde. As far as I know, there haven't been any large-scale gnome incursions into our territory for some time."

"The reason it's not covered at the Academy is because we rooted most of them out a long time ago," Karn said. "But, like vermin, it's really impossible to get rid of them all. Small groups live upon the fringes of our towns, and cities—usually down in the deep dark of the world. We don't go out of our way to bother them and they do the same.

Occasionally there are problems, but usually we tolerate their presence, and they do the same for us."

"There is a treaty that guarantees that," Benthok said as he rejoined them. "Or did you forget?"

"A treaty?" Tovak had never heard of it. "A treaty with the gnomes?"

Benthok gave a nod. "With those tribes that border our territory. It keeps the peace and has for the last hundred years or so." The lieutenant turned his attention to Karn. "We're to scout for four miles, no more. If we find nothing of interest, we report back, so that Karach can move the detachment up. Then we will scout ahead again." Benthok glanced around at the nearest trees, eyeing them warily. "He's also going to send out scouts, have a look back behind us and to the flanks. If anyone is following or watching us, we may find them."

"Sounds like a plan," Karn said.

The lieutenant looked up the path, deep concern on his features. His head was still wrapped in a soiled bandage, from when he had been hit on the head during the enemy's attack on their camp. Blood had seeped through and stained the bandage. The lieutenant reached up and scratched the back of his neck as he glanced up the path.

"Whatever happened to the Second," Benthok said, "it probably happened quickly and not long after the section came through here. The gnome tracks look to me like they were in a hurry. At least, that's what I'm thinking."

"Yes, sir." Karn spat on the ground. "Just our luck then, that the captain and Second wandered into hostile gnome territory."

Benthok scanned the terrain about them.

"Karn, I want you up on the right side of the path"—he pointed—"moving along the slope, just into the trees. Tovak and I will take this side."

"Yes, sir," Karn said.

"Good," Benthok said. "Let's get to it."

Karn tossed his stopped waterskin down next to his pack and moved across to the other side of the path and into the trees and brush, about ten yards away.

"Come on, Tovak," Benthok said as he moved down the slope and into cover on the left side of the path.

The two of them spread about five yards apart and began working their way parallel with the path as Karn kept pace on the other side. They moved slowly, taking their time and making as little noise as possible.

Under the shade of the trees, the temperature was cooler, though Tovak found himself still sweating profusely. The sound of the birds chirping to one another was pleasant enough, as was the wind when it blew lightly through the trees, rustling the leaves overhead. Normally, Tovak would have enjoyed the setting, but not today.

About every ten yards, Benthok and Tovak would come to a stop. They would listen, look around, and make eye contact with Karn before moving on.

Tovak was closer to the path. The gnome tracks were everywhere he looked, even off the path and into the trees. He tried to get a better idea of their numbers but found it increasingly difficult. There were just too many tracks, hundreds of them. Some he judged were old, days, perhaps even weeks, others fresh. There was just no way he could tell how many had gone after the Second.

There was a hissing to his left. He looked over. Benthok had been trying to get his attention. Across the way, Karn had stopped too. He and the lieutenant had just finished using finger speak. So intent had he been on the tracks, Tovak had missed it. The lieutenant moved over and leaned close. "This path we're following is the remains of an ancient road."

"How can you tell?"

"It's raised up." Benthok pointed. "See there? That is a roadbed. It was definitely made, though has not been maintained for years, possibly even centuries."

Tovak studied the path with new eyes. After a moment, he concluded the lieutenant was correct. "What is a road doing all the way out here in the middle of nowhere?"

"At one time," Benthok said, "if I don't miss my mark, this wasn't the middle of nowhere. Long ago, there was a Dvergr nation in these parts. All that remains are their ruins and not much more."

"What clan?" Tovak asked, curious.

"We don't know," Benthok admitted.

"How can that be?" Tovak was perplexed.

"Before we came to this world, it seems another group of Dvergr were here first."

"That's incredible," Tovak said. "So, there could be another kingdom somewhere?"

"We don't believe so," Benthok said. "All we have ever found are their ruins. They either left these parts or died off. It's one of the reasons the warband is out this way."

That got Tovak's attention. He was about to ask a question, when Benthok turned away and raised an arm, catching Karn's attention. The lieutenant pointed forward, and with that, they moved on.

The forest grew thicker the farther they traveled. The path they followed turned from trampled grass and dirt to a crushed carpet of pine needles. The undergrowth became sparser and the trees taller.

Tovak estimated they had traveled nearly a half-mile, when Karn gave an owl hoot to get their attention. When they looked, the corporal was moving backward, away from the direction they were headed.

Tovak and Benthok came to an abrupt halt and knelt down, scanning the trees and brush around them. Nothing. Still in view, Karn stopped behind a large bush that provided him some cover to his front. It was clear his positioning was deliberate. The corporal held up his fist to them as he knelt behind the bush. His eyes were fixed ahead of them.

Ten yards to the front, the trees appeared to thin. Tovak scanned the area. He heard nothing out of the ordinary. He saw no movement either. He turned his attention back to the corporal, wondering what was wrong.

Karn was still on the other side of the path. He gave the sign for them to join him. Motioning for Tovak to follow, Benthok started over to him.

What have you found? Benthok asked the corporal in finger speak.

Clearing, Karn responded and pointed ahead. *Look and see. Careful. Enemy may be about.*

Benthok turned, and with Tovak and Karn following, they crept forward towards the edge of the trees. They found a wide clearing, with low-lying brush interspersed with grass and a handful of small trees. Karn pointed.

Tovak looked in that direction, toward a slight rise in the terrain on the other side of the clearing. There appeared to be a drop-off just beyond it. Tovak's heart stilled as he spotted what Karn was pointing at. There were two bodies clad in skirmisher armor, lying in the brush and tall grass.

Chilled, Tovak slowly searched the area for more bodies. He saw none.

Benthok signed to Karn. *You stay here.* The lieutenant pointed at the corporal's bow and then his eyes. The message was clear and Karn gave a nod.

You—he tapped Tovak on the shoulder—*follow me.*

Hunched over, Benthok stepped out into the clearing. Feeling exposed, Tovak followed. They moved as silently as they could through the low-lying brush while scanning the trees that bordered the clearing to either side. Nothing moved.

The sounds of the birds and insects had gone oddly quiet. Tovak felt as if he was being watched. But there came no shout of alarm or massed charge from the woods by a band of wild gnomes.

As they neared the bodies, it became obvious that a small but fierce fight had taken place here. Several bushes had been torn up, as had some grass. A sword lay discarded several feet from the nearest body.

Benthok moved up to the skirmishers and took a knee. He turned over one of the bodies. Tovak recognized the warrior, but did not know his name, nor the other one, who was lying on his side. Both were incredibly pale, as if the blood had been leeched from their bodies. Dried blood, from numerous wounds on their arms and legs, had caked the ground around them.

"Karvan and Jecksen," Benthok hissed quietly. "Bloody shame. Both were good boys and even better skirmishers."

Tovak noticed a gnome body a few yards off, half concealed by a small bush. He moved over to it and knelt, studying the strange creature. It was tiny, like a child, and terribly thin, as if half-starved. The skin was an ashen gray color and smooth, without blemish. The gnome wore no armor, only a coarse gray tunic and a pair of small boots. It had died by the sword, almost cut completely in half, presumably the work of one of the dead skirmishers.

"Your first gnome?" Benthok asked in a low whisper, coming over.

"Yes," Tovak said.

"Never turn your back on one," the lieutenant said. "They are fast and intelligent. Come on. I found some tracks leading up the slope. I think that's where the rest of the Second went."

Then, keeping low, the lieutenant moved forward towards the top of the rise. Almost immediately, he gave an angry hiss and flattened himself against the ground. Tovak joined him, also flattening himself as he peered over the crest of the rise.

Down below, the clearing continued on the opposite side of the slope. There was a small pond, at least twenty yards away, at the base. On the far side of the pond, forest climbed a steep slope. But for the bodies that lay around the edge of the pond, it was a peaceful setting.

Tovak counted twelve of his comrades below. All around them were dozens of gnome dead. His heart plummeted.

The fighting must have been desperate and hard. There was a trail of bodies on the far side of the pond, leading up to the forest. It looked like the survivors of Second Section had retreated that way and the gnomes had followed, pursuing them hotly.

"Thulla's bloody altar," Benthok whispered, barely audible.

A sudden wash of grief and anger flooded Tovak's heart. He'd been wrong in his feelings towards what had happened. Struugar and Second Section were likely all dead. They must have been ambushed by the gnomes, caught by surprise, and then run down like animals.

He recognized some of the dead. Though they had treated him badly, indifferent to his plight as a Pariah, none of that mattered now. They were his fellow brothers, his comrades in arms.

Benthok patted the armor lightly on Tovak's shoulder, breaking him free from his inner turmoil. The lieutenant looked back at Karn, who was still concealed in the tree line. It took Tovak a moment to spot the corporal.

Follow us, provide cover, Benthok signed to the corporal, *stay hidden. More dead this way.*

Karn acknowledged by giving a vigorous nod.

The lieutenant turned back to Tovak and leaned close, whispering in his ear. "We need information and are going to examine the battle site below. Stay low and move as silent as possible. We don't know if there are more gnomes about. Be on your guard. Understand?"

Tovak gave a nod.

With that, Benthok pulled himself up into a crouch and started forward. Tovak followed a heartbeat later.

As he made his way down the slope, Tovak scanned the nearest trees, searching for any hint that they were being watched. The forest was dark, ominous. He saw and heard nothing. As they neared the pond, Tovak was horrified to see a dead skirmisher submerged under the water, held at the bottom of the shallows by the weight of his armor.

Tovak followed as Benthok moved forward amongst the bodies, checking each he came across. Tovak found it a struggle not to be sick at the sight of his butchered comrades.

Benthok paused for a long moment, crouching over the hewn body of a gnome that wore leather armor. Tovak joined him and saw there was an insignia painted in red upon the gnome's breastplate, three interlocking gears.

Benthok let out a long breath and then, without saying anything, continued on. The lieutenant searched amongst the dead, examining each body, rolling over some. One he paused over for several moments, then moved on. After a half hour, Benthok motioned for them to return to Karn's position, who was on the slope above, watching. The corporal had an arrow nocked in his bow and held it at the ready.

Once they were back together, the lieutenant motioned towards the trees on the other side of the clearing. He led them back the way they had come. From the cover of the trees, Benthok and Karn took a long moment to scan the clearing, looking for signs of pursuit.

The lieutenant blew out a long breath and rubbed at his eyes for several moments. He looked over at Karn.

"I am almost positive the gnomes are Khazagynn—a tribe I thought lived much farther to the north and west." Benthok's expression was grim. "I have no idea why they're here. It looks as if our comrades were surprised and then retreated up the hillside and into the trees." He took another deep breath and then let his eyes shift to the rise at the far side of the clearing.

"Did you see the captain amongst the dead?" Karn asked.

Tovak suddenly felt a wash of guilt. He had not thought to search for Struugar. He had not wanted to look at the faces of the dead.

"No," Benthok said, and then a look of sadness crossed his face as he gazed upon Karn. "Keveen is among the dead. I am sorry."

The corporal's face hardened. A muscle twitched along his jawline. He gave a curt nod, but did not reply.

"Right," Benthok said to the two of them. "Struugar isn't here, so we have to assume he led the survivors on the retreat. We need to find them or their bodies... though, to be honest, whatever happened to Second, I do not think it over yet. I believe there to be survivors."

Karn cleared his throat before speaking. "Why do you say that? After what I saw around the pond, I'd have thought all of Second dead."

"There's a strong chance they are holed up somewhere defensible," Benthok said. "Otherwise the gnomes would have come back for their dead, not to mention the looting of ours. I checked several of the boys and they still had coin on their person."

"You might be right," Karn said, his voice gruff, "at least I hope you are."

Benthok rose and took two steps into the clearing again. "Come on, let's push on and see what else we can learn." He motioned towards the rise a few yards away. "Let's—" The lieutenant froze and turned his ear towards the hillside. It was clear he'd heard something. Then Tovak heard it too.

It sounded like axes at work. The sound was faint and seemed to be carried almost on the wind. Then he picked up something else. Voices, high-pitched and unintelligible, coming closer and not far off.

"Back," Benthok hissed.

The three of them fell back a short distance into the trees and moved behind a growth of brush that would provide some concealment, but still afford a view of the area. Tovak lowered himself to the ground next to the lieutenant and Karn and fell still.

Four gnomes appeared just where he and Benthok had been a short while before on the rise that led to the pond. The gnomes made their way down the rise towards the two bodies of the skirmishes they had first discovered.

The gnomes went to the nearest Dvergr body, Jecksen, and picked him up by the arms and legs. Although the creatures were only half the size of a Dvergr, they seemed to have little difficulty lifting the body between them. They carried him back over the rise and were soon gone from sight.

Benthok and Karn shared a troubled look.

"Does this mean it's over?" Tovak asked. "For the captain and the rest of Second?"

"I don't know," the lieutenant said, sounding deeply concerned. "But we need to follow them and find out for certain. Come on. Let's go."

The three skirmishers spread out and, emerging from the trees, made their way across the clearing and back up the rise. By the time they reached it, the gnomes were already at the tree line on the far side of the pond. Benthok waited until the four gnomes had entered the trees and were out of sight before leading them over the rise and down towards the pond.

The three of them moved across the battlefield. Karn expelled an unhappy breath that was mixed with a groan. He paused to kneel beside a body. Tovak did not know the fallen skirmisher, but the corporal seemed deeply affected by his passing.

"Karn." Benthok had come back to the corporal. "Now is not the time for mourning the dead. That will come later. Keveen would understand."

"I don't want to leave my brother here, not like this," Karn said, a tortured anguish plain in his tone. "He deserves better."

"They all do," Benthok said. "But we must look to the living. If there is a chance Struugar and some of the Second are alive, we have to find them."

"And if they are not?" Karn asked.

"Then"—Benthok glanced towards the tree line a few yards off—"I am certain Karach will see that they are avenged. Your brother will not be left here. You have my word on that."

Karn gave a miserable nod. He patted his brother on the shoulder and stood. Tovak had not known that Karn had a brother. He saw tears in the other's eyes and felt terrible for his corporal's loss.

His gaze going to his brother, Karn wiped at his eyes. He laid a hand on his brother's chest, then looked up at Benthok. The corporal's expression had gone hard as granite. "Let's go find the bastards that did this."

Benthok patted Karn on the shoulder armor. He turned away and started towards the trees. Within moments, all three were back in the forest. The slope rapidly began to increase and in moments became quite steep and rugged. Boulders were strewn all about. With each step upward, the sounds of axes grew steadily louder.

The tree cover thickened, to the point where the forest floor became dim. It was as if they had been plunged into twilight. After what they had seen back by the pond, Tovak found that an ominous feeling. They traveled another two hundred yards before reaching the crest of the hill.

The trees began to thin after that and once again Tovak was able to see sky. In the lead, Benthok advanced a few yards before lowering himself to the ground. Keeping well-hidden amidst tight clusters of undergrowth and trees that filled the forest, Karn and Tovak joined the lieutenant.

The trees continued to thin ten yards down the slope. Beyond that was open ground that had long ago been cleared. Dozens of old stumps littered the area, which traveled another hundred yards to what looked like a dried and sandy riverbed.

The riverbed met a steep, rocky cliff face that was part of the next ridge. The cliff towered above them before becoming heavily forested as the terrain continued to slope upward.

Tovak almost could not believe his eyes. There were hundreds of gnomes below in the open area and in the adjacent trees. A half-dozen gnomes off to the left were working around a large pot full of bubbling liquid suspended on iron struts over a fire. One of them threw a handful of... something... into the pot, which prompted the gnome beside it to smack its fellow hard in the side of its head. The two began an animated discussion in their own language, waving their arms about, clearly arguing.

The four gnomes they had been following had reached the clearing. Tovak watched as they dropped Jecksen's body near the pot. The four immediately began stripping the body bare. Tovak didn't want to think about what they had in mind, but with the boiling pot, the implication was clear to him.

Well off to the right, on the other side of the open area, more gnomes were busy with axes, beating a steady staccato as they worked in teams to fell some of the smaller trees on the edge of the forest. Several dozen trees had already been cut. A good number of these had been stripped of their limbs and piled in an orderly stack nearby.

A short distance off from the axe party, yet another group of gnomes worked on several logs, stripping them of their bark. They worked with axes and saws, cutting the logs apart, efficiently turning each tree trunk into usable, albeit rough lumber.

Yet another bunch of the gnomes was in the middle of the open area. They were busy constructing what appeared to be a medium-sized bolt thrower.

As Tovak watched them work, two little creatures, each carrying a board, ran into each other. They dropped to the ground, clearly dazed. The others hooted in amusement, pointing at them, and jabbered away a bit before returning to work.

Just beyond the bolt thrower was the largest group of gnomes. These were armed with small, rounded shields. They had built a rough earthen wall, topped with fresh timbers, forming a crude barricade.

There were at least a hundred of them. They were doing nothing but standing behind the wall, with only their heads poking above, looking towards the cliff face and what appeared to be a small cave.

A cluster of gnome dead lay before the cave entrance, perhaps as many as fifty. Two skirmishers from Second Section lay amongst them. Tovak could not tell who they were, but he had the feeling the two had made a last stand before the cave.

Just beyond, inside the cave, Tovak could make out four Dvergr from Second Section, as well as two archers. They were crouched behind a pair of boulders.

Tovak felt a wave of elation wash over him. His feelings had been proven right. They had found survivors. He closed his eyes, offering Thulla a silent prayer of thanks, and let out a breath of relief. He opened his eyes and let his gaze shift left, past the big pot and farther along the cliff face. He spotted another open area filled with even more stumps and a gentle slope heading down the hillside.

There was a low hiss from the lieutenant. Tovak glanced over at Benthok, who was signaling for his attention. Benthok's fingers flashed.

Fall back.

Tovak gave a nod, and they moved back into the forest and down the hill, moving in the direction of the pond. When they had grouped up on the edge of the tree line before the pond, Benthok took a knee next to a boulder. Tovak and the corporal joined him. Karn stared at Benthok, grim-faced.

"They have superior numbers," Karn said, "and there are likely more that we don't see. But if we handle this right, we can get the jump on them. We can surprise the little shits."

Tovak had to agree with Karn.

"I didn't see any sentries," Tovak added.

"Neither did I," Benthok said.

"They aren't expecting us." Karn's gaze traveled to his brother's body.

"No, they are not," Benthok said.

"We don't know how many are left alive in that cave," Karn said, "and by the looks of things, it won't take them long to finish that bolt thrower, though I am not sure how effective it will be if they intend to shoot bolts into the cave."

With their numerical advantage, Tovak found himself imagining the gnomes rushing in and slaughtering what was left of Second Section. He went cold at that thought.

"I am not sure what they intend to do with the bolt thrower either," Benthok said, "but it looks like they are boiling oil or something flammable. Using the bolt thrower somehow, they may intend on burning or smoking the defenders out. If anything, gnomes are creative."

"I thought they were going to cook with it," Tovak said. "Isn't that why they carried Jecksen back?"

"I don't think they eat meat," Benthok said, "but with gnomes, who knows? I've never met anyone who can figure them out."

"They might be preparing for some sort of dark cere-mony," Karn said. "That could be why they wanted the body stripped. There may be a priest down there."

Tovak felt a wave of pure and unfiltered revulsion at such a thought. It came on so suddenly, his stomach cramped, as if he'd had bad food. A moment later, it grew into an anger, a near rage that the gnomes would use one of his comrades in such a way. The dead deserved to be honored, not desecrated in some dark rite.

"The sacrifices of the fallen require a full accounting," Tovak said to himself, "and we, the righteous, will see it through until the debt is paid in full and our enemies are vanquished and no more."

Benthok turned to look at Tovak with an odd expression. He was silent for a long moment. "That's a passage from Surn Warbringer, in *Thulla's Blessed Word*, is it not?"

"It is, sir," Tovak said, not realizing he had spoken aloud. He felt suddenly embarrassed. He was equally surprised Benthok knew the passage, for many of their people no longer followed Thulla. In fact, many actively shunned their ancestral deity.

"I had heard you were the religious type," Karn said, though there was no disgust in his tone. "On a day like today, I don't think a little belief would hurt."

"I may not be one for braiding my beard into prayer knots," Benthok added, "but I have to admit, old Surn got it right with that one. We're gonna pay the debt in full. That is for certain."

"So, what do we do, sir?" Karn asked. There was a hungry look in the corporal's eyes.

Benthok turned to the corporal. "We go get Karach, tell him what we found. I am sure he will want to bring the detachment forward to save what's left of Second Section." Benthok sucked in a breath and let it out. "When this is all said and done, I am confident we will be leaving a forest filled with gnome dead, as a message the other tribes in these parts cannot mistake."

That sounded just fine to Tovak, for an accounting was needed.

"I am looking forward to that," Karn said. "I want payback for my brother and what that bunch did to Second Section."

Tovak's gaze moved towards the dry riverbed. "Off on the left, the terrain approaching the riverbed and cave seemed easier than the way we went."

"I noticed that as well," Benthok said. "Before we head back, we will go scout it out and determine if it's indeed easier."

"Regardless," Karn said, "Karach might want to use it. If the gnomes want more of our dead, a party of theirs might stumble across the detachment as it moves forward."

"You make a very good point," Benthok said and then paused, as if thinking. "Let's get moving and check out the approach on the left. I don't think Second has all that much time."

CHAPTER THREE

Amidst the trees and only a short distance from where the bodies of Second Section still lay by the pond, Karach had arranged his warriors into two groups. As they'd formed up, Tovak realized just how much their numbers had dwindled. It bit at him like a hungry animal.

They were going into battle again, and they were likely to lose more, Tovak thought morosely. That worry was set against a stark backdrop of his desire to kill and drive off every last gnome that threatened what remained of Second Section.

To the left of the skirmishers stood the whole of Fifth Company, their patterned, green cloaks a bright wash of color against their dark plate armor. Next to them stood the Baelix Guard's Fourth Section, strikers all. The grim expressions on their faces were a testament to what they too wanted to do to the gnomes.

"You nervous?" Gorabor asked quietly from where he stood beside Tovak.

"I don't know what I'm feeling," Tovak replied in a whisper. Anger, worry, and fear of what was coming—all mixed with a powerful need for revenge. "I want every last one of those gnomes to pay for what they've done."

Gorabor blew out a nervous breath. "I never thought we'd fight gnomes."

"Me either," Tovak agreed. "I did not even think I'd ever see one."

Thegdol, a few paces off, eyed them both and cleared his throat.

They fell silent. Tovak fixed his gaze upon where the officers stood a dozen yards off. Captain Greng of Fifth Company, his lieutenant, Lieutenant Benthok of the Baelix Guard, and Corporal Hilla, who commanded the archer detachment, stood around the warchief in a tight circle.

After they had returned and reported, Karach had moved the entire detachment forward. Tovak had been ordered back to his section while Benthok and Karn had guided the detachment into position for an assault. He felt disappointed at that, but his duty was to follow the orders that had been given to him. Now, they waited while the officers spoke and planned.

As Tovak watched them, Karn emerged from the trees and jogged up to the warchief. He gave a report. None of it Tovak could hear, but he could well guess the corporal had been sent back out to eyeball the gnomes before the detachment went into action.

When Karn was done, Karach nodded and said something to the corporal.

"Yes, sir," Karn replied. He turned on his heel and jogged over to take his position beside Sergeant Thegdol at the head of the Baelix Guard skirmisher formation.

"Join your warriors," Karach said, a few moments later. "It is time."

The officers around him broke up, returning to their respective commands. Lieutenant Benthok strode past Tovak and took up a position beside him at the side of the formation.

Karach moved forward and faced them all, his red cloak fluttering in his wake. He paused for a moment, letting his steely gaze roll across his assembled warriors.

"You all know why we are here," Karach said, raising his voice slightly so they could easily hear. "Several hundred gnomes stand between us and our comrades." Karach glanced up the hill. His eyes seemed to blaze when he turned back. "We're going to get our own and, in doing so, show the gnomes what happens when they mess with our people."

A grumble of affirmation rolled through the warriors, and Tovak felt his heart quicken.

Karach drew his sword. "Officers, you have your orders. You know what to do."

Benthok turned to face his skirmishers. "Skirmishers, right face."

They turned on their heels, facing up the ridge in a marching column.

"March," Benthok commanded and began guiding them up to the right and away from the detachment. The skirmishers of First and Third Sections strode forward briskly, moving up the slope in a column of two abreast, with a steady thumping of boots. As they neared the rise, where the bodies from Second Section still lay, a group of archers, including Gulda, joined them. The archers had caught up to the detachment while Tovak, Benthok, and Karn had been away scouting. Gorabor saw Gulda as she passed by. Tovak's friend puffed out his chest at the sight of her.

"Section, halt," Benthok ordered after they had gone no more than a hundred yards. "Corporal Hilla."

"Sir?" she replied.

"Your orders stand as we move up this hill. If you or your archers see a gnome, kill it. No need to wait for my orders."

"Yes, sir," she replied.

"Listen up," Benthok said, turning to face the skirmishers. "I am sure you've heard, but Struugar and the rest of the Second are holed up in a cave just over the ridge. Karach is positioning the rest of the detachment to hit the gnomes and fix their attention. We're going to come in from what should be behind the action, on the far side of the battle." He paused, searching faces to make sure everyone was listening. "Our job will be to reach the cave and help those from Second Section escape. We are expecting them to be exhausted and to have injured. The main body of the attack should come as a complete surprise. However, these are gnomes we're talking about. If things go badly, and they could, we are to withdraw with the survivors and make our way back to the jump-off point and then to the warband. I know you will all do your duty. Are there any questions before we proceed?"

There were none.

"Good," Benthok said. "Let's get moving. Forward march."

They started off again, continuing up the slope. Benthok led the way, threading his warriors through the trees and up the hill. Tovak's heart pounded, and not just from the exertion of climbing again. Expectation and even trepidation of the coming battle chewed at his nerves.

As they moved up the slope, the growing sound of woodworking almost drowned out the footfalls of the skirmishers. This, in turn, eased Tovak's nerves somewhat.

The *swish-thuck* of an arrow caught everyone's attention, and then there was another *swish-thuck.*

"Halt," Benthok hissed as he spun in that direction, eyes searching the forest.

All eyes turned to where Corporal Hilla stood, just twenty yards off to the left, her bow raised as she drew another arrow from her small bundle she held in her hand with the bow. Just to Hilla's left, Gulda had also fired a single arrow.

Tovak let his eyes follow in the direction they aimed. Both missiles had flown true. Twenty yards ahead of them, through the trees, he spotted two small forms lying on the forest floor, a single arrow stuck out of each. One still moved weakly, rolling on the ground in agony and moaning. Gulda moved cautiously up to the gnome, drew her dagger, and stabbed down. The gnome fell still. Hilla turned to Benthok and gave a thumbs-up.

"Move," Benthok hissed, and the small formation continued up the hill until Tovak, at the head of the line, spotted the rocky cliff face about forty yards through the trees. Benthok marched them to the crest of the ridge, turned, and said in a low tone, "All right, boys. This is far enough."

With that, the skirmishers stopped.

"I want a line here, two ranks," Benthok said, "facing that way, towards the cliff."

Tovak moved and once again found himself in the front rank as the rest of the skirmishers fell in around him. Gorabor was on his left and Karn on the right.

"Draw steel," Benthok commanded.

Seemingly in one smooth motion, every skirmisher drew his blade and held it at the ready position.

"That's it, lads," the lieutenant said. "We're gonna get payback for what the gnomes did. That said, remember our mission. We're here for the Second Section. They come first." He paused and looked over. "Corporal Hilla?"

"Sir?" she said.

"You and your archers will follow us down the hill. Provide an overwatch and take initiative. You don't need to wait for my orders. If I see something I need done, I will tell you."

"Yes, sir," Hilla said and moved over to the right side of the formation. "Girls, on me."

Gulda and the other four archers appeared from their positions amidst the trees and fell in with Gulda.

"Take a knee, boys," Benthok said. "We're waiting for a signal to go in."

The entire section sank to a knee.

"It's likely to get ugly down there," Benthok said to them. "Keep your heads and remember your training." Benthok paused and looked over at Karn. "Corporal, pull your boys from the line."

"Yes, sir," Karn said and stepped aside. "My squad on me."

Tovak felt a keen sense of disappointment as he left the line and joined up with his corporal. He wanted to fight with the formation. Karn turned to make sure the members of his squad—Bettoth, Torimar, Dagmar, Gorabor, and Tovak—were with him.

Benthok moved over to them and addressed himself to the corporal in a hushed tone. "As our line advances, I want you to follow us. When we move in, your job will be going right for the cave. We'll work to provide you cover to get everyone out. Once you get them out of the cave, if they are mobile and capable of joining the fight, see that they do. If not, do your best to get them up the ridge and out of the fight. They might not have had food or water for some time. Expect there to be wounded."

"Yes, sir," Karn said, in a low voice. "We will get the job done, sir."

"I know you will," Benthok said.

There was a high-pitched shout of alarm from the forest ahead and off to the left. The clamor of construction went silent.

"Spears!" a voice boomed through the forest. "Forward, boys, forward."

A battle horn called out a single shearing note, which seemed to rip the air.

"That's the signal, boys," Benthok said. "On your feet."

Below them and through the trees, the gnomes began shouting and shrieking in what to Tovak sounded like outrage mixed with alarm. Then there was the unmistakable sound of steel ringing on steel. Within mere heartbeats, the fight's sound increased dramatically to what could only be described as a full-on raging battle.

"Advance," Benthok ordered.

The line stepped forward as one, moving through the trees and down the slope of the ridge towards the dry riverbed below.

"Come on," Karn said and led his squad loosely after them.

Tovak gripped his sword tightly. His heart pounded. As they advanced down the ridge and through the trees, the battle came into view, and Tovak had to blink several times to make sense of what lay before him.

On the left, there was a wall of Dvergr shields in three ordered ranks. To their front was a mass of gnomes, pressing against the shield wall. It seemed to him that there were more gnomes than they had originally seen when they'd scouted the area. With great effort, the strikers were steadily shoving their way forward against the gnomes, who seemed crazed and eager to get at the Dvergr warriors.

Another force of roughly a hundred gnomes was busy organizing themselves into a rough formation, just behind the raging battle. What looked to be a gnome leader was standing atop a large stump watching the fight. The clash of steel, shouting, and screaming were nearly deafening. The gnome leader turned and spotted Benthok's formation as it moved down the hill. He shouted something, pointing. More than two dozen gnomes separated from the budding formation and started towards the skirmishers.

"Karn," Benthok shouted as he pointed at the cave entrance, "go now. Get the Second."

"Alright, boys, let's go," he yelled to his squad and began jogging away from the formation as Benthok moved the skirmishers to block the oncoming gnomes.

Tovak followed after Karn as the corporal led them towards the earthen wall that hemmed in the cave. Behind them, there was a crash as the gnomes slammed into Benthok's small formation.

Suddenly, there were several gnomes directly to the squad's front. These had remained on the wall, clearly left there to keep those in the cave from escaping. Tovak found himself confronted by a gnome. The creature held a small spear with a wicked-looking point and jabbed it at him. Gripping the hilt of his sword tightly, Tovak hastily dodged and stabbed back. It caught the little creature in the side, opening up an ugly gash that bled heavily. The gnome shrieked in pain and, as if enraged, stabbed again. The tip of the blade bit into his chest armor, but did not go through. Tovak grunted from the force of the strike. He grabbed the spear with his free hand and ripped it out of the gnome's hand.

Badly wounded and bleeding freely, the creature stumbled backward. It fell to a knee and then rolled over on its side, twitching. A heartbeat later, another gnome attacked him, this one with a sword. Dropping the spear, Tovak blocked a strike aimed for his leg. Their blades met in a powerful clang.

Tovak was surprised by the gnome's strength and felt the impact of their swords communicated to his hand, which stung. The gnome shifted and moved its blade around his, clearly preparing to stab at him. Forcing his opponent's sword aside, Tovak kicked out, his boot hammering into the creature's chest. It fell back, hard.

Tovak took two strides forward and drove his blade through the center of the gnome's chest. It gagged as a gout of black blood bubbled up from its tiny mouth. He gave the blade a savage twist. Behind him sounded a scream filled with both fear and agony. He spun around, just as Dagmar screamed again.

"Get it off me," Dagmar cried. "Get it bloody off me!"

Tovak took in the scene in an instant. Dagmar's opponent, although disarmed, had gotten beneath his guard and was now scrambling up the back of the skirmisher's leg. Karn, who had just dispatched his own opponent by decapitating it, turned and looked too.

The corporal was closer, though Gorabor, battling with a gnome, was between him and Dagmar. Karn sidestepped and ran his blade through Gorabor's opponent, drawing forth a bloodcurdling screech from the gnome. Another gnome blocked the corporal's path and jabbed with a sword. The corporal countered.

Tovak began moving towards Dagmar, who was vainly trying to get the gnome off him. He could not pry the creature loose. It appeared to be biting him. In what was clear desperation, Dagmar threw himself backward and onto the dirt wall, slamming the gnome against it. The creature fell off him. Suddenly free, Dagmar rolled away. Tovak could see blood running from Dagmar's backside and down his left leg.

The gnome scrambled and was back on its feet in an instant. It came charging straight back at Dagmar, but Tovak had reached it. His sword was already coming down, hard. The blade connected with the crown of the creature's head. It cleaved through flesh, bone, and brain all the way down between the gnome's shoulders. The head came apart before his eyes and Tovak felt a spray of blood and gore wash over him. The gnome crashed to the ground and lay there, legs twitching.

"Thanks," Dagmar breathed as he pulled himself to his feet. Tovak glanced around, searching for another threat. There were no more gnomes within twenty yards. He turned back to Dagmar, who was clutching his left buttock. "It bit me. The bloody thing bit me in the ass."

Tovak stared for a long moment, then suddenly laughed as Dagmar seemed to dance around in a circle, trying to get a better look at his butt. Absurdly, he found his comrade's antics hysterically funny. It was a moment of madness, it was surreal, and Tovak could not help but laugh madly.

"Tovak, Dagmar," Karn shouted, irritation lacing his tone. "Stop screwing around."

Looking about, Tovak saw Karn with Gorabor standing on the wall. Both went down over the other side.

"You okay?" Tovak glanced at the back of Dagmar's leg and saw a streak of blood. A giggle escaped from his lips. "Are you going to live?"

"I'll be fine," Dagmar replied sourly. "I've had worse. It just bloody hurts."

Tovak stole a quick glance around at the larger battle. What he saw seemed to be organized chaos. Benthok's formation was fully engaged. They appeared to be holding back the gnomes sent against them. Beyond them, the main body was continuing to drive the greater mass of gnomes across the dry riverbed and in their direction.

"Come on," Tovak said to Dagmar and moved, following after Karn and Gorabor. As he clambered over the wall, he saw seven skirmishers emerge from the cave entrance. They were helping four wounded, who were having difficulty moving.

To Tovak's right, Gulda climbed up on the wall. Arrow nocked, she raised her bow and loosed. Tovak did not see where the missile went. His eyes had found the captain, who was still very much alive. Tovak felt a wave of relief. Struugar had a bandaged arm and was helping an injured skirmisher limp from the cave entrance.

"Karn, you are a sight for sore eyes," Struugar said, relief plain in his voice as Tovak came up to them. "We thought we were done."

"Sir," Karn said, "we've been sent by the lieutenant to get you out of here. Gorabor, take Tehent. Help him to the rear."

"Yes, Corporal," Gorabor said and took Tehent from the captain.

"Is there anyone left inside, sir?" Karn asked, looking towards the cave entrance.

"Unfortunately, no," Struugar said. The captain appeared thoroughly worn out, but at the same time there was strength there. "I am afraid eleven is all we have left from Second." Struugar paused a long moment as a look of sadness came over him. "Your brother did not make it. He died like a warrior and bought time for us to escape."

Karn scowled. "We found his body." The corporal swallowed as he looked away. When he returned his gaze to Struugar, he was all business again. "Tovak, Dagmar, the rest of you, help the wounded up the hill and back into the trees."

The squad moved forward. Four female archers had emerged with the skirmishers from Second Section. Like the skirmishers, every single one of them looked like they'd been run through the gauntlet. One's head was bandaged, and another limped on a leg wrapped with a blood-soaked and soiled bandage. Tovak moved up and offered his shoulder to the archer who was limping. They started forward at a slow but steady pace. To their front, Struugar moved up to the dirt wall and climbed up it to see the battle.

"Thank you," the archer said to Tovak as he helped her towards the wall. She looked utterly exhausted and was gritting her teeth against the pain. There was a sheen of sweat on her young face. She was also pale.

"What's your name?" Tovak asked, more to distract her than anything else.

"Serena," she said.

"That's a pretty name," Tovak said as they continued towards the dirt wall.

"Are you flirting with me?" she asked, looking over at him.

Tovak felt himself flush with embarrassment, which caused her to grin at him.

There was a sudden roar of cheering from over the other side of the wall. He glanced around but could not see over the mound of dirt the gnomes had piled up into a wall.

"The gnomes have broken," Struugar said, wearily. "They're running."

Chapter Four

O nce again in the column of march, Tovak, with the rest of the detachment, marched across the rolling grasslands of the Grimbar Plateau. With the survivors of Second Section, the detachment was finally headed home, to the safety of the warband's encampment.

As he put one tired and weary foot in front of the next, Tovak found himself not only greatly relieved to be returning, but also reliving the last sights and sounds of the battlefield around the dry riverbed. It was haunting him.

The wood the gnomes had harvested, along with the partially constructed artillery piece, had been stacked in a pile for a funeral pyre for the dead.

Once it had been lit, a thick column of white smoke had quickly risen into the sky. The air was full of popping as the fresh pine burned, mixing with the sweet, sickly smell of burning flesh. The dead deserved better. They should have been interred in a family crypt alongside their kin, but out in the field, and with the Great March in motion, that was an impossibility. Everything their people had, including the family crypts, was being left behind.

While they had worked at gathering the dead and building the funeral pyre, the gnomes had not disturbed the detachment. In fact, the little creatures had all but disappeared.

Scouts were sent to determine if the gnomes were rallying off in the trees for a counterattack, but found no evidence of them, not even a hint they were still around. Tovak had found that unnerving, for even with his skills as a trained scout, he could not find where they had gone. To their frustration, Benthok and Karn had had no luck either. Tovak had learned from Karn that gnomes were like that.

Karach's skirmishers had arranged two rings of stakes driven into the ground surrounding the funeral pyre. Each one had a small gnomish head jammed down onto it, most with their dead, black eyes open, staring lifelessly into the great beyond. Karach was sending a message to the gnomes, and the image of it had been burned into Tovak's memory. It would remain with him until the end of his days.

As the detachment worked their way down the hills and ridges back to the plateau, Tovak had expected an ambush to come. Nothing of the sort had materialized and now, after several hours, they were within a mile of the encampment. Ahead, a light haze of smoke hung over the warband's camp, like an ugly pall.

The detachment was spread out in a loose column, with the skirmishers taking up the rear. Karach was at the head of the column, with Captains Struugar and Greng at his side.

The heat of the day was beginning to abate, just a little. The last hours of sunlight beat down upon them all, as if to remind them of what was to come on the morrow. In the distance, a line of dark clouds rose ominously across the plateau, well off to the west, carrying with it the promise of rain.

Tovak and Gorabor trudged along, a makeshift stretcher suspended between them. It was their turn to carry one of the injured, Serena. Tovak's arms felt like they were being pulled out of their sockets, and sweat poured from his body. Thankfully, Serena had fallen asleep. The journey down from the hills had been a torment for her and the other injured. Though they had taken care, each step and jolt caused the injured pain.

Excused from litter duty on account of his wound and ankle injury, Dagmar limped beside Tovak and Gorabor. He winced with every step. It seemed the marching was aggravating his injury.

"How's your ass?" Bettoth called out from behind in the column of march. It elicited a chuckle from several. Since they had come down from the hills, Dagmar had become the butt of the company's jokes.

"It hurts," he snapped in an irritated tone. "What do you think? That Thulla-be-damned little monster nearly took a chunk out of my arse." Dagmar gingerly placed a hand on his left bandaged butt cheek. "Bloody hurts."

Corporal Karn had been the one to clean, stitch, and bandage the wound, but not without some good-natured ribbing from the other warriors of the skirmishers. It seemed Dagmar would not be living this down anytime soon.

Amused, Tovak grinned.

The column ahead began snaking its way around a low rise in the plateau. It was an anomaly in the seemingly never-ending flatness. As the column marched around it, he was able to see Karach and Struugar at the head of the column. The two officers appeared to be in an animated conversation. He couldn't hear what was said, but as he watched, it appeared as if Struugar objected to something the warchief had said.

"I wonder what that's all about," Gorabor said quietly.

"You saw it too?" Tovak asked.

"It was kinda hard to miss." Gorabor shifted his grip on the stretcher. "We've taken a pretty bad beating these last few days. Do you think Karach blames Struugar?"

"Who knows?" Tovak blew out a worried breath. "I hope not."

"I doubt there's anything to worry about," Karn said from where he marched a few yards off. He turned towards Tovak. "It's true we've taken serious losses"—the corporal's look became strained—"my brother amongst them, but this isn't the first time a company took it on the chin. You boffers are still new, but there isn't a veteran among us who hasn't seen the like before." His expression hardened, but not in an angry way. "It'll turn out alright. It always does. Karach values Struugar. The captain just has some hard questions to answer, is all. And mark my words, he will answer them to Karach's satisfaction. Now, you two, keep the speculation to a minimum before Thegdol hears. Understand?"

"Yes, Corporal," they both said.

Tovak adjusted his grip on the litter. It was hard not to speculate when things had gone so badly for the Baelix Guard, but he would do as the corporal said.

"I may not be able to carry a litter," Dagmar said, "but I can certainly carry a tune." He pulled his flute from a pocket. "How about 'The Battle of Sul'Drogal?'" Dagmar asked loudly.

"Aye!" several voices rose together from amongst the skirmishers.

Dagmar placed the flute to his lips and poured his heart into the rousing melody. Moments later, several more flutes joined in, and it wasn't long before the entire formation seemed to march with a lighter step.

As they played, Tovak felt his heavy heart lift, at least a little. They'd taken losses, to be sure, and there was still the disturbing vision of what they'd left behind, but they'd accomplished their mission. They had found the Second. It was as good as could be expected, and as they closed the distance to the warband's encampment, he reflected that this was the life of a warrior. It hadn't been like he'd imagined. The victorious made it home, and the dead were sent to Thulla's feasting halls.

"Tighten it up, lads," Benthok shouted from where he marched at the head of the section with Thegdol. A moment later, a similar order was shouted from Captain Greng to his company. The column began moving into orderly rows and columns, sharpening up their appearance.

It didn't take them long to cover the distance to the main gate. As they reached it, a cheer rose up from the sentries along the trench that surrounded the encampment.

"All hail Karach," a number of the sentries shouted.

Tovak and the rest of the formation behind the warchief cheered heartily, with the strikers smacking their swords against their shields. It lasted for a dozen heartbeats, and then everything died down.

"It's good to be back with the encampment," Gorabor said. "I will be glad to put this stretcher down."

"Agreed," Tovak replied. They'd been out in the field for a little more than four days. So much had happened, and in such a short time, too. It seemed to Tovak like he was a different person and had fundamentally changed.

He thought on the maps he'd found in the orc camp. Something deep down told him they would prove vital for what was to come. He didn't know why he felt that way, but as they approached the encampment, he grew more and more certain of it.

A sentry in plate mail, standing atop the gate, raised a battle horn and blew out two notes, announcing the arrival of the warchief. A second horn, floating up from the watch tower at the center of camp, replied in kind, and a mighty cheer rose up from the entire camp.

More stone flutes joined the chorus, and as Karach passed through the gate, every Dvergr in sight stopped what he or she was doing. They stood and watched. Karach led the detachment down the main street of the encampment. Warriors exited their tents to give greeting to their warchief with a cheer or watch the procession pass by. They'd covered about a third of the encampment when a messenger appeared from one of the side streets. The young warrior rushed up to Karach and saluted.

"Column, halt," Greng hollered. The column came to a halt, and the flutes went silent. "Stand at ease."

Karach returned the messenger's salute. The messenger spoke quickly, but it was too far away for Tovak to hear. He and the rest of the stretcher carriers set their burdens on the ground. Tovak rubbed his hands, which ached.

"Gods, that's a relief," Gorabor groaned quietly. "My arms feel like they're two inches longer."

"It almost makes me glad I got bit on the ass," Dagmar added.

"That you didn't have to carry a stretcher?" Gorabor asked to which Dagmar gave a nod.

"Don't let it bother you," Tovak said.

"I won't," Dagmar said.

The messenger saluted again and then left. Karach turned to Struugar and Greng. The three officers had a brief conversation. Struugar nodded once, gave a salute, and moved back down the column as Karach turned away, and headed off towards the center of camp.

"Lads," Struugar said in a clear voice, striding up to the formation, "Karach has ordered Captain Greng and the Fifth back to their tents. The Baelix Guard will carry the wounded to the field hospital." He turned to Benthok. "Lieutenant, I leave the company in your capable hands. I've been ordered to headquarters."

"Uh-oh," Gorabor said under his breath.

"Stow that," Corporal Karn hissed. "I won't have you starting any rumors."

"Yes, Corporal," Gorabor replied.

"Baelix Guard," Benthok called out, stepping forward to face the skirmishers, "pick up the litters, boys. Let's get the wounded to the care they need."

Tovak and the others grabbed their makeshift litters and stood. Tovak's muscles and back cried out in protest, but he gritted his teeth and took it in silence. Serena moaned softly, but did not wake.

Captain Struugar looked over his company, and a strange expression crossed his face. Tovak couldn't tell if it was longing, sadness, or perhaps merely a commanding officer taken by the losses his warriors had suffered. Without another word, he turned and followed in the same direction as Karach.

"Company," Benthok shouted, "forward march." He strode forward, the skirmishers in tow. With the lieutenant leading them, they moved through the camp, making several turns along the way. Every Dvergr they passed, from armored soldier to lowly camp follower, stopped whatever they were doing and turned to watch as they passed.

Benthok led the formation through the camp to the far side, where they finally reached a row of large supply tents full of crates, armor, weapons, and other goods necessary for keeping a warband on its feet.

They came around the tents to find a wide swath of open grass. Several wounded lay out in the open. Beyond them and bordering the grass field were a number of large tents. They had clearly arrived at the field hospital. A handful of healers in the crimson robes of their trade, as well as several priests in orange and tan robes, moved around the area as they tended to the wounded, or were focused on other tasks.

"Halt." Benthok took a deep breath and looked over the formation for several heartbeats. "Place the wounded over there on the grass."

Tovak and Gorabor did as directed, as did the others. Several healers emerged from tents and began working their way over, as did a number of assistants. Serena woke. She looked around wildly for a moment before her eyes focused on them. She made to sit up. Tovak gently held her down.

"Rest. We've got you to the sick tents," Tovak said, taking a knee beside the litter. "You will soon be in good hands and I will offer up a prayer for you."

Serena's eyes narrowed for a heartbeat. She sucked in a pained breath and let it out. "Thank you both and thank you for your prayer."

Tovak stood as a healer approached. The healer knelt down beside Serena and began looking her over.

"Gather 'round," Benthok called. He waited for the skirmishers to assemble around him. "I've got business to attend to. I want you to get back to our own tents, drop your gear, and get some hot food in you. Once you've eaten, I expect you all to clean your kits. Got that?"

"Yes, sir," the assembled skirmishers said in unison.

"Get to it," Benthok said.

"Gorabor, Tovak, think you can find your way back?" Benthok asked as the group broke up. "Or do you need a guide?"

Gorabor hastily glanced around. "I think I can find the way, sir."

"Dagmar," Benthok barked. "Not so fast. You're not going anywhere. Get a healer to look at your wounds."

"Lieutenant," Dagmar said, "you know I don't like healers much."

"That's an order," Benthok said firmly.

"Yes, Lieutenant." Dagmar moved off towards the nearest tent.

With that, Benthok headed off toward one of the sick tents. Tovak hesitated, looking first at Serena and then the rest of the wounded laid out on the grass. A number of healers and assistants were moving amongst them.

"Come on," Karn said to Tovak and Gorabor, "camp's this way."

The corporal led them along the tent lines. There were two groups of sick tents. Tovak saw a couple of haggard-looking healers carrying a warrior from a tent in the first group to one in the middle of the second group.

"Poor bastard," Karn breathed.

Tovak looked over his shoulder. "What do you mean?" he asked.

Karn glanced at the two healers as they disappeared into a tent. A pained expression crossed his face.

"That's where the wounded wait to die." Sorrow filled the corporal's voice. "When the healers have lost all hope of saving someone, they move them to those tents. They care for them—try to ease their suffering and passing—but everyone knows that once you go in there, it's only a matter of time until you are feasting in the ancestral halls."

Karn's words struck Tovak's heart as if they were an orc's blade. Jodin's face flashed before his eyes. He remembered the pitched battle to defend the camp—Jodin appearing out of the darkness to help Tovak—and the belly wound he had taken. Karn had said Jodin's wound was dire, but with everything that had happened, Tovak hadn't had even a moment to think about it. A wave of shame washed over him as he realized he didn't even know if Jodin had survived.

"Are you alright?" Gorabor asked.

Tovak didn't answer at first. An even more painful thought slammed into him. He looked up and locked eyes with Gorabor. "I wonder which tent Jodin is in."

Gorabor paled.

"Corporal," Tovak said, "can I look in on Jodin?"

Karn gave a nod. "Do it and let me know how he is."

"I will, Corporal."

"Come on, Gorabor," Karn said. "Let's go. I don't want you getting lost again."

The corporal started off. Gorabor spared one last look at Tovak before hurrying to catch up with Karn and disappearing around the corner of the supply tents.

Tovak looked about, wondering where Jodin was and how to find him. He did not know who to ask. Lieutenant Benthok stepped out of a tent with an older healer in orange and white robes.

"Thank you, Aggen," Benthok said to the healer.

"Don't mention it," the healer said and moved off, walking away from the lieutenant.

A heartbeat later, Benthok spotted Tovak and raised a suspicious eyebrow before stepping up to him. "What are you still doing here, Tovak?" he asked. "I thought I instructed you to go back to camp with the rest."

Tovak swallowed. "Sir, if it is alright, I'd like to check in on Jodin. Corporal Karn said it would be okay."

Benthok cocked his head to the side, a funny expression overcoming his face.

"He saved my life, sir," Tovak interjected before the lieutenant could think of an objection. "I need to know if he lives or not. I would see him, sir, and thank him."

"I don't see why not," the lieutenant said after a prolonged moment of silence. "Speak to one of the healers. They will point you in the right direction."

"Yes, sir," Tovak said. "Thank you, sir."

"Don't take too long." Benthok turned on his heel. "You and the rest of the company need a good meal, your kit cleaned, and a good night's sleep."

"Yes, sir."

"Very well," Benthok said and left him, moving back towards the healers attending to the newly arrived injured of the Baelix Guard.

Tovak looked around again for someone to ask. He turned his attention to a young healer who was kneeling next to one of the wounded a few yards off. Her loose-fitting crimson robes almost looked like layers of gauze, and she had a wide cloth belt the color of hay. Tovak didn't miss the splotches and streaks of blood that marred her belt or had turned the crimson cloth a ruddy brown in places. She was fair-looking, pretty even. Tovak stepped up to her, just as she covered the fallen warrior's face with his own cloak.

The healer closed her eyes for a moment and bowed her head. Tovak heard her whisper something, although he couldn't make out what. He supposed she was offering a prayer to Thulla, but you could never tell with his people. Most had lost their faith. The sight of the covered corpse tore at Tovak's heart. Before him was yet another one of his people headed for the feasting halls. The cost of war was a terrible price he'd never really considered until he had been harshly confronted by it over the last few days.

The healer opened her eyes and saw Tovak standing there.

"Can I help you, warrior?" Her voice was soft.

"Yes," he said. "I wanted to check in on a member of the Baelix Guard." His eyes shifted to the cloak-covered body and then returned to focus on the healer. "Jodin would have been brought here yesterday, or early this morning." He swallowed hard, remembering the sight of Jodin's blood seeping through his fingers. "He had a bad belly wound."

"I don't know," she said softly. "Let me ask." She rose to her feet and went to the nearest tent. "Father Maragorn," she called out towards the interior. The side had been rolled up. There was an old priest inside. He held a wax tablet in his hands, and Tovak could now see he carried a satchel over his shoulder that contained more of them. Maragorn marked something down with his stylus and then looked up.

"Yes, Belameth?" He moved over to them with the slow, careful strides of the elderly.

Maragorn had gentle eyes of green, and his gray hair was tied back into a single, tidy braid. He had a long dark-gray beard with a streak of white down the center, and it had been tied off prominently with twelve prayer knots of bright orange cloth.

"This warrior has asked about a friend of his," Belameth said, motioning towards Tovak.

"Name?" Maragorn asked with a weary but compassionate voice. He looked to Tovak expectantly as Belameth left them.

"Corporal Jodin of the Baelix Guard, First Section, First Squad." Tovak's heart fluttered slightly, hoping Jodin still remained amongst the living. "He would have arrived yesterday afternoon—or possibly this morning."

Maragorn looked thoughtful. "Jodin, you say?" He slipped the tablet he was holding into his satchel and pulled another out. "Jodin … Jodin." Maragorn ran his finger down several columns of names, and then his expression changed to one of sorrow. "You will find him in that second set of tents, right over there, first column, third row back."

Tovak paled.

Maragorn let out a sorrowful breath. "You know what that means, yes?"

Tovak nodded slowly. "Jodin will soon be feasting in the halls of our ancestors."

"That is not always a bad thing," Maragorn said. "Thulla takes us all when it's time."

Tovak did not reply.

"Come," the priest said, motioning towards the tent. "I will take you to him. What is your name, my son?"

"Tovak."

Maragorn paused. "I have heard that name." He turned to Tovak. "Several of the recently wounded spoke of a Tovak, a Pariah, new to the warband, who braved death to rescue his comrades from an enemy camp. Are you he?"

Tovak hesitated, afraid Maragorn might send him away for being a Pariah. Taking a deep breath, he nodded his head. He was past hiding who he was.

"Thulla bless you, my son," the cleric said, with a good deal of emotion that Tovak took to be genuine. "Your actions … such noble deeds … speak to the character within. They will be remembered by Thulla, who prizes such virtues of the heart."

"Do you truly think so?" Tovak asked.

"I have no doubt." The cleric patted him on the back. "Our god loves us all, even Pariahs."

The night he'd rescued Gorabor and Dagmar flashed through Tovak's thoughts, and he realized he had a perfect opportunity to ask a question that had troubled him since then.

"Father, there's something I would like to know."

"What is it, my son?" The cleric looked at him curiously. "You may speak plainly with me. I will not betray your confidence."

The priest turned away and started walking again. Tovak followed.

"The night of the rescue … I had to—no, that's not right…. I was compelled to kill what I think might have been a dark priest."

Maragorn stopped in his tracks, turned, and placed his hand on the center of Tovak's chest to halt him as well. He searched Tovak's eyes, a concerned expression on his face.

"What makes you say that?"

"I was drawn to him," Tovak said, trying to remember the sensation. He closed his eyes. "It's hard to explain, but when I found him, alone, I was filled with such loathing." He opened his eyes and met Maragorn's gaze. "And looking upon him, I would swear there were black flames running over his body. They were barely visible, and to say it now, I dunno, maybe I was just imagining things."

"Why do you think he was a dark priest?"

"Once I'd killed him, I discovered that he had a spider pendant around his neck. It repulsed me."

Maragorn was silent for a long moment. "The spider is a totem of the goddess Avaya, so he might have been a priest of that vile deity or simply a follower." Maragorn paused, hesitating. "But you say you saw flames?"

"Yes … well, something like flames, but they were black. The sight of him, the darkness that surrounded him, it filled me with such ... rage ... like nothing I've ever experienced before, and that's saying something. I just don't have the words for what I felt." Tovak considered telling Maragorn about the strange pulls, drawing him forward, but he thought it best left unsaid. For all he knew, it had just been his imagination.

Maragorn placed a hand on Tovak's shoulder and searched his face. Tovak found the priest's gaze had become piercing. Perhaps he was wondering if Tovak was mad, or making it up, but his eyes finally softened into a gentle look of concern.

"I don't know what to tell you, my son. Thulla works in mysterious ways. So who knows, eh? I am merely a warband cleric, a lowly priest of Thulla." He gave a slight pause. "Regardless, I would caution you to keep clear of evil priests, if that is, in fact, what you encountered. You have a full life ahead of you. There is no sense in ending it before Thulla has deemed it time to call you to the feasting halls."

Tovak resisted a scowl. It wasn't like he'd planned the encounter with the dark priest. "Thank you, Father. I'll keep that in mind."

The priest scowled as he considered Tovak for a long moment. "Did you touch the pendant?"

"No," Tovak said. "I did not."

"Good." The cleric patted Tovak's shoulder and started in motion again. "Such things can corrupt the soul. Now let us see about your friend. Perhaps a friendly face will ease his passing, at least a little."

A pang of guilt coursed through Tovak's heart. What would he say? What could he do? Corporal Jodin was in the death tent because of Tovak.

"Is there really no hope?" he asked.

"For those who come to these tents, my son, there is little hope of a prolonged life," Maragorn said sadly.

Thunder rumbled off in the distance. Tovak let out a slow breath, looking up at the line of dark clouds that was almost over the camp now. The approaching storm reflected his turbulent mood. He returned his gaze to Maragorn and tried to push his worries aside. He resolved to stay as positive as he could.

"I believe I will hold out hope for my friend until the very end, should it come."

"Good. That is the spirit. From hope comes strength, and there isn't a living warrior here who couldn't benefit from even the tiniest sliver of hope."

Maragorn continued on before stopping at a wide tent, its flaps pulled open. The smell hit Tovak hard. He reflexively turned his head away and tried not to gag. It was the stench of waste mixed with putrescence. Never in his life had he smelled so foul a mix. Teska dung didn't even compare.

He looked inside.

A small fire burned within the darkened tent, with smoke rising up through a hole that had been cut into the roof. A dozen camp cots lay inside. All but three were occupied.

Another priest, this one barely a youth, moved between the cots. He had black hair and a single-braided beard. With a pitcher and cup in his hands, he knelt at a cot and whispered something in the warrior's ear. As Tovak watched, several groans floated up, and then a sucking cough from a warrior at the back of the tent caught his attention.

Anguish struck at Tovak when he recognized Jodin. A desire to turn and run hit him like a lightning bolt. For a fleeting moment, he wanted to be anywhere but here. He closed his eyes, took a breath, and forcefully pushed the feeling away.

"Are you alright?" Maragorn asked with a concerned look.

"I'm fine, Father. Thank you," Tovak said finally. "That's Jodin back there." He pointed at the warrior who had coughed. "May I speak to him alone?"

Maragorn gave a nod. He placed a comforting hand on Tovak's back. "Call for me if you need anything, my son."

Tovak nodded in return, then unclipped and dropped his pack on the ground. He took one difficult step after another, drawing nearer to the comrade who had saved his life. The stench inside the tent made his eyes burn.

When he reached Jodin and got a good look at him, he suppressed a gasp. Jodin's eyes were closed. His face was ashen and his lips a pale white with tints of blue. Small beads of sweat dotted his forehead. Although the blanket covered his body to his throat, his arms lay on top, exposed. There were splotches of dried blood on both sleeves of his tunic. Tovak realized that even Jodin's hands were ashen.

Tovak stood there, staring, with no idea of what to say or do. He knew for certain there was nothing he could do to help Jodin get better. So still was he that Tovak wondered for a moment if the corporal had already passed from the world of the living. He found himself looking to see if Jodin was breathing. He was relieved to see his chest rise slowly—too slowly—and he had to wonder how long Jodin had to live.

At that moment, Jodin opened his eyes, as if he'd sensed Tovak's presence, and slowly focused on the figure above him.

"Hello, Tovak," he said in a hoarse whisper that was barely audible.

Tovak went down to one knee and placed his hand on Jodin's arm. "Hello, Jodin. How are you fee—?" He cut off and closed his eyes for the automatic question that had sprung to his lips. He felt embarrassed for such stupidity. "I'm—I'm sorry," he whispered. "I didn't think—"

"It's alright," Jodin said weakly. "There's nothing to be sorry about." Tovak felt Jodin's hand on his own. "In all honesty, I have felt better." A weak chuckle slipped past Jodin's lips. The chuckle turned into a wet, sickly coughing fit that wracked his body. Jodin covered his mouth with his hand, and he almost sat fully up as the coughing fit took him. He closed his eyes in what Tovak knew was agony. He groaned once the coughing fit subsided. "Thulla's mercy, that hurts." He let his head fall back to the pillow, trembling slightly. Jodin looked at Tovak through red-rimmed eyes. "I appreciate you coming to see me. You have proven yourself to be a true ... friend."

Tovak felt tears prick at his eyes. There was so much in that one word, friend. He and Jodin had hated one another, even fought, beaten each other bloody, savagely, but after everything, it meant a lot for Tovak to be named a friend. It had all started over Tovak concealing who he was, a Pariah. Now they were all past that. Funny though, Tovak could almost still feel the blows from that fight, as if it had just happened.

"It's good to see you too," Tovak said. "And we are, you know ... friends."

It was Jodin's turn to nod.

An uncomfortable silence hovered between them. Tovak didn't know what to say.

"How is the company?" Jodin finally asked, breaking the silence. "Did Struugar ever show up with Second Section?"

How should he answer? Tovak wasn't sure if he should tell Jodin the truth or not. There had been so many casualties, so many losses. After a moment of consideration, he decided Jodin deserved the truth, however difficult it might prove to be.

"Karach led us and one of the infantry companies to go find Struugar," Tovak said. "They had been ambushed by a tribe of gnomes. We rescued the captain and some of the Second. They lost a good number before we could get to them." Jodin had gone still. "We've taken some terrible losses."

Jodin closed his eyes and let out a pained breath, obviously struggling not to cough. Just when Tovak thought he had lost consciousness, Jodin finally opened his eyes and stared at the roof of the tent for a long moment.

"It is the way of things," Jodin said quietly, his voice strained. "We fight and we die, and I'm not long for this world." He turned his eyes to Tovak. "Yet the Great March will continue, without me—as it should."

"What kind of talk is that? You're going to be fine," Tovak said, in a weak attempt to soothe Jodin's mind and give him what little comfort he could. "Where there is hope, there is strength, and I'm not about to give up on you, Jodin."

Jodin reached out and took Tovak's hand. He squeezed lightly. Jodin's hand was ice cold.

"Thank you," he said. Jodin fell silent for several heartbeats, and then a strange, almost embarrassed expression crossed his face. "I would clear the slate between us. I regret—well, everything that happened. I've been doing a lot of thinking. What else am I going to do in here?" He searched Tovak's face.

"I do as well," Tovak said.

"Do you think—I mean...?" Jodin hesitated. "Would you be willing to say a prayer for me, like you did after the battle? I—I was told you prayed over me." He looked sheepish. "Another prayer couldn't hurt, could it? After ignoring Him so long, would Thulla mind? That is another slate I'd wipe clean."

"I don't think He would mind," Tovak said and placed a hand gently upon Jodin's chest, closed his eyes, and bowed his head. Reaching within, he thought on what he wanted to say to his god. "Thulla, I kneel before a noble warrior who seeks Your everlasting love. Like so many others, he has strayed, but in the end has returned home. Turn Your gaze not from him. Show him Your love and bless him, for he is a good person."

Tovak felt something within him seem to bubble up, a light or power. It was unexpected, happened so fast, he found it shocking, and then in a heartbeat it was gone. It left his fingers tingling and had vanished almost as soon as it had come.

He opened his eyes and the tent seemed to sway before him. He suddenly felt terribly weary, exhausted even.

Jodin's eyes were wide as he looked on Tovak. Had he felt it too? Tovak shook his head. No. He'd imagined it all. He was just run-down and tired.

"Thank you, Tovak," Jodin said, his voice sounding slightly stronger. "Thank you for praying with me. I think when you go, I will speak with our lord too."

Another coughing fit seized Jodin. He groaned in pain, covering his mouth with the back of his shirt. When the coughing ended, he pulled back his arm, revealing fresh blood spattered on his sleeve.

"Perhaps I should get a healer," Tovak said, looking around. Both priests had gone.

"No, it's alright," Jodin soothed. "You've done enough. You have given me my faith back. All I can do now is wait till the end."

"And hope," Tovak replied, "and pray."

"And hope and pray," Jodin said. "I feel tired. I think I will take a nap."

"Rest," Tovak said. "I will come see you tomorrow night if I am able."

"I would like that. But I overheard the surgeon saying we were pulling out in the morning. You may not be able to."

Tovak gave a nod. The warband still had a mission, whatever that was. "I will come if I am able."

Jodin closed his eyes and seemed to fall asleep.

Tovak turned away and left the tent. He stood outside for a bit, breathing in the fresh air. He could still taste the stench of death on his tongue. Thunder rumbled once again in the distance.

Thulla, save him, if You can, Tovak pleaded silently. There was no answer. He had not expected one. With that, he started out into the night to find the company camp.

CHAPTER FIVE

As Tovak made his way through the camp, his thoughts and worries on Jodin were interrupted by a flash of lightning, followed quickly by a deep rumble of thunder. The dying light of the day had fully faded. The temperature had finally dropped to the point where he felt cool in his armor. This was probably due to the coming storm. He was tired, weary, and fully worn out.

He heard the whispering hiss of rain as it overtook the camp, pattering softly against the nearest tents. And when he looked up at the dark sky, a light sprinkle of rain hit his face. He had the feeling that before the night was over, the storm would get much worse.

Tovak continued quickly through the encampment. He made one wrong turn, but quickly found his way again. It didn't take him long to return to the Baelix Guard camp. As he passed by Struugar's tent, he saw that the tent flap had been pulled back. A small lamp was lit, but from what he could see of the interior, Struugar was not inside.

As he made his way around the supply tent, he spotted Karn walking away from the water barrels, where Gorabor was busy filling waterskins. Gorabor had removed his armor and wore only his tunic, leggings, and boots. All around his feet lay filled waterskins. His blue cloak was wrapped about his shoulders and covered his head in order to keep off the drizzle, which was slowly picking up.

"Gorabor," Tovak called wearily as he stepped up to his friend.

Gorabor turned, a concerned expression filling his face. Having just filled the last skin, he set it down on the ground.

"Did you find him?" Gorabor asked. "Did you see Jodin?"

Tovak nodded slowly, feeling wretched as he began to say the words he wished weren't true. "He's still alive, but he's in the death tent. They don't expect him to make it."

Gorabor's face paled and he drew in a long breath before letting it out slowly.

Glancing at the back of Struugar's tent, Tovak asked, "Has the captain returned yet?"

"I don't think he has," Gorabor said. "At least, I haven't seen him. Do you believe Jodin's going to die?"

Tovak studied his friend and saw the disbelief there. He gave a confirming nod, and with it, Gorabor's shoulders sagged.

"The conquering heroes return," a voice boomed out behind them.

He and Gorabor turned to see Sergeant Bahr stepping out from the supply tent. He held a wax tablet in one hand and a stylus in the other. Bahr's generally sour expression eased only slightly as he eyed them both.

"I'm glad to see you both made it back in one piece, lads." He set the tablet down on a table just outside the supply tent. "Far too many did not." His eyes shifted to the skirmishers moving about the camp or sitting around fires working at cleaning their gear. Everyone looked tired, run-down, and just plain exhausted.

Tovak looked around as well. There were now far too many tents for the number of warriors present. A pang of loss tugged at his heart. He felt guilty for having survived when so many had not.

"Aye," Gorabor replied.

Bahr turned his gaze back upon them, hesitated for a moment before speaking. "Word around camp is that you two in particular had a rough time of it out there."

"We did, Sergeant," Gorabor said and absently touched his swollen face. "I was a guest of the enemy."

"Uh huh," Bahr said and his gaze shifted to Tovak while he pointed at Gorabor. "I heard you acted quite heroically in rescuing his sorry ass."

Embarrassed, Tovak glanced at the ground and said nothing.

"Or was it stupidity that drove you on? A misguided sense of friendship perhaps?" Bahr asked, his voice hardening. "You, rushing out there all alone to save your comrades. Are you hunting for Legend? Is that it?"

Tovak was surprised by the sudden hostility in the sergeant's tone.

"I'm grateful he came for me," Gorabor said, "otherwise I'd be a goner for sure."

"Shut up, you," Bahr said, his gaze fixed on Tovak. "I am talking to the hero."

On unsure footing, Tovak kept silent.

"I heard from a little bird that you left camp without orders," Bahr said. "Actually, that's not correct. Someone told me you left *against* orders. Going off into the darkness and into an enemy camp by yourself. Are you stupid? Vainglorious?"

Tovak wasn't sure what vainglorious meant. "No."

"No, what?" Bahr asked, in a deadly tone. He took a half step nearer that Tovak found incredibly menacing.

"No, Sergeant."

"Are you a hero, then?" Bahr asked.

"No, Sergeant," Tovak said, after a moment's thought. "I don't think that I am. I wasn't able to save Staggen."

Bahr was silent for a long moment as he regarded Tovak. When he spoke, some of the hardness had left his voice. Though the sergeant had not been out in the field with them, Tovak thought he detected an edge of weariness in his tone.

"In my tablet," Bahr said as he let out a long breath, "heroes tend to get people stone dead, son. They get full of themselves, think they can do whatever they want. Heroes stop playing with the team. So, I'll ask you again. Are you a hero, Tovak?"

"I am not a hero, Sergeant," Tovak said. "I just couldn't leave them out there."

Bahr blew out an angry breath and seemed to soften a little. "Don't make a habit of it."

"We've lost so many," Tovak said softly, glancing around tents, several of which would now be empty.

"Yes," Bahr said, "we did. Our job is a dangerous one, during the best of times. We are the shield for our people. We sacrifice so that others may live. That's why the warband is out here, so our people can survive."

Bahr let his eyes move over to where Karn, Bettoth, and Torimar had emerged from a tent and then turned back to Tovak. "Looks like they're heading to the mess area for some hot food." He glanced up at the dark sky. The rain was coming down a little harder, but had yet to become a full downpour. "You both better get going, get some food in your bellies before lights out."

"Gorabor." Karn stopped and looked over at them as Bettoth and Torimar continued on. "You can finish that up and distribute the skins later. Come, let's get some food while it's hot." He paused. "You too, Tovak."

"I'll be along shortly, Corporal," Tovak replied. "I want to get out of this armor and into a fresh tunic."

Karn nodded and started off. Gorabor joined the corporal. A moment later, they were gone, having disappeared into the night. Tovak watched them go.

"You've been assigned a new tent, with the rest of your squad," Bahr said, pointing to one nearby that the corporal and his two squad mates had just emerged from. "Karn wanted you billeted with the rest of his squad. I trust, this time, with the rain, sharing a tent won't be a problem?"

"Thank you, Sergeant," Tovak said. "And it won't, at least not for me, not now."

"Good," Bahr said, "now get going."

Tovak made his way across the camp to the tent. Pulling the flap aside, he stepped into the darkened interior. A small oil lamp in the shape of a fish had been left burning on the ground. The tent smelled strongly of canvas and waterproofing. He brushed off the rain from his cloak and set his pack and sword down on a patch of grass that was not taken. Removing his cloak, he quickly got out of his armor, which badly needed a cleaning. It smelled of sweat, as did his tunic. He changed into his spare shirt and leggings. They weren't fully clean, but they weren't soaked with sweat, either. The tunic was presentable. He also needed to bathe. Though it would be cold and out of a bucket, after dinner, he resolved to do just that. Wrapping himself back up in his cloak and pulling it over his head, he stepped into the rain, which was light and had become almost misty.

As he started off, he nearly bumped into Dagmar, who was coming the other way.

"What did the healers say?" Tovak asked.

"Don't get bit again," Dagmar said sourly.

That made Tovak chuckle and lightened his mood.

"It hurts," Dagmar replied wearily. "They cleaned it. That was fun, let me tell you. They said it would heal. The ankle will take time too."

"I'm headed for dinner with the rest of the company," Tovak said. "Wanna go?"

"I had some stew in the healers' tent," Dagmar replied. "All I want to do right now is get out of this armor and beneath a blanket." He let out a long breath. "I swear, I could sleep for a week."

"I'm tired too," Tovak agreed.

"No matter that we got the stuffing kicked out of us, they'll be sending us out in the morning," Dagmar said. "I've seen it happen before. Mark my words, there will be no break for us. The warchief needs the Baelix too much." Dagmar glanced sourly around. "I am going to change, clean my kit, and then turn in."

"I'll see you shortly." Tovak turned and then halted. He pointed. "That's our tent there."

"Bahr said so too," Dagmar said and headed off towards the tent as Tovak turned away.

It didn't take him long to reach the mess area assigned to their company. Exposed to the rain, dozens of long tables filled an open space, bordered on two sides by the backs of tents. Another side opened up to the mess kitchen, the very one where he and Gorabor had fetched the dodders before the disastrous expedition that led so many of the Baelix Guard to ruin. Now, that seemed like an age had passed.

There were four lines of warriors who had queued up and were waiting for the cooks to serve them. Most of the tables were occupied by those heartily spooning or sopping up a thick stew, chewing on a hunk of dark bread, or lifting large tankards to their lips.

By the smell, Tovak guessed it was heratta. He let out a long breath. As much as he liked heratta, in all the forms he'd eaten it since joining the Blood Badgers, he was already growing tired of what seemed to be the warband's staple. Still, his stomach rumbled with hunger.

Tovak joined one of the four lines and patiently waited his turn. When he finally reached the serving table, he found an unhappy cook, who dumped several ladles of the thick, gray stew into a wooden bowl, plopped a spoon in, and stuck a thick chunk of bread in the middle. An assistant cook placed a large tankard beside the bowl and then motioned for Tovak to take it and go.

"Thanks," Tovak said, grabbing the bowl and tankard.

The cook merely grunted and dipped his ladle back into the pot while picking up the next bowl. Tovak left the line and looked over the numerous tables for an open spot or someone he knew. The rain had picked up slightly.

"Tovak," a voice called out. His eyes were drawn to a raised hand, and he picked out Gorabor a few tables down. He saw an open spot across from his friend, so he headed in that direction, weaving his way through the warriors coming and going and between the tables. He finally reached the open space to find that Karn was sitting next to Gorabor, with Torimar and Bettoth across from them. Tovak noticed Torimar eying him almost warily as he approached. Quite a few of the Baelix Guard sat in the same general area, eating, drinking, and talking in low voices. The mess area had been clearly assigned to several companies.

Tovak set his bowl and tankard upon the table and sat down beside Bettoth.

"If you'll excuse me," Bettoth said to Karn, rising from the table, and there was no missing the hint of disdain in his voice. Tovak turned to Bettoth and then glanced at Karn, whose face was suddenly an expressionless mask.

"Me too," Torimar added, quickly standing and scooping up his bowl and tankard.

"We'll see you back at the tent, Karn," Bettoth said, picking up his meal. "It's time we got started on our gear."

They both left without another word. And with their going, Tovak found he had lost his appetite.

"What was that all about?" Gorabor asked, looking between Tovak and Karn.

"Give them time, Tovak," Karn said. "They will come around."

Quiet laughter from the next table caught Tovak's ear. He looked to see Logath, Bane, and Mirok from Third Squad exchanging whispers. Logath locked eyes with Tovak, and there was no mistaking the hint of a sneer on his face, nor the deep-seated animosity in his eyes.

"Not that again," Gorabor said. "Tovak's proved himself. Surely they can see it."

"I am still a Pariah," Tovak said woodenly.

Karn dipped his bread into his bowl, soaked up some stew, and then took a bite.

"That doesn't matter now," Gorabor said. "You're one of us. You've earned that right."

"Not fully accepted, but tolerated," Tovak said, and a sad chuckle slipped past his lips. He looked at Karn once again. There was just the hint of ... something ... in the corporal's face. Was it embarrassment? Compassion? Tovak couldn't tell. No matter how much he proved himself, his father's shame would stick to him forever, like a bad smell that could not be scrubbed off. He knew he should have expected nothing less. The stigma of Pariah ran deep amongst his people.

"What? Seriously?" Gorabor asked, looking between Karn and Tovak. The reality of the situation hit him. He turned fierce eyes to Karn. "That's just shit is what that is."

"Gorabor," Tovak said firmly. "It's better than what I'm accustomed to, understand?"

Karn blew out a frustrated breath and set his bread down in his bowl.

"Give them time, Tovak," Karn said. "I won't lie to you. You're not wrong about why they left, but they'll come around …just like I did." His gaze was almost imploring. "They report to me, but I can't tell them how to think or feel about you. Only you have the power to change their thinking."

"I hope you're right," Tovak said with a glance over at Logath, who looked like he'd had one too many tankards.

"I know I am," Karn replied, and there was an easy confidence in his voice that did make Tovak feel better. "Both are good warriors. Trust me on that. Now eat up and stop worrying about it."

Karn picked his bread back up and dabbed it into his stew. He nodded at Tovak's. Tovak spooned up some stew and started chewing. He found it bland, but his hunger had returned, and with a vengeance.

Karn took a bite of his bread. "The cooks outdid themselves with this batch. I'll tell you that."

Tovak looked up, surprised by the corporal's comment. He found Karn grinning at him.

"Gorabor told me about Jodin," Karn said, after several moments of silent eating. "Bad stuff, but with the wound he took, it would take a miracle for him to survive."

Tovak felt sour at the thought of Jodin dying.

Once again, they fell into silence. All around them, there was the general drone of loud talking, laughing, joking, and much merriment. The three of them ate quietly, hungrily, until Karn took a last gulp from his tankard and rose to his feet.

"I'm heading back." He looked at both of them. "Enjoy your meals, and feel free to have another tankard, but don't dawdle too long. Your kit needs to be worked on and it sounds like we will be rousted early. The warband will be back on the move again before the suns dawn."

"Yes, Corporal," Tovak and Gorabor said together.

Karn stood, picked up his bowl and tankard, and strode off.

Tovak and Gorabor ate for a few more minutes, and the silence stretched out between them.

"How do you stand it?" Gorabor asked.

"What?" Tovak looked back over at his friend. "Being a Pariah?"

"Yes." Gorabor set his spoon into an empty bowl. "Now that I've seen up close what you go through daily...." His voice trailed off. "I really don't like it."

Tovak spooned up the last mouthful of stew and chewed thoughtfully, contemplating what sort of answer would help his friend comprehend, even a little, how good things were now, compared to what his life had been before.

"I'm grateful, Gorabor," he said. "Before ... I mean, before the fight with Jodin, I lived a friendless, lonely life. It was faith alone that carried me through it all. My faith sustained me, as it sustains me now." Tovak paused. "I never dreamed I might have a friend"—he searched Gorabor's face—"nor could I have imagined I would be a ...." He glanced around. "Well, mostly accepted as a member of a company and a warband. I had hoped and dreamed it would happen, but that was all. Now...." He looked at the warriors surrounding them. "Well, I'm grateful. I thank Thulla for every blessing I receive, just as I used to thank Him for every painful lesson. My life's journey has led me here, and so far, it's been one well worth taking, especially now that I am a Blood Badger."

"You've earned that right," Gorabor said, "especially after the last few days. You have earned Legend; you've proved you belong. You don't deserve how they treat you."

"I am a Pariah," Tovak said simply.

Gorabor was silent for a long moment.

"You're a better Dvergr than I am, my friend," Gorabor said. "Far, far better."

Tovak took the last draft from his tankard. He suddenly did not feel like another.

"Come on," he said, standing up, "let's get back to our tent. I'm tired and want to get a start on cleaning my gear. I also need to bathe."

"Agreed. That's two of us." Gorabor rose and slapped his belly lightly. "I am full."

Together, they grabbed what remained of their meals and moved out from between the tables. As they did, Tovak almost ran into a warrior nearly as tall as him coming the other way.

"Excuse me," Tovak said, backing up, and then he recognized who it was. The warrior's face was rounded, fleshy, as if he'd never missed a meal in his life. He had beady, almost piggish eyes, a wide nose, and a sturdy frame draped in an obviously expensive tunic and cloak. Five warriors had been following in his wake. They all stopped short too.

Kutog.

He was the insufferable warrior who had given him so much grief during the yuggernok ride from Garand'Durbaad to the warband.

"Watch where you're going," Kutog started, then his eyes flickered with recognition.

Tovak immediately understood there would be trouble, as a sneer crimped Kutog's face.

"Well if it isn't our resident Pariah," Kutog drawled loudly. He looked back at one of the warriors behind him. "This is the bastard I was telling you about, Ferock."

"I can't believe they let such filth eat with the rest of us," Ferock said. The warriors behind him gave a laugh and those at the nearest tables quieted to look around at the drama.

Kutog turned back and narrowed his eyes. "The rumor is you joined the Baelix Guard. Do I have that right?"

Tovak felt the old, suppressed rage bubbling up to the surface. He was done being treated so badly by the likes of such mean-spirited people. No more would he take such blatant abuse without sticking up for himself.

"Tovak," Gorabor warned. "Don't do it. He's not worth it."

Tovak glanced over at his friend. He knew Gorabor was right.

"Well," Kutog demanded. "I'm waiting. What sorry company let you into their ranks?"

"Yes, I joined the Guard," Tovak said simply as he turned back to face Kutog.

"Out there playing with campfires and foraging about for the rest of us, who actually do the hard work and hold the line?" Kutog said loudly. "That sort of work seems suited to a Pariah. It's not real work."

"Hey," Gorabor objected, anger coloring his tone. "How dare you disrespect our company?"

"Shut your mouth," Ferock said to Gorabor. "This doesn't involve you."

"Yes, it does," Gorabor said. "I am a Baelix and if you disrespect one of us, you are disrespecting me as well."

"If you were worth anything," Ferock said disdainfully, "you'd have made it into a line company, like us."

Gorabor's caution seemed to have gone to the wayside. He looked like he was about ready to launch himself at Ferock.

"I also heard," Kutog went on, raising his voice, "that nearly the entire Baelix Guard got wiped out over the past few days."

"I guess what they say about Pariahs is true," Ferock said to Kutog. "They're bad luck."

Tovak struggled to keep himself under control. He wanted so badly to rearrange Kutog's perfect teeth, Ferock's too. Tovak despised bullies.

"I'm going to make you regret those words," Gorabor fairly growled.

"You and who else?" Kutog laughed.

Around them, a number of warriors rose from their tables, kicking back their stools. Tovak looked around and realized that each and every one was a member of the Baelix Guard, and they looked ready to start a brawl. Even Logath appeared pissed, and his gaze was fixed directly on Kutog.

"I think you had best take those words back, boy," Logath said, taking several steps forward and towards them, "before I force you with my fist. That is, if you are even conscious when I'm done with you."

Kutog looked around, suddenly unsure. There was a grumbling assent from the other members of the Baelix present.

"What's going on here?" a voice barked from a short distance behind Kutog.

Benthok stepped through the warriors accompanying Kutog, pushing them roughly aside. There was fury in his eyes as he brushed past Kutog and turned abruptly to face the young warrior. There was no missing the silver trim of his cloak, indicating he was an officer.

Kutog paled as he drew himself up to attention, as did the warriors with him. His back was rigid and chin pushed out. There was worry in his gaze.

Benthok glared at Kutog for several heartbeats, and then Tovak. Looking deeply unhappy, the lieutenant glanced around at the members of the Baelix Guard who stood ready to defend the company's honor. Benthok slowly turned to the now quaking Kutog.

Tovak felt the rage within his heart fade and disappear.

"What company are you with?" Benthok asked in a frosty tone.

"First Infantry," Kutog said. There was a proud note in his voice.

"First Infantry, huh?" Benthok looked Kutog and his friends up and down, as if he were inspecting teska dung.

"Yes, sir," Kutog barked.

"If I see you troubling my boys again, I promise you, I will have a conversation with your captain. Understand me?"

"Yes, sir."

"Go about your evening and let this be the last I see of you."

Kutog offered a crisp salute, which Benthok returned. He and his companions filed by. Benthok watched them until they were out of sight, and then he turned to the Baelix Guard warriors who were returning to their seats.

"Finish your meals and get back to camp. There's gear to be cleaned and sleep to be had." Benthok's tone was harsh.

The Baelix Guard warriors focused their attention on their meals, but not before a few of them glanced in Tovak's direction. Tovak suddenly felt out of place. He knew he was the cause for the problem, but once again, there was nothing he could do about it.

Benthok looked at Tovak, a hard expression on his face. "You do not need to be brawling with members of other companies, nor challenging them to a Circle. You've earned some respect. But that won't count for nothing if you start breaking the rules, not to mention heads too. As a Pariah, it would not go well for you when punishments are handed down. Got me?"

"Yes, sir, I do," Tovak replied. He felt many eyes upon him, the entire mess.

"I expect we will not need to have this conversation again," Benthok said.

"No, sir."

"Now get over to Karach's headquarters," Benthok said. "Struugar sent a messenger for you to report there."

Tovak's insides did a flip. "Me, sir? Do you know what the captain wanted me for?"

"I don't know," Benthok said, "probably has something to do with those maps you found. Do you know where the pavilion is?"

Tovak felt his heart quicken. "Yes, sir."

"Then get your sorry ass over there." Benthok spared him one last irritated look, then turned and strode away. Tovak shared a glance with Gorabor, who could only stand there, a worried expression on his face. He saw Logath a few feet away.

"Thank you for that," Tovak said.

"That wasn't for you, boy," Logath said with disgust plain in his tone. "That was for the Baelix Guard. Gorabor was correct. No one disrespects our own, even a Pariah."

Tovak held Logath's gaze a moment, then grabbed his empty bowl to return it. He had to report to headquarters.

CHAPTER SIX

With the drizzle easing into little more than a mist, Tovak hurried through the camp. His mind raced. He couldn't imagine what headquarters might want from him. He didn't know much more about the maps he'd taken than they could figure out themselves. Then something occurred to him and he almost came to a stop. Had Karach found out about his running off against orders? Had Thegdol told Struugar? He ran cold with that thought.

Was he about to be condemned? Lashed? Forced out of the Baelix Guard? A terrible worry gnawed at him. It was followed almost immediately by a cold, hard resolve. If he was to be punished for his actions, so be it. He would stand and face whatever was in store for him, no matter the cost.

He knew in his heart he had made the correct decision by going to rescue his comrades. And afterwards, if he was to be punished, he would continue to move forward one step at a time, just as he had and always would. To do any less would be to give in, to surrender, and Tovak was loath to do that.

His heart pounding in his chest, Tovak threaded his way through a flurry of activity. As he moved along each street, he realized there was significantly more than he'd seen before. Supplies were being moved around, packed up, and stored away. Warriors were attending to their equipment, and more telling, the cook tents he passed were busy preparing what looked like marching rations for the coming day.

As he moved by one of the artillery parks, he discovered that several of the field pieces had been disassembled and were in the process of being loaded onto two yuggernoks that had been moved into position for towing. Engineers and workers scrambled over several others, dismantling them in preparation for movement.

After what seemed like an eternity but in reality had only been a short while, he reached the center of the encampment. Tovak worked his way around to the small wooden bridge that crossed the defensive trench and wall that protected the headquarters compound.

Two sentries barred the path that led onto the bridge. They eyed his approach. The last time Tovak had passed this way was when he'd first come to the warband in search of an appointment to a company. Though it had only been a few days, it seemed a lifetime ago.

Tovak could remember vividly what it felt like to walk this same path, fresh off the yuggernok and full of apprehension and hope. Every turn winding through the tents of the encampment, bringing new sights, sounds, and smells. Each step had taken him closer to his dream of becoming a pioneer or, in hindsight, closer to that dream being crushed. Captain Dagon from Second Pioneers had quickly disabused Tovak on his hopes of joining an elite scouting company. He had been coldly turned away, and with that dismissal, Tovak's dreams had nearly crumbled. Thankfully, a short time after, Captain Struugar found him and offered him a place with the Baelix Guard.

"Halt," one of the two sentries said, holding up his hand. The sentry seemed bored and it came across plainly in his tone. "What is your business?"

"I have orders to report to headquarters, by way of Captain Struugar Ironfist," Tovak said. "My name is Tovak Stonehammer."

"Written orders?" The sentry looked at him expectantly.

"No," Tovak said. "The orders were delivered to me by my lieutenant. I was told to report immediately."

"Right. Is he on the list?" The sentry glanced over to the other guard, who held a tablet. He consulted it a moment, then looked up and gave a nod.

"He's there."

"You may pass," the first sentry replied and stepped aside. "Go right up the hill to that tent there"—he pointed with his spear—"the main one. The warchief is expecting you."

Tovak passed between them, made his way over the wooden planked bridge, and angled for the wide pavilion that had been indicated, where Karach's Blood Badger banner rose. In the torchlight, the ominous black badger on its crimson background seemed to glare down at him in judgment.

Off to one side, a few paces from the tent flap, stood a group of four warriors in leather armor, sheltering from the rain and talking quietly beneath the overhang of the tent. Directly in front of the closed tent flaps were two guards. Both were warriors in plate armor, decked out with the red and black cloaks of Karach's elite guard.

Tovak approached the two sentries standing outside the warchief's tent. Both guards—a dark-haired giant of a Dvergr and a smaller blond fellow—stepped in front of him, snapping their shields up and staring at him with warning eyes that told him to stop.

"State your name and business," the giant ordered. His voice was deep, almost unnaturally so. Both seemed alert and focused on their duty. Gazing at the giant, Tovak decided he was the tallest Dvergr he'd ever seen.

"I am Tovak Stonehammer, of the Baelix Guard, reporting as ordered."

"We were told to expect you," the other guard said curtly. "Wait here."

They both lowered their shields, and the blond stepped back and opened the tent flap, poking his head inside. "Tovak, of the Baelix Guard, sir."

"Send him in," a stern voice called out from inside. Tovak's heart fluttered. He recognized it as Karach's, and there was no humor there. In fact, the warchief sounded irritated, angry even. Tovak swallowed hard and stood up straight, prepared for whatever the warchief had in store for him. He'd face his fate like a warrior.

The sentry pulled the tent flap back fully. "You may enter."

Tovak took a deep breath, marched determinedly through the tent flap, and ducked inside. The interior of the tent was large, open. A magnificent patterned rug covered the grass. Lamps, suspended from the multiple support posts, filled the interior with warm, yellowed light.

Struugar stood a half-dozen paces inside, before a large central table. The captain's back was to Tovak, but he turned an expressionless face as Tovak entered. With him were Captains Greng and Dagon, along with Karach. All four had been gathered around the table.

The only other occupant in the tent was an ancient-looking Dvergr in the dark blue robes of a scholar. He stood next to the warchief and had a beard that reached nearly to his knees. White hair spilled down from the top of his head and over his shoulders. The hair appeared wild, as if it had not been brushed straight in weeks. It gave the scholar a mad look. And yet, his brown eyes were clear, lucid, and piercing as the scholar studied Tovak.

A series of maps had been laid out on the table. Tovak recognized several as the ones he'd found in the enemy's camp. He stepped closer and saluted the warchief.

"Tovak Stonehammer, reporting as ordered, sir."

Karach regarded him for a long moment before speaking. "Stand at ease."

Tovak recovered his salute and stood to parade rest, hands clasped behind his back. He continued staring straight ahead.

"Easier than that, lad." There was no anger or irritation in his voice this time.

Tovak relaxed his stance, but not completely. He was still concerned about why he'd been summoned.

"I believe you know Captains Greng and Dagon."

"I do, sir," Tovak said, his eyes flicking to the captain of the pioneers. He knew he'd never get past his father's disgrace at Barasoom. People like Dagon would never let him forget. That was okay, for Tovak had accepted who he was, a Pariah.

"This is Grimbok Lorekeeper." Karach motioned towards the ancient-looking scholar. "He is a historian, who at my request has attached himself to the warband. He is also the reason we are out on the Grimbar Plateau. I consider him my personal advisor."

"Yes, sir," Tovak said, not quite sure what else to say.

"Well," Karach said and glanced over at the other officers briefly. His gaze seemed to linger on Dagon for a heartbeat. "Lad, the warband owes you a debt of gratitude. The maps you found have proven incredibly valuable."

"Yes, sir," Tovak said, wondering if there was another boot waiting to drop. "I am glad to hear that, sir."

Resting his hand upon the table, Karach fell silent for several heartbeats as he regarded Tovak.

"I would like to hear your account of what occurred in the enemy's camp." Karach placed a hand on the maps. "Also, tell us, if you would, how you discovered these." Karach glanced at his officers again. His gaze stopped and lingered once again on Dagon. "In fact, I know we all would like to hear how you came across them."

"Yes, sir." Tovak opened his mouth and found he was suddenly hesitant. He wasn't sure where to begin. He took a breath and decided to start at the assault on their camp. Tovak quickly related the tale of the surprise attack on First Section and his trek up the valley to rescue Gorabor, Dagmar, and Staggen. He left out the part about disobeying Thegdol's order, but included that Thegdol had, begrudgingly, granted him permission to make the attempt.

He also did not mention the strange pull that had drawn him up there. He described the enemy encampment, the number of enemy warriors that he'd seen, and how the dark priest had sacrificed poor Staggen. Mention of the sacrifice prompted a low exclamation from Struugar. Finally, he reached the point in the story when he had his encounter in the dark priest's tent. Tovak paused, remembering that moment in vivid detail, as if it had just happened moments ago. He felt a coldness wash over him that made him shiver. He struggled with how much to tell the warchief.

"Well, lad," Karach said, tone softening a tad and bringing Tovak back to the present. "Don't stop now. Continue. I want to hear everything."

"Yes sir, I'm sorry, sir." Tovak took a deep breath and looked up at the warchief. "Everything, sir?"

"Everything," Grimbok said, "within reason."

Tovak gave a nod and decided to relate it all. "You see, sir, when I got a close-up look at the priest, I was filled with a revulsion I've never known before. It was more than just the fact that he'd sacrificed Staggen to a dark god … that was awful beyond anything I could have ever imagined. This was deeper, stronger, and I felt wholly compelled to kill him, to end his life or die in the attempt. In that moment, nothing in the world seemed as important as destroying the … thing … that filled my vision. Not my own life, not Gorabor and Dagmar, not the warband. Not even the Great March mattered. There was only a stain of evil that had to be eradicated, removed."

Tovak sucked in a ragged breath as silence stretched. The warchief ran a hand through his beard as he considered Tovak, then glanced over at the scholar. They shared a look.

"There's more," the scholar said, almost knowingly, "isn't there?"

Tovak gave a nod and hesitated once again. "I saw…."

"Saw what?" Grimbok asked, leaning forward. His hand played absently with his long white beard. His eyes glittered with intense curiosity. "Tell us."

Tovak's gaze went to the Lorekeeper, before returning to the warchief, hoping Karach wouldn't think he was out-of-his-skull mad. "When I gazed upon that dark priest, I … I saw black flames licking around his body." Tovak stared down at the rug that covered the grass and ran a hand through his braided beard. "I don't think it was my imagination." He looked back up at the warchief and met Karach's gaze. "For as long as I live, I will always see him there with that wispy, dark fire burning from within."

There was a long moment of silence. Greng and Struugar shared a long look. Dagon's gaze was still firmly fixed upon Tovak, and in it was clear disbelief.

"I don't think it was your imagination, son," Grimbok said. "What you saw, I believe, was all too real."

Tovak looked sharply at the scholar. So too did Karach.

"You came across a being of pure evil," Grimbok said. "In some of the histories I have read, others, who have been blessed by the gods, recount similar experiences, visions. I have heard it described as a gift from the gods."

"You cannot be serious," Dagon hissed.

"I am," Grimbok said.

Tovak did not know what to say. He felt both relieved he'd not been going mad and at the same time frightened. He had confronted true evil and survived.

"Continue with your tale," Karach said.

"Anyway," Tovak said, "I leapt upon him, struck him down with my blade, and then left with everything you have in front of you now, sir. Once they discovered the bodies, getting out of there with Gorabor and Dagmar was a bit of a race. You know the rest, sir."

Once again, silence filled the tent.

"Flames?" Dagon hissed. "Dark priests? Really? I find all of this difficult to digest." He waved a hand in Tovak's direction. "It is nothing more than the fanciful imagination of a desperate youth, a Pariah, looking to prove himself. He got lucky is all."

Tovak stiffened in anger.

"I don't have any doubts," Greng said, speaking up and looking over at Dagon, "especially after what I witnessed. The lad faced certain death, courted it even, to buy his comrades time to escape. I am inclined to give him the benefit of the doubt. If he says the priest was burning in a black fire, well then, that is what he saw."

"Indeed," Karach said and was silent for a long moment. "Do you feel lucky, Tovak?"

"Lucky?" Tovak asked. "No, sir. My life has been anything but."

"Do you know what I think, Tovak?" Karach asked.

"No, sir," Tovak said.

"In my one hundred and sixty-two years, I've learned to trust my gut. I think you are lucky. Yes, lucky. Fortune favors you. That is something in war you cannot put a price on."

Tovak was unsure how to respond, so he said nothing.

"As I said earlier," Karach said, "what you found has proven invaluable to the warband's mission."

"Our mission, sir," Tovak said and then decided to ask the question that no one seemed to know the answer to. "What exactly is our mission, sir? Why are we out on the Grimbar Plateau?"

Dagon's face hardened and Tovak wondered if he'd overstepped. However, Karach did not seem offended in the slightest.

"Why not?" Karach said. "I think you have earned the truth and everyone in the warband will know soon enough. Until that time, as it becomes common knowledge, you must give me your word that you will not relate anything you hear in this tent... not to your friends, comrades, or anyone else. You will wait for your officers to convey our objectives and mission before speaking on it. Do you understand?"

"The word of a Pariah?" Dagon scoffed. "How can you accept such a thing?"

Karach held up his hand and shot an unhappy look at Dagon. "His word will be sufficient for me. And it should be sufficient for you as well."

Clearly unhappy, Dagon wordlessly nodded his assent.

The warchief turned back to Tovak. "Do I have your word, Tovak Stonehammer?"

"Yes, sir," Tovak said. "You do. I swear by my ancestors, I will reveal none of what I learn here tonight."

"Very well, then," Karach said and turned back to the table with the maps. He considered them for a moment, then returned his attention to Tovak. "You arrived as we were discussing an upcoming operation. So good timing."

"Yes, sir."

"Thanks to your efforts," Karach continued, "the warband now has a proper objective. At least we know where to look for what we seek." He took a deep breath. Tovak could hear the rain pattering gently against the canvas roof of the tent. "As you already know, we've encountered gnomes, orcs, and goblins. It seems gnome territory is to our immediate east in the highlands. While in pursuit of enemy raiders, Captain Struugar discovered that fact the hard way."

"There are also organized companies of orcs and goblins about," Karach said. "That tells us they are from the Horde and not isolated tribes and that the enemy has or is attempting to establish a presence in the area. That is something we had not counted on. The maps you found confirmed this suspicion. We expected the enemy far to the south and west. Are you following me so far?"

"Yes, sir," Tovak said.

Karach turned back to the map, motioned Tovak closer, and pointed to a position northeast of the Grimbar Plateau. "This valley here, is the Keelbooth Valley. What we seek"—Karach looked over at the scholar—"Grimbok and I are firmly convinced is located there."

"You're looking for Grata'Dagoth, aren't you?" Tovak asked, before his mind could stop him. He immediately regretted it. He wasn't supposed to know that name.

Karach's eyes snapped to Tovak, a stern expression hardening his face.

"What made you guess that Grata'Dagoth was our ultimate destination?" Struugar said, eying Tovak, almost suspiciously.

"I've heard rumors of it since I joined the warband, sir."

"Well," Karach said, blowing out a breath, "it is what it is, I guess. It's nearly impossible keeping anything secret in the army." He turned his attention back to Tovak. "If the maps are correct, and we suspect they are, based on other information in our possession, the ancient fortress of Grata'Dagoth lies somewhere within that valley. We also believe the Horde is hunting for it as well, but they do not know its exact location."

"Why do they want to find it too?" Tovak asked.

"That is a good question," Grimbok said, "one we do not yet have an answer to."

"Regardless of their motivations," Karach said, "based upon these maps, as well as the other information in our possession, the warband will be moving with the intention of entering the Keelbooth Valley."

"Assuming they haven't already found Grata'Dagoth yet," Grimbok said.

Karach spared the scholar a hard look. "If they had, their entire army would be in the valley, or at least closer to it. This map here seems to indicate their position to the east, in the mountains, and their garrisons strung throughout the region. It is possible they too have been having gnome problems. Whatever the reason, they seem to be spread thin, which is advantageous to us, at least for the moment."

"Do you know who built it, sir?" Tovak asked, thinking about what Benthok had told him, that an ancient Dvergr nation that had once called the area they were moving through home.

"Grimbok?" Karach passed the question along to the old scholar.

The scholar cleared his throat.

"The short answer to your questions is, yes," he said in a raspy voice. "When our people first came to this world, we found ruins indicating another Dvergr nation had preceded us by hundreds of years, maybe even longer. We've not yet found out if they remain somewhere on this world, or where they went off to. I have spent my entire life studying them. It's been fascinating work. They called themselves the Leghone. Beyond that, we don't really know much about them as a people."

"Get to the important part," Greng said.

Grimbok shot Greng a long-suffering look. "Based upon the information I have discovered through my studies and research, we think that somewhere in the Keelbooth Valley is the entrance to an ancient road, the Ara'Kasan, which leads through the mountains and to the plains beyond. The hidden fortress of Grata'Dagoth guards the road."

"It is our hope this road is still passable," Karach said.

"The Great March," Tovak breathed in, understanding dawning, his eyes going to Karach. He recalled his geography lessons in school. "If we can find it, you want to use this road for the Great March ... to bring our people onto the plateau and to this road."

"It was and is the Thane's hope that we can," Karach said. "With the unexpected fall of the human kingdom of Syrulia to the Horde, our people making the Great March will be at risk for raids and attacks, as we'd need to pass close to the borders of Syrulia." Karach pointed at a larger map that lay on the table. It detailed much of the continent.

95

"Our people would need to work their way around south of the mountains. With so many civilians, it would be fraught with peril. The warbands would have difficulty protecting them all. However, if we can find Grata'Dagoth and this ancient road, the Great March can move north and away from Syrulia, through the Grimbar Plateau, to Keelbooth Valley, and then ultimately through the mountains on the road to safety."

Tovak gave a nod, thinking on the warband's mission. "What's to stop the Horde from following us?"

"The road is not over the mountains," Grimbok said, "but under it. We would bring it down after we use it. The work would be thorough and there would be no following."

"The Horde would be forced to go around the mountains," Tovak said, "a journey of more than a thousand miles, since there is no easy pass or way over them. If successful, it would buy our people time and a chance to put some distance between us and the Horde."

"Precisely," Karach said. "That is why we are out so far from the rest of the army."

"The Horde is looking for the fortress to deny us use of it," Tovak said. "Is that why they are out here?"

"We don't think so," Karach said and pointed down at the map. "I believe the Horde has a different agenda. They did not expect to find us here. That has become all too clear. Captain Dagon's scouts took prisoners that confirmed that understanding."

"They are certainly aware of us now," Struugar said.

"Yes, they are," Karach said, regarding Struugar. "There is no doubt in my mind their knowledge of our presence will complicate things. But there is no helping that now. Besides, it is rather hard to hide a warband marching through the middle of the Grimbar, especially at night. You'd have to be blind not to see our fires from the hills and mountain slopes."

Karach turned back to the map and rubbed his jaw for several heartbeats before looking back up at the three officers.

"As I see it, the pass that leads into Keelbooth and the defensive wall that we were discussing earlier are the immediate problem for us," the warchief said, addressing the officers, as if he'd suddenly forgotten all about Tovak. "It is the only real access into the valley from the plateau, at least for a large force."

"The wall complicated matters," Struugar said. "It will have to be overcome and that will be bloody work."

"You are correct." Karach touched the map again. Someone had drawn a line across where Tovak supposed the wall was reputed to be. "Dagon's boys have confirmed the enemy is occupying it, which is why all three of you are here."

"Do we know how many hold it?" Greng asked.

"At least two hundred," Dagon said. "It is a formidable position. A few hundred more would make the wall almost impregnable."

"We are going to assault and overcome it." Karach paused and looked at the three officers. "We're only three days' hard march away." The warchief looked from Dagon to Greng, then to Struugar. "Under command of Dagon, elements of the Baelix Guard—primarily Struugar's skirmishers, Fifth Company, and Second Pioneers—will move up into the highlands and work their way around and behind the wall. Struugar, you and your strikers will be remaining behind with the warband."

"I don't like that, sir," Struugar said. "I'd prefer to go with my boys."

"I know," Karach said. "However, I need you here. You have more experience than most of my officers do storming a defended wall. You will be personally commanding the assault force."

"I can't say I am happy about it, sir," Struugar said, "but I understand."

"Good," Karach said. "After the siege of Adorana, you have proven your worth when it comes to assaults on fortified positions."

"Yes, sir," Struugar said.

Karach turned back to the other two officers.

"As the warband moves into position and makes the assault," Karach said, "Dagon, Greng, your mission will be to keep the enemy from reinforcing the wall. If there is an opportunity, you are to take the wall from the other side. However, your primary task will be to keep the enemy from reinforcing their hold on the wall. I cannot stress that enough."

"We won't be able to hold long if that enemy army turns up in the valley," Greng said, "or if the bastards have ready reinforcements available."

"Once the warband goes into action, you only need to hold, to delay, for a couple of hours," Karach said. "We will attack before dawn on the third day. I have no doubt the might of the warband can overcome it, but I would like to limit our casualties."

Karach paused once again, glancing down at the map. "The wall and entrance to the valley act as a chokepoint. Once beyond the pass, we'll be into the valley proper. If the enemy is there in force, we will engage them and take the fight forward. If not, we will clear the valley and find the fortress. That is the mission. Once we do that, and determine the road is there, the Thane will reinforce us."

The officers were grim-faced when Karach looked up.

"I know I am asking a lot," Karach said. "The position you will be in is a dangerous one. If I thought I could get away with sending a larger force through the highlands, and around behind the enemy wall, I would. However, greater numbers would increase the risk of detection and discovery. No. We cannot have that. A smaller force is the only way. Should the enemy reinforce the wall, that will translate into blood we cannot afford to spend. I am counting on you."

"We'll get the job done, sir," Greng said.

"Risk a few," Struugar said, "for a greater reward."

"That is correct." Karach hesitated. "Your boys, Struugar, have been through a tough time of it. I would not be asking this of them if the Baelix were not some of my best. Your skirmishers and Dagon's scouts are suited for this kind of irregular warfare. Greng's boys will provide the muscle." Karach paused again. "I can substitute another group of skirmishers, but I would prefer not to. Is the Baelix Guard up to this?"

"They are, sir," Struugar said, without hesitation. "My boys are tough lads. We may be diminished in number, but we have fight left in us. You have my word on that."

Tovak felt a sudden thrill of excitement at what they were about to do.

"Very well." The warchief looked at all three officers. "Dagon, I expect you to march well before dawn. And Tovak goes with you. Though he may be a Pariah, he's lucky. I can tell, and I'll take all the good fortune I can get to see this through."

Tovak wondered if he'd heard correctly. Dagon, on the other hand, looked like he'd swallowed something foul.

"It will be as you command," Dagon said. "I've never failed you and I certainly will not start now."

Karach glanced down at the map. Tovak had the sense that the world rested heavily upon the warchief's shoulders. After a moment, Karach looked up. "It's all in Thulla's hands now."

Tovak found himself surprised by the warchief's reference to their ancestral god. Was Karach religious?

"If you don't have any further questions," Karach said, "you are dismissed."

There were none. The officers and Tovak came to attention and saluted.

"In three days, I will see all of you on the other side of the wall," Karach said.

Almost as one, the officers turned and stepped out of the tent. Tovak followed and found the rain had stopped. The nearest torches burned and hissed, almost noisily, pushing away the darkness. In the distance, the sounds of the warband's encampment carried to them.

Dagon took several steps away from the tent. He stopped and turned to them. "Make sure you bring ropes and climbing gear, in the event it's needed. We will form up around four horns, outside the camp at the east entrance."

With that, Dagon spared Tovak an unhappy look before stepping away into the darkness.

"Good night," Greng said, to Struugar. "I will see you after this is all done."

Struugar did not reply, but he did nod to the other captain, who turned and left.

"Sir," Tovak finally said. "Am I going to be a problem for you?"

"You mean," Struugar asked, "is Dagon going to make it a problem?"

"Yes, sir."

Struugar let out a frustrated breath. "No. Dagon is a professional soldier. He may dislike you, and for good reason, but there should be no significant trouble from that quarter."

Tovak wasn't so sure about that.

"I should add that you have caught the eye of Karach, and from what Benthok and Thegdol have told me, you handled yourself quite well out in the field. No matter your history, you are a credit to the company and I am very pleased I took you in."

"Thank you, sir," Tovak replied, and felt a swell of pride.

"Let's get back to camp," Struugar said and started off.

It was clear to Tovak the captain was not interested in further conversation. He remained silent as they made their way through the warband's encampment. Finally, they reached the company's camp. Struugar stopped before his tent.

"Make sure you get some sleep," the captain said. "You are going to need all that you can get in the coming days. Make no mistake, what lies ahead will be far from easy."

"Yes, sir," Tovak said. "I will."

Struugar spared Tovak a look, as if he were about to say more. It never came. The captain turned away. A moment later, he disappeared through his tent flap.

Tovak stood there, staring at the captain's tent for several heartbeats. He was tired, weary, and run-down. More than anything, he wanted to lie down on his bedroll and go to sleep. Still, there was work to be done, the cleaning and maintaining of his kit, before he turned in for the night.

He walked deeper into the company's camp. Stepping around the corner of the supply tent, he found sputtering torches, closed tents. Most of the company seemed to have already turned in for the night. A handful of warriors were sitting around a lonely campfire. The warriors held tankards or wineskins. Amongst them were Thegdol, Karn, and Gorabor. At their feet lay their armor, which they had clearly finished cleaning. As he approached, they turned to see who was joining them. The group seemed fairly morose. Tovak was still wet and cold from the earlier rain. The fire felt good. He held his hands out for warmth.

Corporals Terogg and Cullor from Fourth Section turned their gazes from Tovak to each other and then back to the fire. There were two other skirmishers present, who Tovak recognized but did not know.

"To the fallen," Terogg said, with a good deal of iron in his voice. He raised his tankard, as did the rest. "May they feast heartily in the halls of our ancestors."

The group drank. Without a drink, Tovak felt out of place. Thegdol handed him his skin. Tovak took a pull from it and found it to be sour wine with a strong taste of vinegar. He handed the skin back to the sergeant.

"To those not among us," Thegdol said, with feeling. He raised his tankard. "They will be missed."

"To those not among us," the others replied together. They drank. Once again, the sergeant handed Tovak his skin to drink.

The circle went silent once again, and each warrior seemed lost in his own thoughts. Though the sergeant had included him, Tovak still felt like he'd interrupted something special. But no one had told him to leave or made plain he was not welcome. He did not sense any animosity or resentment directed his way either.

"Tovak," Thegdol said, "I heard you'd been called to see the warchief. What did he want with you?"

"He asked me about what happened," Tovak said, "when I went after Gorabor and Dagmar."

"That was a ballsy thing to do," Terogg said, looking up from the fire. "Following after an enemy raiding party in the dark. With how orcs can see in the dead of night, I don't know if I would have done the same."

"That's because your balls are on the smaller side," Karn said.

That caused a chuckle around the fire. Tovak even grinned.

"I guess you'd know," Terogg shot back with a grin. "You're always looking at them when I change."

Karn gave an amused grunt.

"And that was it?" Thegdol asked Tovak, sounding a bit surprised. "That's all he wanted, the story of what happened?"

"There was more," Tovak said, trying to evade the question. "But I was asked not to speak on it."

"Come on," Gorabor said. "You can tell us. What else did they say?"

"No, I can't," Tovak said. He would not break his word. To do so would cost him Legend and the little trust he'd earned. "I'm under orders."

"Seriously?" Gorabor asked. "I mean"—he looked around the circle—"it's us."

"I gave my word, Gorabor." Tovak's tone was firm. "I'm sorry."

Gorabor appeared crestfallen.

"Well, lads, that's it for me." Thegdol slapped his hands upon his thighs before he rose to his feet and looked over at Tovak. "If you gave your word, you gave your word. That's the end of it." Thegdol glanced at those gathered around the fire. "It was a bitch of a day and I'm spent. I think you all had best turn in and get some sleep. From the activity going on around the camp, the warband will be marching again in the morning." He eyed Tovak again. "And I suspect you haven't had a chance to clean your kit."

"No, Sergeant," Tovak said. "Not yet."

"Get on it," Thegdol said. "Then get your ass in the sack. That goes for all of you, if you missed the subtle hint."

"Yes, Sergeant," Tovak said.

With that, Thegdol turned and moved off in the direction of the latrines. The rest of the warriors drained their tankards and skins, rose to their feet, gathered up their armor, and filed off. Gorabor patted Tovak on the shoulder.

"Thanks again, for saving my life," Gorabor said and strode off for their tent.

Alone at the fire, Tovak blew out a breath and glanced towards the heavens.

Thank You, Thulla, for the lessons of the previous days, hard though they were. Blessed are those who follow Your word and the Way. Blessed are they who will carry the light to Your people with every breath. I am and ever will be Your humble servant, till that solemn day when I return to Your breast and stand in the glory of Your magnificence. He paused, and his thoughts drifted back to Jodin. And please, if it is within Your heart, grant Jodin his life and a speedy return to health. If not, please make his passing from this life into the next an easy one.

Tovak turned towards the tent. Though he was dead tired, it was time to clean his kit, and that would take some time.

CHAPTER SEVEN

What remained of the Baelix Guard's skirmishers stood assembled in the company area, waiting. They'd been told to don their packs and had been issued four days of precooked rations. Around Tovak, there was a low drone of conversation, mixed with much speculation as to where they were off to as the skirmishers sought to pass the time.

Tovak was tired and in need of additional sleep. He rubbed at his dry, weary eyes, then glanced up at the sky. It was nearly completely black, with a sprinkling of stars visible between the clouds, which seemed to hang low over the warband's encampment. There was no sign of the moon. He figured it was at least two hours from the first hints of dawn breaking across the sky.

Shifting, he stretched slightly. His body ached terribly. He was stiff and sore from the exertions of the last few days. All he wanted was to go lie back down and rest. But that was not to be. Soon, they would be marching. He knew that after a few miles the ache and soreness would work itself out.

Gorabor stood next to him in the ranks. His friend was talking to Dagmar in low tones. Tovak figured both felt the same as he, most likely worse. Gorabor's bruises still looked quite ugly and Dagmar's ankle had improved, the limp barely noticeable.

Around them, the strikers were still in their tents, sleeping, as were most of the rest of the warband. The encampment was quiet, almost still. Tovak found it a little unsettling, unnatural even.

"Company," Benthok called, just loud enough to be heard. It was apparent his intention was not to disturb those who were still sleeping. "Stand to attention."

The conversation ceased, and with it, they all went rigid, chins up and backs straight. Struugar had emerged from his tent and was striding their way. The lieutenant turned and offered the captain a crisp salute, which Struugar dutifully returned.

"Thirty-two present and accounted for, sir," Benthok said. "Twenty-four in the sick tent."

"Thank you, Lieutenant." Struugar turned and regarded the assembled skirmishers for a couple heartbeats.

There were deep bags under the captain's eyes, giving the impression that Struugar had not slept a wink. For the first time since he had met the captain, Tovak wondered on the heavy burden that came with command, the responsibility for so many. He'd not considered it before now.

It was like he suddenly had a window into the captain's soul. He could almost feel it, like it was a tangible thing … the pressure, the anguish, the torment, and the self-recrimination weighing upon the captain's shoulders.

Struugar stepped forward a pace and placed his hands behind his back. His eyes ran over the assembled warriors.

"Boys, you have been taken off foraging duty and selected for an important mission. You will be working with the Second Pioneers and Fifth Company on detached duty." Struugar paused a moment to let that sink in. Though they knew something was up, a ripple of excitement ran through the assembled ranks. "The success of this mission is vital to the Great March." Again, Tovak felt the ripple run through the assembled skirmishers. There was nothing more important than the Great March. "When everything is said and done, it may very well mean the difference between life and death for our people. I cannot stress how important this could be." Struugar paused. "I wish I was going with you. However, I have my orders. The strikers and I will be doing something different. I know you will not let me or the warband down. For now, that is all. With luck, we will see each other again in the coming days."

Around him, there was some low murmuring that was barely audible from some of the veterans.

Struugar turned to Benthok.

"Lieutenant," Struugar said. "Get them moving."

"Yes, sir," the lieutenant said. He snapped off a crisp salute, which again the captain returned.

"Alright, you heard the captain. Company, left face," Benthok ordered. The Baelix Guard turned as one, shifting to a marching column. The lieutenant strode stiffly to the head of the formation and came to a stop next to Thegdol. He glanced back over his shoulder, clearly making certain all was in order. "Forward, march."

And with that, the lieutenant led them out of the company area. Tovak looked over to see Struugar watching. The captain did not appear happy, not in the slightest. Just off to the side stood Sergeant Bahr. Their eyes met.

"Don't be a hero," Bahr mouthed to him. And then, they were by, turning onto the street before the company's camp. Benthok led them through the warband's encampment and over to the eastern gate.

Waiting for them was Fifth Company. They were arrayed in four ranks. The strikers of the Fifth were standing easy. Dagon's Second Pioneers were there also, formed up to the Fifth's right. Dagon stood before his company, talking with a young lieutenant Tovak did not know. The pioneer captain turned and eyed the Baelix Guard as they marched through the gate and approached.

"Company... halt," Benthok called, once they had fully cleared the gate.

The formation came to an abrupt stop.

Captain Dagon separated himself from the lieutenant and stepped forward. Benthok offered the captain a salute. Dagon returned the salute. He scanned the Baelix Guard's skirmishers for several heartbeats, a stoic expression upon his face. It was as if he was looking for someone specific, and then, Tovak knew who, for the captain's gaze stopped upon him. The captain's face remained impassive, cold. He could almost feel the disgust, hatred, and blame radiating outward towards him.

"I have been given command of this operation," Dagon said, his gaze moving off Tovak and sweeping over the formation of skirmishers. "You all know me. We've worked together closely in the past. I expect you to do your duty, just as you would for Captain Struugar." He pointed towards the northeast. "We're headed to a valley called Keelbooth. It is to the northeast and there is something in the valley the warband is hunting for. What that is, I cannot tell you. All you need to know at this time is that what the warband seeks is critical to the success of the Great March."

There was a slight shifting in the ranks at that.

"My scouts have been there," Dagon continued. "The only access to the valley for the warband is a narrow, twisting pass, roughly four miles long. The pass is blocked by a fortified wall. We believe the wall is held by two to three hundred orcs and goblins."

Dagon paused.

"The main force of the Blood Badgers will be assaulting the wall directly. Captain Struugar will be personally leading that attack." This caused a slight stir of surprise that was barely perceptible. "To us falls the difficult task of keeping the enemy from reinforcing their position on the wall, but also, potentially, striking at it from behind. That's the good news." Dagon paused. "Now for the bad news. We have reason to believe there is a sizable enemy presence nearby and possibly in the valley itself. Clearly, our work is cut out for us." Dagon paused once again. "Right, then. I've done enough talking. We have a long way to go today and I want to get started."

Dagon's gaze abruptly returned to Tovak, for only the briefest of moments, before he looked away. Tovak got that same old sinking feeling in his heart. His company had mostly embraced him, but there would always be Dvergr like Dagon who would not.

So be it, he thought. He would prove them all wrong. He would show them his worth, and no matter how many stood in his way, or how pettily they behaved, he would push forward and forge his own destiny, one worthy of great Legend.

"Officers, on me," Dagon called and stepped away.

The march began a short while later, after the officers had conferred. Greng's company was first in the line of march, Second Pioneers came next, and the Baelix followed, bringing up the rear.

The night air was cool, and Tovak thought it a refreshing break from the persistent heat of the last few days. He decided he much preferred marching when it wasn't too hot out.

After the column had gone a mile and passed beyond immediate sight of the warband's encampment, the line of march had spread out and become more relaxed. Talking amongst the ranks had been granted.

Gorabor looked over at him. He appeared troubled, almost hesitant to speak. He knew his friend was working himself up to ask an uncomfortable question. Tovak half suspected what was coming.

Dagmar, Bettoth, Torimar, and Karn were just behind them, having a spirited conversation amongst themselves about noseball and who the best runners and blockers were in the warband. Noseball was a sport Tovak enjoyed watching, but as a Pariah, he'd never been permitted to play.

"What was up with Dagon?" Gorabor asked, in a low tone. "It seemed like it was more than you being a Pariah."

"Saw that, did you?" Tovak asked, looking back over.

"I don't think he likes you very much," Gorabor said. "At least, that's the impression I got."

Tovak shrugged his shoulders, which, given the fact that he was wearing a heavy pack, was more difficult than it sounded. He looked over and gave his friend a weary expression.

"Did I mention that his eldest son was at Barasoom?" Tovak asked.

Gorabor did not seem to understand at first, then his eyebrows went up. "He was killed while under your father's command?"

Tovak nodded.

"That explains a lot," Gorabor said unhappily.

"'With every moment of suffering,'" Tovak said quietly, so that only his friend could hear and not those behind, "we are made more whole. With each pain, and hurt, we draw nearer to Thulla's heart and can tap more fully upon His bountiful and limitless might, until, finally, we become a mountain of strength for others to draw upon.'"

"You're getting religious on me," Gorabor said with a chuckle.

Tovak felt suddenly embarrassed. He'd grown comfortable around Gorabor, perhaps too much. He'd forgotten for a moment that most of his people shunned Thulla.

"It's ... it's from *Thulla's Blessed Word*."

"An idiot could tell that," Gorabor said, looking over at him with an amused expression. "I knew you were faithful. By now, you should know, there's no need to hide it, at least with me."

"Does it bother you?" Tovak asked, worried that he might have crossed a line somehow by preaching.

"Not a bit," Gorabor smiled. "Belief is a personal thing. You either follow Thulla's teachings or you don't. It's not my place to tell you or others what to believe in. That said, I did enjoy the passage."

"Tovak?" a deep voice said from behind him. "You're Tovak, correct?"

Tovak turned to see a lieutenant approaching, walking up the column as it continued to march. He was the one Dagon had been speaking with earlier. From his cloak, Tovak saw he was one of Dagon's officers.

"Yes, sir," Tovak replied uneasily and on guard.

"I am Lieutenant Brund." The lieutenant fell in beside him. "You've been the talk of the warband."

Brund appeared to be only a few years older than Tovak. There was a youthful exuberance about him, an extra bounce in his step that spoke of energy and enthusiasm for his work.

"Yes, sir," Tovak said neutrally, unsure how to take that, especially coming from one of Dagon's officers.

"Benthok speaks quite highly of you," Brund continued, "and he hardly ever speaks highly of anyone. Your lieutenant has always been rather taciturn around the officers' mess."

Tovak glanced in Benthok's direction. The lieutenant was marching at the head of the Baelix Guard, with Thegdol. The two were deep in conversation. Tovak almost missed a step. With them was a priest. He had not seen the priest before they had marched.

"If you say so, sir," Tovak said, still unsure where the conversation was headed. Those nearest had stopped talking and he sensed they were actively listening.

"Aye," Brund said, "after I'd heard about what you did, I wanted to meet you. It took a lot of guts to sneak into an enemy camp to rescue your comrades." He looked at Tovak, studying him for several heartbeats. "Either you are very good at what you do, or fortune favors you."

"Yes, sir," Tovak said, deciding the neutral approach was best.

"Karn." Brund looked back at the corporal. "I see you survived again. I guess there's no killing bastards like you. At least the enemy can't do a proper job of it."

A slight, almost mocking smile tugged on the lieutenant's beard.

"No, sir," Karn said. "So nice to see you again too, sir. Your presence just brightens my day, sir."

"And you're still a bloody liar," Brund said with a laugh.

"Lieutenant Brund," Dagon called back from ahead. "If you would join me."

"Gotta go. Duty calls." The lieutenant looked back over at Tovak. "When we have a moment, I would like to hear about the rescue of your comrades."

"Yes, sir," Tovak said.

With that, Brund picked up his pace and left them.

"Lieutenant Benthok," Dagon called a moment later. "Join me as well, would you?"

"Yes, sir," Benthok said and hurried forward.

Tovak had expected dislike and coldness from Dagon's officers. Brund had been friendly. He didn't know what to make of it all.

"Brund's got too much enthusiasm," Dagmar said, "He's too eager to do his job, but I'll readily admit, he's one of the better officers."

"He is," Karn agreed. "He's fair and knows what he's doing, which is more than I can say for a number of officers I've had the sad pleasure to meet."

"At least he doesn't lord it over us," Torimar added. "He's a bit easier going than Benthok and less intense too."

Tovak found his gaze going back to the priest, who was now walking beside Thegdol.

"Why is there a priest with us?" Tovak asked and gestured ahead.

"Oh," Karn said, "that's just Fenton. He's a surgeon too."

"A surgeon," Tovak said, surprised.

"That means Dagon and Greng expect casualties," Torimar said. "He's along to save lives."

"Save lives?" Dagmar scoffed. "He's a sawbones. They're all the same. He just hides it better beneath his priestly robes."

"Fenton's not that bad," Torimar said. "He doesn't throw his religion in your face all the time. Nor does he beg for money and donations to the church, like the other priests."

"He sewed me up once," Dagmar said. "Hurt something awful."

"Was it your ass?" Torimar asked.

Dagmar shot Torimar an unhappy look.

"I like Fenton," Bettoth said. "He's not afraid to go out into the field with us and share the dangers. You know, I once saw him pick up a sword and stick a goblin clean through with it."

"Really?" Gorabor asked. "He sounds like no priest I've ever heard of."

"I remember that," Karn said, looking over at Bettoth. "What was the name of that gods forsaken village?"

"Delanthus," Bettoth said. "We lost a lot of good mates there."

"We did," Karn said. "It was a bitch of a fight."

They fell silent for a time, the grass crunching under their feet.

"Tovak," Karn said, "why was Dagon interested in you? I saw him glance your way when he addressed us."

Tovak suppressed a sigh. He knew he should have expected others besides Gorabor to notice too. He sucked in a breath and let it out through his teeth.

"When I first tried to get an appointment with the Blood Badgers, I spoke to Dagon. He—he rejected me." Tovak looked back at Karn with pained eyes. He was done hiding who he was. They deserved the truth. "Dagon's son was killed at Barasoom."

"Oh shit," Karn said. "Dagon's son was there?"

"That's just bloody unlucky for you," Dagmar said.

"Yes," Tovak agreed, "it is."

"Dagon's not the kind to forgive easily," Karn said. "He is known for holding grudges."

"Well," Dagmar said, "I guess when it rains it pours."

"Dagmar." Karn glanced up at the dark sky. "Let's not tempt Fortuna, shall we? I don't think we want to be rained on."

"No, Corporal," Dagmar said. "We don't need no rain."

"How about putting that flute of yours to some good?" Karn said. "Play us a marching tune, something to make our steps and hearts a tad lighter."

Dagmar, not needing any further encouragement, pulled out his stone flute. Within moments, he was playing a tune. Shortly, more flutes joined in.

For a while, Tovak's steps seemed lighter. But his thoughts took a troubled turn. As Tovak continued to march, his eyes kept shifting towards the northeast, where Keelbooth lay. He wondered about the Dvergr who had settled these lands and all that had been revealed to him the previous night. Who had they been? Where had they gone? What had happened to them?

He thought on trials and tests to come, what lay ahead. More fighting undoubtedly lay in his future. He was certain of it. What of Dagon? How would the captain of the pioneers complicate his life? He had so many questions, and so few answers. Still, Tovak had the feeling he was marching towards destiny, being inexorably pulled towards something. What that was, he knew not, and that troubled him something fierce.

CHAPTER EIGHT

They marched for two hours before a break was called. By that time, both suns had cleared the eastern wall of mountains and with them the heat had increased dramatically. Tovak had grown warm in his armor, to the point where he was perspiring heavily. They had only been allowed a short break, to drink, eat, and relieve themselves. Then the order had come to don packs and the march had resumed.

It was clear to Tovak that Dagon and Greng wanted to get them off the plateau and up into the hills as soon as possible, for they were marching directly east. The distance passed rapidly, and before Tovak knew it, they were nearing the edge of the foothills, with the steep ridges just beyond. Though Tovak was excited about their mission, he was not so eager to go back up into the highlands, which rose ominously ahead. He felt some trepidation at the thought of what waited.

"I wonder when I'll get to see Gulda again," Gorabor lamented. He marched a few paces off to Tovak's left. They were nearly at the end of the skirmishers' line of march. Karn, Torimar, Bettoth, and Dagmar followed behind them.

"Awww…" Dagmar chided with amusement, "missing the little lady, are we?"

"I am, Dagmar," Gorabor replied, without any venom or hint that he understood Dagmar was being sarcastic. Gorabor flashed a grin at Dagmar. "I understand. You're just jealous because you don't have a sweetheart of your own, that's all. It's okay to admit it."

"You know, Gorabor, you may be onto something. It has been a while since I've spent time with a good, honest, loving lass, and she was a fine one too now that I recollect."

Bettoth barked out a laugh. "An honest lass? Who are you kidding? Then again, I guess we're really talking about the quality of the lady who's willing to share her love with you, eh?"

"Alright, less than honest, then." Dagmar looked over at his squad mates and held his hands out to his sides. "I ask you ... why tie myself down to one, when there are so many to love?"

"For a price, you buy that love," Bettoth said.

Dagmar just shrugged. "The lasses that accept my coin don't judge."

"I can see how that's important to you," Karn said, "especially with your looks."

"Besides," Dagmar said, as if he'd not heard, "if I was to marry, I'd end up paying more just to keep her happy." He raised a finger in the air dramatically, as if making an important point. "And don't forget, a wife would spend all my money before I even had the opportunity. She'd probably want to join the camp followers and be first in line when the paymaster brings out his chest. Now, tell me, where's the sense in that?"

"Your logic, as always, is impeccable," Karn said, with irony dripping heavily from his voice, "flawlessly so."

"My wife likes to spend my money," Torimar said, sourly. "She makes sure we go together to the paymaster when the quarterly payday rolls around."

Amused, Tovak shook his head and listened as the banter continued. Such talk helped to pass the time, along with the miles, and before he knew it, the column of march reached the edge of the grasslands and began climbing up into the hills and ridges. The hills were at first brush-covered, with only a smattering of trees. They climbed one hill after another, each rise seemingly taller than the last, the slopes becoming steeper, more rugged.

Though he was breathing heavily, Tovak's aches and pains had lessened with the passing of the miles. In truth, he found it invigorating to be back out in the field again. And yet, he also found himself once again missing the freedom of scouting. He daydreamed of blazing ahead, searching for threats and the enemy.

A little after noon, around one horn, the march entered a small, narrow canyon, with only a scattering of mountain grasses and small pines nestled in the nooks and crannies of the rock worn by time and weather. To either side, the walls of the canyon were steep and seemed to close in on them. A small stream ran through the base of the canyon, which was barely wide enough for the formation to move through in single file.

The canyon seemed a lonely place to Tovak, primal and unexplored. He itched to explore the entirety of it. However, the march soon left the canyon, following a feeder stream up a steep slope and onto yet another ridge.

"Column, halt," came the call from ahead once the tail end of the march had reached the summit. The column ground to a stop. Tovak was tired. The climb had left him winded.

Lieutenant Brund, along with Benthok, moved down the line from the front, speaking to each corporal and sergeant as they went.

"We're taking a short break," Benthok said to Karn before returning the way they'd come. "See that your boys get something in their bellies."

"Right," Karn said. "Packs off. Make sure you eat and drink. When you're done, avail yourself of the stream. Fill your skins. There's no telling when we might see more fresh water, and it's already bloody hot out. I don't want any of you boffers bumming a drink from my waterskin."

Tovak unhooked his pack and set it down by his side, under the shade of a tree. With a groan, he sat next to it. Gorabor took a seat at his side and leaned his back against a small granite boulder.

Dagmar glanced around the area, which was scattered with brush and trees. "'Bout time we got a break." Rather gingerly, he sat down across from them. Dagmar grimaced, shifted slightly, and then seemed to find a comfortable spot. He let out a sigh.

"Backside still hurts, eh?" Torimar was sitting a few feet away. He shot a grin at Dagmar. "You've literally become a pain in the ass to yourself. What a nice change for everyone else."

Dagmar shot Torimar an unhappy look that promised murder in the near future.

Untying his pack, Tovak pulled out his haversack, which was stuffed full, almost bursting with rations. He peeked inside. When the rations had been issued, there had not been much time to see what he'd been given. It had also been dark. Tovak had simply packed it away in the rush to get ready.

He found a cloth-wrapped bundle of dried heratta, some pork, and a clay jar stopped with a cork and filled with fat for cooking. There were also a number of hardtack biscuits and a dozen dodders. Tovak felt one of dodders. It wasn't hot, or even warm for that matter, but it seemed relatively fresh.

He picked up the dodder and sniffed at it before leaning back against his pack. Taking a healthy bite, he was unsurprised to find it contained chunks of heratta meat. Tovak was hungry and the dodder tasted good. Though he was fast growing tired of heratta, he was grateful for the food and, at the end of each day, a full belly. It hadn't been all that long ago when food had frequently been scarce for him, and even heratta would have been an unaffordable luxury.

Tovak took a drink from his skin, which was less than half full. The water was warm and stale-tasting, but it didn't matter to him. He was parched from the heat and gulped it down.

"Hunger makes the best cook," Dagmar said as he examined his own haversack and, appearing less than thrilled, pulled out a dodder.

Tovak took another bite. He chewed slowly, then washed it down with more water. To his right, through a scattering of trees and back the way they had come, the entirety of the plateau was spread out before them. It was a magnificent view. White clouds floated above the plateau, casting long shadows across the vast grasslands. Tovak felt deeply moved by the beauty and offered up a silent prayer of thanks to Thulla.

For a time, as he ate, Tovak watched the shadows rolling across the grasses of the plateau. Turning to the southeast, he could see the long, mottled streak of what could only be the warband marching across the plain.

In his head, he could imagine the long, thick block-like columns, formed by the marching warriors of the line, trailed by the camp followers and ultimately the warband's supply train. Seeing the warband from his current perspective was inspiring, but at the same time, it seemed to mar the pristine beauty of the plateau.

Tovak heard a scuff of boots on rock and looked over to find one of the pioneers approaching from the direction of the tail end of the column. It was clear to Tovak he had been scouting behind the column. He was undoubtedly one of those charged with ensuring they were not being tracked or followed.

The pioneer wore light armor, like the skirmishers, but colored green and brown. He carried a smaller pack too and had in one hand a stout walking staff that had been smoothed and then covered over with varnish to protect it against the elements. A sword was sheathed at his right side and a dagger on the left.

The pioneer was older, nearly elderly, and had a grizzled and hardened look to him. He wore a black patch over one of his eyes. He seemed unassailably tough to Tovak, intimidating even. Tovak got the sense this was definitely someone you did not want to cross.

"Iger," Karn greeted the pioneer and jerked a thumb in the direction they'd just come. "Spot anything back there?"

"Nah," Iger said and blew out a long breath. His voice was gravelly, like two rocks grinding together. "We did not see anything but wildlife. But I still have to report to Dagon."

Tovak wondered who *we* referred to. He suspected Iger was likely part of a scout team.

The pioneer looked over at Tovak and Gorabor. "Got some new squaddies, I see."

"Aye," Karn said. "That I do."

Tovak hesitated a moment, then pointed at his friend, who was looking up at the fearsome pioneer in what could only be described as awe. "This is Gorabor and I'm Tovak."

Iger fixed his one good eye on Tovak. "Heard of you."

Tovak took another swallow, washing down the last of the dodder he'd been chewing on, as he thought on how best to respond. A fresh mountain breeze blew over them, rustling what few small pines and trees were scattered amongst the rocks and the brush about them. The cool air was more than welcome—it was a relief.

Tovak gave a mental shrug and instead offered up his skin to the fearsome-looking pioneer, almost like a peace offering. He was surprised when the pioneer took it without hesitation. Iger drank a swallow and then passed it back. He seemed to suddenly spot Dagmar across from them and shifted his attention to the skirmisher.

"Heard you got bit by a gnome," Iger said, "in the ass too, if the stories can be believed."

"Don't you have anything better to do, Iger?" Dagmar asked.

"Not at the moment," Iger said matter-of-factly. "Is it true?"

"Yes it bloody is," Dagmar replied, grumpily, before biting into his dodder. Through chews he spoke. "It seems like everyone knows."

Iger grinned at him, showing several bad and missing teeth. "You've got to admit, if it happened to someone else, you'd find it funny as could be."

"I suppose," Dagmar admitted grudgingly and let out an unhappy breath. "I suppose you're right."

"There's no supposing about it," Iger said. "You'd be laughing your ass off, just like the rest of us. Only it was you that got it in the ass."

Tovak could not help but laugh, as did those around them.

"Very funny," Dagmar said. "Very funny."

Iger's gaze flicked back to Tovak before turning out towards the plateau and the warband. "That's a sight I will never grow tired of."

"The warband?" Tovak asked. "Or the beauty?"

Iger glanced over at him before turning his gaze back out to the plateau.

"Both," Iger said and fell silent for several heartbeats. "The warband is just an idea, sonny, a dream, and a grand one at that. Each of us, in our own way, makes that dream a reality"—he glanced over at Tovak meaningfully—"no matter our background. Without us, there is no warband. Without each and every individual blade of grass, there is no plateau, no beauty to behold. There'd only be a vast wasteland before us."

Tovak thought he read something in the pioneer's one-eyed gaze. Was it respect? He wasn't sure. He was about to reply when Dagmar barked out a harsh laugh.

"Spare me," Dagmar scoffed. "You're getting philosophical in your old age, Iger."

"There may be some truth in that," the pioneer said. "As you advance in years, you tend to start thinking more about life and the meaning of things."

"Too much time scouting on your own is more like the cause," Dagmar said.

Iger looked back at Tovak and seemed to have tired of the conversation. "Thanks for the drink."

"Anytime," Tovak said, and with that, Iger moved off, while offering Karn a nod as he passed.

"A tough one, that one," Torimar said, once Iger was out of sight.

"Agreed," Karn said. "A good fighter and an even better pioneer. He's one you want on your side in a fight, that's for sure."

Tovak stared after Iger for a few heartbeats, then stood on legs that ached from the strain of the march. He took a moment to stretch the soreness out of his back. Carrying his waterskin, he made his way to the stream. He splashed some water on his face. It was cold and refreshing. He refilled his skin before stopping it closed.

"Think there are gnomes up here?" Gorabor asked Tovak as he returned.

Tovak looked up sharply at his friend. He had not seen any tracks, but that did not mean they weren't about. He glanced around, thinking he should have a look.

"Relax," Karn said, and seemed suddenly amused by Tovak's discomfort. "The Second has a team of scouts out, screening the march. They're good. Now that we know gnomes are out there, infesting these ridges, Dagon's got boys on the lookout for them. We won't be taken by surprise as easily as the captain was."

"Let's hope not," Dagmar said. "I've had my fill of gnomes."

"You just don't want to be bitten again," Gorabor said. "Maybe next time one will get the other cheek."

That drew a laugh from those gathered around and yet another dark look from Dagmar.

"Next time," Dagmar said slowly, as he shifted his gaze to Tovak, "do me a favor and leave him with the orcs."

"On your feet, lads," Thegdol called from farther up the way. "Break's over. Packs on."

Dagmar groaned. "I was just getting comfortable."

"Get on your feet," Karn said to Dagmar as he got himself up. "Even if you're bandaged like a baby wearing a diaper, I won't have you making the squad look bad by dragging ass."

"It just doesn't end," Dagmar groaned as he pulled himself to his feet. "It's getting old."

"Not for us," Torimar said.

"It'll never bloody end," Dagmar said, shaking his head.

Returning his haversack to his pack, Tovak stood and secured it in its place.

"Fall in," Thegdol called.

The march resumed shortly after that.

"How far do you think we've covered today?" Gorabor asked as they continued working their way along the ridgeline, which was broad and flat. It was covered with long grass and a scattering of trees.

"Maybe eight or nine miles so far," Tovak replied, staring up briefly at the suns. The march had turned in a northern direction.

"How far do you think we're going?" Gorabor asked. "All this climbing, up and down, over broken ground—my legs are starting to kill me."

"As far as we need to go," Karn said from behind. "If you stop talking about it, the miles pass easier, for you and everyone else. Get my meaning?"

"Yes, Corporal," Gorabor said.

They moved from one hill to the next. Sweat once again began pouring down Tovak's face. At times, as they worked their way along the wide tops of the ridges, the ground was rugged and hard. Other times, he found it smooth and easy to traverse, with little undergrowth to catch at the foot.

Throughout the latter half of the day, there were several more breaks, but as the sunlight began to dim, a final halt was called along a broad and relatively flat ridgeline with a scattering of trees. Knee-high grass grew around them. It seemed to whisper when the wind gusted.

"Looks like we will be spending the night here." Karn glanced around. "I doubt we will be permitted fires. That means it's gonna be a cold night."

"Sergeant Thegdol," Benthok called. He was standing with Lieutenant Brund about twenty yards away. "We're gonna need a wall and trench. The Baelix will be responsible for the west side. I will mark it shortly for you."

"Yes, sir," Thegdol said. "Corporals on me."

Karn started over to the sergeant as Tovak unhooked his pack and set it on the ground. He was relieved to have the heavy thing off.

"Tovak."

Tovak turned at the call of his name. Captain Dagon stood a few feet away. He had emerged from a stand of trees and, like everyone else, was sweating heavily. The captain's expression was hard and unforgiving.

"Join me, if you would." It was not posed as a question, but a command.

Tovak saw Gorabor look over with an expression of concern. Dagmar looked over as well.

"Yes, sir." Feeling a deep sense of unease, Tovak stepped over to the captain and came to a position of attention. Since they were in the field, he remembered not to salute.

"I would speak with you in private," Dagon said brusquely, with a glance at the rest of Tovak's squad.

"Yes, sir," Tovak replied, not liking the idea one bit.

"Follow me," Dagon ordered. He turned on his heel and moved off, with Tovak a few paces behind.

Tovak felt a growing sense of dread as they drew farther away from the camp. Dagon stopped while they were still in sight but out of earshot and turned to face him. Eying Tovak for several long moments, the captain of the Second ran his fingers through his beard.

"What you did..." Dagon said, then fell silent. His jaw flexed, as if he was suddenly having difficulty choosing the proper words. Tovak said nothing and simply waited. The silence stretched out ... six heartbeats ... twelve. Tovak remained at attention. He intended to give Dagon no cause to punish him.

Dagon drew in a deep breath and let it out ever so slowly. He narrowed his eyes at Tovak, and then he seemed to reach an internal decision.

"I am not happy with these circumstances—with you under my command, Stonehammer," Dagon said tersely. "Not happy, not one bit. But orders are orders, and I follow mine. While there is nothing I can do about your presence here on this mission, there are some things that are unequivocally within my purview." He paused, as if gathering his thoughts. "Word of what happened before you rescued your comrades from the enemy camp has reached my ears. I suspect them true." He tapped Tovak on the chest armor with a finger. "I once told you I would not hinder you in your pursuit of service. I won't. However, understand that anyone under my command who disobeys an order will receive swift punishment. I will not tolerate you thinking you can do as you wish. We play as a team here or not at all. I will not be swayed in the slightest by a desperate need for you to prove yourself. If you cannot follow orders, there is no place for you here with the warband. Break the rules with me and there will be severe consequences. If you cross me, I promise I will see you whipped, like a dog, and run out of the Badgers." Dagon fell silent for half a heartbeat. "Are we clear, Stonehammer?"

"Yes sir," Tovak said crisply. He kept all emotion off his face, though inside he was roiling with anger and hurt. "I will not disobey your orders, sir."

Dagon eyed him, as if he'd stepped in teska droppings and was looking to scrape it from his boot.

"Permission to speak freely, sir?" Tovak asked abruptly. If Dagon was to speak his mind, Tovak resolved to do so as well.

Dagon's head shifted to the side, and he raised an eyebrow.

"Speak," he said.

"Respectfully, sir," Tovak began, keeping his voice as even and calm as he could, though he was raging with anger on the inside. He could not fully conceal his emotion, for some of it leaked out. "I cannot change the past. Nor can I alter who my father was or bring back your son." Dagon's expression hardened. "I was not at Barasoom." Tovak paused to suck in a ragged breath. "What you heard is true. I crossed a line and defied orders. I did it to save my comrades. If I was to do it over again, I would make the same choice. I offer no excuses for my behavior, for in my mind, it was the right decision. When I made my choice to go, I was fully prepared to accept whatever consequences came my way." Tovak paused. His voice sounded harsh in his own ears. "I understand your anger with my father and, therefore, with me. And now, you know the truth of the matter. Report me if you wish, drum me out of the Badgers if it makes you happy. To my dying day, I will never regret saving Gorabor or Dagmar, sir. My only regret is that I could not save Staggen."

Dagon did not reply. He stared at Tovak for what seemed to be an eternity. His expression had gone blank, almost lifeless. The silence stretched out long enough to become uncomfortable, and still Dagon remained silent. Then the captain sucked in a breath and shook himself slightly before clearing his throat.

"You are dismissed." The captain's voice was barely a whisper. "Return to your squad."

Tovak hesitated a moment, then turned on his heel and returned the way he'd come, leaving Dagon behind. He could feel the captain's eyes on his back as he made his way to his squad. They were already hard at work on the defensive wall, digging away and breaking the ground. Tovak went to his pack and retrieved his entrenching tool, then joined his squad.

"What did Captain Dagon want?" Gorabor asked.

"It's not important," Tovak replied, glancing at Torimar, Dagmar, and Bettoth, who had paused in their work and were looking over, clearly also interested. "I don't want to discuss it."

"Enough talk," Karn snapped, straightening up. "This wall's not getting built by itself."

Grateful that he did not have to speak on his encounter with Dagon, Tovak threw himself into his work and rapidly built up a sweat. The hard physical labor of digging helped him get out his aggression and anger. After a time, he looked up, pausing to stare at the plateau. Out there, no longer in view, was the warband. He thought on Iger's words. The warband was an idea and they all made it a reality, no matter their background. Dagon had been right. He was out to prove himself, but at the same time, he was also a Blood Badger.

"Dig," Karn said.

Tovak turned back to his work.

CHAPTER NINE

On his feet and feeling stiff, Tovak stretched and then
yawned mightily before glancing around. It was still
dark, with the sky beginning to show the very first hints of
color. The moon was up, high above, and the temperature
was cool.

Tovak rubbed at his tired and dry eyes and came away
with sand. He took a knee next to his gear. With a weary
breath, he began rolling up his bedroll, wondering if being
in the army meant that one was perpetually short on sleep.
So far, it was turning out to be that way. Around him, the
rest of his squad was securing their gear.

"I heard a rumor there's been a prophecy of some kind
guiding us all along," Bettoth said as he rolled up his bedroll. "Been thinking about it all night, I have."

"A prophecy?" Dagmar asked, looking up from stowing
his personal belongings in his pack. "Are you serious?"

"Yeah," Bettoth said, "a friend of mine over in First
Infantry said the Thane's High Council knew about
Grata'Dagoth. There's some ancient prophecy that was
found. A scholar discovered it in an old scroll or something
like that."

Tovak looked up at that, thinking of Grimbok.

"That's why we're out here," Bettoth continued. "That's
why the Badgers are in search of the place. Grata'Dagoth

is supposed to be some sort of impregnable fortress that's been hidden for centuries, one the Horde can't crack. Can you imagine?"

"Sounds like a load of teska shit to me," Dagmar said.

Tovak glanced at Bettoth. Before the detachment had turned in for the night, Dagon had spoken to them in depth, providing more details on their mission. He had specifically mentioned the fortress. Notably, there had been no mention that the road to Grata'Dagoth was guarded.

"You're full of it," Torimar said. "If you'd heard such a thing, you would have been crowing about it before we marched."

"No," Bettoth said, "it's true. I swear my friend told me."

"As if you had a friend," Dagmar said. "Who was this imaginary friend of yours?"

"Mikko," Bettoth said.

"I've heard some fantastical rumors from him," Dagmar said.

"I thought he was full of teska shit too," Bettoth said, "until, that is, Dagon spoke to us last night. That's why I said nothing."

Tovak tied off his bedroll and attached it to his pack. He studied the ground where he'd spent the night sleeping on his arms and under the stars. This patch of ground had seemed uncommonly hard and lumpy. Though he had been exceptionally tired, Tovak had still passed an uncomfortable night. Yes, he had slept, but it had been far from a peaceful rest. He had tossed and turned. But it hadn't been the ground either that had kept him awake.

Well, some of it had.

Tovak had strange dreams of a growing darkness. He couldn't fully remember the dreams, but they had kept him restless. That was odd, because Tovak rarely had nightmares.

He yawned as he looked about. The entire detachment had been rousted a short while before. Around him, everyone was preparing for the day's march. The sound of it filled the air.

"You can't keep secrets," Dagmar said to Bettoth, "everyone knows that. Had you heard such a thing, you'd have surely dished on it."

"Look who's talking," Bettoth said, "mister rumor mill. I don't know anyone who loves to gossip more than you."

"Prophecy or not, the warband is headed into a fight." Karn secured his own bedroll to his pack. "And I don't envy Captain Struugar or the boys who will be making a frontal assault on that wall. It's going to be an ugly and bloody business."

"I was with the captain at Adorana," Torimar said, leaning back from placing his things in his pack. "We sieged that human city for months, trying to starve them out. In the end, I think they were reduced to eating each other. When the order came for a final assault on the city's walls, I tell you freely, I was scared witless. The thought of going up those scaling ladders made my knees weak."

"Was it really that bad?" Gorabor asked. "I mean, when the attack was made?"

"Worse," Torimar said, "much worse. The enemy did not give up without a fight. We lost a lot of good warriors that day."

"That was before I joined," Bettoth said. "The captain was a lieutenant back then, wasn't he?"

"Yes," Karn said, "that's right. Dozerg was in command. Struugar had Benthok's position."

"Dozerg was a tough bastard," Torimar said. "When he fell, Struugar stepped up and led us forward. He set the example and gave us the courage to keep on going up those cursed ladders to force the walls. I don't think I've ever seen so fearless an officer as our captain that day. He earned much Legend." Torimar paused, and his gaze became distant, as if reliving the past. "Karn, you were there, too. Tell them."

Gorabor looked to the corporal expectantly, as did Tovak.

Karn had been packing up his kit. He stopped and looked up at Torimar, a haunted expression in his eyes. He said nothing.

"Sturm fell in that battle," Torimar said, filling the silence. "Though we were in different squads, if I recall, you two were close, Karn. He died with the captain."

"He did," Karn said quietly, "and he was my friend, nearly a brother to me."

Tovak saw the look of anguish in Karn's eyes and recalled his corporal had just lost his real brother too. The memory had clearly brought up old wounds to mingle with the new.

Returning to his packing, Karn cleared his throat. "I don't want to talk about it."

There was an uncomfortable moment of silence after that.

"My father stormed several Syrulian fortresses during the war," Bettoth said, a few moments later. "When he got into his cups, he talked about watching comrades on the scaling ladders, pushed back and off the walls, falling to their deaths. He spoke of boiling oil, baked sand, clouds of arrows, and getting skewered by the enemy as he and his buddies worked to get over the enemy's walls. Growing up, I'd thought he was exaggerating. But, having seen combat, I imagine it is as he said."

"An assault on a fortified position is nasty business." Torimar stood up and began putting on his armor.

A heavy silence fell over the squad for several moments.

As he began tying the straps, he added, "I'm just glad we're not the ones who've been asked to storm that wall from the front side."

"Agreed," Karn said. "I've seen my share of such actions. I don't need any more. If we need to hit it, we will be attacking it from the rear, which will make our job much easier."

"The rear? I thought we were talking about the wall," Bettoth said, "not Dagmar."

That caused a chuckle and a lightening of the mood.

"Very funny," Dagmar said. "Ha ha."

"Is anyone else wondering why Captain Struugar was cut out of this operation and the company split up?" Gorabor asked. He had already put on his armor and was tying his bedroll to his pack. "Yeah, he's leading the attack on the wall, but it sort of feels like punishment somehow, for the Baelix Guard getting so beat up."

"You don't know what you're talking about," Karn said, with a bit of an edge. It caused Gorabor to freeze in his work and look at his corporal in alarm. "I don't want to hear any of that kind of talk. Rumors like that cause nothing but no end of trouble. Understand?"

"Yes, Corporal," Gorabor said, sounding chastened.

"We just had some bad luck is all. It happens." Karn softened his tone. "You're still new here. Companies like ours get split up all the time for specialized duties and tasks. We're not like the line companies, the heavy infantry who train and fight together. They are the backbone of the warband and the muscle. Like the pioneers, we are different. We don't fight the way they do. We're irregulars, and as such, we get stuck with all the shit assignments." Karn sucked in a breath. "As to the captain, he has a lot of hard-won experience when it comes to assaults against fortified positions. He's proved that over and over again, especially"—Karn paused and glanced over at Torimar—"at Adorana. He knows his business when it comes to forcing a wall. Where he's being sent might seem like a punishment to someone who doesn't know any better, but he's where he needs to be for the good of the warband. And here"—Karn held his hands out—"is where we need to be, in the field. Understand?"

"Yes, Corporal." Gorabor gave a nod as several pioneers passed them by. All wore packs and were headed for the gap in the wall. Envious, Tovak eyed them. They were clearly on their way to scout.

"Now, all of you, back to work," Karn said, in a near snarl. "It won't be long before they call for the march to resume."

The squad fell into another silence after that. Tovak worked at making sure his gear and personal possessions were securely and neatly put away. Around him, the entire detachment was doing the same. Tovak put on his armor and went to the latrine, which had been dug just outside of the camp. He relieved himself and returned.

He found Karn and Gorabor had finished securing their gear. They were both sitting down and eating a dodder. Tovak pulled out his haversack and retrieved a dodder himself. He had not realized how hungry he was and, barely pausing to chew, quickly wolfed it down.

"Packs on," Lieutenant Brund called over the din of the camp. "Second Pioneers and Baelix, form up outside the walls by squads."

"My company," Greng called. "Assemble outside the camp. Sergeant Greneck, kindly have the squad leaders perform a roll call."

"Yes, sir," the sergeant replied from the other side of the camp. "Get a move on, you maggots. Let's not keep the captain waiting."

With the rest of his squad, Tovak heaved his pack onto his shoulders, secured it, and started moving towards the camp's entrance. They filed through the gap in the wall and began falling into formation, dressing themselves next to one another.

After a quick roll call, and a brief wait while the officers conferred, the march was resumed. Once again, they moved in a northeasterly direction. The march was difficult, and Tovak quickly grew warm, though the day was not as hot as the previous one had been. Dagon pushed them hard and they covered many miles, with only two half-hour breaks during the entirety of the morning.

They were allowed another break for lunch and then, once again, they pushed onward. By mid-afternoon, they found a team of pioneers waiting for them in a small heavily forested valley. It was here that Dagon called a halt for the day. The lake had clean water. Everyone was ordered to refill their waterskins.

Tovak eyed the lake, thinking, if the opportunity presented itself, a dip to bathe would be good. He felt sticky and dirty. Orders were soon passed down for a wall to be built.

"Another cold night without a fire," Dagmar said unhappily as he took his entrenchment tool from his pack.

"You'd rather make it easy for the enemy to find us?" Karn asked, looking up after he'd set his pack down on the ground. "I think I can do without a fire for a few days, if I get to keep my skin in return."

"When you put it that way," Dagmar said, "I guess we don't really need a fire."

"I kind of figured you'd see it my way," Karn said.

"Karn, Tovak," Benthok said, approaching the squad. Though his head was still bandaged, the lieutenant looked fresh, as if the march had hardly affected him. "Both of you are with me. We're going into the field. Bring your packs. We'll likely be out all night."

The rest of their squad stopped what they were doing to look over curiously.

"I've spoken to Sergeant Thegdol," Benthok added. "He'll look after your squad while we are gone."

"Yes, sir." Karn picked his pack up and swung it back onto his shoulders. He looked over at Tovak with eagerness in his eyes. "No rest for us, it seems."

With a soft groan caused by aching shoulders, Tovak did the same and settled his pack in place. Still, he wasn't disappointed. In fact, his heart was racing with excitement and he sensed the same in Karn. They were off to scout. Though he dared not ask, he wondered with no little bit of excitement where they were going. Tovak knew he would learn soon enough.

Karn and Tovak followed Benthok a short distance to Lieutenant Brund, who was talking with Dagon and Greng.

"Yes, sir," Brund said. "I will get it done and before dawn. I'll see that word is sent back on what we learn."

"I'll see you in a few hours then," Dagon said. "Be safe."

"Yes, sir," Brund said.

"Good luck," Greng said.

With that, both Dagon and Greng turned away. Dagon hesitated when he spotted Tovak. An unhappy look, filled with displeasure, washed across the pioneer captain's face. Dagon's gaze shifted rapidly to Benthok, as if in blame, and then he turned away and followed after Greng. Benthok appeared not to have noticed, or if he did, he ignored it, which Tovak thought more likely.

"Tovak," Benthok said, "do you know Corporal Taboth?"

Tovak had not noticed the corporal standing a few feet off from Brund, with a squad of six behind him, all pioneers. Tovak knew none of them, except Iger, who inclined his head ever so slightly in Tovak's direction. Taboth was a little older than Tovak, fit and rugged, with piercing eyes, a brown beard, and brown hair. There was a natural confidence and enthusiasm about him that Tovak could not help but envy.

"No, sir," Tovak said. "I do not."

"Well," Benthok said, "now you do. His squad will be going with us."

"Yes, sir."

"Taboth," Karn greeted. "I see Lieutenant Brund will let just anyone out into the field these days."

"Karn," Taboth said, with a trace of a grin, "good to be working with you again."

"Alright," Brund said, having stepped over and up to Benthok. "Gather 'round." He motioned with his hands. "Come on, gather around."

They made a half circle around the two lieutenants.

"We've got a bit of a hike ahead of us," Brund said. "We're headed for the ridge a few miles from here, where Taboth and I will make an ascent, which will require some scrambling and perhaps even a little climbing."

"Sounds exciting," Taboth said. "It's been a while since we've climbed anything even remotely challenging."

"True." Brund paused, running his eyes around the small group. "Our job is simple. Get some eyes to the top of the ridge. The crest should provide a good vantage of the Keelbooth Valley and the canyon that leads into it from the plateau. From its summit, we will be able to get eyes on the wall the enemy holds that blocks the canyon and, when darkness settles in, be able to spot the enemy if they have an army in the valley. We don't think they do, but this will tell us for sure. The warband needs that information."

Tovak understood the campfires from such an army would be a dead giveaway.

"Speaking of the enemy, we are to avoid contact with them," Benthok added. "However, we can expect patrols in the area we are moving into. Our advance scouts have seen them, so we need to keep an eye out. If we're discovered, we need to kill them all so word about the detachment does not get out. The enemy can't learn that we intend to move a force around behind the wall guarding the pass. If they do, it could spell disaster and make the warband's job of getting into the valley that much more difficult."

"That is correct," Brund said. "We cannot afford to have them become wise to our presence. Part of our mission will be to find an easy route up, over the ridge, and down the other side for the entire detachment to move into position behind the enemy's wall. Understand?"

"Yes, sir," they all replied.

Brund looked to Benthok. "Do you wish to add anything more?"

"No," Benthok said. "I'm good."

"Any questions?" Brund asked, once again running his gaze around the small group.

No one said anything.

"Alright, we're gonna move straight for the ridge in question," Brund said. "Iger's on point. Corporal Taboth, your boys will be on the right. Benthok, you and yours are on the left. Let's get moving. Once we're back into the forest, remain silent, finger speak only, keep your eyes open, and most important, stay alert. I don't want to bump into any enemy patrols along the way. And make no mistake, the enemy is out there. If we do see a patrol, try to be ghosts and let them pass. Let's go."

He nodded to Iger, who turned and strode off, leading the way along the lake's edge. Once they were around the side, Tovak moved out onto the left wing, along with Karn. Karn glanced behind them at the detachment on the other side of the lake, who were working at constructing the fortified camp. He looked back over at Tovak.

"Whenever officers say something is simple," Karn said to him in a tone only the two of them could hear, "it never is."

Tovak sucked in a breath at that. He had an uncomfortable feeling Karn was right. Then they plunged back into the forest. Setting a good pace, they moved as silently as possible as they worked their way deeper into the forest, which was filled with thick hardwoods.

Within a short time, they were soon climbing hills or working their way along the tops of ridges. Tovak searched, as he moved forward, for any sign of tracks, be they orc, goblin, or gnome. He saw none. The farther they went, the more excited he became at what they were doing. This was what he had trained for, and despite being tired from the day's march, he found himself reinvigorated with a second wind and loving every moment of it.

Then, after several miles, Tovak almost stumbled to a stop as something occurred to him. He felt the pull. It was back. Once again, it was tugging him inexorably forward in the direction they were going. He wasn't imagining the feeling. It was tangible and real. There was no doubt in his mind.

Was the pull coming from Thulla? For some strange reason he could not put his finger on, he suspected it was. What was going on with him? Why was his god taking such an interest in him? The last time it had drawn him to confront evil. Was such attention from his god a blessing or a curse? Tovak hoped and prayed it was the former. And yet, with every step, the anticipation grew into a feeling of worry and deep concern that there was something terrible out there, waiting for them.

Or was it waiting for him?

CHAPTER TEN

They moved through the forest like wraiths, silent and wary for any sign of the enemy. Lieutenant Brund led them four miles before they saw their destination in the distance. Through a gap in the trees at least another mile away was a high, steep ridge that rose before them. It was nearly a mountain in its own right. Tovak felt a thrill of exhilaration run through him as he took in the ridge.

Brund led them on an unerring course forward through the forest, down one hill and up the next. When they came upon a swift-flowing river running between two hills, Brund paused and motioned Iger over. The two conferred for a moment before Iger emphatically pointed upstream.

With that, Brund started moving again and led them upstream more than a hundred yards to where a thick, fallen tree spanned the river. It lay a few feet above the rushing water. The river was five yards across and looked deep enough to swallow any one of them. Tovak eyed it warily, as did several of the others.

Brund paused at the tree, eyes scanning and listening to the sounds of the forest for several heartbeats. He scanned the far side of the river, then moved carefully across the log. Brund paused at the other side and took a knee. He flashed a *hold* sign back at them. Then, carefully, he moved ahead, disappearing from view. Tovak began counting in his head.

When he reached two hundred, the lieutenant stepped back into view and gave a thumbs-up. Tovak felt a wave of relief.

Benthok crossed next, moving easily over the log. Tovak watched, like the rest of them. One slip and there would likely be no hope of saving oneself. The water was moving too fast and was strewn with rocks and boulders. Each of the other warriors crossed in turn. Karn and Tovak were last.

The corporal looked behind them. He scanned the forest for a long moment. Karn glanced at the rushing water and then back at Tovak.

"Don't fall in the water." The corporal flashed Tovak a grin and then started across himself.

A wave of nervousness hit Tovak. He wasn't overly fond of water, especially as encumbered as he was with armor, a sword, and a heavy pack. He took a deep breath, stepped up onto the log, and crossed slowly, placing his feet carefully, one step after another. Halfway across, his right foot slipped as some of the bark fell away. Tovak's heart almost stopped as he wobbled uncertainly, waving his arms out for balance. After a moment, he was able to recover. Once again steady, he glanced down at the water rushing by underneath the log and let out a relieved breath. He resumed his trek and made his way over the rest of the log. He hopped off the log and exhaled another relieved breath, as his feet were once again on solid ground.

The party had already spread back out. Tovak fell in next to Karn, who glanced over at him with amusement. He'd clearly seen Tovak almost go over the side of the log.

Brund started off again, leading them in the direction of the steep ridge they had seen through the trees. Moving as silently and quickly as he could, Tovak picked out his own path as they forged their way through the forest. He did his best to listen and scan the surroundings, making certain to leave as little sign of passage as possible.

As they neared their objective, through the trees, the steep slope of the ridge seemed to tower above them, almost ominously. Working their way up the lower reaches of the slope, they began to climb once again. The grade seemed to increase with every step. Tovak found himself breathing heavily as they worked their way through the trees.

Finally, they came upon an extremely steep, rock-covered slope that rose up before them, like a veritable wall. Tovak looked up. He estimated the height from this point was at least five hundred feet to the top.

Brund motioned for Benthok to join him. The two officers put their heads together for a long moment, then Brund made a sign for all of them to gather around. Brund took a knee and pulled out a waterskin. He drank deeply as he waited.

"Alright." Brund wiped sweat out of his eyes. "We've made it. Lieutenant Benthok will form a perimeter around this spot. Stay hidden and silent. Keep watch for any signs of the enemy. Corporal Taboth and I are going to climb up this ridge and reconnoiter the canyon and the valley. We're also going to search for the easiest path for the entire detachment to take to scale this bitch of a ridge. We think we've already identified a likely spot, so hopefully it does not take too long." He glanced up the steep slope. "With luck, I expect we should only be gone a couple of hours, maybe more. Certainly it will be dark by the time we return. That's it." Brund turned to Benthok. "I will see you in a bit."

"Good fortune," Benthok said.

Brund looked to Taboth, nodded once, and then the two of them removed their packs. They pulled out rope for climbing, picks, and other gear. Then, they started for the top. Tovak had to marvel at how easy they made it look as they began scrambling and scaling their way up towards the summit.

Benthok watched for a few moments, then scanned the forested hillside upon which they stood. His gaze traveled from the left to the right.

"I want a line with five yards of separation from each position," Benthok said. "The pioneers will take the right side. Karn, Tovak, and myself will position ourselves on the left. Find a concealed position, stay alert, and remain within sight of each other. Remember, we are in enemy territory. Make no noise unless absolutely needed. We're ghosts. Got that?"

"Yes, sir," they said in near unison.

"Get to it."

They spread out along a staggered line. Tovak ended up in a clump of bushes, almost in the middle of the line, with a good view of the forested slope they'd just come up.

Once in position, he took off his pack, got himself comfortable, and sat down, settling in to wait. The rest was more than welcome. His legs and back ached terribly from the last two days of hard marching, and it felt good to simply not do anything but sit.

For over two hours, Tovak kept scanning the forest in search of any sign of movement. He ate a dodder, drank some of the water in his skin. His mind wandered a little as the boredom increased.

He wondered if Jodin still lived or if he had already passed. Such thoughts were not happy ones and filled him with guilt. He forced them away. He thought on Thulla. He felt the strange urge. It was still there, tugging at him, encouraging him to climb the ridge after Brund and Taboth. He felt somewhat frustrated that he could not. The pulls were increasing in their frequency—and potency. He was becoming more convinced they were coming directly from his god. Where else could they be coming from?

Tovak's thoughts shifted to his Spirit Deck. It was tucked away in his pack. He felt no urge to consult it. He had not since he'd left the camp to rescue his comrades. He knew deep down he would no longer need it. Why he thought so, he wasn't quite sure.

A snapping branch out in the forest to his front broke him out of his thoughts. He rose slowly to a knee and scanned down the hillside. A terrible feeling of foreboding, like a chill wind, washed over him.

The forest was silent, almost unnaturally so. He could hear no birds, or really anything else other than his own breathing. The feeling of foreboding intensified. Tovak unconsciously reached for and gripped the hilt of his sword, his eyes searching for what had made the sound.

Another twig snapped off to the right. It was accompanied by the rustling of brush and fallen leaves. Motion drew his gaze. Among the shadows along the route they'd come, he saw movement through the trees. His heart began to pound in his chest. Someone or something was out there.

He focused on the movement, trying to pick its shape out of the shadows and shade from the canopy above. And then he saw it... well really saw *them*. He blinked several times to make sure he wasn't seeing things. He almost laughed out loud and then remembered they were to remain silent.

Dain.

Three of the six-legged creatures were slowly moving through the forest. Their tannish-gray coats of short fur made it difficult to see them at first, but then they passed

out of the shadows into a more open area, where the sunlight filtered down to the forest floor and fully illuminated
them.

Relieved, Tovak blew out a breath and chided himself.
Dain. He'd gotten worked up over a few foraging dain. He
started to settle back down, but then froze as he realized
that the feeling of approaching danger hadn't abated. In
fact, if anything, it had intensified.

He could feel a presence—dark, malevolent—out there,
somewhere nearby. He recognized the feeling. It was the
same thing he'd felt in the enemy's camp. He found himself
full of the same loathing and a desire to eradicate whatever
the source was. And it was getting stronger with each and
every heartbeat that pounded away in his chest.

He turned, almost as an afterthought, and gave a low
bird call to catch Benthok's attention. A few yards away, he
saw the lieutenant shift slightly and look his way.

Using finger speak, Tovak signed insistently that something was coming.

Benthok signed back, pointing at the creatures to their
front. *Dain.*

Tovak emphatically shook his head.

Not the dain, he signed.

The lieutenant locked eyes with Tovak, and after a long
moment, gave a nod, then shifted his gaze back out into the
forest, searching. A moment later, the lieutenant was looking back at him in question. It was clear he had not seen
anything.

Enemy near, Tovak signed. Even though he'd not seen
them, he felt certain they were out there, somewhere.

Benthok gave him a curt nod, then signed back. *Ready
sling.*

Tovak turned his gaze back to the forest. He still saw nothing, but like a dark cloud hanging over him, the feeling persisted. He realized he'd been holding his sword hilt in a white-knuckled grip. Releasing his hold, he drew his sling. If an enemy was coming, the sling had range. He loaded a single lead shot into the pouch, and while he did, he glanced back towards the lieutenant.

Benthok disappeared through the brush and had moved near the next position. Word of what was happening was beginning to spread. The lieutenant was seeing to that. Tovak looked to his right and saw Karn glance his way before turning his gaze back to the forest before them. The corporal had clearly not missed the exchange. He had drawn his sword and laid it by his side. In his hands was his sling.

With the feeling of darkness growing with each passing heartbeat, Tovak focused his attention back towards the dain and the forest beyond them. It almost felt like his hair was standing on end. The creatures had moved another dozen yards, but then came to an abrupt stop and looked downslope. All three had raised their heads and were turning their ears back and forth as their red tails stood up straight and quivered.

As one, they bolted.

All three leapt forward together and took off through the forest, their six legs scrambling wildly as they bounded and ran, as if in flight from a deadly predator.

Now Tovak was certain there was something out there and it was close. He held his breath, his heart pounding, as he searched the forest for any sign of movement.

Nothing.

What were they running from? He could see nothing. He strained, searching the shadows. He spotted movement.

First, a single orc appeared downslope, moving stealthily from tree to tree, and then there was another close behind.

They stalked like predators on the hunt—slow and calculating. A third stepped from behind a tree, then suddenly there were more. The forest seemed filled with the enemy. Spread across thirty yards, they moved through the trees in threes, covering and watching for one another, while at the same time scanning the forest. Tovak counted nine and then off to his left a ways, thirty yards distant, spotted more. There were eighteen of the enemy, spread out over about thirty yards.

Wearing light leather, with identical chest plates, bracers, and greaves, they appeared to be tracking something. Tovak hoped it was the dain, but he suspected it was otherwise. The enemy had picked up their trail.

Slowly, the orcs moved forward, silent, menacing. And then, one last figure emerged from amidst the trees. At the rear strode a lone orc in black leather armor and a helm that hid the upper half of his face. The helm had six obsidian stones—two large and four small—set above the eye slits, reminding Tovak, almost uncomfortably, of one of the large spiders, a krata.

The instant Tovak laid eyes on him, that familiar surge of revulsion and hatred flowed like red-hot steel through his veins and threatened to consume him.

He knew, without a doubt, he was gazing upon the enemy's leader. He had no evidence this was a correct assumption, but he felt it right, true, and the helmet seemed to confirm it. He clenched his fist, holding the sling, and fought the urge to attack. His breath came in short pants as he struggled to resist the impulse. His heart felt like it was going to leap out of his chest and his pulse pounded in his ears. Tovak forced himself to calm down. He closed his eyes and breathed in deeply, then let it out slowly. The intense feeling subsided.

The enemy's leader, following the line of orcs that was spread out and advancing up the slope, stepped into a shaft of sunshine, and Tovak saw the faintest hint of black flames licking over the orc's body. It was only a flicker here and there, but it was definitely present, tracing along his arms, up his chest, and over the crown of his foul-looking helm.

It was nearly all Tovak could do to simply crouch there, hidden in the foliage, and remain still. He watched and waited. The urge to extinguish the fire burning within the blood of the leader—for that's what he thought must surely be happening—had returned with a vengeance at the sight of the black flames. The orcs at the head of the group moved past where the dain had been moments before.

Tovak held his breath as one of the orcs approached within twenty feet of his position. The leader froze in place, made a hissing sound that was part whistle, and dropped into a low crouch. The other orcs immediately stopped and crouched low, searching the area around them.

The leader turned his head, first downslope and then slowly up the hill, as if he was searching for something. When his gaze came even with Tovak's concealed position, he stopped searching. He seemed to be looking straight at Tovak, staring intently at the brush that concealed Tovak from view. Tovak was certain he couldn't be seen, but he felt as if the leader somehow saw him. Tovak felt a cold sensation slither down his spine. Or was it that the orc sensed him?

But how?

The leader drew two evil-looking, serrated short swords, one from his hip and one from behind his back, and as he did, the rest of the orcs pulled out their long, curved blades. The leader hissed out an order in the guttural language of his people, and the enemy continued moving slowly forward, searching the underbrush.

I've doomed us, Tovak thought as the orcs drew closer. He did not understand how, but the enemy leader could somehow sense him. He just knew it.

"Slings...cast!" Benthok's shout broke the silence and almost immediately the cracks of slings sounded on the air.

With a bang, the nearest orc fell backward, a lead ball having hammered into the creature's helmet. It crashed to the ground, kicking violently amidst the brush. There was screaming and shouting and roars all around.

"Slings!" Benthok shouted again. "Keep it up, boys."

Tovak stood, aimed at the leader, and made a powerful cast. The sling cracked on the air from the force. The orc saw the throw and dodged, throwing himself aside. The bullet missed and hammered into a tree downslope.

The orc leader screamed out an order and pointed one of his swords forward. The orcs charged towards the Dvergr. Tovak pulled out another bullet, considered making another cast at the leader, but an orc was charging right for him from ten paces away. He shifted his aim and, with a sense of desperation, let fly as hard as he could. Again, the sling cracked on the air. The bullet flew true and hit the orc hard in the upper thigh. The creature went down in a tumble.

Lead shot whistled through the air. Several more orcs dropped in rapid succession only a dozen yards away, roaring in pain. Tovak loaded another shot and took aim once again on the leader. He cast and the shot flew true, hammering into the leader's shoulder, spinning him partially around mid-stride. The enemy leader recovered almost instantly and kept on coming, moving upslope towards him. Tovak couldn't believe his eyes. But there was no more time for thought. The time for slings was over.

Tovak dropped the sling and drew his sword. He stepped through the bush as several battle cries filled the air. Four of his comrades rushed forward, meeting the nearest orcs and engaging them. The harsh clash of steel on steel rang on the air.

An orc rushed Tovak. The creature moved between Tovak and the enemy's leader. The attacker raised his blade high and slashed down with a mighty blow, aimed for his shoulder. Tovak raised his weapon in a two-handed grip and parried. Metal clanged like a hammer upon an anvil, and Tovak's hands stung painfully from the impact. With no little amount of effort, he shoved the orc's blade aside, stepped in close, and shot a hard kick into the orc's knee. There was a wrenching crack as the bone in the knee shattered. The orc crumpled to the side, shrieking in pain for only an instant, before Tovak's back-swing cleaved down deeply into the creature's neck with a gush of hot, green blood.

Tovak spun as he yanked his blade free, sensing the leader's approach. He didn't even need to look; he could feel the dark presence coming for him. He spun to face his enemy, who was advancing with another large orc at his side. Tovak could see the black, smoky tendrils clearer now. They were licking around the leader's body. A wave of intense loathing filled him. A battle cry erupted from Tovak's throat.

"Barasoom!" Tovak shouted.

He charged straight at the two orcs, fully intent on killing both of them. One of the pioneers dashed in from the side, slashing at the leader and drawing his attention. The second orc advanced straight for Tovak, with murder in his eyes.

As Tovak charged forward, he saw the leader block the pioneer's swing with one of the short swords. The pioneer drew back and slashed again. The leader parried and then drove the pioneer back with a series of thrusts and parries that put the pioneer on the defensive.

And then the leader's companion was on top of Tovak, blocking his path and view, roaring as he made a sharp thrust with his curved blade. The tip darted in towards Tovak's face. Tovak smashed the weapon aside. The orc stepped back and swung again, with lightning speed, aiming for Tovak's head. Tovak ducked and parried as he took a step forward. He drew back his blade and thrust. The orc side-stepped this strike and then came at Tovak with a flurry of crisscrossing blows that drove Tovak back. The orc's speed was like nothing he'd ever faced before. He was barely able to block each blow.

The pioneer engaging the enemy's leader let out an ear-splitting scream of agony and staggered backward, clutching at a gash along his upper arm. The distraction almost cost Tovak his life, as the orc facing him reversed his swing and came at him from the other side. Tovak blocked at the last instant and felt the tip of the orc's blade scrape against his helm.

Then Tovak saw the opening. He smashed upward with the hilt of his sword, driving the blunt cross guard into the orc's mouth with a crunch of shattered tusk, tooth, and bone. The orc staggered backward, clutching at his ruined mouth.

Tovak side-stepped and swung down, his blade slicing into the thigh and cutting straight to the bone in the orc's leg. Blood sprayed into the air as the orc roared in terrible agony. He staggered on the injured limb as he made a desperate swing at Tovak's body, to ward him off. Tovak easily blocked, then struck.

The orc had just enough time to look surprised before Tovak, in a powerful move, muscles straining with the effort, drove the point of his weapon completely through his light armor and deep into his body. The orc shuddered and, in apparent astonishment, looked down at the blade that had pierced his chest. A heartbeat later, he shuddered, his eyes rolled back, and his arms dropped to his side. He started to topple backward, threatening to pull Tovak with him. Tovak yanked his blade free with both hands and let the orc finish his journey to the ground.

As the orc passed from Tovak's view, he saw the leader standing over the now disarmed and helpless pioneer, prepared to deliver a killing strike. The sight of it filled him with terrible rage.

"Koin'Duur!" Karn shouted from the right. He was charging directly at the leader. "Benthok, there is a Koin'Duur here." Karn crashed into the leader and assailed him with a series of fast slashes. His zjain was a blur as he struck again and again, driving the leader back and away from the wounded pioneer.

Tovak stepped over to the injured pioneer and knelt down. He had lost consciousness, which was odd because, as far as Tovak could see, he'd only been wounded on the arm. Tovak wondered if he'd somehow hit his head when he'd fallen.

The ring of steel on steel close at hand drew Tovak's gaze back to the fight. The leader blocked each of Karn's attacks, alternating with his weapons, left-right-left-right, as he gave ground. Tovak could see the leader was drawing Karn in. And then in a flash, the leader countered, catching Karn's weapon high. He slashed across Karn's thigh with his off-hand, and the corporal let forth a bloodcurdling scream of pain. He staggered back, clutching at his leg with one hand, and raised his sword to block a follow-up attack. It did not come. The enemy was watching Karn with what Tovak took to be immense satisfaction.

Abruptly, Karn fell to the ground, his entire body wracked with convulsions. What magic was this? Tovak felt the rage within his breast swell with intensity. Almost without realizing it, he had started moving forward, but another orc came at him, charging in from the side with a hacking slash aimed for his head.

Something sparked in Tovak, igniting his senses with a fire that coursed throughout his body. His blade came up without even a thought, and he blocked the orc's attack. Fueled by a rage that had been building for a lifetime, Tovak stepped back, swung his blade over his head, and put every ounce of strength and hate into a single blow.

The orc's blade came up, perfectly placed to stop Tovak's swing.

A resonating *ching* of metal breaking filled the air as Tovak's sword shattered the curved blade of his enemy and sliced into his upper arm. The orc roared in pain. Tovak drew back, reversed his swing, and came around again, pouring all his effort into it. The orc raised his ruined arm in a futile attempt to block the killing blow. Tovak's blade passed clean through the arm with a wet *thuck* just above the elbow, before cleaving down into its side. Tovak's blade cut easily through the leather armor as if it were parchment. The orc grunted with the impact, and staggered backward with impossibly wide eyes, before falling to the ground.

Tovak knew he had delivered a mortal blow and sensed no more threat from that quarter. He turned away from his wounded opponent and looked around for the enemy's leader. He spotted him a few feet away, standing over Karn, who was still convulsing violently as if in a fit. Though the fight raged all around, now there was nothing between him and the enemy leader.

"Come on," Tovak screamed. His vision had gone red around the edges. In all the world, for Tovak, there was only this evil creature, who had struck down two of his comrades, one of whom was a friend. He strode forward, his blade held ready.

The orc turned his gaze from Karn to Tovak and bared his tusks at him wickedly. The creature lowered into a fighting stance and waited.

"Tovak." Benthok's warning shout barely registered. "Don't. That's a Koin'Duur."

With every fiber of his body, Tovak hated. He had not known such pure hate could exist until this very moment. He needed to destroy this creature, eradicate its entire existence, no matter the cost.

Like a stone drawn along the bottom of a fast-moving river, the pull dragged him forward. It was as potent as Tovak had ever felt, and he gave himself over to it.

When the enemy was just within reach, Tovak swung a slashing attack. The orc raised his off-hand weapon and side-stepped. Tovak's blade glanced off the block, but he was expecting the orc's main-hand attack. He halted, cut sideways, and blocked the slash of the second blade.

Around them, the battle continued to rage. Distantly, he heard roaring orcs, the battle cries of his comrades, oaths, shouts, and the ring of steel on steel. But in that moment, his opponent existed alone, a pillar of darkness that needed to be destroyed by Tovak's light, which he felt shining within.

The orc came at him with a savage off-hand slash. Tovak stepped back and blocked. A flurry of slashes assailed Tovak's defenses, driving him back. He understood that his opponent was highly skilled, but something within Tovak seemed to have awoken. It made him faster, stronger, fueled his drive. His enemy appeared too slow, and it was almost as if time itself were slowing. He blocked each blow, which came fast and hard. He began angling his blocks, putting more force behind them, pushing those deadly short swords away in an attempt to create an opening.

Again, and again, the orc came at Tovak, but each slash and thrust failed to penetrate the wall of steel Tovak created between them with his blade. Again and again their blades clanged painfully. Tovak parried a wide arcing slash aimed at his midsection. In a fraction of a heartbeat, he saw what he'd been waiting for—the barest opening and a chance to cleave the orc's flesh.

Tovak caught the next attack with a high block as the creature drew back his other hand and prepared to strike. The tip of Tovak's sword dipped as he stepped forward, and he drove it into the orc's thigh. A jolt ran up his arm, along with a dank, sickening feeling that revolted him. He twisted hard as he'd been taught and stepped back, bringing his blade with him.

The orc grunted in pain. Instead of falling back, as Tovak had expected, his opponent came forward and attacked, slashing at Tovak's head. Tovak ducked beneath it and swung his blade straight up as he stepped away. The edge of his blade glanced along the orc's bracer at an angle, sliding down, and sliced into an exposed wrist. Again, there was a jolt of that sickening feeling.

He drew back, parried a weak backslash from the orc. Too late, he realized his mistake. It had been a feint. The orc twisted, slashing with his off-hand, hard. Tovak leaped back, but the blade raked along the edge of his arm, slicing open the flesh.

The wound flared with pain, as if molten steel had been poured onto his flesh. In an instant, the searing burn raced across his nerves. He felt like his body had been set on fire. Angered, Tovak stepped into his opponent and slashed hard. The blade sliced across the creature's neck, thoroughly opening up the throat. Tovak felt a spray of hot blood across his face. He could taste and smell the coppery tang.

"Bastard," Tovak snarled as the orc staggered back. Dropping his swords, his opponent reached for his damaged neck, choking on his own blood. The orc's legs seemed to fail him as he slowly sank to his knees. A moment later he toppled over onto his side, lifeblood pouring out onto the forest floor.

Tovak felt a moment of intense satisfaction and triumph roll over him. He had eliminated the evil from this world, done his part to cleanse it. Then the pain in his arm seared, flaring with intensity, as if he'd been poked with a hot brand. He screamed in agony. Dropping his sword, he gripped his injured arm. His vision began to swim from the pain, only Tovak knew it was more than that. It had to be. The wound wasn't that bad. It was a simple slice and did not go that deep. But at the same time, his arm had gone beet red, as if it were burning from the inside out.

With each pounding beat of his heart, it seemed the pain spread further throughout his body, from his arm up through his shoulder and across his chest. The pain was quickly becoming unbearable.

"Thulla," he gasped, "help me."

He felt himself tumbling backward as blinding agony assailed his senses.

Chapter Eleven

Tovak knew only pain.

Time stood still, contained in a single moment that burned as hot as dragon's fire. Hours, days ... the moment stretched out along a razor-thin line, burning white-hot as it drew itself across a seeming eternity of burning.

At the edge of his senses, a spark of cool, blue light appeared, drifting down through burning currents, the pain, the agony. He had a sense that the spark could soothe the hurt, quench the fire, and end the pain.

Embrace Me, a deep voice said, *as I have embraced you. Serve Me, Tovak Stonehammer. The path is yours alone to walk. The choice must be freely made.*

In burning agony, Tovak reached out with his mind, desperate to wrap his hands around it. The spark was his salvation.

The spark neared, coming ever so close, sifting through the flames with a will of its own. He grabbed it. A sense of love and peace such as he'd never known settled over him. It penetrated his being, filled him up, and as it did, the agony lessened, faded at least enough for him to suck in a breath of air. A wave of soothing energy, originating at the center of his core, spread out across his body. Agony became pain. When it reached the wound on his arm, from which the fire spread, there was a sharp jolt, and then the burning eased rapidly, as if freshly forged steel were dipped into a bucket of water. He could almost sense the steam rising from the wound, floating away.

Pain became ache.

Tovak sucked in a gasping breath. His mind seemed to be shrouded in a fog. Fire still danced along his nerves, but it was muted, distant ...a far cry from the all-consuming agony that had wracked his very being.

And so... the pact has been made and the journey begun....

Tovak took another breath, this one deeper. Through a haze, he blinked. His eyelids seemed heavy and his vision was blurry. It took a moment to clear. Tovak looked around to find his comrades still fighting with the orcs. The battle was spread out all around him. How much time had passed? It didn't make sense. It had felt like forever and yet it likely had been mere heartbeats. His thoughts seemed confused, scrambled. What had happened? Had he hit his head? Then he remembered the voice, the love, the peace, and suddenly felt stronger.

To his right, Benthok fought a desperate duel with an orc.

"Finish the others," Benthok shouted as he fought. "Don't let any escape."

The orc landed a glancing blow on the lieutenant's shoulder armor. Benthok grunted and took a step back. The orc came on and their blades met once again. Both moved fast, their swords barely a glinting blur of steel. Benthok's features were a mask of concentration as he blocked every strike. Tovak glanced over at the enemy's leader. The body lay a few feet away.

I should be dead.

The thought echoed in Tovak's brain. He turned and saw the body of the pioneer a few yards away. The pioneer did not appear to be breathing. Karn lay a few feet away, still and unmoving.

A roar from the orc battling the lieutenant drew Tovak's gaze. The creature sent a flurry of attacks crashing into Benthok's defenses. Benthok gave ground one step at a time, but it was clear he was weakening, tiring.

"Thulla," Tovak pleaded through a ragged breath as he rolled onto his side. "Grant me the strength."

Another wave of cool energy filled him, pressing the pain back further still. He sat up, wincing, and reached out to where his sword had fallen. He wrapped his fingers around the grip, at first rather clumsily, then with more confidence. It felt good to hold the weapon. With effort, he sat up. He jammed the point of the sword into the forest floor and, using the weapon as a crutch, pulled himself up and onto his feet. It was an effort to breathe. Every movement brought back flickers of pain, memories of the agony. He pushed through it and straightened.

Tovak struggled to focus his attention on the orc battling Benthok. He must help. The rage at the enemy surged through him once again, pushing the ache back even further. A wave of dizziness washed over him. Tovak staggered a step and almost fell. Shaking his head, he tried to clear the fog that seemed to cling to his every thought. He took a stiff, wooden step towards the fight between the lieutenant and the orc. Benthok's blade was a blur. So too was the orc's. He took two more steps, closing on the creature from behind. He tightened his grip around the sword and lifted the blade. It felt like it weighed ten times its normal weight. Drawing in every ounce of strength, he thrust as hard as his body was able for the orc's back. The effort was too much. Tovak lost his balance and fell to a knee.

The tip of his blade, however, punched through the back of the orc's calf. The orc roared in pain and half turned. Benthok took that moment and stepped forward. His sword jabbed out, stabbing into the creature's belly. The orc's scream ceased as the lieutenant's blade went deep. Benthok gave the sword a savage twist. Mouth working, the orc gagged in utter agony as he sank to his knees, dropping his sword. Benthok kicked the weapon away and pulled his blade out. The orc stiffened and fell over onto his side, twitching.

The dizziness returned as Tovak tried to stand again. He felt something within him, something new. If he closed his eyes, he could see it in his mind. It was a blue light. Mentally, Tovak reached out for it. He didn't know what to make of it, then realized it was the blue spark. He recalled the voice and suddenly felt very small. His faith in Thulla, however, bloomed beyond the love he had always felt for his god.

What is happening to me?

You have been saved, My son.

Tovak felt a moment of astonishment. Then the fog pressed in once again, wrapped itself around his mind, and swallowed him as he fell headlong into unconsciousness.

Tovak blinked his eyes, but there was only blurry fog.

"He's coming around."

The words floated down into Tovak's consciousness, as if he were at the bottom of a deep well. He recognized the voice, but his addled brain wouldn't put a name to it. With effort, he forced his eyes open, waited several heartbeats for the face above him to come into focus, and then realized he was staring at Lieutenant Benthok. The sky above was dark and the moon was up.

"Sir?" Tovak asked.

"How do you feel?"

It took Tovak several moments to comprehend that he'd been asked a question, and several more to wrap his head around what the question meant. He considered it for a moment. He was exhausted. He knew that much, but what about the rest? He drew in a slow, steady breath. He shifted his legs slightly. There was an ache with each movement, but it was dull at best. He moved his arms. They, too, were stiff and sore. And the back of his right arm, where he had been injured, still burned with fire.

"Tired," Tovak finally managed. His voice was a croak. He cleared his throat. "Stiff and sore." He stared into Benthok's eyes as the fog cleared further. "Alive?"

"It looks that way," Benthok said. "I thought we'd lost you too."

"Too, sir?"

"We lost five, and Karn is still unconscious from that gods-forsaken poison."

"Poison?"

"Yes," Benthok said. "The Koin'Duur coat their blades with it. You and Karn should be dead right now. Though Karn likely won't make it."

Tovak closed his eyes and felt a wave of worry for Karn.

"And what of my wound?" he asked.

Benthok got a curious look upon his face, bordering on disbelief.

"I stitched and bandaged it up. I think you will recover."

A fading memory of what had happened when he was struck by the enemy leader's blade floated through his

thoughts. The ocean of fire ... the blue spark ... the voice ....
Had that all really happened?

"It seems Fortuna favors you," Benthok said.

"Thulla," Tovak said.

"Whichever god you choose to thank then," Benthok
said. "Maybe there wasn't much poison left on the blade.
Whatever the reason, you are damn lucky." Benthok fell
silent a moment. "Killing a Koin'Duur by yourself ... and
then having the strength to come to my aid." Benthok shook
his head. "I think you might be gods blessed, Tovak, or stupid. Of which, I am not sure yet."

"What's a Koin'Duur?" Tovak asked.

"You don't know?" Benthok seemed surprised by that.

Tovak shook his head and almost immediately regretted
it. His vision swam once again, and his stomach felt like it
had flipped. He almost upchucked. It took effort to keep
that from happening.

"They are warriors of skill, courage, and daring,"
Benthok said. "They are also the blessed of Avaya, dark and
malevolent things. They are said to do the dark goddess's
bidding and are imbued with occult powers. Thankfully,
their numbers are few and we don't see very many of them."

"It was evil," Tovak said, his voice a mere whisper filled
with the horror of the memory. He swallowed and locked
eyes with his lieutenant. "I could feel it, Avaya's touch, the
darkness."

Benthok did not reply. His face was a mask, but Tovak
thought the lieutenant's gaze looked troubled. There was a
worry deep in his eyes.

"Did we get all of the orcs?" he asked, wanting to change
the subject. He realized that if any had gotten away, then
the enemy would soon know they'd been there. With the
warband out on the plateau, it wouldn't take much for

someone to conclude they were scouting the ridge for a specific reason. If that happened, the whole mission would be in jeopardy.

"We did," Benthok said. "We're cleaning up the area so nobody can tell easily what happened here. With luck the most they'll know is that a patrol disappeared but not where exactly. If anyone comes this way, they'll probably figure out this is where the patrol ended up. But if we're lucky, by the time they find the battle site, we will be up and over the ridge and it will be too late to stop us." Benthok paused, glanced over at something, and then returned his gaze to Tovak. "We're going to be heading back to camp soon."

A sharp pang of guilt slammed into him. He remembered what had set everything in motion ... what had caused the orc leader to stop and engage them. It had been Tovak. He was certain of it. The Koin'Duur had sensed him, just as Tovak had sensed its evil. It was all his fault. Regret and anguish filled his heart.

Thulla, what have I done?

"It really was a Koin'Duur?" Tovak asked.

"Nasty stuff, servants of Avaya," Lieutenant Brund said, appearing from the other side of where Benthok crouched. "They fight with poison and are dangerous, even without the filth they coat their blades with."

"Sir," Tovak started a bit uneasily, looking between Benthok and Brund, "there's something I need to tell you."

"What is it?" Brund asked.

"I think I might have drawn that Koin'Duur to us, sir."

"What?" Brund's look hardened like cold granite. "You mean you gave your position away?"

"No, sir," Tovak said. "I'm sure they didn't see or hear me. That's not what I mean."

"Then what are you talking about?" There was a harsh edge to Brund's question that indicated he did not have time to play games. "Explain yourself."

"I could sense him, sir." He looked to Benthok. "Really, I could feel him coming before I even saw the enemy."

Tovak blew out a frustrated breath as Brund and Benthok exchanged skeptical looks.

"I swear I felt them approaching," Tovak continued before either could speak, "and when the Koin'Duur got close enough … that last moment … he turned and stared straight at where I was hiding. It was as if he knew I was there, just like I knew he had been getting closer to us."

Brund had turned his gaze back to Tovak. He stared for a long moment, then looked to Benthok. "Do you know anything about this?"

"No," Benthok said. "It's the first I've heard of it. Though, he did alert me to the presence of the enemy and I could not see them myself. He and I had pretty much the same view of the forest."

Brund was silent for several moments before he spoke.

"Have you felt such things before now?" Brund asked. "This … this intuition?"

Tovak gave a nod. "At first, I thought I was imagining it, sir." He took a slow, deep breath and let it out. "I had the same feeling in the enemy's camp. I mean, it's impossible, right? Isn't it?"

"Listen, Tovak," Benthok began. He drew in a breath and let it out slowly. "That poison may have you not thinking too clearly."

"I am not imagining things, sir," Tovak insisted. "This is very real."

"I guess it could be something like Rock Sense," Brund said to Benthok, then turned back to Tovak. "Maybe you did imagine it, maybe you didn't. We'll worry about this later, after our mission is over and the warband has access to Keelbooth. But, that said, I want you to promise me and Benthok something."

"Anything, sir."

"If you ever get a feeling like that again, let us both know immediately."

"I will, sir."

"Good," Brund said. "Also, don't discuss this with the others, at least for now."

"Yes, sir," Tovak said.

"Think you can walk?" Brund asked. "After what happened here, we're all headed back to camp."

With effort, Tovak sat up. Benthok helped him to his feet.

"I believe I can, sir," Tovak said, wobbling a moment before becoming steady. A wave of dizziness hit him, and he lurched forward a step, then became steadier.

The lieutenant stood close to hand, ready to help, but Tovak waved him off. If he could, Tovak wanted to do this himself. He breathed deeply for several moments, trying to gather his strength. He still felt dreadfully tired, but he was ready to do whatever was expected of him. At least he wanted to. He looked around and realized that all of the bodies were gone, as were the casualties they had taken. One of Brund's pioneers was busy sweeping branches over an area about ten yards away, but aside from that, the area had been pretty thoroughly cleaned up.

To his trained eyes, it was clear that something had happened, but most of the boot prints and marks had been smoothed or covered over with leaves and deadfall. Scanning the area, he realized that from a distance, at least, it would just look like more forest with no story to tell.

"Where are those we killed?" Tovak asked, searching. He wanted to see the enemy leader's body. There was almost a need to.

"I had them dumped in the river," Brund said. "The current should take them a fair distance downstream and well away from here. With luck they won't be discovered anytime soon. I also did not want to leave them for animals to discover. That might have attracted some notice."

"And our own dead?" Tovak asked. "Are we taking them with us?"

Brund shook his head. "Buried and covered over with leaves. Like this whole area, nobody will know a fight occurred here, unless they're standing on it and are skilled at reading signs. At least we can hope, anyway."

Tovak gave a nod, feeling a wave of sadness that the dead were not receiving the honors they deserved.

"There's no choice," Benthok said. "We're moving out shortly. It's either we bury them here or carry them back to the detachment to be buried at the camp. As such, we don't see any reason to bring them back with us. This is as good a spot as any. As it is, carrying Karn will slow our pace some."

"It might be better to put him out of his misery," Brund said. "That poison is nasty stuff."

"No," Benthok said, firmly. "Tovak recovered, perhaps Karn will too."

"We can only hope." Brund sounded far from convinced.

Tovak looked around, spotted his sword and pack a few feet away. He moved over and picked up his weapon off the ground. His bandaged arm hurt from the effort, but it was tolerable. He could feel the stitches there, tugging against his skin. The area still burned, but it was more distraction than pain, only a fraction of discomfort compared to the fire that had burned through his entire body when he was first cut.

Tovak turned to Benthok and caught him eying the back of his arm. Maybe, Tovak thought, he'd just imagined the whole thing. Maybe all the pulls and feelings were just his imagination trying to deal with everything that had been going on. It couldn't be real. Could it?

He closed his eyes for a long moment and turned his attention within himself. The light was still there. As if a physical thing, it burned a blue fire inside his chest. As he was reaching out to touch it, Brund's voice broke him out of his thoughts.

"Tovak."

"Sir?" Tovak blinked, focusing on the lieutenant.

"I asked if you were ready to head out. Are you?" Brund eyed Tovak. "Are you certain you're okay to make the hike back?"

"Yes, sir," Tovak replied without hesitation. "I will make it."

"Iger's already on his way back with word of what happened here and what we found," Brund said. "We'll go slow and steady. There's no reason to rush. If you need a break, speak up, understand?"

"Yes, sir," Tovak said. "Did you find a path for the detachment?"

"Aye," Brund said as he picked up his pack and put it on. "We did. Also, it seems the enemy army is not yet in the valley. We saw no evidence they were there in any meaningful strength, which is a good thing." He turned and whistled once to catch the attention of the remaining pioneers who were readying themselves. Two had fashioned a stretcher, upon which Karn lay.

The sight of Karn, lying still and unmoving, filled Tovak with sadness. He let go a breath and offered up a silent prayer that his corporal pull through.

"Let's go," Brund ordered.

Tovak took it slow. He felt exhausted and weary. The going was tough but with each passing step, he became more confident and felt better, recovering a measure of himself. When they reached the river and the fallen tree they'd used before, Brund quickly made his way across. Benthok motioned for Tovak to make the crossing next. The lieutenant followed close behind, clearly to make sure that Tovak did not slip. Once across, Karn was brought over next. Then the diminished party continued on.

The moon rose through the trees and hovered high overhead, shining its light through the canopy of leaves. The temperature dropped and the shadows within the forest grew longer. Tovak was already immensely fatigued, tired, and run-down. A few times he stumbled, either from exhaustion or due to low-lying brush he'd not seen. He vowed to himself to make it all the way without help.

Taking turns, the pioneers and even the officers helped to carry Karn. All throughout their journey, the corporal did not wake.

Please help, Thulla, Tovak prayed, glancing at the darkened sky. Keep Karn alive. Do not let him die.

When they stopped to switch litter-bearers, Tovak took several gulps from his waterskin and re-corked it. The water was refreshing. And then, the march resumed. Pushing his fatigue aside, Tovak continued on.

"One step at a time," he said to himself, determined. "Just one step at a time."

It seemed to take an eternity to reach the camp. When they arrived, there were no fires. Most everyone, barring the sentries, was asleep. It had to have been sometime after twelve horns. They were challenged and Benthok answered. Then they were moving through the gap in the camp's wall and roughhewn gate.

"Send for Fenton," Benthok said to one of the sentries as Karn's stretcher was set down. The lieutenant's tone was low. "And tell me, where can we find Captain Dagon?"

Tovak took a deep breath and struggled to stay on his feet. He shrugged off his pack and knelt down beside Karn. The corporal was pale as fresh snow and covered in a sheen of fever sweat.

"Yes, sir," the sentry said, "I'll fetch the healer straight-away. And the captain is over that way, sir. He's asleep."

Brund set out, walking between and around the sleeping warriors. Benthok hesitated a moment and stepped over, close to Tovak. The lieutenant leaned in and whispered, "I think you should tell the cleric everything that happened. He might have better insight on what's going on with you. You can trust Fenton. He's a good one." And then he was gone.

Tovak stared after Benthok. He turned back to Karn. The corporal was lying deathly still and under the moon-light looked extremely pale, almost as if he had already died. The only hint that he yet lived was his chest rising and falling. Karn's breathing was shallow.

"What happened to him?"

Tovak looked up to see the priest, who knelt down opposite of Tovak. Father Fenton carried a bag with him.

"Koin'Duur blade," Tovak said. "Lieutenant Benthok said so."

"Poison then," Fenton said as he looked over his patient, opening one of Karn's eyes and checking the corporal's pulse.

"It cut me too," Tovak added.

Fenton stopped what he was doing and looked up at Tovak for a long moment. The priest's eyes went to Tovak's bandaged arm. He gave a nod and then turned back to the corporal. He set about removing Karn's bandage and examining the corporal's wound. He checked Karn's pulse again, then wrapped the wound back up. "Not much I can do, other than make him comfortable and hope he can fight off the poison. I would not hold out hope, though. He's pretty far gone, and most people do not recover from Koin'Duur wounds."

Tovak felt a terrible wave of sadness crash over him. Here was another friend and comrade laid low. And to make things worse, Tovak felt responsible. The guilt wracked him.

"Now," Fenton said, and nodded towards Tovak's bandaged arm, "let me see this injury of yours."

"The lieutenant stitched it up," Tovak said, his eyes still on the corporal. Tovak felt absolutely wretched.

"I still want to see it."

Tovak held out his arm.

Fenton carefully unwrapped the bandage, which had been fashioned from some coarse cloth. He turned the arm over to see the wound under the moonlight and scowled.

"What game are you playing at?" Fenton asked, looking up and releasing the arm. "It's only bruised, a bad scrape at best. It's not been stitched up."

Tovak looked at his arm, where he'd been sliced. He blinked, thoroughly astonished. There was no cut. He could still feel the residual pain, but the wound had healed and there were no stitches. It was as the priest said, a bad scrape only.

Fenton glanced down at the unwrapped bandages that lay next to Karn. He leaned forward and picked up what looked like a loop of thin thread. Tovak realized it was what Benthok had used to stitch him up.

What was going on with him?

"Who are you?" Fenton asked, looking back up at him. The priest suddenly grabbed Tovak's arm and poked at the wound with a stiff finger. "Did that hurt?" he asked.

"It did," Tovak replied. "Not too bad though."

Fenton gave him a curious expression. His eyes narrowed.

"How does it feel? The area in general, I mean." He prodded the skin again, this time around the wound, eliciting a wince from Tovak.

"It still burns a little—more like a tingle than anything else at this point. The pain was much worse before."

"Curious." The priest looked from Tovak to Karn and back again. "You were struck by the same blade? Is that correct?"

"I was," Tovak said. "The pain was like nothing I've ever experienced. It radiated throughout my entire body. I thought I would go mad from it. And I think I lost consciousness … I mean, I know I did … it's just that … I um …." Tovak suddenly felt unsure.

"Go on." Fenton's gaze had fixed itself upon Tovak.

Tovak took a deep breath and let it out slowly. He felt like he was being studied by the priest, as one might look at a strange insect. Maybe, like Benthok had said, he could tell Fenton everything, but he was still leery to do so. Tovak had long ago learned that trust needed to be earned. And some priests were better than others. Tovak had encountered a few who, after learning he was a Pariah, had wanted nothing to do with him.

"It's hard to explain," Tovak said, and decided to give a little. "After I was wounded, I only felt pain. I saw a blue spark …."

"A blue spark?" Fenton interrupted. "In the air?"

"No. It was in my mind," Tovak said. "When I reached up and grasped it, I felt a cooling wave flow through me." He looked to the cleric and searched his eyes. "The pain seemed to fade somehow. I don't know how or why, but what could only have been moments later ... it can't have been more than a few heartbeats ... I woke."

Fenton leaned back, studying Tovak. "A blue spark, you say? This is very curious, interesting even. What else are you not telling me?"

"I fought the Koin'Duur." Tovak felt a return of the horror and revulsion he'd felt at seeing the enemy's leader. A coldness ran down his back. "I killed him. Before I could see him, I could sense its evil, the darkness. I felt an almost overpowering need to kill it. I am not sure what's going on with me. Do you know what's happening?"

"Interesting." Fenton's gaze was still fixed upon Tovak. "You are Tovak, the Pariah, aren't you? Iger pointed you out to me yesterday."

"I am," Tovak said, wondering how this would change things between them.

"Many of our people have lost their way," Fenton said. "You, I judge, have not. You are a believer."

"I am," Tovak said again.

"You are not the first Pariah to find comfort in faith," Fenton said. "I sense Thulla's hand here."

"You do?" Tovak asked, surprised. Perhaps he wasn't going crazy after all.

"Yes," Fenton said. "I do."

Tovak nodded, feeling a wave of emotion come over him. He looked away, remembering Father Danik, the cleric of Thulla who had so profoundly changed his life, helped him find faith. Danik had also helped Tovak find the will to keep going. Fenton reminded Tovak of him.

"In the holy books there are tales of Thulla granting His warriors abilities, powers to fight evil," Fenton said. "It is possible, when you needed it, because of your faith, He lent you some strength."

Tovak looked up at that. "I am not a holy warrior."

"No?" Fenton asked, cocking his head to the side slightly. He regarded Tovak for a long moment. He then gestured at Tovak's arm. "You are a believer and faithful. By killing that Koin'Duur, you were doing His holy work. That poison should have killed you, and you said the lieutenant stitched you up. Wounds don't heal that quickly. Only a miracle could do such a thing, and those have been in short supply of late."

Tovak did not know what to say. He needed to think and was tired, exhausted even. He could think after some sleep.

Karn suddenly moaned and Tovak turned his gaze back to his corporal. He felt helpless.

"You will look after him?" Tovak asked.

"He will be in good hands," Fenton said. "You have my word on that. I will also pray for his soul."

"Thank you."

Tovak stood, glanced once more at Karn. He was about to turn away and then stopped. There was the slightest pull, tugging at his mind. It was faint, but by the moment was growing stronger. He slowly turned back and stared at Karn for several heartbeats. As if urged, he knelt, placed his hand upon the corporal's chest, and bowed his head. Tovak closed his eyes. He did not know why he did it, only that it seemed the right thing to do.

"Thulla, it is not my place to ask for Your strength. I fear that, somehow, I might be asking for more than is my right. Karn faced evil bravely and knowing full well what it could mean. I only ask that You deem him worthy as he faces death and fights for his life. To die by poison seems a fate unworthy for such a warrior. Please, I beg You, grant him life or, if not, spare him undue suffering."

Tovak felt a surge from inside him. The blue spark grew into a raging fire. Time once again seemed to slow. The internal fire flared bright and he felt a flow of what could only be described as energy. It moved from the fire within, through his arm, then hand, and into Karn.

Tovak opened his eyes and gasped, astonished. The energy or power or whatever—it seemed to have been holy. He felt soothed by it. The night somehow seemed brighter. Then the fire within faded back into a spark.

Shaken, Tovak rose to his feet. Surely he had felt Thulla's power.

"I could not have said it better myself, Tovak," the priest said. "That was a fine prayer. He's in good hands and I am sure Thulla will look after him."

Tovak stared at the priest for a long moment. It was clear Fenton was unaware of what had just happened. He had sensed nothing. Why? What was going on?

"Thank you," Tovak said quietly, feeling like he might just fall to the ground and dive into a deep sleep. Grabbing his pack, he turned and walked off, threading his way through the camp, in search of his squad. He found Dagmar, Bettoth, Torimar, and Gorabor asleep.

Wearily, Tovak set his pack down and, as quietly as he could, removed his bedroll and blanket. All he wanted to do was lie down and pass out. His eyelids felt like they were made of stone, the weight of the world upon them. He laid his bedroll down next to Gorabor.

"Everything good?" Gorabor asked, eyes opening as Tovak lay down.

"Not really," Tovak said quietly so as not to disturb the others. "We were attacked. Karn was injured and several killed."

"Karn?" Gorabor sat up. "The corporal is injured?"

"Yeah," Tovak said, whispering back, "a poison blade. I don't think he's going to make it."

"Bloody gods," Gorabor hissed in horror. "First Jodin and now Karn."

"It's a long story," Tovak said as an intense weariness washed over him. It seemed his eyes were growing heavy by the moment.

"I'm not going anywhere," Gorabor said.

Tovak let out an exhausted breath. He didn't have the energy to tell the story. "In the morning, I will tell you all. In my entire life, I don't think I've ever been this exhausted. I need sleep."

Tovak lay down on his bedroll with his armor on. He closed his eyes and, within moments, was lost to the oblivion.

CHAPTER TWELVE

The camp was illuminated by the moon, which hung low over the horizon. Almost mechanically, Tovak sat with his squad mates and chewed on a dodder. Without any fires in the camp, it was cold, almost frigid. He was so tired, the dodder was tasteless on his tongue. He felt exhausted, run-down, and thoroughly spent. He knew he needed fuel, energy for the coming day's march, so he ate.

"I'm telling you, Dagmar, you don't know what you're missing," Gorabor said. The two were packing up their gear just a few feet away. Kneeling, Gorabor had rolled up his bedroll and tied it tight. He paused to look up at Dagmar.

"Oh, I do," Dagmar said. "Trust me, I do."

"I doubt that," Gorabor said.

"Is he talking about Gulda again?" Torimar had returned from using the latrine. He took a knee and began securing his bedroll to his pack. "Or is it that he wants you to find a proper lass...someone respectable?"

"Aye," Dagmar replied sourly. "He's trying to get me to reconsider my sinful ways. Can you imagine?"

"As if that will ever happen," Bettoth said. "Perhaps it's not a lass you need, Dagmar."

"Oh?" Dagmar asked, looking over.

"Have you considered a gnome?" Bettoth said. "You could have your very own pain in the ass."

"Funny." Dagmar turned back to his pack. He was returning his haversack and mess kit to their place inside. "Witty too. Who knew you were so clever?"

Tovak was too weary to pay much attention to what followed. Judging from the position of the moon, he'd only managed to grab four hours of sleep, which wasn't nearly enough. By Thulla, he was tired. Tovak took another bite of the cold dodder, while Gorabor and Dagmar continued their back and forth on the benefits of having a relationship with the fairer sex.

Freshly roused, the detachment was preparing to once again march, this time right to the ridge. Beneath a cloudless, starry sky, many were conversing in low tones as they packed up their gear or ate and waited for the inevitable order to fall in. There were laughs and coughs on the air.

As he ate, Tovak tried not to think about how tired he was, or the persistent ache and stiffness that seemed to have invaded his entire body. The moment he'd risen, Gorabor had spilled the beans on Karn. They had peppered Tovak with questions. He had reluctantly answered, telling of the fight and the corporal becoming wounded. He left out how he'd sensed the Koin'Duur. He wasn't sure how he felt about it yet or, for that matter, how they would respond.

Torimar and Bettoth had tried to see Karn, but Fenton had turned them away before they had gotten to the corporal. At the time, Tovak hadn't the energy to do more than pack. He did not want to see the corporal, for he felt terribly guilty that he'd survived while Karn was fighting for his life.

After he'd downed his breakfast, Tovak felt a little better. His mind, however, kept going back to the detachment's mission and what they would be doing this day.

Tovak glanced over in the direction where they would be going, back to the ridge where he'd faced and killed a

Koin'Duur. Memories of the fight nagged at him, the bottomless darkness he'd felt when he'd locked eyes with the creature, Karn's still body lying on the ground. He could still feel the slice of the enemy's blade. The pain that followed would be forever seared into his memory, as if it had just happened.

Tovak moved a small stone around with his boot. Once again, against the odds, he had survived. He was either extremely fortunate, or Thulla was looking out for him. He well understood he could have ended up like Karn, and yet his wound had all but healed. In the near dark, he examined his arm and could detect only a slight irritation. It seemed so unreal, so unnatural. What was going on?

A terrible thought occurred to him and he went cold with it, as if he'd been dropped into a cold pool of water. The tiredness was snapped away. Tovak came to his feet.

"Where are you going?" Gorabor asked.

"To see the lieutenant."

"Why?"

Tovak did not answer. He scanned the camp and spotted Benthok. He moved off quickly, weaving his way around Greng's strikers and Dagon's pioneers as he worked his way towards the lieutenant, who was conversing with Brund. Captain Dagon was with them.

Tovak hesitated a heartbeat as he neared. What he wanted to discuss he was uncomfortable speaking about with Dagon. He thought about turning around and waiting for a better time. Only the march was shortly about to begin and then it would be too late.

"So be it," Tovak said to himself and, stealing himself, stepped closer.

The officers stopped talking and turned at his approach.

"Tovak?" Benthok asked. "What do you need?"

"Lieutenant, sir," Tovak said, "may I have a word please? It is important."

The two lieutenants exchanged a glance and then Tovak's lieutenant looked over at Dagon in clear question.

"We're done here," Dagon said stiffly. "As soon as you are finished with him, get the boys organized. I want to start moving as soon as we can."

"Yes, sir," Brund said.

Dagon spared Tovak a hard look and then strode past, leaving them.

"What is it?" Brund asked.

"Sir," Tovak said, and it came out in a rush. "What if that Koin'Duur did sense my presence? And if he could, what if there are others out there? What if the enemy is able to sense my presence while we're on the ridgetop or something like that? Just by being with the detachment, I could jeopardize the entire mission and give us away."

"Are you saying you sense something?" Brund's eyes narrowed. "Like you did with the Koin'Duur?"

"Ah, no, sir," Tovak said with certainty. "I don't feel anything like that. I just thought you should know about the possibility—in case—"

"In the event we had not considered it?" Benthok asked, finishing Tovak's sentence.

"We had, actually," Brund said. "After we returned, Lieutenant Benthok and I discussed it last night and with the captain too." The lieutenant blew out a tired breath. "You're right in thinking it's a valid concern."

"You told the captain?" Tovak looked in the direction Dagon had gone. He suddenly felt betrayed by the two officers. How would the captain of the pioneers react to knowing that Tovak was getting feelings and urges to do things?

Would he be skeptical? Would he think it was another desperate attempt at gaining attention? Tovak thought that likely. He'd already been warned by Dagon that any breach in discipline would not be tolerated.

"We're taking what happened seriously," Benthok said, seeming to understand Tovak's concern. "If there is even a remote chance what you told us is real, we would be negligent in not informing the captain."

"You don't believe me?" Tovak asked, looking between the two officers. In truth, there were moments when he did not believe himself.

"It's not that," Benthok said. "We actually do believe you. But... you must understand, there is still some healthy doubt. What you are describing is something we've not come across before."

"It's all rather strange," Brund said, "unsettling even. I am sure you can understand that."

"Yes, sir," Tovak said, uneasy. "Does the captain believe me as well?"

"What the captain thinks is unimportant," Benthok said. "He listened and that's what matters."

Tovak thought about that. He decided that Dagon would be highly skeptical, at best. Especially since it came from Tovak.

"How far away do you believe you were when you sensed the Koin'Duur?" Brund asked. "How close was he before you felt him?"

Tovak had to think about that for a moment. He had felt something a short while before the dain had appeared. He walked it back in his head, trying to imagine how quickly the enemy patrol had been moving through the forest and how far away they might have been when he sensed the evil.

"I don't know, maybe fifty yards, sixty, but certainly not more than that."

"And how far away do you think the Koin'Duur was before he sensed you?" Brund asked pointedly. "When did he seem to take notice of you?"

"Ah," Tovak said, "he looked right at my position when he was about twenty-five yards out. It all happened so fast, sir. But I know he knew I was there."

"I understand," Brund said. "Benthok estimated it happening at about the same distance. The Koin'Duur turned right where the dain had been." Brund looked over at Benthok. "Do I have that right?"

"You do."

"So, Tovak, what do you make of that?" Brund asked.

Tovak realized the point the lieutenant was trying to make. It hit him a moment later, like a ton of stone falling on him. Perhaps, if he'd not been so thoroughly exhausted, he might have come to the same conclusion and not have had to bother the officers. He suddenly regretted coming to see them.

"That the range for me to sense the enemy and for them to feel me," Tovak said, "assuming I'm not imagining it all, is too close to worry about for what we're doing."

"Exactly," Brund said. "If we were making a surprise assault against an enemy encampment, for example, with what we know, I'd leave you behind in a heartbeat. You might give us away. However, on something like this, there's no need to do so, as the risk is minimal. There will be a strong cordon of scouts out, so we will know if enemy patrols come near. We're thinking it is not likely going to be an issue. At least we hope so."

"The Koin'Duur are few in number," Benthok said. "With any luck, that will be the only one anywhere near these parts."

"So, don't worry," Brund said. "Let us do the worrying. In fact, we might just have need of someone who can sense those foul bastards at some point."

"Yes, sir," Tovak said, not wholly convinced by their argument. It made him feel a little better, but he was still worried. Then what Brund had said registered. "You do?"

"Of course," Brund said. "If we come across any Koin'Duur, or come near enough for you to sense one, we must kill it. They are very dangerous and not only direct but motivate the orcs they lead. It is a religious thing. Cutting one down early can make the difference in a fight. At least, that is what we're told by those who have faced them in the past."

Tovak had not thought about that. It made sense.

"So," Brund continued, "if you see one, or sense such a creature, tell us immediately."

"Yes, sir."

"I am thinking you are lucky, Tovak," Brund said. "I do."

"Lucky how, sir?" Tovak asked, wondering where the lieutenant was going.

"Fortune favors you," Brund said. "Since you joined the warband, you have lived a charmed life. Good things keep happening around you. Perhaps you are even gods blessed."

Tovak wasn't so sure about that either. From his perspective, what he had experienced was more akin to a continual nightmare. Then, another thought occurred to him.

"What if that's why the enemy came the way they did?" Tovak asked. "They might have followed us because of me. What if they could sense my presence in a general sort of way?"

"That is a lot of what-ifs," Brund said.

"You are overthinking things," Benthok said. "It is more likely the enemy picked up our tracks and simply followed us. You'll come to realize with more experience that often-times the simplest answer is the correct one. Until you know more about this sixth sense of yours, it's wise to assume that your presence only gave us away at the last moment, rather than the reason we were pursued in the first place."

"Yes, sir," Tovak said. It sounded reasonable. He still had so many questions and so few answers. It was maddening.

"We're about to form everyone up and head out," Brund said, signaling the conversation was at an end. "Make sure you are ready."

"Sir," Tovak said to Benthok, then hesitated. "How is Corporal Karn doing?"

"He's still alive," Benthok said. "Fenton thinks there's hope he may pull through. Then again, with poison, who can tell? It is just too early. He will be sent back to the warband along with a report of our progress. There are healers there who can give him better care, and they need to know that we've run into a Koin'Duur. If I hear anything, I will let you know."

"Thank you, sir," Tovak said.

"Don't worry about Karn right now," Benthok said. "We have a job to do and that must be our sole focus. Now, get back to your squad."

"Yes, sir," Tovak said, turning away.

"Oh, Tovak?" Brund said.

Tovak turned back.

"Sir?"

"You were right in coming to us with your concerns," Brund said. "Keep doing it."

Tovak gave a tired nod and left them. He threaded his way back to his squad.

"Form up outside the camp, by company, in two ranks," Sergeant Thegdol called. "Time to get moving, boys."

The corporals immediately took up the call. Tovak returned his haversack to his pack and then cinched it closed. With a groan of tortured muscles, he slung the pack over his shoulders. Around him, his squad mates were doing the same.

"You bunch," Thegdol called to them as he was walking by. He pointed outside the camp wall. "Fall in over there with the rest of the skirmishers on the left. With Karn down, you will report to me and the lieutenant directly. Got that?"

"Yes, sir," they chorused.

"Right then," Thegdol said. "Don't keep the officers waiting. Hop to it. That includes you too, Dagmar. By the gods, don't let me catch you dragging ass."

"You'd never catch me, Sergeant," Dagmar said.

Thegdol gave an amused grunt and continued on.

Tovak and the rest of his squad made their way through the gate of the camp and fell in together. Within a short time, the entire detachment had formed up and was dressing themselves upon one another. Their ranks rapidly became well-ordered. A quick roll call was taken by the corporals and the sergeants.

"Atten-shun," Lieutenant Brund commanded as he strode to the front. The detachment, with the pioneers on the right, the Fifth in the center, and the skirmishers on the left, snapped to attention and turned their eyes to him. Both captains joined the lieutenant. Benthok had formed up with the skirmishers.

Dagon stepped forward.

"By now, you've all heard what happened yesterday with the scouting effort of the ridge," Dagon said without any preamble. "Thus far, we believe the enemy is not yet aware of our presence up here in the hills. They will soon learn a patrol is missing, but we will be long gone by the time that happens." Dagon paused to suck in a breath. "You all know our mission. Our goal is to get up and over the ridge and into the Keelbooth Valley. We will scale the ridge today. The other side is more exposed, and since the enemy is already active in the valley, we cannot risk detection. Once on top of the ridge, we will remain concealed in the trees and wait for nightfall. Then, we will descend the other side and make our way down and into the valley. From there, we will move to block any enemy reinforcement of their defensive wall guarding the canyon and, if possible, make an assault against the enemy's defensive position from behind. I know I can count on each one of you to do your duty. The warband's eyes are upon us."

Dagon turned his gaze to Brund.

"Lieutenant," Dagon said. "Get them moving."

"Alright, then, everyone remember to stay vigilant and call out if you feel something isn't right. We're moving out," Brund said as he paused and eyed the assembled group. Apparently satisfied, he started issuing commands to march. "Detachment, right face. Forward, march."

As they moved by the camp, Tovak spotted four warriors, with two carrying a stretcher back the way they'd come, towards the warband. He knew without a doubt who they bore and said a silent prayer for the corporal's swift recovery. Fenton was not with them. Tovak could see the priest ahead in the column of march.

Within an hour of stepping off, the first of the suns had risen in the east. The light filtering gently through the canopy of leaves overhead made the march easier. The temperature also increased. Tovak's stiffness lessened, along with his aches and pains, as he warmed up. Once again, the skirmishers marched at the end of the column. Tovak was so tired he did not even feel the urge to scout. He needed a good night's sleep, perhaps several, to recover from the events of the last few days. Only he knew that was unlikely.

He focused on the march, placing one foot in front of the other and making sure his feet did not get caught in the undergrowth or an errant root sticking up out of the ground.

The march through the forest to the ridge seemed to take forever. There were many places where the column stopped for some reason and then abruptly started again. At points, wondering what the holdup was, Tovak thought it downright maddening, but at others he was grateful for the break. The crossing of the river proved a choke point. It took some time for the entire detachment to cross over the fallen tree.

As they approached the ridge, he could see it through the trees, seeming to hang over them. Tovak felt no sense of menace, dread, or darkness. Was he imagining things, then? No. Though he had serious questions about what was going on with him, he understood without a doubt what he had experienced had been all too real.

As they neared their destination, Tovak found he became more awake. The exhaustion retreated and he began to feel a keen sense of anticipation and excitement, almost as if there were something waiting for him and him alone, somewhere ahead. With every step, the anticipation grew.

Finally, after what seemed like an eternity, they reached the ridge. Tovak figured they were six hundred yards from where the fight had taken place the day before. As they arrived, he found ropes had been dropped down from above and both the pioneers from the Second and strikers from the Fifth were already climbing.

The slope was steep, but not as bad as what Brund and Taboth had gone up the previous day. Under the direction of officers and sergeants, the tail end of the detachment quickly dispersed into climbing groups and joined existing lines waiting their turn to make their ascent.

Once again, Tovak felt himself waiting. He found it terribly frustrating. He wanted to be up the ropes already. The groups moved forward through the trees until they reached the base of the ridge. Tovak kept looking up, eying the rope and the path he'd be taking. The excitement intensified. The first stretch looked relatively easy, little more than a very steep hill strewn with boulders, a few places of bare rock, some scrub brush, along with a few small pines that grew at odd angles. The second part would be more challenging. Tovak was looking forward to that.

As his turn came, Iger appeared and moved before him. He looked at Thegdol, who was giving the order for each person to begin climbing.

"Mind if I go up next, Sergeant?" Iger asked. "I have to report to the captain."

"Be my guest, Iger," Thegdol said. "Discover anything interesting?"

"Naw," Iger said, in a bored tone. "Just my turn to come back, is all, and give a regular report. You know how it is."

"I do," Thegdol replied. "See you at the top."

Iger took hold of the rope for support and began his ascent with practiced ease. Tovak had to admit the pioneer made it look easy. Tovak stepped forward.

"Just a moment." Thegdol held up a hand to Tovak. "Let Iger get a ways up."

"Yes, Sergeant." Tovak turned to look back at Gorabor. "You ready?"

"I don't like heights none, but with the rope, this should be easy as making dodders," Gorabor said, clapping Tovak's shoulder.

"Tovak," Thegdol said, "you're next. Time to go, son."

Tovak took a deep breath. He grabbed the rope, which was already moving like it was alive from the four people above working their way to the top. He started up. The beginning of the climb was no more than a difficult scramble. He still took his time and worked his way carefully up the slope. Wearing his pack made the job of climbing more challenging. He was concerned that, without a safety harness, there was a serious chance, if he made a mistake, that he could fall. However, Tovak had always loved climbing and was confident in his ability.

Early afternoon sunshine beat down upon him, heating the rocks, almost painfully so. Tovak's muscles soon began to burn with the climb. The rope chafed his hands and he found himself rapidly becoming thirsty. He resisted the impulse to look down and just focused on going upward, climbing. Sweating from the effort, he pulled himself up over a ledge to find Lieutenant Brund standing there, a waterskin raised to his lips. Tovak released the rope and clambered to his feet.

"That's quite a climb," Tovak said.

"It is, isn't it?" Brund said. "I find climbing invigorating, especially on a beautiful day like today."

Tovak looked around and found they stood on a wide ledge he estimated was about three-quarters of the way up to the summit. They were above the tops of the trees, which seemed a long way below them. Tovak was bathed in sweat, and his shoulders and thighs ached. So too did his hands and fingers. As encumbered as they were, he could only imagine what the strikers were feeling wearing all that plate armor.

It had been a difficult climb so far, to be sure, but not impossible. As Tovak looked out, he realized the view made every drop of sweat and every aching muscle more than worth the effort.

They were about a thousand feet above the plateau, perhaps more. He could see for miles under a mostly cloudless sky. He could easily make out the long lines of the warband as it made its way across the rolling grasses and small streams that laced the plateau.

Tovak tore his eyes away from the magnificent view and looked upslope. He spotted Iger above, holding the rope to walk up a slanted chimney of stone. Tovak turned and, looking over the edge, saw the rest of the detachment spread out beneath them, over about two hundred feet of steep incline. Brund looked over the lip of the ledge too.

"We should have everyone up to the top in an hour or so," the lieutenant said. "I think we're making good time."

Tovak did not reply. He spotted Gorabor working his way up. Their eyes met. His friend paused, grinned, and shot him a thumbs-up, then resumed his climb.

"I've been under Captain Dagon's command for almost three years," Brund said, looking over at Tovak. "I know he's not happy you are with us."

"I think that is an understatement, sir," Tovak said.

"He is a hard Dvergr, but one of the fairest, most sensible captains I've ever known." Brund's look was earnest enough. "He's taught me a lot and I owe him."

"Yes, sir," Tovak said, suddenly uncomfortable. Was the lieutenant attempting to excuse Dagon's behavior, justify it? No, that was not likely. Brund did not seem like the type.

"The captain is honorable and takes his Legend even more seriously than most," Brund continued. "Whatever his personal feelings are for you, his priority is his company and, above all else, the warband. I've never seen him behave contrary to that." Brund glanced out at the plateau. "I know his son died under your father's command, a tragedy to be sure. All of Second is aware of it."

"Yes, sir," Tovak said again. He was not sure what else he should say. Though he had been fair to Tovak, he still did not know the lieutenant all that well.

"I've never known him to be vindictive out of spite," Brund said. "I guess what I am trying to say is, you've already changed minds. Keep doing what you are doing, understand? Show him what he does not want to see and is currently blind to."

Tovak nodded slowly, realizing the lieutenant had been specifically waiting for him. "I will, sir."

"That's what I expect." Brund turned towards the steep rock face that rose above them. Iger was almost at the top. "Shall we get a move on?" Brund took hold of the rope again and began pulling himself up, climbing as he went. Tovak waited a bit for the lieutenant to climb some. Then he took hold of the rope and followed after.

Another half hour saw Tovak reach the top of the ridge. The last bit had been the most challenging and had taken some time. Tovak had enjoyed every moment of it.

The crest of the ridge was for the most part wide, almost completely flat, and heavily forested.

Benthok was waiting on the top, standing between two ropes. Brund had moved off into the trees.

"Get into the cover of the trees and out of sight," Benthok ordered. "Take a break. We're gonna be here until nightfall."

Tovak gave a weary nod and took several steps forward as he pulled out his waterskin. He was terribly thirsty. Most who had made it up were farther along and into the trees. They had spread out under the shade.

At the first tree, he took a drink and turned back, marveling at the beauty on display before him. The whole of the Grimbar Plateau spread out in a wide swath of rolling grassland. The view was even more spectacular than the one from the ledge below. He could not have prepared himself for the sight that filled his eyes, and in that moment, he'd never felt closer to his god. His heart swelled at the beauty on display.

The whisper of a cool mountain breeze sifted through pines that covered the top of the ridge. It rustled the branches and cooled him off. The peal of a small bird of prey drifted up from somewhere to his right. With the view and the sunlight warming his face, Tovak suddenly felt at peace. The morning prayer floated to his lips, but he shaped it to more appropriately fit the moment.

"Thank You, Father, for the gift of this day. Blessed am I for the privilege it is to partake of this sight. The beauty of Your creation knows no bounds. I am and ever will be Your humble servant, till that solemn day when I return to Your breast and stand in the glory of Your magnificence."

To his left, at least twenty or more miles away, the mountains were a jagged wall of snowy and formidable peaks. They formed an impenetrable range of unforgiving snow-covered granite that traveled more than a thousand miles to the north and south.

Tovak turned his gaze south to where the Baelix Guard had foraged in the hills and lower ridges. So much had happened there and in so short a time too. It seemed almost impossible to conceive how much his life had changed.

He shifted his gaze back to the warband, which was a dark streak, stretching out over at least ten to twenty miles of grassland. He wondered what it might be like to move along in such a large column. What did it sound like? He could see the choking dust kicked up on the air, as well as the trail of trampled grass that seemed to stretch for miles. How hard was it to march for several hours and then go about the backbreaking work of setting up the main encampment, only to break the camp down the following day and do it all over again? Tovak had thought the constant stop-and-go this day had been frustrating. How much more so would it be for those in the main body, following after thousands who had gone before you? How monotonous?

Looking around at the magnificent view, his appreciation for being part of a skirmisher company went up several notches, and he knew with certainty that he never wanted to be part of the heavy infantry. The life of a skirmisher appealed to him and he felt a sense of contentment. His place was with the Baelix Guard.

The scrape of boots on rock stole Tovak from his reverie. He looked over to see Gorabor moving by. His friend gave him a tired, but enthusiastic wave. Bane, from Corporal Logath's squad, reached the top on another rope, which was tied to a stout tree to Tovak's immediate right. Tovak felt a dampening of his spirit at the sight of Bane, for he was an enemy and an ally, or really a disciple of Logath. Following the direction of a sergeant from the Fifth that Tovak did not know, Bane moved to the tree line. As he neared, Tovak held out his waterskin. He did not know why he did it. The offer just felt like the right thing to do.

"Thirsty?" Tovak asked.

Bane hesitated for just a moment, a strange, almost surprised expression crossing his face. Then he accepted the skin. The skirmisher took a long pull and handed it back.

"Thanks." Bane eyed Tovak for a long moment, almost as if he were seeing him for the first time.

"Of course," Tovak said, realizing there wasn't even a hint of the animosity Bane had shown Tovak previously. "They've ordered a break," Tovak said and pointed to the shade a few feet away where Bettoth, Torimar, Gorabor, and Dagmar sat. "Take a load off with us?"

"I think I will."

They moved over into the shade with some large rocks sticking out of the scraggly grass that grew under the trees. The detachment had spread out over a wide area. Most were lying in the shade or leaning against boulders.

Tovak and Bane sat down near Gorabor, who had selected a boulder a few feet away. Tovak's friend was laughing at something Dagmar had said. Sitting with them were three pioneers, as well as a few others from First Section. Some joke had been passed about, for most seemed amused. Tovak was suddenly too tired to care what it was. The feeling of sitting and resting felt incredible.

"You alright?" Gorabor asked, looking over. "You've not been too talkative today."

Tovak didn't answer at first. Instead, he stared up at the sky through the leaves and breathed deeply. Finally, he turned to Gorabor.

"I don't think I've ever been as tired as I am now," Tovak said.

"Then get some sleep. I'll wake you when they need us to move again."

Tovak nodded gratefully, closed his eyes, and was out in moments.

CHAPTER THIRTEEN

"Tovak." Gorabor shook him on the shoulder. "Tovak, wake up. You are wanted."

Tovak opened his eyes and blinked, looking around, feeling momentarily disoriented. It was dusk and nearly dark out. The sky was still tinged with some remnants of orange light. He felt stiff, sore, and generally ached all over. Even his fingers hurt, likely from the climb and the rope. Yawning powerfully, he rubbed at his eyes and came away with sand. He wanted nothing more than to lie back down and go to sleep. Instead, he sat up.

"What?" Tovak asked, yawning again. "What did you say? How long was I out?"

"You've slept all afternoon," Gorabor said. "Maybe four hours. Thegdol said to leave you be, so we did."

"I appreciate that," Tovak said, stretching. He'd fallen asleep on his pack. He felt tired but at the same time refreshed, better than he had been when they'd arrived. Around them, skirmishers slept. Others were tending to their gear, sharpening blades, or talking quietly amongst themselves. There was even a quiet dice game going a few feet away between Dagmar and Torimar. Dagmar seemed frustrated, for he was scowling at the dice that had just been tossed.

"Maybe we should use mine," Dagmar said quietly to Torimar.

"Everyone knows your dice are loaded," Torimar said, looking up at his fellow skirmisher as he scooped up Dagmar's coin. "Even they couldn't help your luck today."

"I think we should give it a try," Dagmar said.

"Not today," Torimar chuckled.

Terribly thirsty, and with a sour taste in his mouth, Tovak grabbed his waterskin and drank until it was half empty.

"Why'd you wake me?" Tovak looked over at Gorabor.

"Lieutenant Brund is asking for you," Gorabor said. "It sounds like you might be going out on a scouting run. You are to bring your pack."

Tovak perked up at that and glanced around. He did not see the lieutenant. "Where is he?"

"That way." Gorabor pointed farther down the ridge and through the trees. "Thegdol said to get your butt moving."

"Right," Tovak said and stood. He struggled not to groan from the effort. He had thought he was stiff before, but now that he was moving ... his thighs protested angrily. He stretched his back out and legs, then bent down and picked up his pack. It took some effort, for his muscles felt tortured, but he slung the pack over his shoulders and secured it in place. He shrugged his shoulders around for a better fit.

"Stay safe," Gorabor said.

Tovak gave a nod and started over in the direction his friend had indicated. A short walk through the trees brought him to Brund, who was surrounded by six pioneers, four of whom had bows. The only one Tovak knew was Iger.

"Tovak," Brund said congenially. "Glad you could join us. We're heading out to reconnoiter the enemy's position on the wall. I thought you might like to come along."

"Of course, sir," Tovak replied, feeling suddenly excited. What his body wanted was to stay right where he was on the ridge and go back to sleep. The lure of scouting, however, was something he could not ignore. Considering what Brund had said on the climb up the ridge, he absolutely did not want to let the lieutenant down. "I'd like that very much."

"Good," Brund said, looking around at the small group. "The detachment will start following us down in about an hour and a half. It will likely take two hours to get everyone down and off this ridge. That should give us plenty of time to scout and report back on what we discover. I want to make this very clear: Our job is not to fight, unless we have to. Remember, we're poking around a bit. That's all. Our mission is to gather intelligence on the enemy's strength, positions, and possible places to assault the wall. Are there any questions?"

There were none.

The lieutenant clapped his hands lightly together. "Let's get going then."

Brund started off, leading the way and moving deeper into the trees. Very quickly they came to the far side of the ridge. The sky, though clear, had darkened considerably in the time since Tovak had been awoken, which had not been all that long.

Looking over the edge, Tovak saw that it was a near vertical drop-off. In the dimness, it appeared to be a cliff face of sheer rock that dropped straight down, several hundred feet.

Tovak realized he was looking on the Keelbooth Valley. It seemed a vast place. In the dusky gloom, he could barely see the far side, more than ten to fifteen miles away. Keelbooth seemed to be flanked all around by steep ridges, like the one they were now on.

The valley was filled with trees. On his right, the end of the valley seemed to terminate with the snow-capped mountains.

Brund led them along the ridgeline in the direction of the plateau. Tovak followed along with the pioneers. They traversed the ridge for about half a mile, when Brund held up his hand and motioned for them to join him as he knelt by the edge. They grouped up around him and took a knee. A cool breeze blew, whispered through the trees. Tovak noticed a coil of rope at the lieutenant's feet. One end had been tied to a thick tree just a few feet away.

"There's the canyon down there and the wall the warband will be assaulting." Brund pointed away from them, in the direction of the plateau. Tovak looked and saw that another ridge seemed to creep up next to the one they were on, forming a canyon with sheer walls that were too steep to climb without proper gear.

The canyon was wide, at least on this end. He judged it to be over four hundred yards from one side to the other. Ahead in the gloom, perhaps a half mile, he saw the defensive wall, which cut straight across from one ridge to the other. The wall, topped with battlements, was tall, rising several stories above both ridges.

The canyon, like the valley, was filled with trees, though there seemed to be some sort of road that cut down the middle. There were some open areas behind the wall that appeared to have been cleared. In one of the cleared spaces, he could just make out some tents and the edges of several small, roofless buildings made of dark stone. Those were clearly ruins, remnants of the people who had once called this valley home. Tovak supposed the defensive wall was another such remnant.

Around the tents and ruined buildings, the enemy had started a few campfires. These were brilliant spots of light in the growing darkness. Torches along the wall had been lit as well, where dark shapes moved between the pools of light. He could only assume they were enemy sentries. In the failing light, Tovak could barely make out the gate doors, which seemed to be large and barred shut for the night.

He wondered how far the canyon ran beyond the wall to the plateau. Could the enemy see the Grimbar from the top of the wall? Would they be able to see the warband coming? In the darkness, Tovak did not know. He knew that was not his concern, though. It was Karach's, the warchief's head-ache. And Struugar's....

Looking around, it was a wonder to Tovak that the enemy did not have patrols on the ridges themselves. He'd seen no tracks other than those of the detachment. That oversight would soon cost them dearly. Or so he hoped.

Then, something on the edge of his vision caught his eye over the valley. At first, he thought it was a bird, but that could not be right. Silhouetted against the sky to the west, where the suns had set, it did not look quite like any bird he'd ever seen. He could not ever remember birds having tails. He squinted, straining.

"Lieutenant." Tovak pointed, not taking his eyes off the strange creature. "What is that?"

Brund followed Tovak's finger and sucked in a startled breath. The creature was traveling northward and away from them. Its body was black or possibly even a dark blue, though it was hard to tell in the dimming light. He got the sense the creature was much farther away than it looked.

"Thulla's bones," Brund said after a moment. His voice was tinged with a healthy mixture of awe and horror. "It's a wyrm. One of the enemy's, no doubt."

"I don't think so, sir," Iger said. "If I'm not mistaken, that is a full-blooded dragon."

Tovak could not believe his ears. "A dragon?"

"I agree," one of the other pioneers said.

Brund looked more closely. "I've never seen one before, but I believe you are correct." He shook his head. "Amazing, just amazing."

"Is it with the enemy?" Tovak asked.

Brund tore his gaze from the dragon and looked over. He stared at Tovak for a long moment.

"Do you feel anything from it?" Brund asked insistently. "Anything at all? Tell me."

Tovak turned his gaze back to the dragon and studied the creature for a long moment. There was no sense of repugnance, darkness, or anything even remotely resembling a negative feeling. He just felt neutral, beyond the simple awe at seeing such a monster.

"No," Tovak said, turning back and noticing the others were looking at him again. "Then again, it might be too far away for me to get any type of feeling."

"What do you mean by that?" Iger asked. "Feeling what?"

Brund looked at the pioneers gathered around them. "We believe that Tovak is sensitive to evil, or at least the enemy creatures that are favored by their dark gods."

Tovak closed his eyes for a moment. Now everyone would know his secret. In a matter of hours the news would spread throughout the detachment. And when they returned to the main encampment, the entire warband would know. This was a nightmare come to life. When he opened his eyes, he saw Iger turn his gaze slowly from Brund back to him and realization seemed to strike the pioneer. "You sensed the Koin'Duur, before the fight, didn't you?"

There was no accusation in Iger's tone. It was a simple statement of fact.

Tovak hesitated a moment. "Yes. And it could sense me."

"Are you serious?" another pioneer asked. "The Pariah can sense evil. This sounds like magic to me or wishful thinking at best. I am not sure I believe it."

"Believe, for I am very serious," Brund said to the pioneer before Tovak could. "Bellar, this is no joke. We think it is something similar to Rock Sense."

"Rock Sense," Iger said and nodded his head several times, as if it all made sense now. "My brother had Rock Sense. He could just tell where the best veins of ore were by closing his eyes and thinking about it some. Made himself rich, he did, by sinking his own mine into the deep dark before he told anyone."

All of the pioneers' gazes were now focused upon Tovak. Tovak felt a growing sense of personal discomfort.

"You all know now. It's out in the open and it is all true, every word the lieutenant said. I sensed the Koin'Duur before I killed it." Tovak suddenly felt miserable. Not only was he a Pariah, but now they'd see him as having occult powers. How much more of an outcast would he become? Well, it did not matter much now. He'd made his choice by telling the officers, and now he'd have to live with the long-term consequences, whatever they turned out to be.

"Aye," Iger said. "We do."

"So," Tovak said, turning his gaze back to the dragon and wanting to change the subject, "is the dragon with the enemy?"

"Wyrms, yes," Brund said, "dragons, no, at least generally not."

"How can you tell the difference?" Tovak asked.

"Between a wyrm and a dragon?" Brund asked.

202

Tovak gave a nod.

"Dragons have four legs, wyrms have two," Iger said simply. "And wyrms are generally much smaller and less intelligent. That"—Iger pointed—"out there is definitely a dragon. It's not the first I've seen. And I pray to the gods it takes no interest in us or the warband."

They were silent for several heartbeats. Since they had spotted it, the dragon had continued on, in an unerring course northward, flying into the night.

"Is that a rider on top of it?" Bellar asked. "I think I see one."

As impossible as it seemed, Tovak thought he could make out someone on the back of the massive creature.

"You're right," Brund said, sounding deeply unhappy. "There's a dragon rider. That is not good news."

Tovak looked over in question. The lieutenant's gaze was still focused on the dragon.

"Why?" Tovak asked.

"There's only one race we know that rides dragons," Iger answered, "and that is the Vass."

"The Vass?" Tovak had heard of them. They were an ancient enemy of his people. Beyond that, he did not know much more.

"I didn't think any were on this world," Brund said, in more of a whisper to himself than anything else.

"At least we know they're not working with the Horde," Iger said. "The Vass hate them more than they hate us."

"There is that," Brund said, "a bright spot at least."

"If that is a rider, what are the Vass doing here?" Bellar asked. "And at the same time the warband is about to storm this valley. It can't be a coincidence. Can it?"

"I don't know," Brund admitted, sounding troubled. The lieutenant was silent for several heartbeats as he studied the beast. He ran an absent hand through his braided beard, then seemed to reach some inner decision. "Bellar, go inform the captain. Tell him there might have been a rider on the dragon. He'll know what that means. Ask him if he wants us to proceed or hold off on scouting."

"Yes, sir," the pioneer said and dashed off the way they'd just come.

"Well, at least it's headed away from us," Tovak said.

"And if it wasn't, the warband has weapons for such things," one of the pioneers said. "Big bolt throwers."

"Those are for wyrms," Iger said emphatically, "not dragons. Those beasties are a different matter altogether and are much more dangerous. I doubt the dragon killers would be very effective against a full-blooded dragon. Their younger cousins, wyrms, yes... but not against something like that."

"Let's hope it doesn't come back," Brund added, glancing around. "Well, now, we wait for orders."

It turned out the wait wasn't all that long. Red-faced and breathing heavily, Bellar returned.

"The captain says to hold off on the scouting mission," Bellar said between breaths. "The entire detachment is being readied. The captain wants to get everyone down and into the valley as soon as possible. He said to tell you that, sir. They will be here shortly."

"Really?" Brund was clearly surprised. "The detachment was to head down at three horns and not sooner."

"I know, sir," Bellar said. "Once they heard about the rider, both captains seemed pretty insistent and of one mind on the matter. They must have their reasons, sir."

"No doubt," Brund said. "Are we to return or wait here for the detachment to move up?"

"Wait for the detachment, sir," Bellar said.

"Very well," Brund said. "Alright, boys, take a load off. It will take them time to get organized and move up. Might as well get what rest you can before the fun begins."

Tovak slipped out of his pack and set it down on the ground, then sat with his back to a tree. He tried not to let out a sigh of relief but failed. The dragon had gone from view and the sky had turned completely dark. To the left, a partial moon was just climbing over the horizon. He was still tired and felt generally run-down. He decided the only thing to do was catch up on some sleep while they waited, for he suspected it would be a very long night. He closed his eyes and drifted off into oblivion.

A gentle hand shook Tovak out of a deep, dreamless sleep that clung to his thoughts like thick cobwebs.

"They're coming," Brund said. "Time to get up and get ready."

Tovak stretched. It felt like he'd just shut his eyes. He searched the sky for the moon. Based on its movement, not much time had passed, maybe half an hour at most. Brund moved on and shook awake the other pioneers who had taken the opportunity a grab some shuteye.

Through the trees, Tovak could hear the detachment coming as he pulled himself to his feet. From the sounds of it, they were making one heck of a racket. Moments later, the first of Dagon's pioneers emerged from the darkness. There were six of them and they came at a jog, clearly in advance of the others. Each was carrying a large coil of rope that had been slung over a shoulder.

"Right here, boys," Brund said to them and pointed towards the other rope. "Five feet of separation between each line. Find some good trees and drop the ropes over the side and then get down yourselves to make sure there is no problem on the way down, nothing in the way of the ropes."

Without needing to be told twice, they immediately set to work, first locating a tree for each line and then tying the rope securely about it. Tovak watched, fascinated, as the pioneers worked. At the Academy, he had always enjoyed climbing training.

"You will be returning to your squad," Brund said, coming up to him and drawing his attention.

"Yes, sir," Tovak said. It was too bad there wouldn't be a scouting mission.

Several of those with the ropes, having tossed the ends over the ledge, started down the side of the cliff face, rapidly disappearing into the darkness as the rest of the detachment began arriving, with Dagon's pioneers at the front. Tovak stepped back and out of the way as sergeants and corporals moved forward. Dagon and Greng moved by without seeming to notice him. They began directing the climbers into lines. Brund left him to help bring order from the chaos.

Tovak watched for a moment, then hoisted his pack onto his shoulders. He began moving back against the tide coming forward, until he found Gorabor with the rest of the squad.

"Tovak," Gorabor said, sounding both pleased and surprised. "Thought you might be off on some super secret adventure."

"If only," Tovak said. "We were going scouting, then saw a dragon. Things changed after that. I'm still not totally sure why."

Tovak fell into line with them as they waited to move forward to the ropes. The skirmishers were behind Greng's company, and Tovak suspected the wait would be a long one.

"Yeah," Torimar said, "some of the sentries saw it also, and it caused quite the stir."

"Wish I'd seen it," Gorabor said, "a real dragon. I thought they were no more than tall tales told over drinks."

"Surely you've gone and seen the dragon bones at the Thane's palace," Torimar said in surprise. "Everyone I know has seen them."

Tovak had as well. He well remembered the reconstructed skeleton of the dragon. It had been unbelievably huge. The story was that it had tried to take his people's home from them, forcing them out of the mountain.

"Big Beth?" Gorabor asked.

"Yeah. Thane Hoggarth killed her himself," Torimar said. "I think I've gone a dozen times or more to see it. The size of the skeleton never ceases to amaze me. That thing must have been a real monster in her day. Honestly, I don't know how the Thane did it, killed it I mean."

Tovak agreed. Beth had been so large, he could not imagine just one person bringing such a dragon down. The story must have been embellished.

"Well," Gorabor said, "as a child, my parents took me to visit it, but I didn't think much of it at the time. I was rather small."

Bettoth gave an amused grunt at that.

"I pray we never meet a dragon." Torimar looked up into the dark sky, searching. Tovak knew that if the dragon he'd seen earlier was up there, in the darkness, it would be almost impossible to see. The thought of it made him nervous.

"Like you'd know anything about dragons," Dagmar scoffed. "You ever seen a live one?"

"No," Torimar admitted grudgingly, "I've not."

"I didn't think so," Dagmar said.

Tovak glanced at Dagmar. He seemed more surly than normal. In sudden insight, he realized that Dagmar was nervous about what was to come. He looked around at his comrades and, despite the lighthearted conversation, they all seemed tense.

"But my grandpa did," Torimar said. "He talked about it all the time when I was a wee lad. Said they were nasty stuff and I believed him … still do."

"Uh huh," Dagmar said. "He probably made it up, got into the drink and decided to boast some or had bad spirits or something like that, maybe ate the wrong mushrooms, hallucinated it all. Have you thought of that?"

Torimar bristled at that and shot a hard look at his fellow skirmisher. "Dagmar, one day your mouth is gonna buy you more trouble than you'll be able to pay."

"Are you saying dragons don't exist?" Bettoth asked Dagmar. "Because I am pretty sure the sentries think they do."

"He's just doing his best to be disagreeable," Gorabor said. "That gnome bite did nothing to improve his disposition. I think it made it worse."

"I saw it," Tovak said, drawing their attention, "the dragon, and it looked like someone was riding on its back."

"Really?" Gorabor asked.

"A dragon rider," Torimar said in awe. "It's said the Vass ride dragons."

"That's what the lieutenant said too," Tovak said. "I don't know much about them."

"Like dragons," Torimar said, "they're nasty business too."

"Imagine what it would be like," Gorabor said, "soaring like a bird and all. I bet it would be marvelous."

Tovak looked over at his friend. "I thought you didn't like heights."

"I don't," Gorabor said. "Maybe you are right, it's not for me."

"It'd likely be bloody cold," Dagmar said, grumpily, "especially on a night like this one. Bah, we have no business flying like birds." Dagmar shivered as a cool breeze blew through the trees. He rubbed his hands together for warmth. "Gods, what I wouldn't give for a fire." He stomped his feet and raised his voice a tad. "I'm bloody chilled to the bone. Maybe they could hurry things up, get us down below and out of this wind."

"Quit your whining and talking so loud." Thegdol's voice came from the darkness. He was somewhere ahead. A moment later, the sergeant came into view, walking back along the column. He paused next to Dagmar and eyed him for a long moment. "You'll warm up once you start climbing. And if you keep jawing, and the enemy hears, they will give you an even warmer welcome when you get down."

"Yes, Sergeant," Dagmar said and clamped his mouth shut.

The sergeant eyed them all and then moved on.

Thoughts of what they were about to do caused Tovak to look back out onto the valley. His eyes searched the darkness for any sign of the enemy. The canyon and defensive wall were not in sight from his current position in line. It was concealed not only by the trees, but also by those out in front of him, waiting to go down the ropes. In the valley, he'd expected to see at least several campfires signifying a larger enemy camp, certainly not an entire army, but more beyond what he'd seen by the wall. Tovak didn't see anything, no lights, nothing. It was as if the entire valley was empty. Only it couldn't be, could it?

He considered that the trees in the valley might be concealing an isolated camp or two. It seemed odd to him the enemy would take possession of the wall and not have more forces in the valley, for surely they must. What were they guarding? Had they already found Grata'Dagoth? He hoped not, for much was riding on the warband getting to it first, wherever it was….

It took nearly an hour of waiting to reach the spot with the ropes where he'd been with Brund and the pioneers earlier. In the near darkness, as they moved forward, he watched as those ahead were directed to a line and took hold of the rope. They made their way down into the darkness, disappearing from view as if they'd never existed. The partial moon had risen higher in the sky, but it did not provide much light.

"You scruffy boffers are with me," Thegdol said. The sergeant had positioned himself by a line. He beckoned to them as they came forward. Tovak had seen Lieutenant Benthok just go down the same rope, walking his way down the cliff face. "Use this rope here. Dagmar, you are up first. I'll follow just after you've all gone down and pick up the pieces."

"Awww…Sarge," Dagmar said as he stepped up to the rope and took hold, "your concern is touching. It just warms my heart. Really it does."

"If you don't get that gnome-bitten ass of yours down that rope," Thegdol said in a growling tone laced with clear menace, "you'll find my concern for your welfare reach new levels, as in a charge and punishment detail. I'll be sure to come up with something really creative to keep you busy for the next year. Understand me?"

"Understood," Dagmar said with a grin and began lowering himself down the rope. Tovak realized Dagmar's grin was forced. His comrade was feeling anything but amusement. That, Tovak thought, was sobering.

Gorabor stepped up to the rope next, grabbed it, and glanced down into the darkness with what Tovak thought was more than a little trepidation. There were no safety harnesses that the Academy used in training, and it was a near vertical drop. What they were doing was incredibly dangerous. They were a mountain people and were trained as children to climb, but one mistake would still mean death.

"Get moving," Thegdol said, and with that, Gorabor started down, following a few yards behind Dagmar.

Tovak waited for Gorabor to get several yards ahead before taking hold of the rope himself. He sucked in a deep breath of the cool night air and looked down into the darkness below beyond his friend. He wondered, with no little concern, on what the coming hours had in store for him, for all of them. He started down.

CHAPTER FOURTEEN

Mountaineering at night was tricky business and more difficult than Tovak had supposed. Even with the light from a partial moon, which wasn't all that much, he still found it a serious challenge. In some places, the going was steeper than he expected, becoming a complete vertical drop. The face of the rock was in places smooth and slippery with lichen. Tovak moved carefully, slowly, and worked his way steadily down.

The rope gave an unexpected jerk that was quite violent. Tovak's feet slipped against the weather-smoothed rock and with it his hold on the rope gave slightly. Instinctively, he grabbed hold hard, as tight as he could.

Thankfully, the rope was knotted. His grip slid only a couple of inches and stopped at such a knot. Holding on for dear life, with his feet dangling precariously over open space, Tovak looked down. Fear of falling tore at his heart. Reason returned a heartbeat later, and he hastily wrapped both feet around the rope. He shifted his weight from his hands to his feet on the rope.

For a moment he felt like he was swinging free, hanging from one of the thick forest vines. Gazing down again, he saw Gorabor was looking up at him in clear concern. It appeared as if his friend had slipped too, which had caused the rope to jerk in the first place and nearly knocked Tovak to his death. Gorabor had just gotten his feet back on the rock. A moment later, Tovak's friend began to continue working his way down.

Heart hammering in his chest and pulse seeming to thunder in his ears, Tovak remained where he was for a moment, frozen. Looking down beyond Gorabor, he still could not see the ground. The darkness and the trees obscured it. He got the sense that it was still a long way down. Any type of fall would clearly be lethal. There was no doubt in his mind about that. He tried to mentally calculate how much distance he had traversed. It couldn't be much farther, could it?

Taking a calming breath, he let it out slowly through his nose, then swung his feet back onto the rock and once again began walking his way down, eager now more than ever to get to the bottom and plant his feet upon solid ground.

"What I wouldn't give for the safety ropes and harnesses we used in training back at the Academy," Tovak said to himself.

Step by step and hand over hand, Tovak continued to make his way down the rope. Sweat beaded his brow and made his hands slippery. It seemed to take hours before he reached the canopy of leaves, then he climbed down through the branches. The ground finally came into view and Tovak felt an intense wave of relief at its sight. His feet touched solid ground a few heartbeats later. Tovak released the rope and rubbed his hands together, working the hurt from his palms. They felt slightly burned from when he had caught himself. His forearms also hurt. He rubbed at those too.

Tovak looked around. The forest spread out before him, dark and impenetrable. Lieutenant Brund was standing between the rope Tovak had come down and the next one over. As climbers came off the ropes, he was directing them on where to go.

"You are to gather over there," he said in a low hiss to Tovak, "with the rest of the Baelix." The lieutenant pointed. "You'll find Lieutenant Benthok that way."

Tovak started off in the direction indicated. He found Lieutenant Benthok directing the skirmishers into position. They were being arrayed in a line that faced out into the valley. Benthok was organizing them into groups of threes and placing each group a few yards apart.

The line of skirmishers, as far as Tovak could see, covered about sixty yards of forest. There were hardwoods all around, many with thick trunks. The trees appeared old to Tovak, perhaps even ancient. Some of the trunks were twisted and gnarly with the weight of ages. They gave the forest a sinister feel.

"I want you with Gorabor and Dagmar over there, at the end of the line," Benthok said in a low voice to Tovak as he came up to the lieutenant. "Take cover, keep your eyes open, and wait for orders to move out."

"Yes, sir."

With the darkness, he could not see Gorabor or Dagmar from his current position. He began moving along the line indicated and passed by Logath, who was moving between two positions. Logath paid him no mind as he stopped and knelt down next to three skirmishers already in position.He started speaking to them in a low whisper that Tovak could not hear.

Tovak continued on and quickly found Gorabor and Dagmar where Benthok had told him they would be, on the extreme right side of the line. They were about forty yards from where he'd come down the rope.

Gorabor had taken a knee behind a large granite boulder located next to an even thicker tree. The boulder was almost as tall as Tovak. Gorabor was peering around the side of it, scanning the darkness to their front intently. Dagmar kneeled by the tree, doing the same.

Tovak knelt beside Gorabor and realized they were on the edge of what looked like a narrow cart path, just on the other side of the boulder and tree. In fact, now that he'd noticed it, the path seemed to run across the entire front of the line. It clearly traveled in the direction of the canyon and defensive wall. In the opposite direction, the path moved deeper into the valley.

Fresh wagon ruts in the dirt exposed hard-packed soil, along with what looked like paving stones. These mostly had become partially buried. Poking up out of the dirt at odd angles, a few of the stones appeared to have come loose with age. That the path had once been a paved road, Tovak thought, was eye-opening. It meant there had once been a people strong and skilled enough to not only build the wall that protected the valley, but also pave what had once clearly been a major road. Once again, he wondered on the people who had lived in these parts so long ago. Those same people had likely built Grata'Dagoth.

"Sorry about the rope," Gorabor whispered to him. "My feet slipped and I almost fell."

Tovak glanced over at his friend. He was surprised that he was not angry about coming so close to death. "Don't worry about it. One day we will laugh about it over drinks. The important thing is we made it down in one piece."

Gorabor looked like he was about to say more. Tovak forestalled this by placing a hand on his friend's shoulder armor.

"I will talk on it no more tonight. We have more important things to worry on."

Gorabor gave a reluctant nod.

The moon had traveled farther into the sky and by the moment was beginning to illuminate more of the land. To his left, and through the darkness, Tovak could just barely make out Dagon's pioneers, where they had taken up a position and were extending the line along the road. He had to assume Greng's strikers were off to the left of the Second, but he wasn't sure. It wasn't his problem to worry on.

Tovak turned his gaze back to the front and scanned the dark forest ahead on the other side of the path. Nothing moved or seemed to stir. The forest around them was unnaturally quiet. He strained every sense, searching, scanning, listening… nothing.

Dagmar moved over to them.

"So, what do we do now?" Dagmar hissed.

"We wait for orders." Tovak thought it was obvious. Though at the same time, he was beginning to understand Dagmar was feeling the stress and tension of what was to come. Tovak looked over at his comrade, his face lined with worry. This veteran, with all his experience and time with the company, was seeking reassurance from two recruits nearly fresh off the yuggernok. It was an eye-opening insight that worried Tovak.

How many others tonight felt the same way that Dagmar did? Were they just concealing it better? It was something to think on.

Dagmar gave a grunt and returned to his original position. Gorabor shot Tovak a strange look, but then turned his gaze back out to the forest.

Even though he was well secluded behind the boulder, mostly shrouded in the darkness, Tovak felt the tension too.

He really did. It was as if they were being watched. It seemed unnatural to just do nothing. He wanted to do something, anything. But, as he'd just told Dagmar, there was nothing to do but wait for orders. And so, Tovak settled in and waited as patiently as he could.

A half hour passed with no orders.

Tovak tried to mentally reconstruct in his head what he'd seen of this area from above with Brund and the pioneers before it had gone completely dark. If he had his bearings correct, to the left, about three to four hundred yards, the canyon began as the two ridges started to come together. About six hundred yards beyond that was the large wall the enemy held and the camp with the ruins behind that. He could not recall any features around where they were currently positioned, other than forest. Heck, he'd not even seen the path from above. It had been completely concealed by the tree canopy.

Movement to the left drew Tovak's attention. A pioneer was working his way behind the line. He went up to Benthok and knelt at the lieutenant's side. The two put their heads together for a long moment. The lieutenant gave a nod as the pioneer stood and then returned the way he'd come.

Benthok signaled and motioned for Thegdol and Logath to join him. The two sergeants made their way over to the lieutenant and took a knee beside him. Benthok began gesturing towards the front of the line, clearly giving them instruction.

"Here it comes," Dagmar hissed. "We'll be moving out in a short bit."

Tovak had no doubt about that. It was clear something was in the wind.

Going separate ways, the two sergeants left the lieutenant. Logath began moving down the left side of the line, stopping at each grouping of skirmishers, while Thegdol went to the right side. He too stopped at each of the skirmisher positions, said something, and then moved on.

"Alright," Thegdol said as he joined them. "On the lieutenant's signal, we're going to move forward, cross the path, and then advance a hundred yards. At that point, the line will pivot, or really wheel, to the left, so that all three companies are facing the canyon. Once that's done, we will hunker down and wait."

"Wait for what?" Dagmar asked.

"Orders, you fool," Thegdol hissed. "Remember, our job here is to screen and not only keep word from escaping about the assault on the defensive wall, but also stop or delay reinforcements." Thegdol fell silent for a long moment, then let out an explosive breath. "If you must know, while we're busy doing that, the Fifth are going to push forward and try to storm the wall from behind as the warband makes their attack. I expect that bit to happen sometime around dawn."

"As long as we're not the ones doing the storming," Dagmar said. "Assaulting a wall sounds hazardous, Sarge."

Thegdol spared Dagmar a hard look that spoke volumes. For a moment, he looked like he would respond, then he turned his attention to Gorabor and Tovak.

"After the Fifth moves forward, both the pioneers and Baelix will be extending our lines," Thegdol said. "There will be more ground to cover with less. That means you will have to keep your eyes open. Nothing can get through our net, understand?"

Almost as one, they gave a nod.

There was an owl call to the right. It was Benthok. He stood, made an exaggerated movement with his hand, pointing forward, and began advancing across the road. The entire line of skirmishers came to their feet and started moving with him. Thegdol left them, moving behind the line, clearly with the intention of making sure no one, in the darkness, was left behind.

Tovak crossed the road, eyes searching the shadows for threats. So intent was he that he almost tripped on a partially buried paving stone. Pausing, he glanced back at the boulder they had been behind and almost missed a step. The face of the rock was illuminated by the pale moonlight. The stone, though weathered, had been carved into. Gorabor saw it too and hissed out a surprised breath.

The carving was of that of a Dvergr warrior, beard braided neatly and complete with prayer knots. He wore armor that looked nothing like anything Tovak had ever seen. Once again, Tovak found himself wondering on the people who had lived here. They were his people, cousins to be sure. What had happened to them? Where had they gone?

That was a puzzle for another day. He turned back to the job at hand and continued forward. As he crossed the road, with his boots crunching on the dirt and small stones, he itched to draw his sword, but the order had not been given. He saw no movement amongst the trees, nor even a hint that they were under observation, which made him even more edgy. He found it deeply unsettling. One step at a time, they moved slowly, cautiously forward. Then they were off the cart path and back into the forest.

Amongst the trees, there was undergrowth, but it wasn't too bad, as the hardwood canopy made it difficult for much to grow in its shade. The forest floor underfoot was a mix of rotting leaves and thick beds of moss.

With the moonlight filtering through the thick layer of leaves and branches overhead, the forest had a spooky, almost surreal feel to it. Tovak felt like he was being watched, but he knew that was just his imagination. It had to be. The enemy did not know they were here.

There was another owl call, and with it, the line came to an abrupt halt. Then the lieutenant set about pivoting the line around, wheeling it, so that they were facing the canyon. When they came to a stop, Tovak placed himself behind a large tree. Gorabor knelt down beside him. Dagmar took a position on the other side of the tree. They searched the forest with their eyes and listened. No one spoke or, it seemed, dared to breathe for several moments.

With a slight rustling of leaves, Thegdol returned to them. The sergeant took a knee behind the tree.

"Your position is the end of the line," Thegdol told them in a hissing whisper. "There is no one to your right. Keep that in mind and stay alert. Got that?"

"Yes, Sergeant," Tovak said, eyeing the darkened woods to their right. The other two gave a nod.

"When we move forward to the mouth of the canyon, being on the end of the line should not prove much of a problem, as it will be more difficult for someone to flank you, what with the slope of the ridge ahead," Thegdol said. "That said, no one can get by you. If the enemy tries to do so, don't wait for orders. Understand me?"

"Yes, Sergeant," they said quietly.

"Packs off," Thegdol said. "We should be here all night. I will check in on you later."

And with that, the sergeant left them, going back the way he'd come. Tovak shrugged gratefully out of his pack, as did Dagmar and Gorabor. It felt good to have the heavy thing off. He, along with the rest of the skirmishers of the line, settled in to wait.

The night turned out to be one of the longest in Tovak's life. Sitting around in a dark and unexplored forest was stressful enough, especially with the enemy nearby. Waiting for the action to begin just added to the tension, especially when there was nothing to do but sit there, listen, and watch. Every breeze that rustled the branches out in the forest drew their attention, as did any little sound.

Tovak imagined a horde of the enemy coming out of the darkness, rushing them, but none came. Time passed and with each hour, Thegdol stopped by for a brief visit to check in on them. Tovak found the sergeant's presence and calm demeanor comforting.

They were ordered to drink and eat. Though Tovak did not feel like either, he downed a dodder. Afterwards, it seemed to sit heavily in his stomach, refusing to be digested. Eventually, the sky began to lighten, then the first streaks of pink appeared.

The rough peal of an orcish horn shattered the dawn, sounding from the direction of the wall. It startled everyone. Tovak froze. The horn was rapidly joined by another. Both sounded like a desperate call to arms.

He had been sitting down, as had Gorabor and Dagmar. They shared a look as they came to their knees. The fight at the enemy's wall had likely begun or was soon about to. Tovak could only imagine how difficult that would be.

An owl hoot floated out of the trees somewhere ahead. It seemed wrong for an owl to hoot at this time in the morning. Since the lieutenant had used the same call earlier in the night, Tovak was sure a bird had not made it. He searched but saw nothing. He suspected it had been made by a pioneer.

Lieutenant Benthok gave out a matching hoot to get everyone's attention. All eyes turned to the lieutenant as he raised his hand and signaled for them to stay hidden and be ready. The lieutenant also made a show of drawing his sword.

Tovak drew his own sword. Dagmar and Gorabor followed suit. The rest of the skirmishers along the line were doing the same. Then, motion caught his attention through the trees. He squinted and spotted two goblins jogging along the path that was now about a hundred yards away from them.

When the goblins were about twenty-five yards from the line, the twang of multiple bows rang out. A heartbeat later, the goblins crashed to the ground as several arrows hammered them. One of the goblins squealed and began screaming in a high-pitched tone that was almost painful. Sword in hand, a pioneer stepped out from cover and onto the path. He efficiently slit the throat of the screamer before dragging each body out of the way and off the path.

Benthok rose to his feet, whistled, and motioned in an exaggerated manner with his sword, pointing it forward for the line to move. Beyond the lieutenant, Tovak could see Dagon already in motion, leading his pioneers forward, off to the left. Greng's strikers were gone. Before it had become light, they must have moved forward in preparation of storming the wall from behind. Or they might have simply been out of his view.

Tovak, Gorabor, and Dagmar moved with the line, slowly, cautiously through the forest in the direction of the canyon. Tovak heard distant, faint shouts that sounded like cries of alarm, but he could not be certain. With each step, the shouts grew louder.

After about two hundred fifty yards, the steep slope of the other ridge came into view, seeming to tower over them. As they continued forward, through the trees, the ground began to incline steeply upward to their right as they entered the canyon. It became rocky and broken. Tovak knew it would be difficult to traverse.

The foundation of a building appeared to their front. It was small, box-like, with a slight depression. The stone walls of the foundation rose only to knee level and were covered with moss. Tovak climbed over the wall and into what had once been the building itself. He wondered what it had been, a farmhouse, storage? With the forest all around him, there was simply no telling. It was now a ruin, a monument to the past that no one remembered. A few steps later, he climbed out the other side. There was another foundation a few yards away to his left that looked suspiciously like it had belonged to a barn.

There were more shouts ahead, drawing his attention. They were closer now, as was another horn call that sounded desperate. It blew several times. In Tovak's mind, he could well imagine the warband's lead companies, led by Captain Struugar, moving through the canyon, preparing to assault the wall, if they had not already begun to do so. Then, from ahead, in the trees, there was a harsh shout, almost animalistic. Benthok held up his hand. The entire line stopped and then crouched down.

There was another shout close by. It was followed by the distinct ring of steel on steel. Tovak found that shocking and it set his nerves on edge. There was a bloodcurdling scream and then silence.

A heartbeat later, half a dozen orcs wearing black leather armor burst through a stand of trees and brush ahead. When they spotted the line of skirmishers, they came to a halt, suddenly uncertain.

"Shoot them!" Dagon roared. "They cannot escape! Bows...."

The thrum of bowstrings from the pioneers filled the air. An orc dropped, while another was thrown to the ground with an arrow in his side. He roared with pain. The injured orc staggered back to his feet and shouted something in his guttural language, while pointing ahead with his bloodied sword at the line of skirmishers. Shouting war cries, the other orcs charged forward. The leader, badly wounded and with an arrow sticking out of his side, managed two steps before three more arrows hammered into his leather chest armor and knocked him down. He did not rise again.

The surviving four orcs, closer to the path, continued at a run for the skirmisher line. Another orc was hit by an arrow. Though staggered by the missile, he kept moving forward at a run. Then they reached the line, attempting to go through a gap between groupings of the skirmishers. Thegdol and Benthok were moving to intercept them, as were the nearest skirmishers. Tovak, Gorabor, and Dagmar were just too far away to do much other than watch, and Tovak could not risk using his sling and hitting a friendly. Besides, their responsibility was to hold their position and keep any other enemy from slipping by them. So they, like most of the others along the line, simply watched the drama unfold.

Tovak saw Bane reach the enemy first, bodily positioning himself in the path of one of the orcs. The skirmisher swung his sword in a powerful slash towards the orc's midsection. The orc blocked the strike, knocking it aside. However, the creature's momentum carried him full on into Bane. They both went down in a tumble. Then Thegdol was there, as was Benthok, along with two other skirmishers. The melee was violent and ugly. Two orcs went down in rapid succession.

One shoved a skirmisher roughly aside and sprinted forward, breaking through the line. He got five yards before an arrow hammered into his back. The creature went down hard. This was followed almost immediately by an agonized squeal of pain that reminded Tovak of a pig being slaughtered. Then Bane pulled himself to his feet. The skirmisher had lost his sword, but he held a bloodied dagger in his hand, and he was fairly coated with the orc's green blood. All of the enemy were down. It had happened incredibly quickly, almost shockingly so. The fight was over and done.

Then Benthok abruptly looked Tovak's way, only that wasn't right. The lieutenant was looking beyond him. He pointed. Tovak, Gorabor, and Dagmar turned. While they had been focused on the fight, two orcs had gotten behind them and were scrambling into the trees along the steep slope of the ridge. Tovak felt a surge of horror at the lapse. He cursed himself. He should have been watching the area around them, not the fight. To the orcs' front was an old wall that was overgrown with ivy. They were both moving towards it.

"Tovak, Gorabor, Dagmar, get them," Benthok shouted. "Don't let them escape."

Tovak began running. A quick glance behind told him Dagmar and Gorabor were following. Weaving through the trees and dodging boulders, they began climbing the slope as they pursued the enemy. Both orcs reached the wall, glanced back, and then hastily pulled themselves up and over the other side. Dropping down, they were gone from sight.

Tovak increased his pace, pushing for all he was worth. A few heartbeats later, he reached the wall, which was about six feet in height and about twenty to thirty feet long. It was covered with ivy and moss. The stone had once been cemented together and then plastered over. Only remnants of the cement remained and some plaster. There were easy handholds. Sheathing his sword, Tovak began climbing. The stones shifted but held his weight.

He reached the top and glanced over. He felt his heart plummet. Both orcs were gone. It seemed almost as if the forest had swallowed them up. He pulled himself over and dropped down to the ground below, which was strewn with stones that had come down from the wall. A heartbeat later, Gorabor joined him. Scanning the trees to their front, Tovak pulled out his sword.

"Where'd they go?" Gorabor asked, searching the forest as well.

Tovak did not know, but he knew what he had to do. He had to find and kill them, before they could spread word of the warband going for the wall. Tovak wasn't helpless either. He knew he could find them, track them down. He turned his attention down to the ground, studying the area intently. After a moment, he spotted tracks amongst the leaves. He pointed to the right. "They went that way."

He started forward, with Gorabor following. Behind them there was a heavy thud, followed by a grunt.

"Bloody gods," Dagmar hissed.

They looked back to find Dagmar on the ground cradling his ankle, the one he had injured days before.

"Bloody gods," Dagmar groaned. "I have the worst bloody luck."

"Are you alright?" Tovak asked.

"I've gone and bloody twisted it again," Dagmar said, through gritted teeth. He attempted to stand and clearly couldn't. He looked up at them. "What are you looking at me for? Go get the bastards."

That was enough for Tovak. He turned, with Gorabor at his side, and started forward, following the enemy's trail.

CHAPTER FIFTEEN

Tovak moved through the forest with Gorabor a few yards behind him. With every passing moment, it became brighter out, easier to see. The enemy were making no effort to conceal their tracks, and Tovak was moving at a good jog, nearly a full run, as he followed their trail. The previous season's leaves rustled under his feet as he ran.

After they had gone five hundred yards, the two creatures came into view. Both had stopped running and had clearly paused to take a breather. Almost immediately, they spotted Tovak and Gorabor and as one turned and broke into an outright run. It became a full-on race after that. Tovak's legs kept pumping beneath him and pretty soon he was sucking some serious wind. He had to assume the enemy were doing the same. At least he hoped so.

As he chased after them, he soon realized he had left Gorabor behind, somewhere back in the trees. He considered stopping, but to do so would see him lose sight of the enemy, and he couldn't allow them to escape. He decided there was nothing to do but keep going. He hoped Gorabor would be able to follow.

His heart pounded in his chest. His legs burned from the effort. His body was covered in a sheen of sweat, and his breath came in heavy gasps as he pushed himself to the limit … and then beyond.

Tovak was beginning to tire and the distance between him and his quarry grew from twenty yards to thirty. He began to lose sight of them as they ran, the trunks of trees temporarily blocking his view. The distance increased to forty yards, fifty. Then, as he went through a tight stand of young pine trees, he lost sight of them. When he emerged through the pines, the two orcs were nowhere to be seen. A deep fear crept into his heart. Had they gotten away? Had he failed?

Slowing to a walk and desperate to get his wind back, he searched for their trail amongst the scattering of leaves and moss on the forest floor. There was no disturbance or evidence they had even come this way. He could hear nothing, other than the breeze moving through the trees and stirring the leaves overhead.

When he caught up with them, if he did, it would be two against one, and he was rapidly becoming spent. Tovak understood his only hope was that both orcs would be just as exhausted as he was.

He knew they were close by but could not find their tracks anywhere. He retraced his steps but saw nothing other than his own boot prints. As he neared the stand of trees, he recovered the orcs' trail. They had turned to the left there, likely to throw off pursuit. Feeling a thrill of excitement, he pressed forward, following and making his way through the trees as quietly as possible, despite his breath coming in short gasps.

As he moved forward, the forest began to thin around him. He came upon a low wall of dark stone with thick blocks. The wall formed the remains of a foundation. Lichen and moss grew over it. Stepping up to the wall, which was chest high, Tovak looked beyond.

There were dozens of ruined buildings ahead. Tovak took a moment to scan about. It looked as if he had found the remains of an ancient town. He saw no movement, so he stepped around the end of the wall. The other four walls of the building had collapsed, falling inward into a disordered pile of shaped stones. Vegetation had grown up over it all. Tovak paused again and surveyed what he could see. It appeared as if the forest was doing its best to claw back the remnants of civilization in this place. He had the sudden feeling that nothing in the world held permanence, and that made him feel slightly sad.

Moving forward slowly and holding his sword at the ready, he followed the tracks deeper into what was left of the town. The farther he went, the more structures he saw, parceled out around him. Mostly, all that remained were walls, foundations, or collapsed piles of stone that vines and vegetation had taken over.

Stepping along what had once clearly been a street, but was now scattered with large oak trees, Tovak came to a small square, where several streets had converged. There were what appeared to be the remains of a rectangular well in the center of the square. Or perhaps it had been an aqueduct-fed fountain where the residents would come to fetch fresh water. He could no longer tell. He moved up to it and glanced down into the hole or basin, whatever it had been. It went down a few feet, then stopped. He saw no water. It might have intentionally been filled in, or maybe time had done that job, with layers of leaves from uncounted years.

As he quickly followed the tracks, he glanced around the square. What had happened to the people who had lived here? Where had they gone?

He was surrounded by what was left of a large Dvergr town, perhaps even a small city. He was sure of it. The stonework of the buildings was too similar to what his own people built. There was no telling how far the ruins extended out into the forest, but he suspected they were extensive.

Holding his sword at the ready, he continued on, scanning the ground, following the tracks. They led him down a narrow street, and then onto a larger one, straight ahead into the middle of what he decided must have been the town center, a central square of sorts.

It was good-sized, easily two hundred feet across. Here would have been the center of the community, where the government and holy buildings would have been located. If it was anything like his people's towns, farmers from the countryside would have come to this place to sell their produce and goods. Important meetings would have been held here and news read by officials.

Tovak tried to picture what it might have looked like in his head and had difficulty doing it. Too much time had passed, and so very little was left, just the remnants of who these people had been to mark their passing.

In the center of the square were a large pedestal and a fallen tree. The pedestal was of the kind used to mount statues. But of the statue there was no sign.

Tovak continued forward. A few feet into the square, the trail stopped, as if both orcs had vanished into thin air. There was silence all around. Not even the birds chirped. On guard, he glanced around, wondering where the two creatures had gone. The buildings that had hemmed in the square had all been large structures, and there were plenty of places to hide amongst the fallen columns, collapsed walls, and trees that grew up throughout it all. Tovak took a moment to get control over his rasping breath as he scanned carefully about. His heart was still pounding in his chest from the exertion.

He could see nothing that stood out to him, no movement. But he had the sense the enemy were close by. It was a distinct possibility that they were lying in wait, maybe even watching him. He looked down at the tracks again and back the way they went. He decided they had doubled back on their own footprints. It was a clever move and it told him his quarry were not stupid, mindless beasts. They were thinking individuals, capable of higher reasoning. That made them even more dangerous.

After a moment, he started forward, deciding not to play their game. He moved deeper into the square, stepping around a couple of large oaks that grew close together. He continued to carefully scan the area about him as he moved. He stopped at the ruined pedestal. It was taller than he was by a head and at least six feet wide. He realized after a moment that what he had thought was a fallen tree was in reality a massive marble statue that had fallen and then become overgrown with vegetation. The statue had broken into several pieces and, with the overgrowth, was nearly unrecognizable.

For a fleeting moment, as he looked around, Tovak felt very alone. There was no sign of Gorabor, and the only sounds were his own faint footsteps as he moved about, exploring, and the occasional gust of a breeze. But, in truth, he wasn't alone. He'd never been alone. He had his faith and always would.

Blowing out a determined breath, he moved around the statue and continued forward a half-step at a time to the far side of the square. He decided to circle around behind the ruins bordering the square. He would pick up their tracks that way and, if they were planning on an ambush, possibly gain the upper hand on them.

As he moved past a medium structure with multiple columns that had fallen outward and split into large chunks, he hesitated. The columns had partially sunk into the forest floor. He wondered if this might have been a temple at some point in the distant past. A temple to his god, perhaps?

Then he heard a rustling of leaves to the left. Tovak turned just as an orc, who had been hiding behind a stone wall five feet away, emerged and charged him, shouting a guttural war cry as it came on.

Tovak raised his weapon and took two steps back to gain space. The creature's blade crashed down into his sword, forcefully driving him back another step. A roar filled the forest, this one coming at him from behind.

Tovak spun and dodged desperately sideways, narrowly avoiding a slash that swung down at him and slammed into the ground. The second orc's blade kicked up a spray of dirt.

Tovak scrambled backward, moving away from the center of town and down what had once been a narrow street, perhaps even a side alley. Both orcs came after him. Tovak continued to back up, moving off the street and up what seemed to be a small hill. He had to watch where he was going so that he did not bump into a tree or trip over a root.

The two orcs followed. They held long, straight blades at the ready, and their eyes were filled with what he could only describe as cunning and intelligence. They rushed him together, slashing at him. He parried one swing and dodged the other as he continued to back up the hill. One of the orcs snarled something in their own language to the other and lunged at Tovak, the blade coming in fast and low. Tovak blocked. The clang of steel on steel rang out almost painfully on the morning air. He took another step back. The other orc swung his blade high, aiming for

Tovak's head. He blocked that blow as well and moved back another step.

Step by step and thoroughly on the defensive, he blocked, parried, and dodged one blow after another as he continued to give ground. He knew he was in real trouble. There was no doubt about it. He could already feel himself tiring and that was dangerous, for that's when mistakes were made.

He took a quick glance behind him and saw a small wall about a foot high that ran around the crest of the hill in a sort of ring. It was only about a foot high and two feet wide. Increasing his pace, he stepped over it. As one of the orcs went to follow, Tovak lunged forward, striking out. The orc stumbled on the wall as he hastily attempted to back up, almost tripping and falling. The tip of Tovak's blade slipped past the orc's guard and sank into the exposed flesh of his shoulder, punching easily through the creature's leather armor. Lightly wounded, the orc hissed in rage and swatted Tovak's blade away, then made a lunge of his own. Tovak gave ground as he was forced back once again.

Warily, both orcs crossed over the wall and closed on him slowly. One angled out to come at Tovak from the left side. The first orc came straight on and attacked. Tovak again blocked. The second slashed and Tovak dodged by stepping aside. The sound of steel on steel echoed throughout the ruins as they came at him, relentlessly attacking. He decided that both orcs were not skilled fighters, but they had just enough training to keep him off balance and on the defensive. Tovak's hands stung from the repeated impacts. He could feel his fingers beginning to go numb.

The first orc swung hard. Tovak blocked. Out of the corner of his eye, Tovak saw the other orc raising his blade for a killing blow. Tovak dredged up every ounce of strength he had left and shoved the first orc's blade away, but he knew he would not be able to turn in time to fully block the second attack.

Tovak's head snapped up as an unintelligible battle cry filled the air, and with it, a thick body crashed into the second orc, sending them both tumbling to the ground.

"Gorabor," Tovak shouted in elation as his friend and the orc thrashed together and then separated. They both quickly rose to their feet, facing one another.

The first orc that had been facing Tovak took two steps back and glanced about, while keeping an eye on Tovak. It was clear he was wondering if there were any more Dvergr about.

Gorabor charged like a berserker, slashing violently at the orc and driving him back. Then Tovak had no more time, for the orc he faced recovered from the surprise appearance of Gorabor and attacked, pressing him tightly. Tovak managed to block several attacks. He side-stepped another quick slash, dodging, and stepped back, giving ground. Again and again, the orc pressed him. Tovak counter-lunged. The orc parried and drove his blade in towards Tovak's belly. Perhaps he was more skilled than Tovak had originally estimated.

Tovak barely managed to block this time, but he could feel himself seriously tiring. He took a nick on the arm from the orc's blade. It stung. His own blade was becoming heavy in his arms. He knew the orc was stronger and slowly getting the better of him. The creature sent another flurry of slashes at his head. Tovak fell back a step, until he stood on the very crest of the hill, barely able to defend himself.

With a mighty swing, the orc slammed Tovak's weapon aside, knocking it free of his left hand. The blade went flying and landed several feet away. The orc leaned his head back and roared in triumph as he drew his blade back for a killing blow. In desperation, Tovak yanked out his dagger and, rushing forward, shot his left hand up, grabbing the orc's sword wrist. His arm quivered as the orc, clearly surprised by the move, pushed down with incredible power in an attempt to break his grip. Tovak drew in a last burst of strength and drove his dagger into the orc's belly, just beneath the lip of his chest plate.

The orc grunted before screaming out in agony. They stood there frozen for a protracted moment, looking at each other. There was clear recognition in his enemy's eyes that the wound was a bad one. Then the creature roared in rage and pain, baring his tusks. The orc released his sword and wrapped his arms around Tovak's body tightly, as if to squeeze the life out of him. Tovak struggled to break the bear hold the orc had on him and could not. It was frightfully strong and Tovak felt his feet leave the ground as he was lifted into the air and shaken violently.

Still holding the dagger that he had plunged into his opponent's belly, Tovak gave it a savage twist. Hot blood rushed over his hand as the blade ripped open the creature's belly. He pushed it deeper into the orc's stomach and felt it hit the spine. There was a physical pop that was communicated through the hilt of his dagger as bone snapped and the spine was cut. The orc groaned, shivered once, and, still holding him tightly in a bear hug, fell backward to the ground like a toppled tree. When they hit, there was a strange snapping sound, a splintering of wood, and then a crash. The ground opened beneath them both, and they tumbled into a black void.

Tovak woke to near darkness and a sense of chilling cold. His whole body ached. The back of his head felt like it had been flattened, and there was a persistent ringing in his ears.

"I hurt," he mumbled to himself and his voice sounded distant in his own ears. He wondered how long he'd been out. He tried to focus on what lay within his field of vision.

Dark gray motes of floating dust drifted in a weak light that seemed to have no source. He blinked and shifted his head slightly. Even the tiniest effort hurt. He realized he was lying on cold stone. His vision swam. Tovak blinked several times. As his vision cleared, he realized the wall and floor were a uniform gray and covered with a thick layer of dust. He turned his gaze upward and winced in pain as he shifted and discovered where the light was coming from. A wide shaft of daylight shined at a shallow angle through a seven-foot hole more than thirty feet above in the ceiling.

Had he fallen that far?

He blinked again, not quite believing his eyes. Almost impossibly, the orc he'd stabbed was suspended ten to fifteen feet above him. The creature was unmoving and thick gobs of blood dripped down to the floor next to him. It took Tovak a moment to understand what had happened. With that understanding came a terrible dread. The orc was suspended in a thick web, one cast by a spider, and clearly a large one at that.

He looked around the room, which appeared to be circular. It was big, twenty yards from one side to the other. The walls, from the opening high above to the chamber that surrounded him, were covered in thick, gray sheets of webs that could only have been created by the mother of all krata, or, worse yet, maybe even one of giant super-predators, a krow.

He peered into the darkness around him, his head pivoting in all directions, wondering if one of the giant arachnids was lurking in the darkness somewhere. Now that his eyes were adjusting, he could just make out a sort of tunnel that shot off at the back of the chamber. Unlike everything else, it wasn't filled with curtains of web that seemed to stretch away into even deeper darkness. He rolled onto his side and groaned in pain and discomfort from the effort. Everything in his body seemed to hurt. He pulled himself to his knees and reached for his dagger.

"Oh no," he said in a horrified whisper. He had stabbed the orc with the dagger. He looked up and saw the weapon still stuck in the creature's stomach. His sword was nowhere in view either. It was probably still up on the surface. Tovak was weaponless and in a den of death. He hoped that the spider was long gone, and the webs were old.

Tovak sat up, groaning with the effort. His left side was particularly sore. Once he and the orc had hit the web, Tovak must have been thrown free and fallen the rest of the way down. He realized he had landed on his left side. His throat felt dry like a desert. He checked his right hip where he'd tied a skin. It was half full. He unstopped it and drank a few mouthfuls of water. It felt wonderful going down.

He looked around. The floor was smooth stone and so too were the walls. He was in what looked like a rounded chamber with a domed ceiling. It did not appear anything like what he would expect from a spider den. This looked like a room that had been carved from the very bedrock with two hands, hands much like his own.

He turned his gaze up towards the ceiling, where he'd fallen through. He couldn't be certain, but it looked like there had been some sort of wooden door overhead, the sides of which hung at odd angles. Splintered wood lay all about him. It must have been a trapdoor that had rotted through. Around him, he could see what looked to be the remains of a pulley system. A rusted wheel, with a portion of rope still tied around it, lay off to his left. Where the rest had gone, he had no idea. There were also several broken boards scattered about that had clearly been used to help raise and lower things. He knew with a sinking feeling there was no getting out that way. The walls were smooth and rounded, with no handholds. The trapdoor lay at the very top of the dome.

He turned his attention back to the chamber itself. As he peered deeper into the darkness, he saw something that made him deeply unhappy. Within the curtains of webbing was a grisly assortment of heavily webbed, desiccated bodies. Some were large and some smaller. Most were clearly animals, but a couple looked suspiciously like orcs.

Careful to make as little noise as possible, he pulled himself to his feet. The effort was painful, as his left arm hurt terribly. He experimented with moving it. Nothing seemed broken. He took a step closer and saw more bodies, smaller ones that were about the size of children. Gnomes.

There were at least a half-dozen gnomes mixed in with the desiccated animal carcasses. He hoped the bodies were old because the alternative was that the spider was still alive and down here with him.

A surge of sudden panic threatened to overwhelm him. He very much wanted to get out. But how? He stepped up to the wall, inspecting it closely. The webbing that covered the smooth stone was old, very old, and heavily coated with the dust of time. He reached out and grabbed some of the finger-thick strands that snaked their way around the room. It was dry and had no stick to it. He looked up, wondering if he could climb it. If the web could support the spider, which was undoubtedly large, perhaps it could hold his weight. He tried to pull himself up. The web quickly broke away. Disappointed, Tovak decided he would have to find another way out.

"Tovak!" Gorabor's voice echoed down from above, filling the chamber with his friend's voice. The sound filled Tovak's heart with relief. Then he felt a wave of panic. What if the spider was still around?

"Shush," Tovak hissed back up as Gorabor's head appeared over the edge. "I think there is a krata or krow down here."

"Gods," Gorabor hissed back. "Look at all that web. Are you okay?"

"That depends upon how you look at it," Tovak called back. "I'm alive, which is better than the alternative. Unfortunately, there's no way for me to get up there … unless you brought a rope I don't know about."

"Nope, no rope," Gorabor said. "What do you want me to do?"

Tovak blew out a frustrated breath. Gorabor was his one connection to the surface. Without him, Tovak would have to find another way out, and up was clearly not an option. "Go back and get help," he finally said. "Bring rope."

"Are you sure?" Gorabor sounded uncertain, obviously not happy about leaving Tovak alone.

Tovak stared up at his friend for a few moments. "Yes, I'm sure, and I don't see any alternatives," he finally replied. He looked around the chamber. He really wasn't happy about his situation. Then another worry hit him. "Think you can find your way back? We came a long way."

"I believe I can manage," Gorabor said. "I'll be back as fast as I can with help."

Tovak nodded. "Alright…. And, Gorabor…."

"Yes?"

"If I don't see you again … may your Legend never fade."

"What kind of talk is that?" Gorabor scoffed. "I'll be back as soon as I can. You just sit tight, okay?"

Tovak nodded again, and then Gorabor disappeared from sight.

Now, Tovak really felt alone, more isolated than he had felt in his entire life. He let out a long breath and inspected the chamber one square inch at a time with his eyes. As he did so, he noticed in the dimness several bulges sticking out of both sides of the wall to his left, only a few feet from where the pile of corpses began. The bulges were elongated and fully covered in what looked like a sheet of webbing that hung from the ceiling. It ran over them and down to the floor. The bulges' bottoms started at about his waist level and reached to just above his head.

Wondering what the webbing concealed, he moved over and pulled away the thick coating of webs that covered one of the bulges. As he yanked the fibers away, he exposed an ancient torch. Any oil that might have been soaked into the torch head would have long since become unusable. If nothing else, the torch might be used as a cudgel, if it was stout enough. He pried away the last of the webbing.

The base of the torch looked to be made of solid oak. It had been set into the wall. He gripped the shaft to pull it free. As his hand closed around the torch, the end glowed. Tovak pulled his hand back, as if it had been burned. The light went out. Tentatively, he reached out again and poked the torch with a finger. Nothing happened. He then gripped it. The torch glowed with a steady light. It pushed back against the darkness, filling the chamber with bright yellow light that, at first, hurt his eyes.

"Magic," he hissed to himself, absolutely stunned. "It's magic."

Magical artifacts were rare and expensive. This wasn't the first time he'd seen true magic. There had been the like in the great caverns of Garand'Durbaad. But beyond that, only the very wealthy could afford to own such powerful and rare artifacts. His father at the height of his own personal success would not have been able to purchase a magical artifact.

Tovak reached out to the light, which was still encased in a thin layer of webbing. He removed the web and discovered a crystal or glass cylinder the size of his fist underneath. It was from this that the light emanated. He touched it and found it cool, cold even.

The thing glowed more brightly than any torch Tovak had ever seen, but there was neither flame nor heat emanating from it. Not knowing what else to call it, he decided to simply think of it as a torch. It was truly a marvel and, if he escaped this underground pit of death, one he fully intended to bring with him.

The bright light cast the web-wrapped and desiccated corpses a few feet away into sharp highlights and shadows. He could see now that there were dozens of them, piled haphazardly. There was really no way for him to tell how long they had been down here. But one thing he did know: whatever type of spider had consumed them was capable of catching and killing a grown orc, which meant it was very dangerous. He could see no weapon amongst the bodies.

He suddenly cursed himself. He should have thought to have Gorabor toss down his sword or a weapon of some kind. Frustrated with his failure to think ahead, Tovak lifted the torch up into the air, turning around in a circle and surveying the chamber more closely. He moved over to the hole in the wall to his right. Something had clearly dug its way into the chamber. Could spiders do that? The hole was large enough to crawl into, but Tovak wanted to go nowhere near it.

He moved away, surveying the rest of the space. The back of the chamber had a thick wall of webbing covering it. He thought he could see almost through it. There appeared to be some sort of a cavity beyond.

And then he felt it—the urge to discover what was behind the wall of web. The pull was unmistakable, and it was strong, almost demanding. Tovak paled at the thought of going through the web, and yet the pull drew him onward, beckoned to him with an intense growing urgency to climb over the corpses and carcasses, scratch and scrape his way through the webs and into an even deeper and completely unknown darkness.

He closed his eyes as a passage from the Fifth Saga of Uliand Stormhand came to mind.

"At all costs, fear must be ignored, for it has no bearing on courage of the heart and can only serve to prevent us from doing what must be done."

As he voiced the passage, he felt his fears fade, at least a little, and the burning spark within blossom. It seemed to fill him up. With his eyes closed, he reached out and touched the burning spark and was comforted by it. A sense of pure calm and peace descended over him.

Tovak opened his eyes and scanned the wall of webs before him. While he desperately wanted a weapon better than a magical club, he wasn't all that keen on the idea of climbing over the desiccated bodies and digging through the wall of webbing.

Go forth.

The urge slammed into his thoughts, and without thinking about it, he moved forward towards the bodies and animal carcasses. He began climbing over them. He put his hand on the limb of an orc. It felt dry and shriveled under the web.

Reaching the area where the cavity was, he found the webs thicker and harder. They seemed fresher than the rest. Some of it clung to him as he tore it away with his hands. He even used the end of the torch to stab and punch his way through it. The web resisted at first and then gave way with the sound of tearing fabric. He then worked on creating a hole big enough for him to crawl through, which was harder than it sounded.

Once it was done, he could just barely make out the outline of a stone passage beyond. He held the torch out before him and found himself staring down a long hallway of gray stone.

A dozen yards ahead, he saw what looked to be alcoves cut into the walls. The alcoves were stacked two high on either side of the hallway. The bottom ones were only a few inches from the floor, while the upper ones were just above waist height.

He felt a strong draft of cool air coming from the passage that blew by and around him. He glanced behind him at the hole in the ceiling, then around the round, domed room. Tovak turned his gaze back to the hole he had created, suddenly unsure whether to proceed or not. Maybe this would lead him out? Perhaps that was why the urge, the pull, was wanting him to go this way. He really didn't want to stick around and wait for the spider to return. Then again, there might no longer be a spider.

Wait for help? Or go explore and possibly get out?

He felt another strong nudge. That decided it.

Raising the torch, he moved forward, climbing through the hole he had created. Despite the draft, the air in the hallway was dank, full of moisture, and smelled of decay. The floor, ceiling, and walls were all covered with a thin coating of webbing, somewhat different, not as thick as what he'd just cut his way though.

Holding the torch up, he shined the light outward. Not far down the passageway, he picked out the wet glisten of water seeping in from the ceiling above. The passageway angled downward at a steep grade. The water ran along the edge of the floor, disappearing ahead into darkness. What caught his attention, however, was what occupied the alcoves on either side of the hallway.

They were burial shelves. He was in an ancient catacomb system. That much was now clear. The chamber behind him had likely been an access point. He started slowly, almost tentatively walking forward, then stopped and peered into the nearest alcove. He moved onto the next. Each one held Dvergr bones, along with scraps of clothing. These may not have been his direct ancestors, but they were of his race and therefore his people. Here were laid to rest the honored dead.

Tovak wondered how long it had been since one of his kind had come here and visited the dead. The urge tugged at him again, encouraging him to get moving, to stop wasting time.

The urges that had been dragging him into trouble were growing stronger and more difficult to ignore with each passing day. They were becoming a force of will in their own right. He didn't know what to make of them, but he was becoming increasingly worried that one day they would end up getting him killed …and perhaps sooner rather than later. Then again, he was almost fully convinced they were coming directly from his god. And if so, how could that be a bad thing? Surely Thulla had a plan for him.

"From now on, Thulla," Tovak resolved, speaking softly, "wherever You lead me, I will follow."

The spark within him warmed noticeably. It was Thulla. His god was acting through him and, as crazy as it sounded, sending him messages. Tovak was now sure of it. He let out a long, excited breath. The spark continued to grow, warming him against the cold of the underground. Tovak felt his heart swell. He would move forward, as was his god's wish, and face whatever challenges were set before him.

"Thulla, ever am I Your humble servant. I find myself surrounded by darkness. Guide me to the light."

You have already found it, My son... you have already found it.

Tovak froze. He had heard it, the words—only they were in his head. He knew without a doubt he had not imagined them. Thulla had spoken to him. His faith had been rewarded.

Resolved and raising his torch, he strode boldly forward into the unknown. The hallway descended farther into the ground, and as he walked, he passed by hundreds of alcoves. The bones that rested in each were covered in the dust and grime of ages.

He continued down the passage, glancing left and right at the bodies interred along the way. Occasionally, there were smaller spiders living in the alcoves, but Tovak knew them not to be threats. They shied away from the magical light as if it caused them pain.

After a time, he came upon a fork in the catacombs. Tovak shined the torch light in either direction. Both passages looked the same. However, the draft was coming from the right. He was about to turn that way when the urge tugged at him to go left.

"As You wish," he said softly and turned to the left. He walked forward, the sounds of his footfalls echoing around him. There was not much he could do about that other than try to walk softly. The problem was the hobnails on his boots and the stone floor. After two more turns, he encountered something he had not expected. At the edge of his light, the hallway appeared to open up onto a platform of sorts. A carved stone railing waited, along with steps.

A thin layer of webs covered everything, and there were curtains of web caught up in the supports of the railing. Anxious about what might lie beyond, he approached slowly. The air seemed somewhat fresher, although he could feel no breeze whatsoever.

He moved forward and exited the hallway. Tovak found himself on a landing, with a long spiraling stone staircase about six feet across. The steps went up to the right and down to the left and ran around a cylindrical shaft of carved stone about twenty yards across.

His torchlight revealed the walls of the shaft had been carved with hundreds of portraits. Every face was unique and lifelike. Some were larger than others. He saw blacksmiths holding hammers and weavers with looms. There were warriors, sculptors, farmers... the list of occupations was numerous. At the bottom of each was a line of what seemed to be Dvergr script. The letters were familiar, but at the same time not. It was a language he'd never seen before and could not read. Tovak assumed the letters represented the person's name.

"Incredible," he breathed, lifting his torch to get a better view of the portraits. "Truly incredible."

Most of the sculptures depicted people in their golden years, but he found several younger faces scattered throughout, as well as a cute little girl, barely more than a tot, shown clutching a beloved doll in her arms.

Tovak found himself deeply moved. Here was a window into the past, a view of those who had lived and passed onto the ancestral feasting halls. There were hundreds of generations of people before him, portraits covering the walls of the shaft and disappearing around the curves with the steps, as far as his light reached. He'd never seen anything like it.

The urge pulled him up the stairs. Reluctantly, Tovak turned away and made his way up the stairwell. He had a feeling that every Dvergr who had been interred in the catacombs must have had their portrait added to the wall of the shaft. Astounded by the sheer scale of it, he stopped at the next landing, where the stairs ended and led into another corridor with alcoves to either side.

Tovak turned back for one last look at the sculpted and painted portraits. They were so lifelike they seemed to be watching him. After a moment, he turned away and, holding the torch before him, started down the corridor where hundreds of people had been laid to rest. Keelbooth must have once had a massive population, or the people had lived here for a very long time.

His aches and pains were forgotten. He passed the occasional dead spider. Smaller ones about the size of his foot moved about, drawing away from the light.

Then, he reached a wide hallway where the webs grew thicker. The walls were covered with heavier strands, and as he looked around, he discovered the desiccated remains of small forest animals and insects, cocooned and sequestered in small clumps here and there. Tovak immediately felt on guard. It was clear the spiders hunted on the surface. It was a ray of hope that they were topside and not down here in the catacombs with him.

He continued down the hallway, when he came upon a small chamber with three passages shooting off from the other side. The pull led him to the right, where the webs started to get even thicker. They also seemed fresh, for when he brushed against them, they stuck to him. He realized, almost belatedly, there were no more alcoves along the walls. Instead, he discovered the faint outlines of frescoes. These were mostly covered by the increasingly thicker strands of web, but every now and again, he could just make out the figures of Dvergr and scenes of a great city, especially if he held the torch close. Some were warriors, some not, but in each fresco, it seemed as if a story was being told.

The webs continued to grow thicker the farther he went. Tovak moved slower, more cautiously. And yet, he kept pressing forward, drawn along by that insistent pull from his god.

CHAPTER SIXTEEN

The passage opened up into a larger rectangular chamber that was at least twenty yards long and ten wide. Holding up the torch high so he could better see, Tovak stopped at the entrance and looked around. Webs covered almost everything. In addition to that, there were shriveled animal carcasses piled up along the far wall.

There were tracks in the dust on the floor too. These were nearly round and smallish, as if someone had used a crutch. That worried Tovak, for there were hundreds of such prints, clearly large spider tracks.

A passageway led off from either side wall. Tovak's eyes were drawn to the walls of the chamber. Behind the webs, there were floor-to-ceiling frescoes. He entered the room and moved closer to one and examined it, brushing away the dust and some of the old webs so he could see better.

The fresco seemed to depict a battle between Dvergr warriors and what looked like humans. The work was exquisite in detail. There was a heroic cast to it that had Tovak wondering if the artist had ever experienced real fighting. Looking it over for a long moment, he also found himself wondering how long it had been down here. There was no telling. Everything around him had an ancient feel to it.

He moved deeper into the room and peered down the passageways that led off to the right. He had assumed there would be more alcoves with bones. But there weren't. The hallway leading off the chamber was about ten feet long. In the darkness of the room beyond, there was a faint pool of light, just enough for him to see that some sort of large stone structure lay at its center.

He felt a pull forward, a tug, a nudge, call it whatever. Thulla wanted him to forge ahead and, in a strange way, he felt like he was being drawn towards his destiny.

Tovak moved down the hallway. There was a sculpture on the wall to the right, just before the entrance to the room. Tovak paused, studying it in fascination. This one was marble. The carving was of a warrior, stern, with a hard-looking face. He was middle-aged and had a neatly braided beard complete with prayer knots.

He wore plate mail of a design Tovak had not seen before. It did not match the carved statue he had seen in the forest. Like the other sculptures in the catacombs, this one had been painted lifelike. The warrior looked very real to Tovak's eyes, almost as if a slice of time had been captured in its image. The eyes seemed to be staring right at him, piercing his very soul. Under the sculpture's fixed gaze, Tovak thought he detected approval.

There was a pendant around the warrior's neck. It seemed to have a blue aura emanating from it, shining outward. Tovak leaned closer and saw Thulla's emblem...well, an older symbol, one not seen very much these days. Tovak could only ever remember seeing it in the oldest of the temples and holy books, a mountain lion, fierce and baring its teeth in a silent roar. Again, he could not read the writing that had been stenciled under the carving.

"What I would give to know your name, noble warrior," Tovak said quietly. "But it is an honor to meet you nonetheless."

Tovak turned back to the room and, moving up to the entrance, held his torch out. When his light reached the center of the room, he saw that part of the ceiling had caved in, carrying with it a good deal of soil and several large boulders. A small beam of sunlight came through a hole in the ceiling fifteen feet above, and it highlighted the center of a large and now shattered sarcophagus. There was no way for Tovak to reach the hole or, for that matter, climb through it. It was just too small. But at least he knew the surface wasn't that far off.

Part of the ceiling had fallen and cracked off part of the top of the sarcophagus, breaking it open. Tovak moved forward towards the sarcophagus. It was plain. There was nothing remarkable about it other than it being the only thing in the room.

Through its shattered cover stone, he saw there was a skeleton inside. It was clearly a warrior, for in repose, he held a two-handed sword, a volzjain, across his chest. Bony, fleshless fingers interlocked around the hilt. Though the sword was covered in dust, it was clearly a work of supreme art, a masterpiece like none other. Tovak looked upon it in awe, for only a true master could have forged such a sword and he thought it a thing of beauty.

At the base of the sarcophagus, on the near side, was Thulla's crest, complete with a lion and similar to the medallion in the sculpture out in the hallway, only larger. The lion looked more magnificent, fearsome even. Within the crest was the symbol he was more familiar with, a hand with two fingers held up. Tovak glanced at the skeleton and ran a hand through his braided beard. Could this have been a holy warrior of Thulla?

The scriptures spoke of such warriors. Father Danik had told him there had not been one such divinely blessed warrior amongst his people for centuries, perhaps even thousands of years.

That was how far his people had turned from the light of Thulla. The great god had stopped helping them, sending them divine aid. It broke Tovak's heart. Many thought divine warriors nothing more than old tales. And yet, here was strong evidence they had been all too real. Was Thulla honoring him by bringing him here to this place? He suspected Thulla was, and when he looked inside himself, feeling for the truth, Tovak knew it to be so. He took a knee before the tomb and bowed his head respectfully.

Thulla, he prayed, I am humbled by this honor. My faith grows with each passing day. Thank You for blessing me so.

He stood slowly, and then stepped forward, placing his hand upon the cool stone of the sarcophagus. There were no webs covering it, not even small ones. Tovak carefully looked around the room. The webs ended several inches from the base of the sarcophagus. It was as if the spiders that called the catacombs their home had chosen to avoid it ... or had they been driven away, repelled by Thulla's majesty and this warrior's purity of heart?

He eyed the sword several moments, desiring very much to take it, to own such a fine weapon, but could not bring himself to do it. The weapon was not his to claim. The sword had clearly been important and belonged to the holy warrior it had been buried with. Tovak leaned over and looked into the sarcophagus, shining the light inside. The warrior was nothing more than a collection of bones now. He had not been buried with his armor. Whatever clothes he had been dressed in at the time of his interment had long since deteriorated to dust.

Oddly, the warrior's beard was almost completely intact. Though it was covered in a thick layer of dust, it was clearly brown and had been braided and secured with a dozen prayer knots.

Tovak stared at the warrior, trying to remember what Father Danik, his old mentor, had once called them. Warriors such as these had had a name, and each had belonged to the same holy order within Thulla's church. Tovak could not recall the order's name, but what the holy warriors had been called was on the tip of his tongue. He could feel it.

"Tala," Tovak said in a near whisper, as if speaking louder would somehow violate the sanctity of this place. "No, that's not it." He ran a hand through his beard, wracking his brain. "Talapin?" Then it came to him. He snapped his fingers. "Paladin. You were a paladin."

Had this warrior truly been a paladin, invested with Thulla's divine power? Tovak searched his feelings within, reaching out to the spark that now burned in him. It seemed as if his assumption was correct, for it simply felt true. This had been a paladin of Thulla, a true-to-rights holy warrior, who'd had a direct connection to his god. The mere thought of it filled Tovak with not only awe, but sudden hope. His people needed to know of the warrior who lay before him. Here represented the embodiment of faith, and a future, one built on a foundation of belief in Thulla, the Forger of Worlds. Was this the reason he had been brought here? Tovak hoped it was.

He looked around, remembering he was trapped underground. Tovak had to get out to spread the word, and that meant finding an exit. He spared one last look at the warrior and then turned almost regretfully away. Thulla had granted him an incredible honor, one he felt wholly unworthy to have received. He felt spiritually restored and revitalized by the experience, almost as if he had been reborn in his faith.

He walked back down the hallway to the main chamber with the webbed bodies. He stopped and gazed at the other hallway across from him. Was there another paladin there too? He suspected there might be, but there was no pull, no nudge to go forward. Still, he wanted to see what was there.

Tovak was about to go look, when he heard a noise to his right. It was a slight scraping sound. He froze, going abruptly cold. It had come from the back of the chamber, where the webbed bodies had been piled. He held the torch up, shedding its magical light on the pile, and saw nothing, no hint of what had made the sound. He almost jumped when one of the web-wrapped bodies shifted ever so slightly.

Heart hammering like a smith beating metal, and holding the torch before him, he moved forward tentatively to investigate. The body, which was small, shifted again. One step at a time, he drew closer. Then he saw it wasn't a body, but something else moving a webbed and desiccated her-atta. He held the torch closer to get a better look.

"A gnome," Tovak exclaimed softly. The little creature had been hiding behind the carcass.

Tovak took a step back, fearful the gnome would attack him. Instead, the creature drew back from him, holding its hands before its eyes, clearly shielding against the magical torchlight, as if it was painful.

Concern washed over Tovak. He glanced around. Where there was one gnome, he had learned, there were more. And yet, he saw no others, but he knew that meant nothing. They could be nearby. He looked down at the stone flooring and cursed himself. The gnome's small footprints led from the other hallway into this one. Amongst the hundreds of spider prints he had missed it, and that, for a scout and tracker, was an unforgivable breach.

The gnome stood and, though it had been hiding, seemed unafraid.

"No kill," the gnome squeaked in broken Dvergr. "You no kill me. I no kill you. Deal?"

"What?" Tovak asked, shocked the gnome spoke his language. "You speak my tongue? How?"

"Shush." The gnome held a finger to its lips. "You too loud. Big spiders hear. Big spiders come back and eat you. Big spiders kill us both. No want that."

Tovak felt his heart run cold. He glanced nervously around, probing the shadows.

"You lost?" the gnome whispered.

Tovak turned back to the gnome.

The little creature was eying him speculatively. It pointed an accusing finger at him. "You lost?"

"I am right where I am meant to be," Tovak said, and that was the truth. Thulla had led him here.

"Hah. I knew, I knew. You be lost." The gnome wagged the same finger at him and snickered, before growing serious. "We no lost. I show you out. If you help? You help, yes? I show way out."

"You know how to get out?"

"Yes, yes," the gnome said. "You help, I show."

"Help you—how?" Tovak asked and then became concerned. "Wait, what do you mean, we? You are not alone?"

"We." The gnome turned to one of the web-wrapped bodies and pointed. This one was not a gnome. It was big, larger than any orc Tovak had seen, only it clearly was not an orc. In the shifting shadows under his magical light, he had missed it, for several smaller animal carcasses had been piled on it. Tovak took a step closer. Under the webbing, whatever he was looking at appeared to have fur and it was lying on its side. Some of the web around it had been pulled away, as if the gnome had been working to remove it.

Tovak realized what had happened. He looked over at the gnome. It had unblinking black eyes with no pupils and stared back at him without any fear. Tovak now understood he had surprised the gnome when he had arrived in the chamber. The creature had simply hidden amongst the carcasses. He turned back to the large webbed body, then looked back at the gnome.

"You want me to help you carry that out?" Tovak asked in clear disbelief, pointing at the body. "It's dead."

"Greku no dead," the gnome said firmly. "Greku lives. You help. You help me free, yes? I show you way out. Deal?"

Turning back to the body, Tovak felt himself scowl. How could it be alive? Leaning closer, he shined the light over the webbed body, trying to see the creature better. It was hard to see what was under the webbing. While he studied it, the gnome began to pull away the web, almost frantically, and as it did, the creature wrapped up inside seemed to give a shiver. Whatever it was, the gnome was right; it was still alive. Tovak made a snap decision. Even if this turned out to be a race enemy, he could not leave it down here for the spiders to feed upon. That was a fate no one deserved. Besides, Tovak did not like spiders and never had.

"Hold this," Tovak said and held out the torch to the gnome.

The small creature took it and as soon as it did, the light extinguished. They were both plunged into darkness.

"Stupid Dvergr magic," the gnome hissed, with clear indignation. "Never works when you need it."

Tovak took the torch back and it instantly flared to life. Did the magic only work in the hands of his people? The web-wrapped creature gave off a moan, followed by some speech that was muffled. Tovak turned back to it and, one-handed, began pulling the web, ripping it away. It was fresh and sticky. The web clung to him as he worked. He rolled the creature onto its back. There was a muffled sound from its face, which was completely covered in webs. How it could manage to breathe, Tovak had no idea. Carefully, he began removing the web from around the face. He lifted the last layer off and then stood in horror as the creature before him gasped a huge breath of air, seeming to gulp it in.

He was looking on a feline face, like Thulla's lion, but different. The creature had orange-and-black-patterned fur, yellow eyes, a mean-looking disposition, and a vicious set of teeth on display as it breathed deeply.

The creature's eyes were fixed on him.

"Are you going to kill me, while I lie helpless?" the creature asked in Tovak's tongue. The language sounded rough, and heavily accented, but easily understood. "Perhaps I was mistaken. I thought you people had honor, Legend."

"What?" Tovak asked, suddenly put off guard. "Me, kill you?"

"Yes. If you are going to kill me," the creature said, "do it now. Don't waste my time. I hate waiting."

"No," Tovak said. "I don't know what you are, but I have no wish to kill you." He looked over at the gnome and then back on the creature. "He said your name was Greku. Is that correct?"

"Yes." The creature grunted as it made an effort to break free of the webbing. The webs flexed but did not tear. "If you aren't going to kill me then free me. Get me out of these cursed webs."

"How do I know if I do, you won't kill me?"

"Hess and I will be in your debt," Greku said simply. "I would not incur my god's wrath through such a disservice. A debt is a debt until fully paid."

"Hess?" Tovak asked, looking over at the gnome. The little creature gave a nod.

"I Hess the Mighty," Hess said, puffing up his chest and hitting it with a tiny fist.

"Hess the Stupid," Greku said.

"I not one who got bit by spider," Hess snapped back, in an angry tone. "You stupid cat. Want to play with spider, like ball of string, and get bit. Stupid kitty."

"When I get out of here," Greku growled deeply, "you and I, gnome, will have a talk, one that's been long in coming."

"Right," Tovak said and began working at freeing Greku from the restricting web. He worked quickly and within moments had freed one of Greku's arms, which was fur-covered and muscular. He was about to start on the other, when he heard a soft chattering sound that filled him with an almost uncontrollable terror. It echoed up the hallway from behind him, the one through which he had originally come.

He froze, as did the gnome and Greku.

The chattering increased in volume, and then it was joined by another ... and what seemed like another. There were multiple spiders out there. As Tovak turned slowly, he saw ... three of them ... stalking down the passage he had come through. He felt his heart sink as he took them in.

Krata.

Their bodies were only about three feet long, with their eight legs spreading out almost four feet across. They were covered with a thick layer of soft, brown fur streaked with green and red that turned pale on their undersides. Long, black, spiky hairs stuck out of their legs, looking almost like barbs. Under the light of his torch, they seemed to glisten. He could not see their fangs, which were tucked beneath, but he knew they were there, and he knew that any one of them could kill him with a single bite, as the fangs were filled with venom.

Sucking in a breath, Tovak made a decision. He turned back to Greku.

"Lie still," Tovak said quietly. The gnome was gone. It was as if Hess had vanished into thin air. "Pretend you are dead. I will distract them. You are almost free. If I die, when they leave, escape."

Greku gave a nod.

Tovak turned back to the spiders, which had clearly spotted him. What terrified him the most were their eyes. Just above the venom sacks was a row of four obsidian orbs the size of walnuts. Above those were a pair of *buurl*-sized, iridescent black eyes focused squarely upon him, and above those, set a little wider and farther apart atop their rounded heads, were two smaller obsidian orbs that seemed to be staring off into nothing. Their gaze was one without feeling, and that filled him with terror. They did not view him as an enemy, only as food.

"I will not be your food today," Tovak said, standing. "Do you hear me? You will be my food."

Undeterred, one crept forward slowly along the center of the passageway, another was just behind it and to the side, while the third made its way above them both, crawling from the floor to the wall and then along the ceiling. They were almost into the chamber.

These were krata, pack hunters, and they were incredibly dangerous. He glanced at the torch in his hand and knew in an instant that he could not possibly kill all three of them. The torch's shaft was stout, but against these killers it would not be enough. Tovak had no illusions on his chances of survival, but that did not mean he was going to give up. No, he'd fight with every ounce of strength within his body. He would go down fighting.

Despite his resolve, Tovak's heart pounded in his chest with barely controlled terror. All three spiders entered the chamber. Tovak gripped the torch tighter. The light seemed to intensify. The spiders shied back for a heartbeat, as if suddenly afraid. Then, after a hesitation, they continued towards him.

"You are not going to eat me," Tovak said firmly to them. "If anything, I am going to eat you."

The krata in the middle of the passage paused for a moment, seeming to study him. Its forelegs rose slightly into the air, quivering. Its back legs lowered and its body went into a crouch.

It leapt straight at Tovak, flying through air.

Tovak reflexively swung out with the torch as he scrambled backward. The torch hammered into the giant flying arachnid like a club and sent it sideways, crashing into the floor.

It landed on its side and then teetered for a moment, before falling onto its back. Tovak moved towards the wall and the side passageway. He needed a better weapon, and the only one he knew that was handy was the paladin's sword. He hoped the long-dead warrior would not mind if he borrowed it for a short while.

One of the spiders moved to counter him, while the one that attacked scrambled madly to right itself. Tovak kept his eyes on both spiders that were still right side up. The one moving to counter him climbed onto the wall. Seeing an opportunity, Tovak sprinted for the passageway. As he did, the spider overhead lunged for him, jumping and spinning in midair.

He dodged to the left and slid painfully into the wall. His arm and shoulder, which already hurt, cried out in agony with the fresh impact. The spider crashed to the ground next to him. Tovak swung the torch as hard as he could down upon it. There was a clunking sound as the butt of the torch hammered into the carapace. The powerfully delivered blow knocked the spider off its legs and onto the floor. It squealed painfully.

The other spider had not moved from its spot on the wall. It seemed to be watching. Tovak sprinted again for the passageway. Legs clicking on the stone loudly, it gave chase.

In a panic, with the spider close on his heels, Tovak entered the warrior's tomb and threw the torch back at the oncoming spider as he crashed hard into the sarcophagus. The tomb was plunged into darkness, save for the small beam of sunlight shining down from above. He reached out towards the weapon. As he did, he thought he saw the skeletal warrior lifting its bony hands towards him. The spider hissed, almost on him, as Tovak's fingers wrapped around the pommel.

There was a brief shock of icy cold, as if he had connected the world of life with the underworld and the great beyond. The chill coursed up his arm and across his entire body, freezing the life within. Then something countered that. The spark inside him seemed to blossom into a full-fledged fire that roared like a lion, pushing back the terrible and biting cold of death.

Time seemed to slow. A distant bell tolled, deep and ominous. The darkness around him lifted slightly, becoming brighter. Dust motes that had been moving through the beam of light from above froze as if caught in amber. Tovak seemed frozen with them, only he wasn't; he was still moving, bringing the large sword around.

With a snap that was almost audible, time began moving again. Having yanked the volzjain free, he rolled out of the way. The krata leapt towards him and slammed into the sarcophagus. There was a flash of intense light, followed by a snapping and sizzling sound. The spider screamed. It was a terrible sound that tore at the ears.

As Tovak came back to his feet, he saw the spider attempting to crawl back the way it had come, only half of its legs were not working. Smoke rose from its carapace. The stench of burned spider was on the air. Without hesitation, Tovak swung. The blade came down with a gruesome *THUCK*. The heavy weapon easily cleaved its carapace in two, splitting it straight down between its eyes and halfway through its body. He was sprayed with gore as the sword made a crunching sound.

Mortally wounded, the spider screeched. Its legs flailed beneath its body uncontrollably. Tovak pulled the sword back out. The krata flopped around beside the sarcophagus in a slap-dancing patter of legs. He was about to finish it when another spider entered the hallway.

"Come on, you bastard," Tovak said, turning to face it and raising his sword. Tovak hefted the volzjain in his hands. Though the weapon was a heavy one, it felt light, almost as light as his regular sword, and it was perfectly balanced. No weapon had ever felt so good in his hands. He had always preferred the volzjain, and felt more comfortable with it.

The spider came scrambling straight towards Tovak and, without hesitation, leaped at him. Tovak swung the weapon in a flat arc in front of his body. The blade caught the krata in mid-air, cleaving off three of its legs and slashing deeply into its hardened carapace. The strike caused the creature to fly sideways, where it hit the wall.

"Barasoom!" Tovak roared as he moved towards the stunned creature. He raised the sword and drove it point-first down into the center of the krata's head and between the eyes.

The blade passed completely through, the tip making a clanging sound that echoed hollowly in the tomb as it bit into the stone floor. The krata's legs shook, quivering as the creature died. Another chattering sound and clicking of many feet forced Tovak to turn just in time to see the third spider launch itself into the air straight for him.

He dropped down and ducked beneath it. He felt the tips of its legs on his back armor as it flew by. The krata hit the wall and dropped to the floor, its legs a blur as it recovered its balance and spun around. Wrenching his weapon free from the spider he had just killed, Tovak backed up. It lunged for him. Tovak thrust with the sword, meeting it and jamming the blade into its body.

Badly wounded, it gave out an ear-splitting screech and pulled away from him. As the sword came free, it made a sucking sound and pulled the spider's insides out with it. The spider gave off a whining sound. Not willing to give it any time to recover, Tovak followed, raising the blade above his head in a two-handed grip. The spider hissed at him and made to lunge again. He swung down and caught the krata in the middle of its body and stabbed hard, pressing downward with all his effort. The blade passed clean through. He gave the weapon a savage twist.

The krata's legs spasmed and then went limp as it collapsed to the stone floor. It seemed to give a hissing sigh and then expired. Gasping for breath, Tovak pulled the sword free. He looked around. All three spiders were dead. He could not believe he had not just survived, but bested them. He had killed three krata by himself and, as impossible as that seemed, he would live to tell the tale. Only, Tovak thought, no one would ever believe him.

His heart, hammering away in his chest from the exertion of the fight, felt like it was going to leap out or explode. The terror of the moment began to drain away, leaving him tired and spent. Tovak lowered the magnificent weapon to the floor, allowing it to rest point-first on the stone. He noticed that his hands were shaking badly. He looked down at his hands and contemplated them for a long moment. He was fairly coated in gore. He had survived. Tovak blew out a shaky breath …. He had survived.

He suddenly doubled over and vomited, spilling out what little had been in his stomach in a violent gush that splattered onto the floor at his feet. He heaved again … and again … and again.

Finally, when the dry heaves stopped and the terror faded to the point where he could think straight, he stood up and wiped his mouth clean with the back of his arm. His breathing came in desperate gasps. He turned back towards the sarcophagus and dropped to his knees. He bowed his head.

"Thank You, Thulla, for placing this fallen warrior in my path. Thank You for granting me the strength to face these vile creatures and emerge victorious." He turned his attention to the sarcophagus and placed a hand upon the stone. "And thank you, my friend, for allowing me the use of this fine weapon. Without it, I would surely have joined you in death."

Tovak rose to his feet and hefted the volzjain, examining it slowly. It was soiled from the fight. He wiped it clean against the hem of his tunic. There wasn't a spot of rust or a single nick in the blade, not even at the point where it had contacted the stone. It was perfect, beautiful. As he inspected the weapon, he saw small etchings just above the hilt in the form of Thulla's lion. Beneath them were symbols or characters that were similar to what he'd seen in the catacombs. It was both like and unlike his own. He was certain they were script from a long lost Dvergr language.

The blade was, without a doubt, the most magnificent weapon he had ever laid eyes upon, let alone held. It was perfection in the extreme and felt like it had been made just for him. He loathed the thought of parting with it. But the weapon was not his and he did not have a right to claim it. He was unworthy of such a magnificent weapon.

He stepped back around the sarcophagus. He was no grave robber, and the idea of taking something from a noble servant of Thulla was not an act he felt right about, no matter how perfect the weapon was in his hands. As he stepped around to the open side of the sarcophagus again, he froze in his tracks. A chill ran down his spine.

He remembered the shock of cold he had felt when he'd pulled the volzjain free. He blinked several times to make sure he wasn't seeing things. When the view didn't change, all he could say was, "Thulla be praised."

The warrior's skeletal hands had been raised and were held forth as if it had given something away. Had the paladin really handed Tovak the weapon?

"It can't be," Tovak whispered. "It just cannot be."

The weapon is yours, My son, and fairly earned. Wield it with honor and My blessing as others doing My service have done.

Tovak froze. He felt a wave of rapturous joy, not from the fact that the sword was now his, gifted to him, but that Thulla had blessed him greatly. He bowed once more, solemnly, thoroughly overwhelmed. He took in a deep breath and let it out slowly. He saw that there was a scabbard fixed to a harness inside the sarcophagus, where moments before there had not been one. He reached in and pulled it out. The leather felt supple in his hand, fresh. It was of the highest quality and something he would never have been able to afford.

He knew this was a miracle. All of it was. Thulla had seen to it.

He slid the harness over his shoulders and onto his back. It was a perfect fit. Then, carefully, he sheathed the sword in the scabbard. It felt natural against his back, as if he had always been meant to wear it. Glancing down at the paladin, he considered that might not be far from the truth, for surely this day, with Thulla's help, Tovak had truly begun to forge his own destiny.

He looked around, then bent down and picked up the torch where it lay on the stone floor. It immediately lit, filling the room with a brilliant light. Tovak suddenly recalled Greku and Hess. He turned away and made for the hallway. There was a heavy grinding behind him. It shook the floor, and he had to lean a hand against the wall to stay on his feet. Dust cascaded down from the ceiling. He turned back to look.

As impossible as it seemed, the sarcophagus was rebuilding itself. He stood in awe, watching it happen. This was a true miracle, and he felt blessed by witnessing it. The transformation lasted only a span of ten heartbeats.

When it finished, the sarcophagus was whole and looked newly made. Its sides were painted white. The lid was no longer smooth, plain stone. A warrior in stone lay in repose on the lid. He held a likeness of the sword that was now sheathed on Tovak's back. A blue light glowed upon the stone paladin's chest. Tovak stepped closer and saw a medallion there, set deeply into the stone. It was Thulla's lion, and it shone forth with its own light.

He looked up as the shaft of sunlight overhead disappeared. The fallen rocks, the boulders, and the opening to the surface were gone. The room looked new, as if freshly constructed. Even the spiders were gone. Their bodies had vanished. The webbing on the walls had disappeared too. In its place were brilliantly colored frescoes, telling the story of a holy warrior of Thulla.

Holding the torch high, Tovak walked around the tomb, studying the frescos, committing the story to memory. It started with the warrior's birth, in what seemed like abject poverty, his life of crime and debasement, then transitioned to being saved, discovering faith, and being given a second chance by a noble lord. It continued on and covered the growth of the warrior's faith, devotion to service, ultimate blessing by Thulla, and the elevation to becoming a paladin.

Tovak found himself moved by the warrior's story as he followed it from one wall to the next. Several of the great deeds the paladin had performed were detailed as well.

It all ended on the far wall to his right, in a tomb. Tovak went cold, for he saw what he thought might be himself rendered in the fresco. He blinked and leaned closer. A chill ran down his spine. The fresco showed the paladin handing the sword to another figure. There was no mistaking what that figure was, but Tovak still could not understand it. It was him! The last image was of the paladin handing Tovak the sword to confront darkness and evil.

There the story stopped. In a way, Tovak realized the paladin was passing the torch of faith to him, for that was what the message seemed to convey. The sword now strapped to his back represented faith and belief in Thulla. Tovak would wield it with pride and honor. He would care for it, as had the warrior before him. With all his strength, he would strive to live up to the standard that had been set for him.

He cleared his throat. "Thank You for this, Thulla," Tovak breathed and then turned away.

Right behind him was Hess. The gnome was completely still, and his gaze was fixated upon Tovak. Had he seen everything? Tovak suspected he had. He decided it did not matter, not one bit. Tovak was not meant to hide what had just happened. He knew that with all his being. He was to share it and his faith with the world.

"Let's go free your friend," Tovak said to Hess and strode by the gnome.

Hess shook himself slightly and followed. "He—no my friend. He no anyone's friend."

Tovak stopped and turned back to the little creature. "Regardless, I will not leave him down here for the spiders. Come on."

CHAPTER SEVENTEEN

As he entered the chamber, with Hess following close behind, Tovak found Greku had finished freeing himself of the constricting webbing. He had sat up and was holding a hand close to his side, as if shielding something.

Under the full light of the torch, Tovak had a better view of Greku. What he took in was terribly concerning, frightening even. Greku was completely covered in orange-and-black-patterned fur. Two ears on the top of his head flicked this way and that, as if listening to every sound. His face was cat-like and animalistic. He made Thulla's lion look almost tame. Greku was powerfully muscled, and he looked at Tovak like he was prey about to be taken down. To say the gaze was intense would be an understatement. It was a challenge, or really a dare, to keep staring, and yet Tovak refused to look away and back down. He was done backing down from anyone, and that included Greku.

What was he?

"You killed them?" Greku asked after a moment, stern expression fading. A look of what Tovak took to be curiosity seemed to steal over him. "Of course you did. Otherwise, you would not be here. I must admit I am impressed, very impressed. I had not thought there was such strength in your people."

Greku winced and almost doubled over. He pressed his hand to his side tighter. Dark red blood seeped out from between the furred fingers.

"You are injured," Tovak said.

"I am," Greku admitted and bared his teeth in what looked to be an expression of pain. He wore black leather armor and matching black pants. His leather boots were a dark brown.

"Can I help?" Tovak said.

"No." Greku shook his head. "No, you cannot."

"What happened?"

"A krow got me good," Greku said, almost with embarrassment.

"Krow?" Tovak was surprised by that.

"I told you," Hess piped up from Tovak's side. He was wagging a finger at Greku. "No play with krow. Bad—very bad."

"I wasn't playing with them, you fool," Greku snapped at the gnome. "I was trying to kill them."

"A krow," Tovak said and pointed back towards the paladin's tomb. "Those were krata."

"A good observation," Greku said and removed his hand to look at his wound under Tovak's magical light. It was a round hole that bled freely. He probed at it with a finger and winced. "It could be worse. It's not too deep, nothing more than a painful poke."

Tovak felt a wash of cold run down his spine. He looked about as realization slammed home. "This is a krow lair."

"Another good observation," Greku said. "Had there been only one, it would not have been much of a problem. Unfortunately, I happened upon a mating pair. The second one surprised me and stuck me"—he bared his teeth again, which were wickedly sharp—"but not before I killed her."

Hess said something in another language to Greku.

"I am not going to die," Greku said, "you infuriating little bastard. And no, you can't have my things."

The gnome let out an unhappy sigh.

"A krow bite is poisonous," Tovak said.

"Not to my people." Groaning, Greku, with no little effort, pulled himself to his feet. He was so tall that when he straightened, he towered over Tovak and the gnome. His head almost hit the ceiling eight feet above. "At worst it incapacitates us for a few hours and, as you can see, the venom causes great pain. I will recover just fine. The spider, however, will not."

"Who are your people?" Tovak asked.

Greku looked at him as if he could not believe Tovak did not know. "I would think that obvious."

"It's not."

"He Vass," Hess said helpfully. "Big stupid kitty."

"Enough from you," Greku snapped and took a menacing step towards the gnome, who scuttled behind Tovak's legs.

Greku pressed forward. Tovak took a step back and almost tripped over the gnome behind him. He was reminded of Dagmar being bitten in the ass by a gnome. He pushed Hess away to the side, then recalled he faced a Vass. Turning back to face Greku, he felt a strong desire to draw his sword, but he resisted the effort and forcibly calmed himself. Greku, for his part, seemed amused by Tovak's reaction.

"I take it I am the first Vass you've seen?"

"No," Tovak admitted. "I've set eyes on another of your kind."

"You have?" Greku seemed surprised by that. "We are few in number on this continent. If you had seen one of my kind, how is it you did not recognize what I am?"

Tovak did not immediately respond, as he felt a wave of weariness wash over him. After the last few hours, he was spent. All he wanted to do was sit down and rest. But he could not do that, not until he escaped back to the surface and safety. Even then, there may be no rest. There was no telling what was going on with the assault on the wall. Then again, it might all be over.

Greku turned and started looking around the area where he had been lying. He kicked aside several of the carcasses. "Bah. No sword."

"It is where spider got you," Hess said.

Greku rounded on the gnome. "And you did not think to bring it?"

"Too heavy," Hess said with a tiny shrug of his shoulders. "Too big and if I drag, like spider dragged you, they hear and eat me. I no like that."

Greku shot a hard look at the gnome, then blew out a heavy breath that sounded like more of a snort than anything else. "You were right to leave it. We will have to go and get it. That sword has been in my family for generations. I take it my pack is there too?"

Hess nodded. "I no touch and spider no care."

"Good, because if you had, I'd kill you."

Again, Hess gave a shrug of his shoulders.

Greku abruptly turned back to Tovak. "I asked you a question. How is it you did not recognize my kind?"

"I saw another of your kind from a distance and was told the person riding the dragon was likely a Vass," Tovak admitted. "At the time, it was a long way off."

Greku stilled at that. After a long moment, he gave a nod, as if thinking on what Tovak had said.

"Was this recent?"

"Last night," Tovak said.

"I thank you for that information. It is most welcome. It means I've not been forgotten." Greku paused, eyeing him for a long moment. "What is your name?"

"Tovak."

"I am glad you happened by, Tovak," Greku said and glanced around the chamber, examining it. He turned to Hess. "How far was I dragged? How far from where my sword and pack are?"

"Not far," Hess said. "Short walk, short walk."

Greku turned his attention back to Tovak. There was an unspoken menace in his gaze. "I think we both know it is no accident you are here in this place."

Tovak did not immediately respond. He studied the Vass for several heartbeats, then spoke. "Just as it is no accident you are here either."

Greku gave a huffing laugh that caused him to wince and grip his side. "That is true."

"Are you certain I can't help you?" Tovak asked, wondering how bad Greku's wound was.

"My people heal rapidly," Greku said. "Though it is painful, I have had worse. I will tend to it after I get my pack. The supplies I need are inside."

Tovak was not convinced. He feared the wound was a bad one.

"There was a time when your people and mine worked side by side."

Tovak did not say anything to that. He only knew the Vass to be ancient enemies, and not much more.

"I ...." Greku stopped, his jaw working, as if what he intended to say was causing him physical pain. "I am in your debt."

Hess said something in another language, drawing Greku's attention. To Tovak it was a long string of rapid babble. When the gnome finished, Greku flexed his jaw again and turned back to Tovak.

"*We* are in your debt," Greku said. "Hess and me."

"No," Tovak said. "I don't think so. I would have done the same whether you were orc or goblin. I'd not leave anyone to be fed upon by spiders. No one deserves that fate."

"Regardless, a debt is owed and must be paid. Such is the way of my people and"—Greku huffed out a breath, gesturing towards Hess with a hand—"his too."

Hess spoke again to Greku. It was yet another long stream of speech, at the end of which Hess responded in the same tongue, though slower.

"Hess says you need the way out," Greku said.

"Why did he not just say that, then?" Tovak asked. "He speaks my language well enough."

"Probably because he answers to me," Greku said, "and thought the information would bring me an advantage in the coming negotiation. What he says is true, yes?"

"It is. I came to be down in these catacombs by accident," Tovak said, glancing around, "but I believe I would have ended up down here anyway."

"The gods work in mysterious ways." Greku's eyes had narrowed. "Still, we know the way out. In repayment of our debt, we will guide you out of the catacombs instead of killing you."

Tovak stilled. He swallowed before speaking. "I find that acceptable."

"You should." Some of the menace left Greku's tone. "You are part of the Dvergr army headed here to this valley?"

Tovak did not say anything.

"By your presence here," Greku continued, "I assume your people have already entered the valley in strength. It is either that or you came in advance of your army, as a scouting party perhaps?"

Again, Tovak chose to not reply. He remained stoically silent. It was not his place to give potentially vital information to an enemy, especially one who had just mentioned killing him.

"Your silence only confirms my suspicions," Greku said. "Perhaps we can help each other?"

"What do you have in mind?" Tovak asked suspiciously, knowing there was no way he could trust Greku. Only, he knew he might have to.

"If you permit me to leave after we guide you out," Greku said, "and guarantee your people will not interfere, I will give you information on your true enemy, the Horde. They are our enemy as well. Helping you, I think, will hurt them, which, in a way, advances both of our interests somewhat."

"What sort of information?" Tovak asked.

"There is a hidden pass that leads into the valley. My guess is your people do not know of it. And no, I am not talking of the pass that leads in from the Grimbar." Greku regarded Tovak for several heartbeats. "Might its location be of interest to you and your army?"

Tovak reluctantly gave a nod.

"The only conceivable reason your people are here in this ancient land is for Grata'Dagoth," Greku continued. "If the enemy pours unchecked into this valley, you will never find it or, more correctly, reach it and what it guards. Your people will be in a difficult position."

That Greku knew what they were looking for set off alarm bells. What was more concerning to Tovak, though, was that there was another way into the valley, a pass, and it was unknown to the warband.

He wondered if the Vass was telling the truth. It was quite possible he was intentionally misleading Tovak to gain his trust and support in escaping the catacombs. Still, he knew he could not take that chance. And, there was something about Greku, a feeling, that told him the Vass was not lying. He was speaking the truth.

"If they are keeping their current pace, the Horde will enter the valley in strength soon. Tell me, are you interested in that information?"

"I am," Tovak said, knowing the warchief would need it.

"If you agree to let me and the gnome go after we show you the exit to this place, then I will share this information with you. Regardless of what you decide, due to our debt, I will guide you out. Do not agree to my terms, and this added information remains with me and you risk the destruction of your warband."

Tovak thought for a long moment. "I cannot bind my people to that. I do not speak for them."

"We wish no trouble with your people," Greku said. "I personally want no trouble, nor do I seek to cause you any difficulty. But I will take your personal word on the matter. Agree and we have a deal."

"I just told you," Tovak said, "I cannot bind my people to that. There may be those who choose to disregard whatever agreement we make here. In fact, I am quite sure they will."

Tovak could only imagine how Dagon would respond to such an arrangement.

"They would go against your word?" Greku seemed thoroughly astonished, aghast even, by the thought of that alone. "I find that difficult to believe."

Tovak felt himself scowl at the Vass. "Greku, I am a nobody, a Pariah to my people. I am a soldier, with no rank, nothing more."

Greku took a step forward, studying him intently, as if in disbelief. "I know this word, Pariah. How can that be? You are clearly no such thing."

"Oh," Tovak said, feeling a sudden flood of embarrassment, mixed with terrible bitterness, "but I am. My father disgraced himself at a place called Barasoom. All my life I have lived with his shame, dealt with it as best I could."

"Your people think differently than mine," Greku said and then fell silent, eying him for several long heartbeats. He was clearly weighing Tovak's words. "Still, if you give me your word, you will do everything within your power to see that we are allowed to go free, that shall be enough. As I've said, I have no desire to trouble your people. Do we have a deal?"

Tovak thought it through. The information Greku was willing to trade could prove vital to the warband's interests. He could not pass it up. He knew that. He had to agree and do what he could, even if it meant he might be punished for his actions and giving his word to an enemy. It might see him expelled from the warband or worse, condemned to death.

"We do," Tovak said, "upon my Legend, I promise you to do all that I can."

"Good enough." Greku seemed immensely pleased with himself. "Bargain fairly struck, paladin."

"What?" Tovak asked, not quite believing what the Vass had called him. "You are mistaken. I am no paladin."

"You cannot deceive me," Greku said. "There is no point in deception now. We have entered into an agreement. You cannot renegotiate. It is done and final."

"I am being honest," Tovak said. "By Thulla, I swear that I am no paladin. I would not deceive you in this. My faith is too steadfast to allow me to do so. Thulla would never forgive me for such temerity."

Greku cocked his head to the side as he regarded Tovak. "No matter what you say, you have been blessed by your god. My people have the ability to sense such things. It is in you. I can feel your power. I can sense it radiating outward. You are a holy warrior of Thulla. On that I'd bet my life."

Tovak felt rocked by Greku's words. He took a step back, his gaze going toward the paladin's crypt. Could it be true? Could Greku be right? No, it simply could not be. He knew he had been blessed by Thulla, but this seemed too much, too great of an honor to even contemplate. He found his mind going back to the fresco inside the crypt, with his own image detailed there. Was he, Tovak, continuing the paladin's journey?

"It can't be," Tovak breathed in a near whisper. "It just cannot be."

"Though our people are not friends, you offered to protect Hess and me, against three krata no less," Greku said plainly. "Would another of your people have readily done the same? Would they have had the moral courage and fortitude to do so?"

Tovak looked to Greku and just shook his head.

"I thought not," Greku said. "You bested three full-grown krata by yourself. When you left us, you had no weapon in hand, other than a magical torch. I saw you draw them into that crypt. And yet, only you emerged alive and with that magnificent weapon now strapped to your back. If I do not miss my mark, it is mogan steel, a treasure worthy of a king, and a tool fit for a paladin."

Tovak blinked. His sword was mogan steel? He'd never seen a blade to match its like. Now that Greku said so, he could easily imagine the sword was made of the fabled steel. Such weapons were incredibly valuable; the secret of making them had been lost to the ages. He knew the Thane had a mogan steel axe, but beyond that … no other Dvergr to his knowledge owned one.

"This day you were surely tested by your god and found worthy," Greku said. "You went into that crypt, a skilled and blessed warrior to be sure, and came out even more honored, or cursed, depending upon how you look at it. I even felt you use your power. You may not be a full-fledged paladin yet, but a paladin you are nonetheless, a holy warrior of your god, a knight even. You are no Pariah, not anymore." Greku closed his yellow eyes and held a hand forth towards Tovak. "The *will* of Thulla burns strongly within you. I can sense it, taste it even. Your ability, the potential to use *will* is raw, untempered, but it is there." Greku opened his eyes again and they were intense as the Vass's gaze bored into Tovak. "I know you feel it, the change. You cannot deny it."

Tovak opened his mouth to speak and then closed it. It was as the Vass said. He could feel the change, the burning spark within, and Greku's words felt right to him, more than right. Was it just wishful thinking on his part? A Pariah wanting to fit in, find his place in a harsh and uncaring world?

He shut his eyes, reached out to the spark, and searched for the answer. The Vass's words felt true. Funny that an outsider should show him the truth of things … and yet all throughout Tovak's life, he had been an outsider to his own people. How strange.

Tovak opened his eyes and was startled to find he was no longer in the chamber. He was outside. The sky overhead was brilliantly blue. There was not a cloud to be seen. A strange yellow sun that seemed overly bright hung high overhead. Its light felt warm against his face, comforting. Gone was the cold sap of the underground. Exotic and colorful birds flew through the air. Small insects flitted about.

Metal clanged on metal to his right, harsh and jarring, breaking the serenity. He looked over and saw a blacksmith with a long neatly braided, fiery-red beard hammering away on a sword he was tempering. Next to the blacksmith in the grass lay a dog, shaggy, sad-looking, and seemingly asleep as it enjoyed the warmth of the sunlight. It was the largest hound he had ever seen, almost as large as the blacksmith. It picked its head up and regarded Tovak with droopy brown eyes, wagged its tail once, then laid its head back down and promptly went back to sleep.

The blacksmith looked up from his work and their eyes locked. In them, Tovak felt a deep eternity that seemed bottomless and a divine spirit, powerfully strong, fierce. He was rocked by it as the spirit rolled over him in pulsing waves of power. Tovak wanted nothing more than to fall to his knees but could not. He was frozen in place, caught locked in his god's gaze.

"Welcome to Olimbus." Thulla's voice was deep, confident, and firm. "Few come here these days. Not many are permitted such an honor, not anymore, and fewer in the days to come."

Tovak tried to speak but could not. The god's power and majesty were overwhelming. It battered against his soul and mind, radiating outward in waves. Tovak felt tears prick his eyes.

Thulla held his hammer lightly in his left hand. In the other he held a piece of glowing steel that was partially forged. "Very much like this sword I am working on, your journey as one of My holy warriors has only just begun. Like those you have already faced and conquered, there are trials and tests still to come. Show a strong heart. Continued faith and courage will see you through them."

Thulla turned back to the sword and began hammering away at it. Glowing sparks flew into the air with each hammer strike. Tovak was watching the Forger of Worlds work. He felt incredibly honored and at the same time wholly unworthy. After a moment, Thulla stopped his hammering and examined the glowing shaft of metal. A satisfied expression on his face, he looked back up at Tovak.

"My people on your world have turned from Me. Few worship at my altar, and of those, even fewer are pure of heart." The god seemed deeply saddened by this. Tovak felt the sadness keenly in the god's power that continued to radiate forth like the heat of the forge. He could not help but weep as the sadness rolled over him. "Many peoples have strayed from the light, scorned their gods, and suffered for it on your world." The god's sadness turned to burning anger. "It is time for that to end. You, Tovak, will set the example. Even though they are presently blind, you will be the burning light, the beacon in the darkness My people need and have been craving. With the torch of your unquenchable spirit, you will light the way for them to rekindle their own faith. Can you do that for Me? Can you try to make a difference? For without faith, My people will remain lost and trapped by the spreading darkness."

"I will do as You ask," Tovak said, finding the ability to speak. "I will do everything in my power to see Your will done."

"That is why I have chosen you. Though your life was shattered by the hands of others, your spirit remains unbroken and your faith true. That is why I have endowed you with mana and My everlasting love."

A large bucket of water materialized next to the forge. The god plunged the glowing steel into it. Steam hissed forth from the bucket.

"Know that you may no longer heal others. That is a power that is henceforth denied to you. The battle over life and death of the faithful and unfaithful, pulling them back from the edge of the great beyond, is not yours to fight nor contest—not anymore. Your battlefield will be a different one and your journey as a warrior, a knight in My service, has only just begun. As I have said, additional tests, terrible trials lie ahead. Have faith and do as your heart wills and you shall pass them."

"Thank you for this honor, my lord," Tovak said.

Thulla regarded him for several moments.

"When next we meet, Tovak Stonehammer, your life's journey will have run its course and you will have crossed over. I look forward to that meeting, feasting with you in the ancestral halls, hearing of your tales and seeing you reunited with loved ones. Until then, the rest will be up to you. I will not directly interfere—I cannot, not anymore. Use the gifts I have bestowed upon you, learn to manipulate your *will*, and lastly, search and listen to your feelings, for that is how you will know not only My love, but My desires as well."

"I will," Tovak breathed as the god's power continued to pulse forth in ever stronger waves. Tears once again rolled down his cheeks and into his beard.

"Good," Thulla said. "Know that you are but the first of My faithful that I shall lift up. On your journeys, keep an eye out for them, for those with true faith are rare. Aid them where you can, inspire them through action and example, open their souls fully to My spirit."

"I will," Tovak promised.

"Good." Thulla hesitated a moment as he regarded the sword in the bucket. Steam was still rising from it. "Barasoom is not as it seems, but that is a mystery, a puzzle for you alone to figure out. Now, it is time for you to go back from whence you came. I must return to My work, forge this sword, for it is meant for another, just as yours was destined for you."

Tovak felt a powerful wave of love emanate from his god. Then Thulla turned back to the forge and the weapon, which he drew from the bucket.

The world before his eyes shimmered, as if he were surrounded by steam. Tovak blinked and found himself back in the underground chamber with Greku and Hess. He staggered, feeling a profound sense of loss at the breaking of the connection with his god.

He rubbed at his eyes and then glanced down at himself, for all was not as it should be. He seemed encased in something. With no little astonishment he saw that he was wearing plate armor.

Where had it come from?

The armor was perfect as could be, as magnificent as the sword, and it felt incredibly light, almost as if it were a second skin. On his chest was emblazoned the lion of Thulla. It had been etched into the armor and was the same one he had seen in the paladin's crypt, only larger. Utterly rocked to his core, he stared first at himself and then at the Vass.

He was speechless.

The armor encased his chest, legs, and arms. It seemed polished to an impossible degree, where it reflected the magical torchlight in brilliant flashes that shone against the walls.

"That transformation was something to see." Greku chuckled, thoroughly amused. "And now, you know the truth of things, paladin. You are, without a doubt, a holy knight of Thulla." Greku smiled at him and it was a fearsome thing to see. "Let me be the first to congratulate you."

Tovak could only shake his head in disbelief.

CHAPTER EIGHTEEN

With Hess leading the way, Tovak followed, the torch held high in his hand. It lit the passageway ahead in a steady and constant light. Greku followed just a few steps behind.

The corridor the gnome was leading them down had no burial alcoves along the sides. The walls seemed to be set a little farther apart and the ceiling a tad higher than the rest of the passageways he had been through. Why it had been constructed like this he did not know. But there had surely been a reason, one lost to time and the ages.

A strong draft continually blew around and by them. Tovak sniffed when he caught a familiar scent. It was the faintest hint of pines and fresh air. The smell was not terribly strong, but there was no mistaking the outside world. That told him they were likely close to the surface, or there were ventilation shafts nearby.

After another three hundred yards and four turns, the gnome brought them to a thirty-foot passageway that ended in a wall of silken-white webbing that had a large oval opening in the center. It was just big enough for them to step through. Seeing it made Tovak feel terribly uneasy, for it had an otherworldly feel, as if it were the border from his world to a strange and fantastical place. He had a sense that he would not like what he found on the other side. It was more like a premonition than anything else.

Stopping just before the web, the gnome pointed ahead and then made a walking motion with his fingers at the same time. The meaning was clear enough. Tovak glanced back at Greku, who nodded grimly.

The Vass still had a hand pressed tightly to his side where he had been injured. He had stoically refused all offers by Tovak to help or craft even a rudimentary bandage. With almost every step, he was grimacing or gritting his teeth. It was clear he was in a great deal of pain. Tovak feared Greku had been hurt far more seriously than he was admitting to.

"Ahead is the female's lair," Greku hissed in a low whisper to Tovak.

"The one you killed?" Tovak warily eyed the wall of web ahead.

Greku gave a slow nod.

"With some good fortune," Greku said, "the male will be gone, perhaps out hunting."

Tovak thought about that. Greku did not sound wholly convinced by his own words.

"Where I found you was the male's lair, right?" Tovak asked.

"It was," Greku admitted. "The two are a mating pair."

"Meaning there is likely a nest with eggs somewhere in there," Tovak said, gesturing ahead.

Greku nodded at that. "Yes, there are eggs inside."

"You don't really think he's out hunting," Tovak surmised, "do you?"

"He's in there," Greku said, then gave a slight shrug of his shoulders. "He should be, at any rate. If he's not, we retrieve my sword, along with my pack, and go."

"And if he's in there," Tovak said, with a sinking feeling in the pit of his stomach, "we have to kill him."

"That's right," Greku said, "for not only will he defend the eggs, he will most certainly come after us. Krow are highly territorial."

"So, what you are saying is he will not be pleased to see us."

"No," Greku said, with a trace of what passed for a grin. "I don't think he will be."

Resigned, Tovak drew his new sword. It felt good to have it out. He spared Greku one last grim look, then with one hand holding the torch and the other his sword, he began inching forward towards the webbed portal ahead. He stopped before it, his unease mounting to new degrees of intensity. He almost couldn't quite believe what they were about to attempt.

The wall of web, as well as the floor beyond, was made up of the thickest blanket of webbing he had encountered thus far, and it seemed to cover every visible surface ahead. There was a massive space beyond the portal. Holding his torch out, Tovak poked his head through the hole and peered outward.

The space that opened up beyond the entrance felt truly cavernous. It swallowed the sound of his breathing and stretched out farther than he could see. A tingle of fear crawled down the back of his neck. A large body lay in the darkness ahead. Legs curled up, the spider lay on its back. It was clearly dead, but the size of it was impressive. It was easily four times as large as the krata he'd fought.

The rational part of him wanted to turn back, for he knew another krow lay somewhere ahead. He could almost sense the primordial hunger of the spider, lurking out there in the darkness, just waiting to ambush them. Carefully, Tovak stepped through, into the chamber beyond. The light of his torch pushed back against the darkness, almost as if it were fighting the black.

He found himself in a chamber at least one hundred feet across and the same wide. The ceiling was high above and seemed to hover just at the edge of the light. Every square inch of the interior, from floor to ceiling, was entirely covered by a thick layer of webbing. Some of it clung to his boots.

At the center of the room stood what appeared to be a large rectangular structure with an arched roof. It looked to be a crypt, almost two stories in height. Like everything else, it was also covered with webbing. Dim light filtered through a hole in the ceiling, giving a twilight cast to the chamber.

A scuff of boots caused Tovak to look around. Greku had climbed through. He glanced around briefly, surveying what lay before them. He did not appear to like anything he took in.

"Your work?" Tovak asked, pointing with his sword to the corpse of the large spider. Tovak still could not believe how large it was, almost the size of a full-grown teska.

"Yes," Greku said. "The male is even larger. I am thinking it dragged me back to its liar out of habit."

Tovak gave an absent nod, hoping the male had not now decided to make this place home. There were numerous web-wrapped cocoons all around. Many were too thickly coated to easily identify what might be inside, but here and there he picked out the shapes of orcs, goblins, and gnomes. He also spotted dain, stags, and even what he thought was the long sinuous form of a murinok.

"Hess," Greku hissed, looking back. "Come on."

Tovak glanced back when Greku's expression hardened. The gnome was standing on the other side of the portal of web. He was shaking his head firmly in the negative.

"Not coming," Hess hissed back at them. "I not stupid like you. You kill spider. Then I come."

"Have I mentioned he's a bit of a coward?" Greku whispered to Tovak. "At least when it comes to spiders. I think all gnomes fear them."

"I fear them," Tovak said.

"I thought you were Hess the Mighty," Greku hissed back at the gnome. "Hess the Weak-Kneed, is more like it."

"Hess the Living," the gnome replied without any hint of embarrassment.

"He's got you there," Tovak said.

Greku looked back towards the crypt ahead, scanning the chamber. "Hess may be the only sane one down here." Greku raised a hand and pointed. "My sword and pack should be by the crypt."

Deciding there was no time like the present, Tovak started cautiously forward. He approached the crypt slowly, his eyes scanning in every direction. He saw nothing. When his light reached the back right corner of the chamber, he could just make out a thick tube of even thicker webbing along the wall that climbed up at a steep angle and intersected the ceiling. The tube was six feet wide and hollow. The spiders had attached it to the wall and reinforced it with sticks and dirt all along the outer surface. A wide network of thick supporting webs held it aloft and maintained its shape.

It led to where the light overhead was coming from. Tovak understood that was how the spiders got to the surface to hunt. His eyes followed the webbed shaft back downward, but his view of the base was blocked by the back of the crypt.

They moved by the body of the spider Greku had killed. He could not see any obvious wounds, but a pool of liquid had spread out on the webbing around it, staining it dark, before drying. Was it spider blood? Tovak gave it a wide berth.

Greku caught his attention and pointed towards a large pack that lay before the crypt's entrance.

"My sword should be behind the crypt," the Vass hissed to him. "Let's get that first, so that we are both armed."

Tovak gave a nod. They stood a better chance if the Vass held a weapon. Still a dozen feet from the crypt, he sidestepped slowly to the right as they advanced deeper into the chamber. He wanted to bring the back of the chamber behind the crypt into his light and view.

As they continued forward, there were more desiccated bodies, and the webbing underfoot seemed to become thicker and possibly older, for it did not cling to his boots.

Then the base of the webbed shaft came into view. It opened up at floor level, and the entrance leading into it was easily several feet taller than Tovak. With Greku at his side, and his heart hammering in his chest, he kept moving inexorably forward.

He glanced over at Greku. It seemed so extraordinary, outlandish even, that he should find himself in a krow lair with a Vass at his side and in the company of a gnome too. Heck, this entire day had not gone the way he had thought, not one bit.

Shaking his head slightly in disbelief, he returned his attention to the matter at hand and focused his mind, looking and listening for even the faintest movement or sound. They continued forward. A deep alcove that had been cut into the back of the chamber came into view.

Numerous cocooned and desiccated bodies filled the area on either side. They had been stacked up in piles, several of which were taller than Tovak and even Greku. Many of the bodies were embedded into the webbing of the floor, or stuck to the walls. One of the bodies, somewhat visible through the web shroud, an orc, looked as if it had been sucked dry of all its insides and now was a shriveled mockery of its former self. It was possibly the most gruesome thing Tovak had ever seen.

The sight of it all sent a chill through him, but that wasn't what almost stopped his heart. An involuntary gasp escaped his lips and he blinked in startlement. Folded up at the back of the alcove was the largest spider Tovak had ever seen. Curved, foot-long fangs glistened under the light of his magical torch. What served as its head was as large as Tovak's torso, and its black, furry thorax was at least eight feet across. Its abdomen was lost in shadow behind a cluster of folded legs.

Tovak's breath caught in his throat and he dared not breathe, for the spider seemed to be resting, possibly even sleeping. The monstrosity twitched slightly. Like a great lumbering monster, the krow shifted its body, turning ever so slightly so that its head faced him squarely. Black, soulless eyes, each the size of an orc's fist, glittered from within the shadows. Tovak felt a deep knife of terror stab at his heart. The monster was most definitely not asleep. Its full attention was now wholly focused upon him.

Tovak took a step back. The creature shifted again within the alcove, and he could just make out the massive stalks of its legs, flexing against its body. Each one was thicker than his own leg.

Tovak's heart, already hammering in his chest, began pounding harder, if that was possible. Despite the chill of the underground, he felt sweat break out on his brow. All he wanted to do was run, only he knew he could not. He must face and kill this terrible nightmare. It was either that or die trying, for that's what he had come here to do.

The krow shuddered once, issuing forth a rasping hiss, and then began shifting its legs inside the alcove. Tovak took another step backward, as did Greku at his side.

"Are you going to eat this one too?" Greku asked.

Tovak glanced over at the Vass and realized that it was a poor attempt at humor.

"Let's just make sure it doesn't eat us first," Tovak replied, returning his gaze to the monster.

"From your lips to our gods' holy ears," Greku said fervently. "May it be so."

Making an almost angry, guttural hissing sound as its legs unfolded, the creature stood. The legs extended almost a dozen feet around its black body. Underneath where it had been lying, Tovak saw thick webbed orbs that he suspected were eggs.

The spider hissed at them again.

Greku growled in reply. The sound of it raised the hair on the back of Tovak's neck and caused him to jump slightly. As he did, he almost dropped the torch and, for a moment, plunged them into near darkness. He gripped the torch tighter and the light brightened. The spider seemed to flinch back at the flaring of brilliance. The hesitation lasted but a moment. Then, it began advancing towards them, its legs rising and falling in a maddening order that was almost frighteningly hypnotic.

"I wonder." Tovak glanced at the torch in his hand and recalled the smaller spiders in the catacombs flinching away from its light. He waved it before him, as if it were a burning brand. The krow stopped, hesitating again. It hissed at him. He backed up another step, and as he did, he glanced over at Greku and almost dropped the torch again. The Vass was nowhere to be seen. He quickly looked around.

Greku was gone.

Hard realization struck home. Tovak had been left to face the spider alone. He felt a stab of bitter anger at having been tricked and then abandoned so callously.

The spider issued another terrible hiss that drew his attention back to it. The creature's entire focus seemed to be on him. It resumed its advance. Tovak waved the magical torch wildly in the air before him. Again, the spider hesitated for a heartbeat, then continued forward, slowly and deliberately. Tovak began backing up faster and raised his blade in a defensive stance.

To Tovak's left was the web-covered wall of the tomb. As he backed up, the spider followed, coming closer and closer. He moved nearer the crypt. As the creature neared, it seemed to tower over him. The spider stood almost fifteen feet tall and Tovak wondered how he could possibly fight such a monstrosity. Who single-handedly could?

Its razor-sharp jaws clicked as they snapped together. The spider continued to move forward, almost hungrily, as if anticipating the meal to come. Tovak could imagine it wanting to feed upon his web-wrapped body until he was nothing other than one more desiccated corpse in this forgotten tomb.

"That will not happen to me, you bastard," Tovak shouted at it.

The shout seemed to be what burst the dam. The spider surged towards him with shocking speed. Tovak took several rapid steps back and swung his sword out before him. His blade connected with a leg, halfway up to the joint, and with a *THUK* cleaved neatly through.

The krow hissed in surprise and what was clearly pain. It drew the injured limb back, rearing on its hind legs as it raised the front part of its body off the ground.

"How did you like that?" Tovak shouted at it. "Not used to your food fighting back?"

The krow uttered another terrifying hiss and then surged forward again. Dodging to the right, Tovak ducked, just as it jabbed its fangs at where his head had been moments before. He thrust upward with the volzjain, aiming for the krow's fangs, hoping to cut them off or damage them. As he was off balance from dodging, the effort was poorly done. He missed and felt the blade bite into its armored shell, but only with a glancing scrape along the spider's underside.

The creature took several steps back, as if startled, eyed him for a long moment, and then lunged forward. It happened so quickly, there was no dodging. Tovak could not believe that something so large could move so fast. It jabbed its fangs into his chest. There was a hard clacking sound that echoed around the chamber. The spider jerked back, hissing angrily and flexing its fangs.

Tovak glanced down and, to his astonishment, saw that his armor had held. There was not even a scratch or dent upon it, but a splash of some liquid, which he took to be venom. Though his armor had protected him, the blow had hurt. It felt like he had been punched powerfully in the chest. It had almost been enough to steal the wind from him.

The spider attacked again. Tovak managed to jump out of the way by throwing himself to the left. He hit the ground and rolled. Tovak came up to his feet and found himself before the front of the crypt. The spider had clearly lost sight of him. It was turning in a circle, searching. Then it saw him. Tovak turned and sprinted for all he was worth, dodging around the far side of the crypt. He half expected the spider to follow, but it didn't.

He continued along the side of the crypt, moving towards the back of the structure, where the alcove was located. Turning the next corner, he put his back against the wall of the crypt. Heart hammering and breathing heavily, he froze, trying to hatch out some sort of a plan against the creature.

The chamber had gone silent. Then he heard it, the krow's footfalls, echoing off the cavern's walls. They sounded as if it was now following him around the building. He looked back around the corner of the crypt, the way he'd come.

Nothing.

The spider was not there. Where was it?

He cursed Greku for abandoning him as he looked to his right and strained, listening for the monster. The footfalls had stopped. The cavern was once again silent, except for his pounding heart and ragged breathing, which he was doing his best to suppress.

Where was it?

As if in answer, a droplet, or really a gob, of liquid passed in front of him and spattered onto the floor at his feet. Tovak cursed himself. He should have dropped the torch. Of course it would know where he was, based on the light. Another gob of liquid passed by his face to the floor.

He looked up and saw the spider atop the crypt, hovering over him and poised to attack. Blood or something like dripped from the severed limb. Tovak felt a terrible dread steal over him as he looked into its black and uncaring eyes. Then the spider jumped and Tovak threw himself once again to the side. He landed painfully on his left arm, which already was hurting. There was a heavy thud from where he'd been standing. He rolled and lost the torch. The chamber was plunged into dimness, the only light source now high above.

The spider did not hesitate and did not seem to be affected by the lack of light. It spun and came on, striking out at him. Tovak rolled to the side. Less than a heartbeat later, fangs punched down into the ground next to him. One attack after the other, flashing almost faster than Tovak could see or react. More than once, the fangs hammered into his plate armor. Tovak realized he was still holding his sword. Gripping it with both hands, he blocked the next attack, knocking the fangs away, then dodged the attack after that.

A leg hammered down to his immediate left. Tovak swung hard, as hard as he could. There was a *crunch* as his blade carved through the leg. The spider screamed. Then he was hit by something large in the chest and tossed into the air, like a child's toy. He slammed down on the ground. The spider was on him before he could react. A leg hammered down and clipped the side of his helmet. The blow hurt and a flash of light filled his vision. He felt the warmth of his own blood sliding down his temple from under his helmet.

Ignoring the pain, almost impossibly, he still held his sword. He scrambled to the right and, desperate almost beyond reason, stabbed up at the creature, which seemed to be standing almost completely over him. The sword hit the creature's carapace but did not penetrate it. The carapace seemed hard as forged steel and Tovak felt the impact communicated through the blade. The spider hissed at him in reply. He punched the sword up again, this time harder, with more strength behind the strike. There was a crack and the sword punctured the carapace just a little. Tovak almost shouted out in triumph, but the krow beat him to it, screeching in what sounded like a mix of rage and pain. It backed up and away from him. Tovak scrambled to his feet and held his sword out before him, point towards the massive creature.

"Come on!" he shouted at it. "There's more where that came from. Come on."

Hissing, the spider moved to attack again. As it did, there was a shout from above. As if materializing out of thin air,

Greku jumped from the roof of the crypt. He had a large sword in his hand. Landing atop the spider's back, he drove it into the creature, stabbing deeply. The spider screamed again and spun around, as if trying to reach its tormentor. Only Greku, holding on tightly to his sword hilt, was firmly latched onto its back. The creature began to buck in an attempt to throw the Vass off.

Tovak saw his chance.

He charged forward and swung mightily at the nearest leg, about halfway up its full length. The blade sliced through, showering him with a spray of dark liquid. The krow screeched again, but he ignored it and stepped forward, swinging with all his might at another leg. He severed that one closer to the body. A gout of thick liquid coated him. He could taste it in his mouth and found it quite foul.

Still bucking wildly, the krow sidestepped and attempted to scramble awkwardly away, as if it now comprehended the danger it had placed itself in. Another slice and the spider, squealing, collapsed to the ground. Greku stood upon the spider's back, pulled his sword out, and stabbed down deeply again and then again. Each time, the sound of his sword punching into the spider's carapace cracked around the tomb in a sickening echo.

The spider shivered as the sword went in a fourth time and tried to stand. Tovak stepped up and, putting all his effort into it, drove his sword right through the center of the krow's thorax. The spider seemed to give a hiss of escaping breath, shuddered violently, and then fell still.

Tovak pulled his blade out, took two steps back, and then fell to his knees. He was thoroughly spent. He wiped his face free of the sticky liquid that had sprayed across it. He wanted a drink to wash the foul taste of the spider out of his mouth but knew his waterskin was dry.

He lay his sword down on the ground and then looked at his hands, which shook under the dim light from above. In fact, now that he realized it, his entire body was shaking, trembling uncontrollably. He could not believe he had once again beaten the odds and survived.

Greku jumped off the back of the spider. He regarded it for a long moment, then turned to Tovak.

"Well fought, paladin," the Vass said. "Facing the krata was a difficult challenge. This"—he gestured at the krow with his sword—"was different, more impressive. Even amongst the Vass, not many would willingly face an adult krow like you did. That was bravely done, and I see now why Thulla has taken such an interest in you. This day you earned what I think your people call Legend."

"I thought you left me," Tovak admitted.

"Never," Greku said and managed to sound offended. "We have entered into an arrangement and I mean to keep it. To do otherwise would dishonor me and my family. I would rather die than see that happen." He pointed at his sword. "While you were distracting it, I snuck around behind the creature and retrieved my sword."

"Spider dead?" Hess asked, from their right. The gnome had come up to them and was eyeing the spider's body with serious wariness.

"Yes," Greku said. "It's done. No thanks to you."

"You no pay me to fight," Hess said. "That cost more."

Greku grunted at that but still seemed far from impressed. "I don't pay you at all."

With a groan, Tovak dragged himself to his feet and stood there, staring down at what was surely the greatest of all krow. He couldn't believe he'd just helped to kill it. Nobody would ever believe him, not in a thousand years. They would think he was mad. He wiped his blade clean off the hem of his tunic and then slid the weapon back into his scabbard. Tovak glanced around and spotted the torch, lying where it had been dropped. He went over and picked it up. As his hand wrapped around the shaft, the torch flared to life, filling the chamber with its magical light.

Turning back to the monster of a spider, he sent up a silent prayer, thanking Thulla for seeing him through this ordeal.

"This was a good kill." Greku threw his head back and gave a mighty roar. He shook his sword and pounded his chest with clear satisfaction.

Tovak just watched. He was weary, spent, and wanted nothing more than to leave this cursed underground and return to the surface.

"It was a very good kill," Greku said.

"You done?" Hess asked Greku, his squeaky voice filled with clear irritation. "Can you make louder noise? Or does the dumb kitty want to play with more spiders? This underground bad place."

Greku looked over at the gnome, clearly unhappy, but he said nothing. He seemed almost to deflate, and his hand returned to his injured side.

Tovak glanced around. "I vote we go."

"I need my pack first," Greku said and started for the front of the large crypt.

"What is this place called?" Tovak asked, following after the Vass. "Do you know?"

"You are in what was once the kingdom of Askamatu," Greku said. "This tomb belongs to a past king, Hargana or something like that."

Tovak looked at the large crypt that towered over them as he followed the Vass around to the front. "You mean thane? We don't have kings."

"I mean king. Askamatu once had kings, Dvergr kings."

"My people don't believe in kings," Tovak said.

Greku moved to his pack that lay on the ground and knelt before it. The Vass looked back at him as Tovak came up.

"They did." Greku pointed at the crypt. "Your cousins moved on long ago." Greku opened the pack and began sifting through the contents inside. After a moment, he gave a soft sigh and his shoulders seemed to sag with clear relief. He tied the pack back up.

"Do you know where they went?" Tovak asked, glancing back towards the crypt.

"Some think they went to the west, across the sea. I am not really sure." Greku stood and hefted the pack onto his shoulders. He winced as he did it. Dark blood was freely running down his leg. The Vass followed Tovak's gaze and looked down at the injury. "When we get to the surface, I will need to bandage it. I'd rather do it up there than down here, if you know what I mean."

Tovak did understand. They both wanted out.

"Across the sea?" Tovak asked, thinking through his geography. He could not remember there being such a thing nearby.

"There is a great ocean," Greku said. "I have never crossed it myself, but others I know have. They say there are more of your people on the other side, a lot more."

Tovak felt his heart beat faster at that. His own people had come to this world centuries ago with the Horde pursuing them. They had thought themselves alone and on their own. Now, he knew they weren't. Tovak fully realized this information might change everything, including the Great March. Perhaps, if they could find a way to cross this ocean, locate their cousins, they might even be able to push back against the Horde or at the very least combine strength to hold the enemy at bay. It was definitely something to pass along to the warchief.

Wondering on the king who was buried here, Tovak glanced over at the crypt. With the torchlight, he saw that the webbing over the doors had been torn away. The metal doors stood ajar, forced open, and recently too, if he was any judge. He could see the Vass's tracks in the dust, leading up to the door. He looked over at Greku and felt a wash of hot anger that the crypt had been desecrated, broken into. Was Greku nothing more than a grave robber? That thought had not occurred to him. Dvergr tombs were sacred. His anger, like a bird in flight, soared.

"I do not wish to fight you, paladin." Greku met his gaze levelly. "If you make me, I will."

"What did you take?" Tovak asked.

"Nothing of consequence to you, but something that long ago was ours. It belonged to my people and we—*I* have spent years searching for it. Rest assured, I did nothing to disturb the king's rest, only took what was rightfully ours."

"Tell me," Tovak insisted, taking a step forward. "What was it?"

"No," Greku said firmly. "That was not part of our agreement. For better or worse, you gave me your word on letting me go. There will be no renegotiating now."

Tovak closed his eyes in frustration. He did not want to fight Greku either, but Legend was at stake here, his people's Legend, even if these people were not his own by blood. It fell to him now to uphold their honor. By breaking into the tomb, Greku had crossed a line, an inviolate one.

He took a deep breath through his mouth and let it out through his nose. He recalled what Thulla had told him to do and he searched his feelings on the matter, for he wanted to find a way out that did not involve fighting. He was so exhausted, he wasn't sure he had the energy to challenge the Vass.

The spark within flared, and with it, Tovak felt his exhaustion, aches, and pains lift ever so slightly. There was no compulsion to contest whatever it was the Vass had taken. In fact, it seemed the opposite. Thulla clearly wanted him to help Greku. He was sure of it, for there was a friendly warming sensation when he thought on the Vass. What was going on here?

"I will not fight you." Tovak released his hold on the spark and opened his eyes. "Whatever you took, you can keep it."

"Your god does not mind?" Greku seemed surprised by that.

"Not that I can tell," Tovak said. "In fact, I think he wants you to take it. Perhaps our paths were meant to cross down here."

Greku gave a relieved nod and relaxed. "In a way, I suppose that makes sense."

"I hope whatever you found was worth it."

Greku bared his teeth at Tovak in a wicked-looking grin. He issued forth a low growl.

"Very worth it."

"Great," Tovak said. "I am happy for you."

He glanced up the webbed tube that led to the surface. He was not looking forward to going through it. But getting out was what mattered.

"Can we go now?"

"Yes, but not that way." Greku had followed Tovak's gaze and then pointed to a dark passage off to their left. Tovak had not seen it before now. Clearly eager to leave, Hess was already moving towards the passageway. "We go that way."

Tovak turned and started walking. Greku fell in at his side.

"Was that your first krow?" Greku asked.

"And krata too," Tovak admitted. "Hopefully, that will be the end of it. I can go the rest of my life without ever coming across another." He glanced back over his shoulder at the monstrosity they had felled. He still had the foul taste of it in his mouth. "I don't think I will ever be able to bring myself to eat spider again."

Greku gave a huffing laugh and slapped Tovak on the back. "Never say never, friend."

"The worst I've ever faced was a near full-grown murinok," Tovak said, "but I think this krow was worse, much worse."

"You killed a murinok?" Greku seemed surprised by that.

As Tovak glanced over at the Vass, he expected disbelief. Instead, he saw no skepticism in the other's gaze. There was just a growing respect.

"Aye," Tovak said. "It almost took my life."

"You survived," Greku said as they came to the entrance to the passageway. They both stopped, with Greku turning to face him. "That's all that matters. 'Almost' has nothing to do with it. You survived and lived to tell the tale, just as we both did today. Take heart in that."

Tovak gave a nod. He held up the torch, shining the light down the passageway. Hess was several yards ahead. The gnome had stopped and with an impatient air was looking back at them. Along either side of the passageway, there were burial alcoves. A draft of air was blowing strongly down the passageway. Tovak could smell the outdoors. He longed for a return to the sky.

"How far is the exit?" Tovak asked.

"Maybe a hundred yards," Greku said.

Tovak thought on all that waited above on the surface for him. He had no idea on how the assault on the wall had gone. Had the warband been successful? Was it even now pouring into the valley in strength? Had Gorabor reached help? Were they attempting a rescue effort? Tovak had no idea on how long he had been in the catacombs. At the very minimum, it had been several hours.

He knew there would shortly be a return to authority. He wasn't quite sure how he felt about that, especially after all that had happened. He was a holy warrior of Thulla now. How would his people react? He had so many questions.

Turning, he glanced back at the crypt. In the shadows, he could just make out the bulk of the krow's body. To get this far, he had faced terrible, almost nightmarish trials. Tovak understood keenly that even more difficult ones lay on the journey ahead. Thulla had even told him that.

Tovak nodded to himself and started forward into the passageway, moving to catch up with the impatient gnome. Greku followed after him.

CHAPTER NINETEEN

Tovak stepped out into daylight, and as he did, he breathed out a sigh of relief. Though he had grown up underground, that had been a Dvergr city and not a long-abandoned catacomb filled with nightmarish monsters come to life.

He glanced around and saw he was inside the remains of what had once been a large structure now badly over-grown with vegetation and dotted with trees. What it had once been, he had no idea. The passage of time had erased any hint of that.

The foundational walls were thick and tall. They had clearly been designed to hold significant weight. The remains of all four walls were higher than he stood, with a gap on the far end. That had likely once been an entrance of some kind.

The interior of the ruin, despite being heavily overrun with vegetation, was littered with large stone blocks that Tovak recognized as carved granite. There were also the shattered remains of clay tiles lying all about. Those had likely come from the roof.

Tovak set the magical torch down on a large stone block. Rubbing at his tired and weary eyes, he breathed in, enjoying the clean smell of fresh air. No one was about or in view. He wondered how far he was from where he had fallen into the underground catacomb system. Hopefully not too far.

He looked up at the sky, judging the position of the two suns. They were already well along in making their descent for the evening. Tovak realized with a start he had been underground most of the day. He figured it to be about an hour or two from nightfall.

Behind him, Hess emerged with Greku following close behind. The Vass stopped and took a moment to gaze about before stepping over to a large block. He shrugged off his pack and set it down at his feet. He bent rather painfully and then opened the pack, rummaging through it for several moments.

At first, Tovak thought he was searching for a bandage, but the Vass pulled out what looked like a large brown river stone that, under different circumstances, would have been unremarkable. That the Vass was carrying it around made it a curiosity.

Greku brought the stone to his lips. He seemed to whisper to it for several moments before returning the stone to his pack. Then he straightened and looked up. Their eyes met.

Had Tovak just witnessed a religious ritual? He did not know. Afraid he might have intruded in something personal, he turned away and walked over to the nearest wall. Several large blocks had fallen down next it. Tovak was able to climb up onto them without too much trouble, until he could look over the wall.

He found himself in the same ruined town where he had fought the two orcs, before falling through the hole into the underground. In fact, he could see the main square, just forty yards off.

He felt his heart leap. There were several pioneers, along with a number of skirmishers, gathered around the small hill and hole he had fallen into. One of them was coming up with a coil of rope. To his right, motion drew his attention. Through the trees, about a hundred yards off, a company of strikers was moving by in a long column of two. They weren't Greng's boys either. A standard with a murinok symbol told him that. Tovak felt his heart soar. The warband had successfully taken the enemy's wall and now they were moving into the valley in strength. Otherwise the company of strikers would still be outside the valley and on the Grimbar.

Tovak wondered how the strikers of the Baelix had done. Was Struugar still alive? Had he been injured leading the main attack? There was just so much he did not know. Though it had only been a number of hours, he felt like he had been cut off for ages.

Tovak looked back towards the pioneers and skirmishers gathered around the hole in the hill. He recognized Gorabor and Dagmar amongst them, along with Lieutenants Benthok and Brund.

Tovak cupped his hands to his lips. "Over here. I am over here."

Gorabor turned and pointed. Tovak waved. Almost instantly, they started moving in his direction.

"Why'd you do that?" Greku demanded harshly as Tovak climbed back down. With his pack at his feet, the Vass had sat down on the stone block. He was nearly hunched over, his hand pressed tightly to his wound. As he spoke, he grimaced. "You just had to complicate things, didn't you? Now they won't let me go."

Tovak had not thought about that possibility. There was a strong chance Greku and Hess would not be allowed to leave. But, as he gazed upon the Vass, he knew without a doubt the wound was a serious one. Greku's pant leg was slick and dark with blood. He needed help, and the only ones who were near at hand and could assist him were Tovak's own people.

"You need medical attention," Tovak said. "You are losing a lot of blood, too much I am thinking."

"I am," Greku admitted sourly. "The spider got me good."

"If you don't get help soon," Tovak said, "I think you might bleed to death."

"Has anyone ever told you that you are a true master of observation?" Greku asked.

"Master of obvious, he is," Hess said.

"You don't have bandages in there, do you?" Tovak asked.

"No, I don't," Greku said, with a breath laced heavily with exhaustion. It seemed to Tovak that the Vass was weakening. "But help is on the way, isn't it?"

"My people may be able to help you," Tovak said. "We can find you a healer."

"Your people?" Greku said. "That's a laugh. I ask you, who amongst your people has ever treated one of my kind?"

"It's better than no treatment at all," Tovak said.

"The thought of a Dvergr treating me makes me ill."

Tovak considered Greku before he replied. "I don't want to see you die. I will get your wound tended to, then see that you are free to go, as we have agreed."

Greku eyed him for a long moment. There was a sad look in his gaze. "Do you think your people will honor our arrangement?"

"I will do what I can," Tovak said, then felt a firm resolve steal over him. "No, I will make them honor our agreement."

"It seems I am in your power, paladin." Greku glanced skyward, as if searching for something. "At least for the moment."

"Tovak."

Turning, he saw Gorabor approaching at a jog. He had come through the entrance to the ruins. Behind him were Dagmar, Benthok, and Brund, along with Iger. Dagmar was limping badly.

Gorabor slowed to a stop when he saw Greku and Hess. His mouth opened in astonishment. Then his gaze slid to Tovak, clearly for the first time seeing the armor and sword strapped to his back.

Dagmar and Iger drew their swords. Greku did not react. He continued to sit there, his yellow-eyed gaze resting sullenly on the newcomers. Hess, on the other hand, began backing towards the entrance to the underground. It looked like he might flee back into the darkness.

"It's alright," Tovak called hastily, placing himself physically between them and holding his hands up, palms facing the Dvergr. "They are with me."

"Move aside, son," Iger said. "That there is the enemy."

"No," Tovak said, "they are friends."

"Tovak, what is going on here?" Brund demanded, his eyes on the Vass and the gnome. There was horror there and worry too. Then his gaze shifted to Tovak. "What are you wearing?"

"It's alright, sir," Tovak said again. "They don't mean any harm. They are with me."

Benthok seemed to take it all in, his gaze studying the Vass and then the gnome before moving to Tovak.

"Put your swords away," Benthok said in a steady tone.

Dagmar and Iger looked to the lieutenant in question. They were surely wondering if he had lost his mind.

"There's a gnome," Iger said. "Need I remind you what they did to Struugar and his boys?"

"I don't need any reminding," Benthok said.

"Then there is the Vass, sir," Iger said. "They are dangerous."

"Usually that would be correct," Greku said, drawing their attention. He lifted his hand off his side and displayed his wound for all. "But, as you can see, I am injured and slowly bleeding out. A krow stuck me when I wasn't looking." He gestured towards Tovak with a bloodied hand. "We ended up killing it."

"A krow?" Iger's gaze went to Tovak. "You killed a krow?"

Tovak gave a nod. "Not to mention an orc and three krata. You could say it's been a challenging day."

They all looked at him in apparent disbelief, all except Lieutenant Benthok. The lieutenant was studying Tovak's armor. Tovak could almost see him mentally piecing things together.

"Dagmar, Iger, put your swords away," Benthok snapped in a brusque tone. "I should not have to ask a second time."

"Yes, sir," Iger said, and with clear reluctance, he and Dagmar sheathed their weapons. Iger moved around behind them. He placed himself between the underground entrance and the Vass. Hess did not appear too pleased by the move, for the gnome's eyes were on the pioneer.

Benthok took several steps nearer to the Vass, eyeing him carefully. Greku had placed his hand back over his wound and pressed down hard. The Vass met Benthok's gaze levelly.

"Iger," Benthok said, glancing over. "Go fetch Fenton. Tell him we have a patient that needs his attention. Have him bring his bag. He should be with the captain, back where we left the rest of the detachment in that smaller square."

"Are you sure, sir?" Iger asked and jerked his head towards the underground.

"I am," Benthok said firmly. "Go now."

"Yes, sir," Iger said and moved away, returning the way they'd come at a steady jog.

Having sensed the tension pass, Tovak suddenly felt a wave of exhaustion settle over him. He took several steps to a large rectangular block that had fallen over on its side. He sat down across from Greku, facing the Vass. He noticed Dagmar staring in what Tovak took to be concern at Hess.

"Don't worry, Dagmar," Tovak said, "Hess doesn't bite. At least, I don't think he does."

"He better not," Dagmar replied guardedly and patted the hilt of his sword. "He bloody better not."

The little gnome looked between them, then abruptly smiled at Dagmar, showing tiny needlelike teeth. Dagmar took an involuntary step back and his hand came to rest on the pommel of his sword.

"You really killed a krow?" Gorabor asked, stepping nearer Tovak. His friend kept shifting his gaze from Greku to Hess with a mixture of nervousness and curiosity.

"Aye," Tovak said, tiredly. "I helped, at least." Tovak glanced down at himself. He was fairly coated with gore and spider guts. His new armor needed a good cleaning. Heck, he needed one too.

"He delivered the final blow," Greku said, looking over at Tovak, "after drawing its attention to him. It is one of the bravest things I've ever seen."

"Tovak," Benthok said, almost gently, as he came nearer. His eyes roved over Tovak. "Are you okay? Are you injured in any way?"

"Tired is all," Tovak said, looking up at the lieutenant. He could hear the bone-numbing fatigue in his own voice. "I am exhausted, really. The last few hours have been very trying, to say the least."

"I am beginning to see that," Benthok said with a glance over at Greku. "What matters is that you made it out, understand? You are back with friends."

"Did the warband take the wall, sir?" Tovak asked. Having seen the heavy infantry, he thought that was the case, but he still felt the need to ask. He wanted to hear it said.

"The warband was successful," Benthok said, "and it seems we stopped any word from getting out about the assault. As we speak, the warband is moving through the canyon and into the valley."

Tovak gave a weary nod and then gestured over at Greku. "He says there is a hidden pass into the valley and the enemy is planning on using it. They are coming in strength, sir."

Benthok looked over sharply at Greku. "Is this true?"

"It is," Greku said.

"Tell me where this pass is located," Benthok said.

"Tovak and I came to an arrangement," Greku replied after the barest hesitations. "If it is honored, I will divulge the information you desire. If not... well, you will just have to live with the consequences."

"I promised we would let him go, sir," Tovak said. "In return, he will tell us where this pass is located."

Benthok sucked in an unhappy breath, then turned his gaze back to Greku. "He doesn't look like he's going anywhere, at least anytime soon."

"Don't be so sure about that," Greku said. "I am a Vass. I go where I will."

Benthok eyed Greku for a long moment. The lieutenant's gaze was a hard mask. Greku did not seem to care in the slightest. He returned the lieutenant's look as if it were a challenge.

"Whether you go or not," Brund said, "that will be for the warchief to decide."

"Now that," Greku growled deeply, "is unacceptable. He gave me his word and I took it on good faith."

"I don't care what he promised you, Vass," Brund said. "Tovak is under our command. He answers to us and ultimately the warchief."

"Not anymore." The words slipped out before Tovak could stop them. It was as if he'd almost been compelled to say it. He closed his eyes, knowing the mistake he had just made. When he opened them, he saw Benthok had stiffened and was looking at him, his expression was inscrutable. Brund had turned a hard look to Tovak as well. There was understandable fury there.

"What did you just say?" Brund demanded, taking a step nearer.

Tovak blew out a resigned breath and turned his weary gaze towards the lieutenant from the pioneers. He understood he had made a terrible mistake, but as he thought on it, the words were more than correct. He could no longer be part of the warband. Thulla had made that decision for him, taken away his opportunity to serve any other master. Tovak had thought he had found a family with the Baelix, a home, a place where he belonged. Only, now, that was not to be. The mere thought of it was wrenching, hurtful. But at the same time, he now served a greater purpose.

"I'd say he no longer reports to you," Greku said, sounding suddenly amused. "There has been a change in command."

"What does he mean by that?" Brund demanded, taking another almost menacing step closer.

"Look at his armor," Greku said. "A higher power gave it to him. I was there. I was blessed to have witnessed a miracle. It is not every day I get to see such a thing happen."

Benthok turned his gaze from the Vass back to Tovak. His eyes slid down to Tovak's chest and Thulla's lion. He became very still and then his eyes shifted and locked with Tovak's.

"Is this true?" the lieutenant asked in a near whisper. Tovak thought he detected a touch of awe in Benthok's tone, maybe even a sliver of hope. That, for some reason, made him feel uncomfortable.

Tovak suddenly felt deeply moved as he thought back on what had happened, his visit with his god. Standing in Thulla's presence had been an unbelievable honor, overwhelming even, for he felt undeserving. Not trusting himself to speak, he gave Benthok a simple nod.

Benthok brought his hand to his chin as he considered Tovak. "I knew it was more than just luck."

The last was whispered so low that only Tovak could hear it.

"I just knew it," Benthok said, a little louder.

"Is what true? What did you know?" Brund asked, looking between them. The lieutenant seemed highly irritated. "What the blazes are you talking about?"

"It's more than just luck," Benthok said. "It is what we talked about. He is gods blessed."

"Oh," Brund said, as if suddenly comprehending. "Oh my."

"What's going on?" Gorabor asked.

"I think it best that I speak with the warchief," Tovak said. "Do you think he will see me?"

Benthok ran a hand through his beard. "I believe he will want to make time for you."

Tovak felt a burden lift from his shoulders that he had not known was weighing him down. He looked down at his feet for a long moment. Then looked back up at Benthok.

"Thank you for believing me, sir."

"You found him?" a voice demanded harshly.

They turned to see Dagon and Fenton coming their way. The captain looked to be in a thunderous mood as he approached. His gaze went to the Vass and the gnome, and his features hardened even more, if that was possible. Dagon stopped a few feet from Tovak. He studied Greku for a long moment. Fenton was doing the same with a look of what could only be described as horror. Then, the captain's gaze slid over to Tovak.

"What are you wearing?" Dagon demanded, looking him up and down.

"Armor, sir," Tovak said plainly.

"Stand when you talk to me," Dagon hissed.

Tovak eyed the captain for a long moment. He already did not like where things were heading. Resisting a groan, Tovak stood, his tortured muscles protesting the move.

"What happened to the kit you were issued?" Dagon demanded harshly.

"I don't know, sir," Tovak admitted, and that was the truth.

"I am told you fell into the underground," Dagon said, in a tone that made it clear he did not believe it, nor Tovak's previous statement. "Are you a coward like your father? Are you a shirker? Did you think to avoid the fighting by hiding down there while the rest of us put our lives on the line?" Dagon pointed to the opening of the underground.

Tovak did not know what to say. He was shocked that the captain was accusing him of not doing his duty. For a moment, he just stood there, thoroughly dumbfounded by the turn of events.

"Tovak and I were fighting orcs, sir," Gorabor said, speaking up in a nervous and hurried voice. "I saw it happen. He killed the orc he was fighting and they both fell into a hole. The body is still hanging in the web. You can see it plain as day if you want to look, sir."

"I did not ask you," Dagon said in a harsh tone, shooting Gorabor a look that told him he did not know his place.

"I ordered Tovak, Gorabor, and Dagmar to pursue two of the enemy who got by us, sir," Benthok said calmly. "They followed them on my orders."

Dagon spared the lieutenant a stern look.

"There is a burial system under our feet here, sir," Tovak said and pointed towards the exit they had come out of a short while before. "Dvergr once lived in these parts. The catacombs are quite extensive. I've never seen anything like them. I've been stuck down there for several hours." He gestured at Greku and Hess. "They helped lead me out."

Dagon turned his gaze briefly to Greku and then Hess before returning his attention to Tovak. He did not appear impressed.

"I assume you found that armor down there," Dagon said, "and that sword strapped to your back."

"In a manner of speaking, sir," Tovak said wearily. The exhaustion was becoming worse. It was an effort to keep his eyes open, let alone stand. "I did."

All Tovak wanted to do was sit back down and rest. He did not see the slap coming. The back of Dagon's hand hammered into his cheek. The blow brought tears to his eyes and he tasted the tang of copper in his mouth. Tovak staggered back a step. Stumbling over a small granite block, he almost fell.

"You are a disgrace," Dagon said, spitting with rage. "You disgust me."

Tovak did not understand the problem.

"Sir," Benthok said, "I believe you do not have all the information. Perhaps you should listen to what he has to say and then judge."

Reaching up to his cheek, Tovak felt a cut. He saw the captain wore a silver ring on his index finger. The ring had likely opened his cheek. The wound bled freely down onto his armor. Tovak eyed the captain. His startlement shifted over to heat as his anger mounted, and he straightened up.

"Listen to him? Listen to the pathetic excuse of a Pariah? Lieutenant, are you seriously telling me I don't have all the information I need?" Dagon asked, looking over at Benthok. "He undoubtedly stole that armor from a crypt, the sword too. Open your eyes and see him for what he is. Desecration, grave robbing, is one of the worst crimes amongst our people. It has never been tolerated."

"I am not so certain about that, sir," Benthok said.

Dagon turned his attention back to Tovak as if he had not heard Benthok speak. "I should have expected nothing better from a Pariah." Dagon spat at Tovak's feet.

"He is beginning to bore me," Greku said to Tovak. "Tell him to go away."

Dagon turned a disgusted and infuriated look upon the Vass. "I will deal with you soon enough, beast."

"Good," Greku growled, "because now you are really beginning to bore me."

Ignoring the Vass, Dagon instead returned his heated gaze to Tovak. He stood there staring at him. Tovak could feel the captain's anger radiating outward, as if it were a hot sun.

"What do you have to say for yourself?" Dagon demanded. "How do you answer the charges I've leveled against you? It better be a good excuse, because if it isn't, I will see you executed for grave robbing, Stonehammer."

"I did nothing of the kind," Tovak said firmly. His own anger was threatening to overcome his reason, and with it, his exhaustion had retreated. He took a step closer to Dagon, meeting the captain's gaze with firmness of his own. "You are wrong, sir." Tovak saw the captain smile without warmth. "You judge me too harshly, and I think before you accuse someone of acting without Legend, I suggest you find a mirror first."

Dagon's cheeks went red. When the next slap came, Tovak was ready for it. He grabbed Dagon's wrist in an iron-clad grip with a clapping sound. He had stopped the captain's hand a bare inch from his face. Despite his rage, he suddenly and oddly felt pity for the captain.

Locking eyes with Dagon, Tovak had what he could only describe as an insight into the captain's soul. Perhaps it was the personal contact and his growing powers or maybe it was just plain intuition. Tovak did not know, but he saw things clearly as he had not seen them before.

Losing his son had been the worst blow of Dagon's life. Tovak could see it in his eyes, feel it even. The loss had ripped him to his core and almost destroyed him and his sanity. In response, the captain had turned all his energies to his work, the only thing he had left, commanding Second Pioneers.

Tovak could only imagine the wound he had ripped open when he'd shown up at the captain's tent just weeks ago, looking for a place in Second Pioneers. He could see all that now, as if it were written plainly on a piece of parchment. Dagon was letting his anger at the loss of his son get the better of him, placing the pain and hatred for Barasoom at Tovak's doorstep.

Tovak's anger drained away. It was replaced with sadness, pain, and a feeling of terrible, almost incalculable loss.

He wanted to weep, but instead, he felt an urge, a need to help Dagon. This all flashed before him in a heartbeat.

"I am truly sorry your son died." Tovak held the captain's wrist in an iron grip. "But I had no hand in what happened. Taking out your anger on me will not bring him back. It will not make things better or ease your pain." Tovak remembered a line from scripture. "'Revenge is but an empty vessel that, when poured, will never sate one's thirst.'"

"Unhand me," Dagon said quietly, his eyes burning with unconcealed hatred and fury. "I will ask you one more time to unhand me, Pariah, or I will kill you where you stand and save the executioner some time."

Tovak felt the spark within him surge. Time seemed to slow as the power roared. Dagon's eyes widened ever so slightly, and his pupils dilated. Tovak understood Dagon felt the power as well, Thulla's direct touch as it poured through him into Dagon. Then, as rapidly as it had come, the power died away. With it, Dagon's anger went. Tovak could feel it leaving, evaporating on the air, like a morning mist burned away by the newborn sun.

He released his hold on the captain's wrist. Dagon staggered back two steps, appearing to have been rocked to his core. His gaze was still locked on Tovak. His mouth opened to speak and then closed. He tried again and it came out in a strangled whisper.

"I heard my son. He spoke to me. I felt his—his touch ...." The captain trailed off, looking at his hand and then back at Tovak. "Oh gods. What have I done?"

"Such is Thulla's will," Tovak said quietly, understanding what he must do, what his god wanted of him in this moment. Tovak took a step closer to the captain.

"What just happened?" Benthok asked, looking between them.

"Captain," Brund said with clear concern, "sir, are you alright?"

Tovak ignored the lieutenants. His gaze was on Dagon. He took another step forward, feeling the captain's deep sadness, the heart-wrenching loss. Tovak did not have any children, but he understood loss and how terrible it could be. He had a flash of his mother's body, the day she had killed herself, lying there pale and lifeless. The empty cup by her side. He knew pain keenly, as it were an old friend. Knowing one's pain allowed you to feel another's suffering and sympathize.

"Your son feasts with Thulla in the ancestral halls." Tovak held out his hand. Dagon looked at it but did not move. He extended his hand farther. "Take it, take my hand. You son waits for you."

As if afraid, Dagon swallowed and hesitated.

Tovak could feel Dagon's son, his soul, the longing for his father's touch. Tovak had become the connection, the bridge to the other side. That was, if Dagon was willing to take a leap of faith.

"Heghon is waiting for you," Tovak said quietly, not knowing how he knew Dagon's son's name. "Thulla is granting you a chance to say goodbye. I beg you, do not waste it or spurn this opportunity, for it shall not come again."

"My son," Dagon whispered, reaching out, tentatively at first, then with a need, almost desperately clasping Tovak's hand. Again, the spark within him flared. Dagon closed his eyes. The surge lasted only a moment, perhaps not more than two or three heartbeats, but Tovak understood that for Dagon, a significant period of time had passed. Again, how he knew, he was not sure. He just did.

The surge faded, and with it, Dagon almost reluctantly released his hand. The captain of the pioneers took several wooden steps back, then slowly sank to his knees. Tears streamed down his cheeks and into his beard. He gave a wrenching sob filled with utter agony. No one moved. It was almost as if they were afraid to breathe.

"Though he is no longer in this world," Tovak said gently, "know your son is never far from your heart, as you are not far from his. Such is the way with souls and love."

Dagon looked up at Tovak, cheeks wet from his tears. He cleared his throat. "Thank you—thank you for that, for opening the eyes of a bitter old warrior. I can never repay you."

"It is as Thulla wills," Tovak said, "nothing more and nothing less. Your gratitude should go to Him."

Dagon wiped his tears away, then pulled himself to his feet. He cleared his throat. "It will. You have my word on that."

Tovak gave a nod. He felt no ill will towards Dagon, not anymore, only terrible sadness at the captain's years of pain and suffering. But with luck, that was in the past now. Tovak fervently hoped he would be able to live again and take some joy from life.

"I regret how I treated you, Tovak Stonehammer." Dagon said Tovak's last name without any hint of derision or scorn. "Can you find it in your heart to forgive me?"

"Your faith and devotion in our lord will be forgiveness enough," Tovak said and meant it. Thulla had given him a mission to spread the faith, and it started here with Dagon.

The captain of the pioneers gave a curt nod, then bowed his head respectfully. "Till the end of my days, He shall have it, Father Stonehammer."

Tovak sucked in a breath, startled by the title Dagon had given him. It didn't feel quite right. He felt as if he still had to earn it and was not quite worthy of such a title.

He glanced back towards the entrance to the catacombs and thought of the paladin's crypt. His quest to reclaim his honor and rise above being a Pariah had become so much more than he could have ever dreamed. He was not a full paladin yet. Tests and trials lay ahead. Thulla had pretty much told him so.

"No," Tovak said firmly. "Just call me Tovak. I am not ready for that, not yet."

Dagon gave a nod.

Tovak glanced over. The others were watching him. The priest, Fenton, had fallen to his knees and clasped his hands before his chest. His lips moved with a silent prayer. The sight of the healer caused Tovak to remember Greku's injury.

"Father Fenton," Tovak said, "we have need of your services."

Fenton did not move. "What are you?"

"He is a Lion of Thulla," Greku huffed, "a paladin, blessed by your god, Thulla, Builder of Worlds. His armor, especially with that lion, should have been your first clue. By the gods, you Dvergr are thick-skulled."

The priest gasped audibly. Tovak wanted to strangle the Vass, for the others were now looking upon him in what could only be described as awe. Tovak knew he did not want that. He wanted people to see him as he was, who he was, flawed and imperfect like everyone else. He did not deserve their reverence, did not feel he had a right to claim it. Such honors should go to Thulla, for the god had made Tovak who he was.

Greku groaned in pain.

"Father Fenton," Tovak said, "he has lost a lot of blood. Can you stop the bleeding or bandage the wound?"

Fenton tore his gaze from Tovak and looked at the Vass. Gabbing his bag, he moved over, first with alacrity and then cautiously, as if afraid Greku might attack him.

"I won't bite you," Greku said and removed his hand for the priest to examine the wound. When he did, the blood began flowing again, thick and red. "Just bandage it tight. You can't stop the bleeding. I will seek aid from my own people. They will be able to treat me."

"I can try to stop the bleeding, maybe sew it shut," Fenton offered.

"No," Greku growled, "just bandage it tight. Eventually the bleeding will stop on its own. Only my people can help me after that."

Fenton looked to Tovak, who gave a nod.

"I need to remove your armor," Fenton said.

"It's ruined anyway," Greku said, gesturing at the hole in it. He lifted his arm and exposed laces down the side. "Untie it if you would."

The healer did as asked, and after short work, pulled the leather armor off the Vass. The pattern of orange and black fur continued underneath. There was a patchwork of scars along Greku's chest that looked like old sword wounds. Where there were scars the fur did not grow. Greku looked up at Tovak and shrugged as if he did not care.

Fenton pulled out a bandage from his bag and began working on Greku, wrapping it around his torso and tying it tight. Greku winced as the healer worked.

Glancing around, Tovak saw his people still staring at him. It made him feel terribly uncomfortable. The weariness had returned, greater than before. He suspected that using his power and connection with Thulla had drained him. He blew out a weary breath and sat back down again on the stone block. He undid his helmet and removed the heavy thing. He set it in his lap. It was a relief to have it off.

The helmet was not the one he had started the day with. It matched the armor he wore and was square-ish, almost block-like. Roaring lions were stenciled on each side. Like the armor, it was incredibly beautiful, a work of a master to be sure. Had Thulla forged it? Tovak decided he liked the thought of that.

He reached up and felt his scalp. His hair was matted with dried blood, a result of the fight with the krow. His head hurt. Heck, most of his body ached. He found a small cut on the side of his head. It no longer bled but was painful to the touch. Tovak felt the need to bathe. He was sticky and filthy, almost beyond belief, coated with dirt, blood, spider guts, webbing, and dust. He was sure he looked like a right mess.

Tovak became aware that Hess was standing next to him. The gnome did not say anything, only reached out a tiny hand and then patted his, in what seemed like a gesture of comfort. Then, he stepped back and walked over to watch Fenton finish tying the bandage tight over Greku's wound.

"That should slow the bleeding," Fenton said.

Greku looked over the healer's work. "Thank you."

"Is it true?" Gorabor asked, moving over to Tovak. "Are you a paladin?"

"Yes," Tovak said, hoping almost desperately his new status would not jeopardize their friendship. "It is."

"From Pariah to gods blessed," Gorabor said, with a trace of a grin. "That's quite a jump."

Tovak could only agree. He spied Gorabor's waterskin tied to his hip. It looked full.

"Might I have a drink?" Tovak asked. "Mine ran dry hours ago."

Gorabor untied the skin, unstopped it, and handed it over. Tovak drank deeply, then passed it back.

"Thank you."

There was a flash of something large overhead. Looking up, Tovak felt the passage of a strong wind. He blinked, thoroughly astonished, not quite believing his eyes. Even in a day full of firsts and shocks, this was almost too much to comprehend.

"Dragon!" Dagmar yelled, yanking out his sword. It was almost immediately followed by a terrible roar that seemed to shatter the very air.

The dragon was almost impossibly huge. Tovak could not believe something so large could fly. It was magnificent and fearsome all at the same time. The creature swung around, tilting to the side, banking. Before Tovak could even react, it was flapping its wings, slowing its rate of descent. A moment later, its claws reached out and connected with the ground, landing just yards from them, by the entrance to the building. The ground shook and part of the wall to their right collapsed in a rumble of stone.

Tovak found himself on his feet and could not remember standing. He was ready to draw his sword, only he felt no threat from the creature. It gazed down at them with eyes that spoke of a deep intelligence. The dragon's jaw parted slightly. Tovak had a glimpse of rows of serrated teeth, each one far larger than he stood tall.

There were shouts and cries of alarm from the nearby woods, panic even. Tovak could only imagine the alarm the creature had caused. He felt it himself. Then, his eyes were drawn to the figure riding on the dragon's back. He was sitting in a saddle and wore all black armor, with the exception of a helmet. It was clear that this too was a Vass. Was it the same one he had seen the night before? Oddly, Tovak sensed a power of sorts within the rider, a spark very much like his own, almost emanating outward.

"My ride," Greku said and, with effort, stood. He hoisted his pack onto his shoulders. Greku looked down on the priest. "Thank you again for bandaging my wound."

Tovak turned to Greku and now understood. "The stone. It was some sort of a summoning tool."

"A very good observation," Greku said. "It is a relic from a bygone age, called an Agaggi Stone." The Vass looked towards the dragon and the Vass on its back, then stepped closer to Tovak. "We have an arrangement."

"We do," Tovak agreed.

"I would discharge my obligation to you," Greku said. "In truth, I would have told you anyway. We Vass consider the Horde the enemy."

"I see," Tovak said.

"The pass is to the north. Look for a good-sized and fast-moving stream that comes out of the mountains. There is a ruined aqueduct at the point where it enters the valley. Follow the stream up onto the ridges. It will lead you to the pass. You cannot miss it."

"Thank you," Tovak said. "I appreciate the information."

"I would not wait too long," Greku said. "The enemy will be there soon enough. They might even be there now."

"I will pass it along," Tovak said. "I am sure the warchief will act upon this intelligence."

"Very good," Greku said and was about to turn away. He hesitated. "What you seek, Grata'Dagoth, is to the west. That fortress is sealed magically, but I have no doubt you will find a way in." Greku seemed amused. "You are a paladin after all."

Tovak gave a nod, then looked towards the dragon and the rider. "Who is that?"

"My boss," Greku said, looking briefly towards the rider, "a Knight of the Vass, Ugincalt. I am thinking he will be very pleased by what I have recovered. One can hope anyway."

"You still won't tell me what it is, will you?"

"No." Greku turned to regard Ugincalt again. "But—it may even make up for some of my past failures."

"Past failures?" Tovak asked. He seriously doubted Greku had many of those.

"Perhaps our paths will one day cross again, paladin."

"I'd like that," Tovak said.

"I would as well." Greku started for the dragon. He paused after a few feet and looked back. "Hess," Greku said. "Let's go."

"I stay," Hess said insistently, "with Tovak. I stay and help Tovak. No like dragons anyway."

Greku seemed surprised by Hess, perhaps even more so than Tovak.

"I don't think dragons like gnomes either," Greku said after a moment. "She will likely be pleased you are not coming. They consider your people vermin."

"Try not to be too curious, dumb kitty," Hess said. "Don't play with string."

"Oh no," Dagmar groaned, looking between Hess and Tovak. "You can't be seriously considering letting him stay."

"Are you sure you won't come?" Greku asked Hess.

"You found what want," Hess said, "deal over."

"Very well." Greku turned his gaze to Tovak. "He's your headache now." Greku paused and looked once more at Hess, then turned back to Tovak. "Take care of him, will you?"

Tovak glanced down at the gnome, who had moved to stand by his side.

"I be good," Hess said. "Yes, yes. I promise. I help. No trouble. No trouble. You see. None at all."

Tovak wasn't sure how he felt about the gnome staying with him. He sensed no menace in the small creature, only a desire to help.

So be it.

When he looked back up, Greku had turned away and was walking over to the dragon. When he reached the massive creature, without any hesitation, he climbed up the side of the dragon and settled himself onto its back, right behind the knight. There seemed to be a saddle there as well, which he quickly secured himself to.

The dragon unfurled its wings and with several large beats took to the air, almost leaping upward and flying right over them. The wind generated by its wings was nearly enough to knock them over. Tovak had to brace himself. Then, the dragon was gone from view. Shouts of alarm from all around were still sounding out amongst the trees. Tovak could hear officers shouting orders as they worked to restore order.

"Well," Dagmar said, "that is something you don't bloody see every day."

As he sat back down, Tovak thought that an understatement. He looked up at the sky, which was perfectly blue, with not a cloud in sight. The temperature was beginning to cool down as the evening approached. Tovak reflected that it had been a long and challenging day.

Oddly, he found himself thinking on Serena, the wounded archer he had helped carry back to the warband. He hoped she was doing well. He had a desire to see her again a surprisingly strong desire. Once the warband set up camp for the night, Tovak decided to make a point of visiting her in the sick tents. His thoughts shifted to Karn and Jodin and he recalled what Thulla had said.

Know that you may no longer heal others.

Had he given them some healing? He suddenly had the feeling he had. Would they survive their injuries? It was an intriguing thought. He would also make a point to look in on them as well. The least he could do was give them some company.

Yes, Tovak thought, still studying the magnificent sky and reflecting on all that had happened, the day had been a challenging one, but in truth, it had been a good one too. He thanked Thulla for that and hoped that there would be many more good days to come.

The End

Tovak's adventures will continue in **Paladin's Light**.

Important: If you have not yet given my other series—
<u>Chronicles of an Imperial Legionary Officer</u>, <u>Tales of the Seventh</u> or <u>The Karus Saga</u>—a shot, I strongly recommend you do. All three series are linked and set in the same universe. There are hints, clues, and Easter eggs sprinkled throughout the series.

Give them a shot and hit me up on Facebook to let me know what you think!

You can reach out and connect with me on:

Patreon: www.patreon.com/marcalanedelheit

Facebook: Marc Edelheit Author

Facebook: MAE Fantasy & SciFi Lounge (This is a group I created where members can come together to share a love for Fantasy and SciFi)

Twitter: @MarcEdelheit

You may wish to sign up to my newsletter by visiting my website.

http://maenovels.com/

Or

You can follow me on **Amazon** through my Author Profile. Smash that follow button under my picture and you will be notified by Amazon when I have a new release.

Reviews keep me motivated and also help to drive sales. I make a point to read each and every one, so please continue to post them.

Again, I hope you enjoyed *Forging Destiny* and would like to offer a sincere thank you for your purchase and support.
Best regards,
Marc Alan Edelheit, your author and tour guide to the worlds of Tanis and Istros.

Enjoy this preview of Lost Legio IX, Book One in The Karus Saga.

By Marc Alan Edelheit

LOST LEGIO IX

Chapter One

There was a loud rap on the hardwood door. Karus looked up from the scroll he'd been reading, feeling somewhat annoyed. He was seated at a rough wooden table scattered over with a variety of scrolls.

"Come," Karus called.

Karus sat back as the door scraped open to reveal Centurion Tacitus Cestius Dio. A wash of cold air from the outer corridor flooded into the already chill room.

"Am I interrupting?" Dio flashed Karus a lopsided grin.

"Yes," Karus said.

"Good." Dio stepped into the small room, closing the wooden door behind him.

Though spring had arrived, the morning temperatures were still quite bitter. The small brazier that sat in the corner of the austere room did little to combat the cold, even before Dio had opened the door. Karus had no idea how the locals managed to thrive.

Dio glanced about the small room. Karus followed his friend's gaze. Except for the table, everything was neat. Karus liked it that way. There were two simple trunks and a camp cot. A sputtering yellow lamp hung from the ceiling. Another lamp sat on the table and provided light for Karus to read by. A thin stream of black smoke trailed toward the ceiling, where the numerous drafts caught it and swirled it about.

Karus's armor, maintained to perfection, hung from hooks on the back wall, as did several spare tunics. His shield rested against a wall. It prominently displayed the bull emblem of the emperor's Ninth Legion, Hispana.

Dio's eyes scanned the floor.

Karus knew there was not a speck of dirt or a particle of mud present, unlike the rest of camp, where dirt seemed to cling to everything. He had swept it clean.

"Is this an inspection?" Karus was being ironic. Dio was junior to him in rank.

"For the legion's senior centurion, you read too much." Dio's gaze traveled back to Karus. Dio reached down and picked up one of the open scrolls, narrowing his eyes as he studied the script. "Is this Greek?"

"Yes," Karus said with a sour note, "it is."

Dio made a further show of examining the scroll, though Karus well knew his friend was unable to read it. As it stood now, Dio could barely read Latin, and only enough so that he could manage his duties. Being able to read and write was required for promotion to the centurionate. After a moment, Dio lost interest and laid the scroll back down upon the table.

"A proper soldier should not read so much," Dio said. "It is not natural for those in our line of work."

"Only a fool ignores the histories," Karus said, "particularly those focusing on *our* line of work."

"So, I am a fool then?" Dio asked with a hint of a smile.

"Let's just say you are my kind of fool." Karus began to roll up the scroll he had been reading, along with the others scattered about the table. No matter how much he desired to continue reading, he had duties to attend to. It was time he began his day. "You should try reading sometime," Karus suggested. "You may learn something for a change."

"How to speak, and read, like a Greek?" Dio chuckled. "No thank you. I am a soldier, not some dishonest merchant. Besides, thanks to your brother, you are now of the equestrian class, with aspirations of nobility. I understand from good authority that all respectable patricians learn Greek. So, I find it fitting in a way that you can read this stuff."

Karus spared his friend an unhappy look as he finished securing the scrolls of the book he had been reading. He tied each off with a bit of string. Satisfied, he leaned over, stool creaking, and carefully placed each into a small trunk, which was filled with similar scrolls.

"What were you reading?" Dio asked curiously when Karus snapped the trunk closed.

"Polybius's *Universal History*," Karus said. "I have all forty books."

"All forty," Dio teased him. "You sound rather proud of that."

"I am," Karus admitted, and it was the truth. It had taken him years to collect all the historian's books. They were now the pride of his collection, and he was quite confident another complete set did not exist anywhere in Britannia.

"What does old Polybius have to say?"

"A great many things," Karus said.

"Such as?" Dio pressed.

"I was reading on Governor Galba, and his tenure in Hispana specifically."

"Galba?" Dio said. "Never heard of him, though I guess our legion has something in common with him."

"He was a bit before our time." Karus stood. He groaned with the effort, using his hands to help push himself upright and off the stool. He massaged the old wound on his thigh a moment, then glanced up at Dio. "What say we grab some grub? While we do, I will tell you all about him."

"I thought you would never ask," Dio said.

Karus was already dressed. In truth, he had been waiting for Dio. Over the winter, as in others past, this had become their morning routine. Though these days Karus's responsibilities were greater, the two still made the effort to continue the practice. Karus was the legion's senior centurion, the primus pilus of First Cohort. Dio, on the other hand, commanded Second Cohort, and was that unit's senior centurion.

Officially, a cohort numbered around four hundred eighty men. A cohort was lucky to come close to that number. The emperor's legions were always understrength. This was due to a number of factors, some of which included death, disability, retirement, or sickness. Or, in the Ninth's current circumstance, a lack of recruitment.

First Cohort, Karus's own, was a double-strength cohort and, out of all the formations of the legion, was maintained as close to full strength as possible. The First was the backbone of the legion and boasted the greatest concentration of veterans. Not counting those on the sick list, Karus commanded nearly eight hundred men.

He glanced back at the spare tunics hanging from pegs on the wall opposite his bed. He considered slipping on a second one. It was not uncommon in cold weather for legionaries to wear multiple tunics.

A quick glance at Dio changed his mind. His friend was wearing only one tunic, and besides, Karus was of the opinion that the men should see their centurions as tough, unflappable bastards whom even the frigid morning air failed to disturb.

Dio led the way out of Karus's quarters and into the short hallway beyond. Unlike standard cohorts, Karus shared the barrack with the five other centurions from his cohort. Each commanded a double century, which consisted of a hundred sixty men, instead of the normal eighty. The doors were all shut, as most elected to sleep until the morning horn called the legion to assemble.

The two men stepped out into the bitter cold of the quiet early morning. His breath steaming, Karus glanced up at the sky, which had barely begun to lighten. Within the next hour, the legion would be roused from its nightly slumber, the quiet shattered. They started walking in the direction of the officers' mess.

"I bloody hate Britannia," Dio hissed as a bitter gust of wind whipped down a pathway between the buildings. It struck Karus like a slap on the face.

The legion was stationed at Eboracum, a permanent garrison town. Eboracum represented the northernmost point in the empire. It was almost as far away from Rome as you could get, and as such, it seemed to Karus as if the High Command had more often than not forgotten them.

"It is too damned cold out, that's for sure," Karus agreed as the two men weaved their way between buildings, following the pathways of the fortified camp toward the officers' mess. "My days could be spent in warmth and comfort."

Dio glanced over at him, amused. "Sicily again? I can't ever see you retiring."

Karus grunted in reply.

"You," Dio jabbed a finger at Karus, "love your job too much, as do I. Though to be perfectly honest, on a bitch of a morning like this, a warmer climate has some appeal."

Karus chuckled.

Dio was right, of course, but in truth Karus was thinking more and more on retirement. He was nearing the age when his usefulness to the legion would come to an end. Karus found that he was beginning to think on his responsibility to family over that of the empire. He could not admit this, of course, but he found himself dwelling increasingly upon his life after the legion.

"Trade army life for one of comfort and indolence?" Dio waved his hand dismissively. "Bah, you'd be bored in a week, and you know it."

"It might take more than a week," Karus chuckled.

"At least you have something to look forward to besides your army pension and a plot of land in some poor veteran's colony," Dio said. "You know it's not every centurion that has a brother who is exceptional at business."

"I don't know about that," Karus said.

Dio shot him a skeptical look. "You are seriously trying to tell me your brother is not good at what he does? He grew a small, shitty farming interest your father left him into one of the largest plantations on the island of Sicily."

Karus shrugged, admitting defeat.

"That's what I thought," Dio said. "Your father raised two exceptional sons, I think. Both became very good at their respective professions."

"I will agree to that," Karus said, reflecting upon his brother's success. There was an open invitation for Karus to join him, to help manage not only the plantation, but the family's growing investments.

Karus had put in twenty-two hard years of service. With each passing year, his aches and pains increased. This past winter had been especially trying for not only Karus, but the legion.

"Too much mud, wet, and cold," Karus grumbled unhappily. His toes had quickly become moist from the numerous small puddles along their path, a result of the half-thawed mud.

"Agreed," Dio said as they reached the officers' mess. He pulled the door open and held it for Karus. Light and warmth flooded out, as did a number of voices. A brown camp cat with white paws had been waiting for the door to be opened. It darted in as Karus stepped through, with Dio right behind him. The other centurion slammed the door closed as a gust of sucking wind attempted to keep it open.

The officers' mess consisted of a medium-sized common room filled with well-worn tables, basic stools, and benches. A kitchen, complete with several ovens and a fireplace for cooking, had been added as an afterthought. The kitchen was separated by a simple wooden door, which had been wedged open so that the heat from the ovens could warm the common room. Compared to the chill cold outside, the warmth was more than welcome. Karus's fingers and toes began to quickly ache. As the door closed, half a dozen heads turned toward them, looking up from their meals.

"Morning, Karus." A grim-looking officer in his late twenties nodded a greeting. The man's face had once been fair, but was now marred by a myriad of scars, the result of the previous summer's campaign. Valens had once been an extremely personable and outgoing officer. Hard action and unfortunate luck—which led him into the hands of their enemy—had changed his outlook on life, and his view of the locals.

"Valens," Karus returned the greeting, nodding to the prefect. "And how is the Ala Agrippiana Miniata this morning?"

Valens commanded the legion's cavalry wing, an allied auxiliary cohort.

"Still sleeping the night blissfully away along with the rest of the legion," Valens replied. "Though soon enough I will have my boys in the saddle."

"There is nothing quite like a day filled with drill and exercise." Dio clapped his hands together and rubbed them for warmth.

"Entirely correct," the cavalry officer replied, raising his cup of wine in toast to Dio. "Train 'em hard and often is what I say."

"Valens," Karus said, "as a proper infantry officer I freely admit to a ready dislike for the cavalry. That said, I've always found your attitude toward drill and training your men toward perfection somewhat refreshing."

The officers in the mess chuckled, and Valens gave Karus another nod as he sipped at his wine. The young officer had long since earned Karus's respect, which was not an easy thing to do. Unfortunately, after his rescue, Valens had developed a deep-burning hatred of the Celts. Friend or foe mattered little to the prefect. He hated them all just the same.

Valens was seated with another auxiliary prefect, Arminus Autun Otho, who commanded the First Nervorium. The First was a light infantry cohort. Otho's men had distinguished themselves over the last few years, primarily working as skirmishers and scouts. Otho, on the other hand, was a recent appointment, having transferred over from Second Legion, which was stationed farther south. Karus did not know him all that well. He hoped to change that, as Otho seemed competent enough. Only time, and hard action, would tell the man's true worth.

Karus received a few other nods and a handful of greetings as he and Dio made for a common table that had been set with bread, cheese, and jars of wine. He poured himself a cup of wine, which he knew was well-watered-down. The officer's mess fee, a meager charge, paid for it. If he wanted better-quality stuff, he had to go into town and pay for it himself. Karus took a battered wooden plate, grabbed a half loaf of bread, and then poured himself a liberal helping of garum sauce from a jar. Dio did the same, but instead took honey. They settled on an empty table with two benches along the back wall.

Karus saw Dio grimace as he dipped his bread into the sauce. Karus took a large bite and chewed thoughtfully as he contemplated his friend. It was the same old story.

"You have to be the only legionary I know who is not overly fond of fish," Karus commented out of the side of his mouth, chewing. He loved garum and for the life of him could not understand why his friend loathed the stuff. In Karus's mind, the sauce was a gift from the gods. It simply made everything taste better.

"I believe that real men were meant to eat animals that walk the land, not swim in the sea," Dio replied with a look of distaste.

"It isn't because you can't stand the taste of fish, is it?" Karus asked, deliberately dabbing up some more of the sauce with his hunk of bread. He took another bite and chewed, raising an eyebrow.

"Fermented fish sauce is a taste that I fortunately have never acquired." Dio wrinkled his nose at the ripe smell coming from Karus's plate and dipped his own bread into the honey before taking a healthy bite. "You know perfectly well that summer we spent on those bloody ships cured me forever of fish."

"There was plenty to eat, that's for sure." Karus grinned, thinking back to the time they had helped to hunt down a small band of pirates operating along the coast. "I miss rays, and boiled lobster."

Dio grimaced again, shook his head, and then changed the subject. "Tell me about this Galba."

"He was governor of Hispana a few years back." Karus took another bite and waited 'til he had swallowed before continuing. "He forced this tribe, the Lusitanians, to surrender. They were real tough bastards and had been a thorn in Rome's side for some time, interrupting the imperial silver and lead supply. They even killed tax collectors."

"The usual stuff then," Dio joked, then sobered. "Worse than the Celts we have here in Britannia, do you think?"

"Now that is hard to say," Karus said, taking a deep breath as he thought on it a moment. "It is possible they were worse, but I doubt it. Anyway, after a difficult campaign, our friend Galba managed by force to finally convince the Lusitanians to come to heel and negotiate."

"I like these stories," Dio said, "where hairy-arsed barbarians get it into their thick skulls that it's easier to simply submit to Roman authority than resist."

"Well, they did."

"Quite sensible of them," Dio said, taking a pull of wine from his cup and washing down some bread. "I wish our bloody Celts had as much sense, but assuming they had any would be charitable."

"Well," Karus continued, drinking a swallow of the watered-down wine, "Galba made some demands. The Lusitanians met them and came as an entire tribe—men, women, children, entire families—to the governor and his army to submit. At the agreed upon spot, Galba ordered his legion to surround the tribe and made them turn over all of their weapons." Karus paused as he thought on what it would have been like. Romans typically left conquered peoples armed. In a ceremonial surrender, the key figures usually handed over their weapons. It was far better to allow the tribes and local kingdoms to deal with internal problems rather than have the Romans police all issues, such as banditry, in a province.

"Once the Lusitanians had given up their weapons," Karus continued, "the governor ordered the legion to move in and put the tribe in its entirety to the sword."

Dio paused mid-chew, eyeing Karus for a long moment. He continued to chew, though more slowly. He swallowed.

"Women and children too?"

Karus nodded.

"That is a bad bit of business," Dio said quietly. "Maybe they *were* worse."

"Perhaps," Karus said and took a small bite from his bread. They were quiet for a few moments.

"I would not have enjoyed that task," Dio said, "even if these Lusitanians had it coming."

"Neither would I," Karus agreed, "but this act by Galba represented more than simply the act of wiping out an entire people."

"How is that?" Dio asked, cocking his head to the right slightly. "They were enemies of Rome, and apparently got what was coming to them. Otherwise, the governor would not have executed them all. Am I wrong?"

"Galba's decision was flawed," Karus said. "Once the Lusitanians had surrendered and agreed to submit to Roman rule, they were no longer our enemies. There is the practicality of reputation to consider."

"How so?"

"Don't you think it sensible for Rome to honor her agreements?"

Dio thought on it, and then nodded. "By honoring our agreements, no matter how much the bastards deserved it, you are saying that it would help with future negotiations?"

"Exactly," Karus said, pleased that his friend had grasped the meaning of Galba's betrayal, which had really been to Rome herself. Despite Dio being barely literate, he was sharp as a finely edged weapon.

"So, by going back on his word...other peoples and tribes might not be so willing to negotiate with Rome?"

"Which would likely translate into more fighting," Karus said.

"More bleeding and dying by our boys then?"

Karus nodded somberly.

"Then Galba was a fool," Dio concluded, chasing down some bread with a liberal dose of wine.

"It was indeed bad business," Karus said. "Polybius wrote it down—"

"Wait," Dio said, holding up a hand. "I think I've heard this part before. Long ago, he wrote it down so that future generations would not make the same mistake. Is that what you were about to say?"

Karus chuckled. "You know me only too well."

The two officers ate in silence for a bit.

A pretty woman in her early twenties emerged from the kitchen, carrying a small pitcher. She caught Karus's eye, and he flashed her a smile of greeting. Dio turned slightly as she placed the pitcher on the serving table behind them.

"Morning, Keeli," Dio said, waving at her with his hand holding the hunk of bread.

"Dio," she said in a soft voice and then returned to the kitchen.

"A nice girl," Dio said. "Easy on the eyes too. I can understand why Felix likes her."

"He finally got around to buying her," Karus said. Gallus Felix was the senior centurion for Fourth Cohort, another close friend and old comrade.

"About time too," Dio said. "They've been sweet on each other for far too long."

"He's saved for six months," Karus said. "When the headquarters staff gets around to it today, Keeli will be his."

"I suppose he still plans to free her?"

"Yep. He's also petitioned to the legate to make her an honest woman."

"Well," Dio said, raising his cup in a toast, "I hope they make each other very happy."

"They both deserve happiness," Karus said with a glance at the open kitchen door. "Though I rather suspect she will have her hands full with Felix."

"Has it occurred to you it might be the other way around?"

Karus chucked.

"How are those new recruits coming?" Karus looked at Dio as he took a pull on his cup of wine.

"The other freed slaves?" Dio asked. "Well, they just finished their basic training. Surprisingly, none washed out, which I suppose is as good a sign as any." Dio frowned. "To be perfectly honest, I was not expecting the manumitted when I put in the request last fall for replacements. I tell you, it's just not right enlisting freedmen. Our recruits should be citizens."

"They will be when they complete their service. You'd reject a hundred eighty fresh recruits?" Karus asked him, already knowing the answer. "Just because the emperor saw fit to free a bunch of slaves, who had earned it?" The emperor had made legionary service a condition of their freedom.

"Well, when you put it that way, of course not," Dio said. "I'd never question the emperor's wisdom. Freed slaves or no, we will make proper soldiers out of them."

"I have no doubt you will," Karus said, speaking out of the corner of his mouth as he chewed.

"It is a good thing we have some time," Dio said. "This winter was rough and the legion needs work."

"Nothing that can't be fixed with drill, exercise, and training," Karus said. "Though the campaign season is fast approaching." Karus paused to take a sip of wine. "You should feel lucky, you know."

"I should?" Dio looked up at him with an amused expression.

"Half of Felix's recent batch washed out," Karus told him. "The legate sent the washouts to an auxiliary cohort somewhere down south, near the coast."

"Seems like recruits these days just don't measure up." Dio made a disgusted look. "Kids today are all soft types, raised on the government's dole back in the capital and expecting everything to be handed to them. They don't understand that nothing worthwhile comes easy. They have an inkling we lead a life of adventure, and they want that, but are not willing to work for it. It is sad."

"We don't lead an adventurous life?" Karus asked with a sudden grin.

"Bah," Dio said and tossed the remnants of his bread back onto his plate. "We seem to get only weak-kneed, spoiled children or, worse, convicts…and now slaves. It's not like when we enlisted. I tell you, standards have fallen."

"I fear you are correct."

Karus had enlisted at age fifteen. His father before him had been a centurion, who had mustered out after taking a near-crippling wound. Raised on stories of legion glory, unlike his brother, Karus had known he wanted to be like his father. When he grew old enough, his father had seen to it that Karus had a place with his old outfit, the Ninth.

"Nothing worth doing comes easy," Karus said, quoting a saying that centurions were fond of telling their men. "Though I can think of a recruit who once thought he had all the answers."

"You and Centurion Sadius beat that out of me," Dio said with a straight face. "But, as only age can confirm, I now know I have all the answers."

Karus chuckled.

"Who got your two new centuries?" Karus asked, leaning back on his stool.

"Cestus took the Fifth, and Mika the Ninth."

"Good men," Karus said with approval, "solid soldiers, and suitable choices for centurions."

"Say," Dio said, lowering his voice so only the two of them could hear. "What is going on with Julionus?"

"The legate?" Karus asked, and his mood darkened. "Nothing that I know of. Why?"

"When old Tarbo died, you should have been promoted to camp prefect."

Karus dipped the last bit of his bread into the dregs of the sauce on his plate. He was deeply unhappy about this subject, and did not answer. The camp prefect was, technically speaking, third in command of the legion. The last camp prefect had caught sick over the winter and had not recovered. Tarbo had been a good man, someone Karus respected.

It had been over a month since the new legate had arrived. As the senior centurion in the legion with the most experience, Karus felt that by rights the position should be his. However, for some unknown reason, Julionus had put off appointing the next camp prefect.

"Tarbo was one tough bastard," Karus said, unwilling to follow the path Dio had started down. "I was sorry to see him pass from this world."

"He was a good man," Dio agreed, taking the hint and looking down at his plate. "Remember that time he caught me sneaking those girls into camp?"

"I do." Karus chuckled at the memory. "He should have busted you back to the ranks."

"Only he couldn't without embarrassing himself," Dio said with a matching grin, "seeing as how one of them beauties was the girl he'd been seeing, bragging on for months."

"She was a looker," Karus said, thinking back on a happier time. "What was her name?"

"Cylenia."

"He got a little angry over that."

"I'd say." Dio's grin grew wider. "I'd be mad too, if I found out my girl was a common prostitute."

A muffled horn sounded in the distance. Both men looked in the direction of the door, as did those other officers present. The officer of the day had given the order for the legion to be roused.

"Well," Karus said, standing stiffly. He waited a moment for the discomfort in his thigh to subside, then gathered up their plates and empty cups. He placed them in a wooden bucket by the kitchen door. Most of the other officers in the mess were doing the same.

Dio stood and stretched out his back.

"Duty calls," Karus said loudly to those centurions who had not yet moved from their tables. "Time to earn your pay, ladies."

"The legate will be with you shortly," the clerk said. He spared Karus a bored glance, then returned to his stool at a small table cluttered with scrolls and tablets. The clerk picked up a bronze stylus and began writing on a wax tablet. A scribe to his left wrote using ink on vellum.

Karus chewed on his lip as he looked around the headquarters. Half a dozen scribes and clerks worked feverishly at various tasks. To his eye, they seemed unusually busy. He idly scratched an itch at the back of his jaw as he studied them. Something was on the wind, he was sure of it.

He strolled casually over to one of the tables, where two clerks were working diligently. Both were legionaries who had been assigned to the headquarters staff because they could read and write. Rarely would the legate's staff be asked to fight, and it was a good thing, as their kind generally went soft after a few years of sedentary work. The physical requirements, though the same for every legionary, saw these men repeatedly excused from regular training and drill, something Karus despised.

He glanced down at one of the wax tablets that had just been placed aside. Reading it upside down, Karus saw it was an order to the legion's cooks to prepare pre-cooked rations. Interestingly, it detailed how much each man was to receive: four days' worth of salted pork, a portion of dried beef, a measure of bacon fat, vinegar, salt, cheese, hardtack biscuits, and wine.

Hardtack biscuits were an unfortunate staple of a legionary's life. Hardtack had the unique ability to remain unspoiled for quite some time and was the perfect wheat ration for extended marches. Despite that, Karus hated the biscuits, but had to admit when rations were short it beat starving. The biscuits were so hard that it was nearly impossible to chew without first soaking in some water or wine. A few years back, Karus accidently discovered another use for hardtack when he had once used an uncut block of the stuff to brain an enemy unconscious during a difficult moment. The incident was still the talk of the legion.

He glanced toward the closed door of the legate's office and wondered what was going on. Had the legion received movement orders from the governor? Surely the campaign would not start so early in the year. The ground was only partially thawed, far from firm. It had only recently gone from being frozen solid to having a soft and wet top layer. This time of year, individual cohorts could easily move about if needed, but not the legion in its entirety. Any type of massed movement would prove problematic, as the local road network would hardly hold up under the strain. The only reliable roads were all legion-built, and those were far to the south.

"Can I help you, sir?" One of the clerks had looked up from his work. Karus glanced down on the clerk, who had flipped several tablets over so Karus could not read their contents.

"No," Karus said curtly and stepped away. Something was definitely up, and it was likely the reason he had been summoned to headquarters right after the morning parade.

Well, Karus thought, he would just have to wait on the pleasure of the legate to learn more. He placed himself near one of the large braziers that had been set in the corners, providing the room its warmth. From the terrible smell, Karus recognized coal as the fuel source.

Coal was one of the truly rare commodities of value that Britannia had to offer. It provided more heat than wood, but was expensive. While the legate got coal, everyone else had to make do with peat, dried cow droppings, or wood.

Karus leaned his back against the wall and settled in to wait patiently, allowing the brazier to share some warmth. One lesson the legion taught every recruit was how to hurry up, and how to properly wait, for those seemed essential requirements for serving the emperor.

Just moments later the door to the legate's office opened, and out stepped a Celtic noble, dressed in a rich fur cloak over a chainmail shirt. Karus blinked in surprise. He knew most of the local nobles. All of them were arrogant, though some had adopted Roman ways, including dress. This one he had never met.

The Celt, a man in his late twenties, was tall and heavily muscled. He looked every part the barbarian, complete with gold jewelry, tattoos, and long black hair tied off in a single braid. He had the way of a born fighter.

The man spared Karus a disdainful glance as he retrieved his sword from one of the guards by the door. The Celt slipped the long sword's scabbard over a shoulder before turning away and stepping through the door, leaving the legion's headquarters behind.

"Is Centurion Karus here yet?" The legate's high-pitched voice reached out from his office. One of the clerks scurried from his desk to the door.

"He is, sir." The clerk turned and hurriedly motioned for Karus.

"Well, man, just don't stand there. Send him in."

Karus was already moving before the clerk could say anything further. He stepped through the door into the legate's office. It was a large room, easily five times the size of Karus's own personal quarters. A table had been placed near the back wall and served as the legate's desk. Several large trunks lined the walls. As the legate had his own personal quarters, these, Karus assumed, were for important papers. Another smaller table with two chairs had been placed off to Karus's left. Two braziers, burning coal, smoked lazily at the sides of the desk, providing a modicum of heat and a mildly nauseating smell in the closed room. The small windows were shuttered to keep the cold out.

Wrapped up in a heavy blue cloak, the legate was seated behind the desk. He was a slight man, and the cloak hung awkwardly on his bony frame. Papers, scrolls, and wax tablets were scattered haphazardly across the table. The legate was bent over a small map, studying it intently.

Julionus reminded Karus of a bird. The man had a large hooked nose, similar in shape to a beak. His eating habits had only reinforced that impression. Karus and several of the other senior centurions had recently been invited to dine with Julionus. The legate had the most annoying habit of picking through his food with his index finger and thumb until he found a choice morsel that he judged worthy enough to consume. It was a delicate gesture, but oddly reminded Karus of how a crow picked at the flesh of the dead, looking for the tastiest portion.

Karus marched toward the table. He straightened into a position of attention and saluted.

"Centurion Karus reporting as ordered, sir."

"Close the bloody door," the legate roared around Karus at the clerks and then bent back down to his examination of the map. There was the sound of hasty footsteps behind Karus, and then the door scraped closed. Karus remained at attention. After a moment, the legate looked up and straightened.

"Stand at ease."

Karus relaxed a fraction. The legate was still relatively new to the legion. Karus did not know the man well enough to take any liberties, lest he offend his new boss. Vellius Rufus Julionus commanded the legion in the emperor's name. His word was law.

Karus's eyes took in the map, which detailed the region north of the Ninth's garrison. No matter what official maps claimed, just a handful of miles farther to the north, imperial authority, and civilization as Rome knew it, came to an abrupt end. And whether they desired it or not, the legions were here to pacify the tribes and bring civilization to the island the Celts here called home.

"You want the job of camp prefect?"

Karus blinked, considered his reply for a fraction of a second, and then gave a mental shrug. Honesty was in order.

"I do, sir."

"You feel you have earned it?" There was a scheming look in the legate's eyes.

"I do, sir." Karus wondered where this line of questioning was going. He kept his face a mask.

The legate considered Karus for a long moment, saying nothing further. Julionus had access to his military record. There was no need to recount his battle honors and justify his fitness for the position. Besides, he was primus pilus of First Cohort. Only one who had repeatedly distinguished himself could ever hope to attain such a prestigious and coveted position.

"We don't fully know each other yet," the legate said. "I have read over your service history, but it tells me little about the man himself."

Karus refrained from frowning. The service record, in his opinion, told much.

"What would you like to know, sir?"

"I would not dream of putting you on the spot." The legate studied him for another long moment. Karus was becoming irritated. Julionus was playing a game with him. For what purpose Karus could not fathom, so he waited.

"Your service to me will tell me everything I wish to know," the legate finally said. "Effective immediately, you are promoted to 'acting camp prefect.' You will handle this additional duty along with your current responsibilities, those of leading First Cohort. This will continue at least long enough for me to determine a suitable replacement for the First."

Karus blinked, at first unsure he had heard the legate clearly. He almost asked for clarification, but bit his tongue as he struggled to contain his rage. There should be nothing "acting" about the position. By rights it should be his. He swallowed and cleared his throat.

"Thank you, sir," Karus said, doing his best to keep the anger from his tone.

"Good, good. I see you are moved by my magnanimous gesture." The legate gave him a smile that smacked of insincerity. "In a month's time, after we have worked together under some trying conditions, I hope to make your appointment permanent."

"Yes, sir." Then what the legate said registered. The fighting season was at least two months off. Something was definitely up, and he was about to find out what. Despite his rage, Karus leaned forward slightly, eager to learn more.

"Karus, an opportunity has presented itself." The legate's eyes fairly shone with excitement. "The Caledonian tribes are gathering just to the north of us, here in this valley." The legate pointed to the map on the table.

Karus leaned over to examine the spot where the legate was pointing. The location was uncomfortably close to Eboracum. The terrain in that area was extremely rugged, with rolling, misty hills. Karus had led a few patrols through those same hills. There were two large villages in that valley and another just beyond.

Though not yet imperial territory, the previous legate had found it was best to show Roman strength by marching a cohort or two through the valley on a regular basis. In fact, that very same valley had claimed the entirety of Sixth Cohort over the winter. The legion had learned of the Sixth's fate when they found the heads of the officers mounted on wooden stakes before the gates of the garrison.

Tarbo's death, coupled with the loss of an entire cohort, had been a body blow to the men of the legion. Morale had been low ever since, and it had not picked up with the arrival of the new legate. Karus knew in time it would recover, but he found he was increasingly tempted to submit his retirement request despite his desire to achieve the most coveted position a ranker could reach, that of camp prefect. He sensed the day fast approaching when he would finally put the life of the army behind him.

Karus looked back up at the legate. He had lost more than a few friends in that ambush and wanted some payback.

"They intend to launch an attack against us here, before the campaign season begins. I understand they hope to catch us before the might of the governor's army can assemble," the legate said.

"I would be shocked if they could overcome the walls of the garrison," Karus said matter-of-factly. "Our enemy fights better in the field than against fortified positions. Courage is no substitute for technical knowhow and discipline."

"Agreed," the legate said with a nod. "That is my thinking as well."

"Besides," Karus continued, "attacking us here won't help them."

"What do you mean?" A frown line creased the legate's brow, and he cocked his head to the side.

"Well, sir, they could easily enough besiege us," Karus said, thinking it obvious but working carefully to keep it from his tone. "There is plenty of loot to be had in the town outside the walls. However, our supply depots would allow us to hold out for some time. Once the ground hardens, the governor will bring up the rest of the army to lift the siege. They won't stand a chance and will ultimately be forced to flee back to their mountains with little gain to show for their efforts."

"Yes, exactly," the legate said with a snap of his fingers. "That is why we must strike first."

Karus blinked in surprise.

"Strike them first, sir?"

"Yes," the legate said, full of the excitement of the moment. "That is the brilliance of my plan. You see, we strike them before they are ready and have fully assembled. By doing so, and smashing what forces they have gathered, we can scatter them to the winds before they can move against us. That way, when the governor brings up the army, the summer campaign will have a much easier time of it, courtesy of the Ninth, of course."

Karus thought it through, and was silent as he did so. After a moment, he noticed the legate looking at him with an odd expression and realized he had been frowning.

Karus, like most of the legion, wanted payback for the Sixth. The only problem was that Karus felt anything but excitement at Julionus's plan. In fact, he felt dread at the thought of taking the field so early, and without any ready support. The Celts knew those misty hills and mountains far better than the Romans.

"Sorry, sir," Karus said neutrally. "I was just thinking it through."

"Yes, well," the legate said, looking down at the map again, before glancing back up. "It is a rather bold and audacious plan, isn't it?"

"Yes, sir," Karus said, and then a thought occurred to him. The legate was new to the legion. He was the authority in the region. He determined when, and where, the legion moved. However, surely even he would not act without the governor's direct orders. Had he even consulted the governor? Karus considered how best to approach the matter.

After a moment, Karus continued. "Sir, I am sure the governor will bless your plan."

"He will," Julionus said, glancing back down at the map. "Once I have won my victory."

"You have not informed the governor?" Karus was so surprised that the words spilled from his mouth before his brain could catch up.

"There is no time for that," the legate snapped, clearly irritated that Karus had questioned him.

Karus said nothing. Julionus was new to Britannia and was clearly looking to make a name for himself back in Rome. It was an old story, and a dangerous combination.

"If we don't march immediately," the legate said, visibly calming himself, "the opportunity will be lost. Waiting for word from the governor will take too long. Karus, this is a once-in-a-lifetime opportunity. Even Tribune Saturninus recognizes it. Surely you can see that we must do this?"

"Sir," Karus said, and gestured at the map. "I feel it only prudent to point out the ground is not yet firm enough for the entire legion to march. The roads to the north are poor and in short order will be reduced to mud. We will be unable to cover ground quickly. At best, we will be moving at a snail's pace. If that occurs, and I expect it to, the element of surprise will be lost. We know the enemy has spies in the town. They will get wind of our intentions the moment we march through the gates, if not before. Once we get into those hills, that ground up there is rugged, hard, and difficult. It is their ground, sir, not ours. They will be waiting. They will have the advantage."

"I have intelligence that they have only managed to gather a few thousand warriors so far," Julionus said. "Regardless of whether they know we are coming or not, we should easily outnumber them."

"What if the intelligence is wrong, sir?"

"They are barbarians," the legate countered with a heavy breath.

"Who wiped out Sixth Cohort this winter, in that very same valley. They may be undisciplined barbarians who wouldn't know how to use a latrine if instructed in advance, but that does not make them any less dangerous. And, sir, they are incredibly dangerous."

The legate's look hardened. Karus realized that he had gone too far.

"Do you fear the enemy?" Julionus asked, a contemptuous expression crossing his face.

Karus resented the implication. "No, sir. But I do have a healthy respect for them."

"They are nothing but uneducated and illiterate barbarians," the legate said. "I have studied them extensively and met with their representatives, including their nobles. My intelligence sources are unimpeachable. We are prepared, and they are not. All it will take is one quick lightning strike to the north. They will not expect such a bold move, before the traditional coming of the campaign season. There is no way they can stand against the might of this legion, especially with me in command." Julionus paused for a breath. "You may not know it, but back in Rome I am considered something of a tactician."

Karus could not believe what he was hearing. The legate had no military experience that he was aware of. The man had not even served as a junior tribune. Rumor had it Julionus's connections, and a hefty bribe, had secured him his current post. Thoughts of Sicily came to mind. Karus considered for a moment submitting his resignation.

Would the legate even accept it?

His thoughts hardened. Karus loved the Ninth. The legion was his home, and she was going into danger—mortal danger, if Karus was correct. How could he abandon her now?

"Did you know that the emperor is on his way to the island?" the legate said.

"Hadrian is coming here, sir?"

"It is not widely known yet, but indeed he is." The legate picked a cup off of the table and sloshed the contents around a moment before taking a liberal sip. "Before I left Rome, barely three months ago, he told me himself." The legate paused. "I fully intend to present him with a victory. You, Centurion Karus, will help me deliver that victory."

"Yes, sir," Karus said stiffly. The legate saw only the glory of a victory, the adoration of Rome, and further advancement waiting within his grasp; perhaps that even included the purple toga. Julionus would not be the first legate to crave the emperor's chair. He was gambling with the legion and their lives on a fool's errand, and Karus did not know how to stop it.

"I have no doubt we will bring the enemy to battle," Julionus said, a fervent look in his eyes. "I have had the omens read. They are auspicious for a victory. The gods are on our side."

Karus said nothing.

"Have no fear. We shall prevail."

"Yes, sir."

The door opened, and both men turned.

"Ah," the legate said in a delighted tone. "Tribune Saturninus, I am so pleased you could join us."

The tribune had arrived with Julionus. He was young, in his twenties, and handsome. The tribune had a ready smile and wore an expensive, thick fur robe over his tunic. He was no different than many of the other tribunes who came to serve with the legion—rich, powerful, and well-connected. For Saturninus, serving with the Ninth was a stepping stone to public office or higher military command.

"It is I who am pleased, sir," Saturninus said. A clerk closed the door behind him. "Why, Karus, my favorite centurion, it is good to see you."

"Sir," Karus said neutrally. Since the first moment he had met Saturninus, the tribune had been nothing but friendly to him. That worried Karus, for Saturninus was clearly a player of politics, and such games were dangerous. Roman patricians rarely played nicely with each other. When their politics became violent, bystanders frequently suffered in their stead.

"I trust I have not missed anything?" Saturninus turned back to the legate.

"No, no," the legate said, waving a negligent hand. "It is nothing we did not cover last evening. I've just explained my plan to the centurion."

"And what do you think, Karus?"

"It is a bold plan, sir," Karus said, and Saturninus turned his gaze on Karus, regarding him curiously. He was half tempted to bring up his objections again, but common sense intervened. He remained silent.

"Yes, well," Julionus said, "I do have a talent for strategy."

The legate went to a side table, where there was a fine ceramic pitcher, and poured some wine into two cups. He then walked back and handed one to Karus and the other to Saturninus before picking his own back up from the desk.

"A toast, to our success and victory." The legate held up his cup and drank deeply. Karus hesitated a moment before taking a sip of the fine wine the legate had provided. He found it tasted like ash but, not being one to ever waste any type of wine, forced it down with a single gulp. The legate took back the cup with a disapproving expression.

Saturninus sipped his own. "A very fine vintage, sir."

"Thank you," Julionus said, looking down at his own cup. "Sentinum is my favorite wine. I brought it with me all the way from Rome."

"Sentinum, really?" Saturninus took another sip and appeared to savor it. "Perhaps you would be kind enough to spare me some? Good-quality wine is hard to come by on this miserable island."

The legate looked uncomfortable with the idea, and then caught Karus's eye. He flashed another insincere smile Karus's way.

"Fear not, Centurion," the legate said, returning the cup to the table with the pitcher. "I have planned everything out. We even have the benefit of local guides to show us the way. Between the legion and my overstrength auxiliary cohorts, we will have over thirteen thousand highly trained men. With such a powerful force at my command, the enemy cannot hope to stop us."

"Yes, sir," Karus said. He wanted to object, but it was not his place. The legate had made up his mind. Karus, no matter how much he disagreed, was bound to support Julionus in his mad fantasy.

"Serve me well, and when we return, the position of camp prefect will be yours," the legate continued.

"Thank you, sir," Karus said, almost biting the words out. *If* we return, he wanted to say.

"Very good," the legate said, seemingly pleased with himself. "I will have orders issued within the next few hours. We march in two days."

Two days? Karus was rocked by this news. His mind raced over all that would need to be done. Supplies had to be drawn from the depots. The legion's train had to be put together and packed. That alone usually took a week of careful planning, supervision, and work, especially after a long winter with little activity. Not to mention the time needed to check equipment and ensure that anything found deficient was repaired or replaced. There were a million things that needed doing, and with his new responsibilities, much of that would fall on his shoulders.

"Now, I am sure you have a lot to do," the legate said with another smile that Karus felt had been intended to reassure. It had the opposite effect. "You are dismissed."

Karus drew himself back up to a position of attention and saluted crisply. The legate did not bother to return his salute, but had turned back to his map and his fantasies. Karus eyed Julionus for a long second, then turned on his heel and left the office, remembering to close the door behind him. Before he closed the door, he saw Saturninus, cup in hand, walking over toward the fine ceramic pitcher.

Karus passed the clerks, barely noting their frenetic activity, and stepped out of the headquarters and into the street. The chill snap of the wind was a shock, yet Karus paid the cold no mind. He glanced around and saw Dio waiting for him just a few feet away. The other centurion had been leaning casually against the cracked, plastered wall of the headquarters building, flipping a silver coin into the air. A brown cat nosed its way around Dio's feet, rubbing itself on one of his legs before walking off. Clearly his friend was hoping for a scrap of news.

"That bad?" Dio pushed himself off the wall and approached with a trace of a lopsided grin. He rolled the coin absently over his knuckles. "You look like your pay was just docked."

"He promoted me to 'acting camp prefect'," Karus said. "And we march in two days."

"What?" Karus could see Dio was genuinely shocked at this news. "Is there trouble to the south?"

"No," Karus said and gestured in the direction the legion would be going. "We march north."

Dio was silent as he absorbed this new information. "In two days? The entire legion?"

"Yes," Karus said unhappily, and began making his way back toward his quarters. Dio fell in beside him, looking as troubled as Karus felt.

Karus's mind raced as they walked. He had to get not only his own cohort as ready as possible, but the entire legion. Just thinking over all that needed to be accomplished in the limited amount of time available made him weary.

"It's going to be a nightmare," Dio said. "The ground is far from firm. Add a few thousand sandals, carts, horses, and hooves... it will be a bloody quagmire. We won't be moving anywhere fast."

"I know," Karus said.

"Does the legate understand that?"

"I did my best to convey my concerns," Karus said. He was unhappy with himself for not being more assertive. However, he also realized that had he done so, the position of camp prefect would have gone to someone else. At the very least, the position was his, even if it was only in an "acting" capacity. As camp prefect, in the days ahead he might be able to do some good. Perhaps he might even be able to mitigate some of the potential disaster that he felt was in store for the legion.

"Are we to have any support?"

Karus stopped and looked over at his friend. There was genuine concern in the other centurion's eyes.

"No," Karus said heavily. "We will be on our own, with only our auxiliary cohorts."

"Madness," Dio whispered.

"Nevertheless," Karus broke eye contact, turned away, and started moving again. "Those are our orders."

Dio did not follow.

Karus took a deep breath of the cold bitter air as he walked. He resolved to make an appropriate sacrifice to the gods. If he did right by them, hopefully they would do right by him. A little fortune, he reasoned, might just come in handy.

Printed in Great Britain
by Amazon

59170571R00227